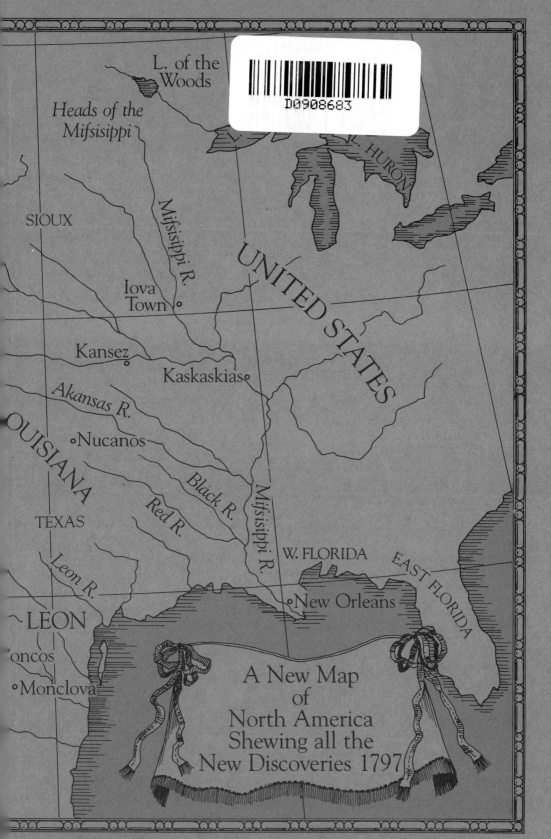

L. of the
Woods

Heads of the
Mifsisippi

L. HURON

SIOUX

Mifsisippi R.

UNITED STATES

Iova
Town

Kansez

Kaskaskias

Akansas R.

OUISIANA

Nucanos

Black R.

Red R.

Mifsisippi R.

TEXAS

Leon R.

W. FLORIDA

EAST FLORIDA

LEON

New Orleans

oncos

Monclova

A New Map
of
North America
Shewing all the
New Discoveries 1797

After Jedidiah Morse, *The American Gazetteer* (Boston, 1797)

YELLOWFISH

YELLOWFISH

John Keeble

HARPER & ROW, PUBLISHERS

NEW YORK

Cambridge
Hagerstown
Philadelphia
San Francisco

1817

London
Mexico City
São Paulo
Sydney

Everything is real and, where given, no
names have been changed, not of mountains, rivers, roads, cities, women, nor of
men.

FIRST EDITION

Designed by C. Linda Dingler

Endpaper map by Paul J. Pugliese

Library of Congress Cataloging in Publication Data

Keeble, John, 1944–
  Yellowfish.
  I. Title.
PZ4. K2538Ye   [PS3561.E3]   813'.5'4   79–2651
ISBN 0–06–012292–7

80 81 82 83 10 9 8 7 6 5 4 3 2 1

For my mother and father,
immigrants . . .

For their early reading, Ransom Jeffery and Fred Newberry; for support and aid given in various forms, for certain "ideas," Kwaku Dadey, Ed Dorn, Ken Halwas, Mrs. Charles H. Hine, Sr., Mademoiselle Liu, Jim McAuley, Stephanie McAuliff, Tillie Olsen, Jay Rea, Grant Smith; and my wife, Claire; and my dear friends and fellow travelers, Charles Hine and Deshika Desilva Hine; and my agent, John Sterling; and, for his editorial counsel, Ted Solotaroff: to all these who have instructed me in what John Steinbeck called "the gift of receiving," I can only hope that I have practiced my lessons.

Their leading ideas
come directly from the landform

Ed Dorn, *Recollections of Gran Apachería*

The fog, they say, its density and in winter its bitterness, is worst in Chinatown of all places in San Francisco. Its bitterness is traditional. The fog is used here as a measure of divination as the moon's aureole is used elsewhere, or the snow level on a mountain, the radiance of a distant glacier, the depth of a creek, the anxiety of cattle in a pasture, the crick in one's knee joint. Complaints about the fog when it is bad become collective and, thus, certain. In such certainty one finds relief.

It was not winter. It was spring, April of 1977, and nearing 8:30 in the morning, a Thursday in Chinatown, but the fog was raw and cold for April. The people wore heavy coats and hurried up and down the steep sidewalks or unloaded crates from trucks or vans or station wagons—parked with two wheels above the curbs to allow passage—and carried the crates with numb hands into the shops and restaurants. The people seemed to be blunted, substantial shadows in the fog, like ghosts of weight. Crevices, doorways, landings, and the mouths of alleys were laden with fog and divested of color, stiff and resistant like the skin between the nose and a squinting eye. Here and there, overhanging balconies and pagoda-like façades of the high, narrow tenements pierced through a weakening in the fog.

At regular intervals traffic flooded the streets—Washington and Clay—on either side of Chinatown's park, Portsmouth

Square. Held up out of sight by signal lights, then released, the traffic came on suddenly from nowhere. An astonishing mass, raucous and hissing in the moisture, the closely packed cars stormed the two streets, but then, controlled by the unseen signals, they vanished just as abruptly as they had appeared. The silence was as startling as the clamor.

The sounds heard then came as if from the other side of a wall: a lid pried off a crate, nails wailing in wet wood, a mother crying out from a window above an alley, a trolley bell ringing several blocks away. These dislocated sounds heightened the sense of space without dimension. Faintly, the traffic could be heard toiling down in the financial district, collecting behind the lights, invisible at the foot of an invisible skyline, but mounting for another surge.

A red Datsun slowed, knotting the traffic behind it, then whipped off Washington Street into the parking lot next to the Golden Phoenix restaurant and directly across the street from the park. The car pulled up to the wall and stopped. The taillights, glowing in the fog, went out. When the driver cracked his door the dome light switched on and four heads were visible, three of them dark and low above the tops of the seats, two in back, one in front. The driver's head nearly touched the ceiling of the small Japanese car. A white man, he bent his large frame nearly double to get out. He shook his trousers off his legs, arched his back, and stretched his arms up over his head.

When he came to rest he looked around through the fog with a startled expression, fixing on two Chinese teen-agers in pea jackets who stood side by side across the street in the park, then on a slender Chinese man in a knee-length coat some distance from them. The man, slightly stooped, his hands clasped behind his back, gazed at the sky, or at the fog, or at nothing. He stood on the low slope just above the shrubbery that lined the edge of the park. He seemed, because of the tricks the fog played, to be standing on the shrubbery, or he looked like a figure in a picture of a man standing by magic on the tips of the shrubbery's slender, uppermost branches. Something about the man, his immobility,

2

the calm he communicated, or the dark angulation of his body against the gray, fulfilled the white man's expectations of how people should look here.

One of the two teen-agers in the park turned and called out. Momentarily, a young boy materialized and stood beside the two teen-agers. The three of them stared at the white man, Wesley Erks. Erks opened the trunk of the car, then leaned around and rapped on the rear window. Inside, the three dark heads moved at once. Three doors opened. Three Chinese youths stepped out and gathered around Erks at the trunk, and removed their bags, three small and identical green plastic suitcases. Erks removed his bag, a worn leather valise held shut with an elastic "tie-down." Fastened to the "tie-down" and flush against the side of the valise was a short crowbar, which would seem here, in the city, a good deal more like a weapon than a tool. This was in fact the case.

The three youths waited in silence while Erks closed the trunk and returned the keys to the ignition. He had showered and changed into fresh clothes at a truck stop in Vallejo, but the plaid wool coat which he took from the seat and put on was deeply creased from the long journey. He had shaved in Vallejo, too, and the fog stung his skin. He raised the collar of his coat around his neck and put on his hat, a beige Western hat, and drew it down close to his eyes. One of the two teen-agers in the park bent and spoke to the young boy. Instantly, the boy began running. Erks looked up. His eyes narrowed beneath the brim of the hat as he watched the boy's image recede in the fog. The sound of running feet continued for a moment after the image had vanished, then was overcome by another surge of cars on Washington Street.

In the park the two teen-agers stood near a memorial to Robert Louis Stevenson, the famous adventurer, who, when he sojourned in San Francisco in 1879 and 1880, had passed many hours in Portsmouth Square, but all that was apparent of the memorial now was the bronze statue of a frigate which in the fog appeared to be at sea, afloat above the heads of the two teen-agers who stared directly at Erks and the three youths. The man

3

in the knee-length coat still gazed upward into the murk. Below him the bushes quivered, then shook violently, and another man emerged, feet first, his torso following the soles of his shoes as he sat up straight and rubbed his eyes—a derelict hatched from sleep.

Erks removed a sheet of paper from his shirt pocket, unfolded and studied it. The paper, on which were written an address and a diagram of streets, curled in the damp. He put the paper away and picked up his valise. The three youths picked up their suitcases. When he moved away from the Datsun and up the sidewalk, the three youths followed in a row, shoulder to shoulder, matching his pace. No one spoke.

The boy ran straight for three blocks, scarcely pausing as he crossed the streets, then turned the corner and stopped in front of a diner. He cupped his eyes with his hands and pressed against the window, peering inside, fogging the glass with his breath. A lean man, sweeping the floor, saw him and gestured upward. The boy entered a side door and climbed to the second floor and knocked on the door at the head of the stairway. The door opened abruptly, snapping against the chain. A face, or a vertical third of a face and one eye, appeared. The door shut and re-opened fully.

"They're here," the boy said in English.

"Who's here?"

The man was stocky, the face below the mouth as broad as his forehead. Two deep creases ran diagonally down and away from the mouth, bracketing the chin. The chin was like a dumpling, but harder, like a fist. A long scar ran down one cheek and crossed the corner of his lips and threw his expression to one side. He wore a loose-fitting double-breasted suit and vest. The dark cloth was expensive and brushed clean.

"The three and the American, Mr. Jui."

The man, Jui, leaned forward on his toes and scrutinized the boy. The boy, afraid, stepped back. "Who says so?"

"John Hoy."

Jui reached into his vest pocket and produced a fifty-cent

4

piece, with which he performed the knuckle trick. He turned the coin deftly from knuckle to knuckle, then produced it between thumb and index finger and pressed it into the boy's palm. He closed the boy's hand on the coin and smiled, or leered, showed his teeth, the lines of his cheeks and chin tight, rapacious, and thrown to the side of the scar. The boy turned and fled.

Jui stepped back into the living room of his apartment, which, despite the storefront below and unswept stairway, was elegantly furnished with flowered rugs, ornate furniture, wrought-iron stands, vases, statuettes. . . . At one end of the room stood an altar that was crowded with paraphernalia: in the center a large wooden tub painted red and filled with white rice, and surrounding the tub several ceramic tablets with pictures of animals, an abacus, two cardboard footprints inscribed with Chinese figures, a dozen or more small flags in stands, an incense tray, a jade statue of Buddha, a rosary, a bloodstained white robe, a red club, a dagger, a carved wooden pistol, a coiled rope. . . .

A cigar smoldered in the incense tray. Jui stopped in front of the altar, picked up the cigar, lifted the head off the jade Buddha, tapped his ash inside it, and replaced the head. He paused, puffing deliberately on the cigar, then turned and walked the length of the room to a large window.

Beneath the window was a telephone stand. Jui expected the telephone to ring any moment. On the adjacent wall was a photograph of some twenty gentlemen standing in two rows, the board of directors of the Chinese Six Companies. The photograph had a sheen given by the window, the light turned silver by fog. Jui leaned toward the photograph and studied it, his hands clasped behind his back, the burning cigar wedged between short fingers and the smoke fanning upward against his thick back.

He himself was among the gentlemen, his face in the photograph composed, cold, and—it pleased him to see—dignified. He was the youngest member of the board, elected several years ago through the strength of his position in his family association and the influence of another man in the group—the oldest, extremely old, in his nineties when the photograph had been taken, a slender, ascetic-looking man with the high brow and delicate features of a scholar—Chiang Taam. On the one hand, Jui's own election to the board was his crowning achievement. On the other hand, it was meaningless. Most of his colleagues he regarded as old women, out of touch and harmless. There were too many men of power not among them—Robert Liu, Chan Tatming, Joe Ng, Mak Yen-muk, Hiram Chow. . . .

Chiang Taam had died a month ago. His funeral parade— band, dancers, and mourners—had filled two Chinatown blocks to the walls of buildings, a mass of people, but some among them —Jui knew well—had cursed the honor paid the old man, the old liberal, old merchant, old socialist, old Triad man, the remnant of the old scholar class whose life stretched back to the days when the tongs still held sway in Chinatown and long before the days when the Six Companies themselves had lost power. Among the dignitaries and businessmen at the head of the parade were some who had hated Chiang, and of those who remained, most had at once been awed by Chiang and distrustful of him. As to Jui himself, he regarded Chiang as a father, as more than a father, as a spiritual grandfather.

Jui was a Triad man. He didn't have old Chiang's ancestral ties with the Hung Men, or Red Sect, or Triad Brotherhood, the secret society said to have been founded years ago at the Shao-lin monastery in the province of Fukien. Few Triad members did. He didn't have old Chiang's preoccupation with politics, either —Sun Yat-sen and the Manchu dynasty, Mao, Chiang Kai-shek, the People's Republic, Taiwan. . . . All that was a generation, two generations, even three generations removed from Jui—a hinterland of idealists. But Jui's face softened as he remembered how Chiang used to bait the businessmen who made up the board of directors of the Chinese Six Companies, of the Chinese School, and of the Chinese Cemetery, by advocating certain social or educational reforms, or by suggesting that it made no difference where a body was buried or how, or by refusing to attend a Taiwanese embassy function, or by reminding them that Taiwan was not the true China. . . .

Jui ran the illegal conduit for the transport of young men— or boys, Triad initiates—from Hong Kong, Singapore, and Tai-

6

wan to the West Coast. He'd risen to this since working for Chiang, who'd given him his first job when he was ten years old. Jui believed that he owed his position in life to Chiang, and—though in most ways an opportunist—he was deeply superstitious over such matters as personal attachments, loyalties, and obligations.

Now the time had come to repay Chiang. Chiang's son, Ginarn Taam, who'd been in exile in Red China for seven years, was wanted here both by the government and by the Triad. The Triad had an execution order out on Ginarn. And old Chiang's business interests were on the block, including a casino in Reno, which Chiang's widow planned to sell to a Triad interest at a reduced price in exchange for her son's safe return and a lifting of the execution order. Jui had found the buyer—Hiram Chow—and had made the arrangements for Ginarn's return, although he had long hoped to own the casino himself, to legitimize himself and enhance his standing. Also, he endangered his own position by aiding Ginarn, one who had taken actions and committed a crime which Jui considered a betrayal, even heinous. . . .

Jui was profoundly inconvenienced.

It was a riddle.

He was in a snarl from which he couldn't extricate himself until just the right moment.

In the photograph he saw the face of the younger man, Ginarn, creeping through the features of the dead man, Ginarn's face broader than Chiang's, softer, and the eyes sharp, the face suddenly there and immovable as if Ginarn had sent his spirit—his shen—on ahead of his body to trouble Jui.

Jui turned away. He puffed on his cigar and waited for the telephone to ring. He gazed through the window, which, by coincidence of the placement of buildings, of years of razing and fire and reconstruction, commanded a vista of the city, or, now, of the slowly dwindling fog, the half-concealed great gray buildings of the financial district just below Chinatown.

The three youths, following Erks in a row up Washington Street, had about them a singular air of attention, receptivity, uncertain curiosity, the air of travelers, which was what they were, who have reached their destination, which they had, a place to which they have never been before, a strange place. Or rather the topography was strange, the air, the architecture. The language of signs and people was familiar, if corrupted, if antiquated and emblazed in neon, and if its dialect could not be fully understood, its cadences at least they had heard before. The youths were slender young men between the ages of sixteen and nineteen, Chinese, natives of Hong Kong though they, too, traced their ancestry to Fukien—their parents refugees from the revolution. They appeared younger and more fragile than they were. They wore tight-fitting denim outfits and rough Oxford shoes with heavy soles like clumps on their lightly moving feet. They were like reeds, like cattails, slender but heavy at the head.

Erks felt that he had come too far and stopped abruptly in front of a jewelry shop. The youths stopped behind him and stepped deferentially to one side when he turned around. Erks moved back down the sidewalk, searching for the name of the alley they had just passed. The three youths were like hydrae, rooted, pliable at the stalks, the organs of reception alerted. Their faces, though immobile, were given the countenance of activity by the eager movement of their eyes and a quickened, translucent hue of skin.

Erks found the name—Ross—painted on the corner of a brick building. He stood in the mouth of the alley and spoke to the three. They did not respond. Erks gazed at them, amused. They understood no English. He understood no Chinese. He pronounced their names, or the names he had been using for the last two days, taken from the sheet of directions given him by Lucas Tenebrel. Erks had thought that any three words would suffice: "Wong, Low, Choy."

They turned and Erks gestured for them to follow. They moved as one, straight and delicate as maidens, holding their plastic suitcases in their right hands, following Erks into the alley and past an appliance shop from which came muted strains of Chinese music. Out on the main streets the atmosphere had begun to burn clear, but here the fog still choked the light that shone through the windows of the appliance shop and an adjacent flower shop. Beyond that point the alley grew dark. Two women passed in the opposite direction like boats in the night, discerned only as they came abreast. Erks groped along the wall, pausing and bringing his face close to the doors in order to see the numbers. The quantity of doors was startling, one every four or five paces; the quantity of people who lived behind the doors would be equally startling: a matter of history—he knew—through years of crowding wrested by race and economics upon the immigrants, forced here years ago by white fear of Mongolians possessing the entire Pacific Slope, fired by the railroads, squeezed out of the mines, driven off the farmlands, and held within the Chinatown margin by a reign of terror, and now by the residue of that history. . . . Their tenements accommodated themselves well to density.

He found the door. On it was a sign directing prospective renters to see Mr. K—— at the address of a certain association. As instructed, Erks tried the knob. It turned and the door swung open and he and the three youths found themselves on a landing immediately above a large room with a wide entryway through which could be seen rows of sewing machines. Women worked at the machines, thirty or forty of them, and the air was filled with clicking and a thick, abrasive, pulsating hum. The women's hands guided cloth and their backs were hunched, their skin sickly-looking in the fluorescent light. It was a piecework factory. A man in a vest and shirtsleeves paced the aisles. He stopped and looked up furiously at Erks.

Erks turned away and started up the stairway to his left. The youths followed him. They climbed to the third floor, then walked down a narrow hall to the farthest door. He knocked lightly. It was cold in the building, colder, it seemed, than the outdoors. The three youths waited at his back. For a moment the only sounds were a vague vibration—from the factory, he guessed—and breath quickened by the climb, his breath heavier, that of the three youths short, light puffs of air as if from exerted

9

puppies. He knocked again. Footsteps approached the door from within.

A block away, the boy sat at a Formica table in the diner below Jui's apartment. The lean man emerged from the kitchen with a plate of steaming noodles and a pot of tea, a cup, chopsticks. Smiling broadly, he placed the articles before the boy.

"You are lucky," the lean man said, gesturing at the fifty-cent piece that lay on the table beside the teapot. "Mr. Jui favors you."

The boy nodded. The lean man returned to his work in the kitchen. Every night and every morning the floors were swept, the tables washed, the ovens and griddles wiped clean. Two old men in hats sat in a booth across the room, gazing with deliberation at the empty table between them. The boy ate voraciously, scooping masses of noodles into his mouth, scarcely chewing before he swallowed. For his services as a messenger, he was permitted to eat here without charge. In time, if all went well, he might ascend to the level of John Hoy, his brother, one of the two teen-agers who had sent him here. His brother's duties the young boy scarcely understood. He knew that his brother attended meetings on the sly, that sometimes he skipped school, that at times he would leave at night and not return until dawn. His brother carried a long knife with a white handle in his boot. Once, his brother had let him hold a heavy black pistol.

As to Mr. Jui, he was unfathomable to the boy. The boy held him in awe.

Footsteps could be heard pacing to and fro on the floor above the diner. The boy, having finished his noodles, listened. He wondered if these were Jui's footsteps or those of another man, superior perhaps even to Mr. Jui. His brother, John Hoy, had told him of these powerful, unseen superiors who sometimes arrived from overseas. Perhaps Jui was receiving an order. Perhaps the room upstairs was crowded with men. The boy looked up. The floor seemed to sag with the weight of secrets. So much was alien to the boy, as if he were a stranger. So much activated his imagination. He covered the fifty-cent piece with his hand and gazed at the ceiling.

A woman in a tweed skirt and jacket opened the door. Erks stepped back and allowed the three youths to enter before him. A man was inside the room with the woman. He immediately addressed the three youths, each in turn. The youths' replies were brief. Erks presumed that they spoke of the journey, of the long drive from Vancouver, of the voyage by sea from Hong Kong, or perhaps of their family, mutual acquaintances, news from the homeland. Maybe they spoke of arrangements to be made or of a contract to be fulfilled. Erks did not know. The room was bare of furniture except for a small desk which held a telephone, and near that a straight-backed chair and a lamp; desk, chair, lamp, sills, and the cobwebs that hung from the corners of the ceiling were coated with dust. Their shoes scraped the dust on the floor. The youths stood in a row like toy men, holding their suitcases. Erks shifted his valise with the crowbar strapped to it from one hand to the other, uncertain as to whether or not he should set it down. The man spoke at length, gesturing with his palms. His voice was low, soothing, and monotonous. The woman listened closely. A well-kept, hard-looking middle-aged woman, it was she, despite her silence, who was in charge, a matter of importance to Erks because he expected now to be paid.

She held a small black book open before her waist, a ledger. One page had been filled with numbers and words in both Chinese and English, the numbers contained, the words spilling outward and overwhelming the margins. The woman's body inclined forward; the very motion of her solid, compact body, her hands gripping the book, and the expression on her round face, fixed and intense, the circles of rouge on her cheeks heightening a hectic appearance, brought an abrupt end to the man's apparently decorous chatter. He took one step back and smiled at the youths, whose expressions grew furtive. A silence filled the room and in it Erks felt himself growing larger, more conspicuous. Uncertain as to what was expected of him, as to whether or not

11

he should speak, or for that matter what he was even doing here
—the entire proceeding, words, bodies, conduct, and transaction,
was a cipher to which he had not a clue except that Lucas had
said money would be paid him here—he hung on to his valise as
if it were his anchor. Nearly a foot taller than the others in the
room, he felt like a giant in the silence, big and as white as a
beluga whale.

The youths—he knew—were illegal aliens. That was why he
had been hired. They entered Canada on tourist visas. He had
driven them across the border at an unchecked point. It was a
simple maneuver and the risks seemed slight. His employer—
Lucas Tenebrel—had told him that the business was called "yellowfish" after a trash fish of Chinese waters eaten by the poor.
Those who so entered the country were called yellowfish because
they lacked the money to immigrate legally. They had something, though, some kind of fancy connection. Lucas had mentioned the Triad. Erks knew nothing about that.

He knew this: The Immigration Act of 1965, advocated and
signed into law by Lyndon Johnson, had been intended to replace eighty years of quotas based upon nationality or class or sex
or race, but in fact it restricted Chinese immigration again, particularly from Hong Kong. More history: a history of Chinese-
American relations, of expanding and contracting trade, of the
attraction in the 1850s of gold fields for the Chinese, their homeland impoverished and torn by war, and men coming over to
send earnings back home, fathers without wives, without children, sons without fathers, so-called paper sons, paternity coun-
terfeited by "uncles" in exchange for indenture, and a history of
the use after the Civil War, by a rising West Coast capitalist class,
of Chinese labor, and of the hostility of white labor toward cheap
Chinese labor, economic at its roots, racist in its flowering. Coo-
lies, johns, opium smokers, slaves, harlots, infidels, idolators, pa-
gans, they were called in speeches and tracts, heathen Chinee,
jackass rabbits, the yellow peril.

The history was of punitive immigration laws—no Chinese
women allowed to enter, no families, no resident status granted,

no Chinese except of professional classes, no Chinese at all, deport them—and, following the Chinese revolution, of the entry under Eisenhower and Kennedy of refugees and "displaced persons" from Taiwan and the crown colonies. Johnson's Immigration Act attempted to regularize immigration. It established quotas according to place of birth, irrespective of race or nationality. It granted twenty thousand visas each year to each independent nation, but counted Hong Kong as a part of Great Britain, the lot of these people not to exceed one percent of visas issued to Great Britain, and thereby reenacted, strangely, the "paper sons" and "uncles," Hong Kong F.O.B.s (fresh off the boats) entering surreptitiously from the north much as Mexicans, Colombians, Guatemalans, and Ecuadorians enter from the south —kitchen help and pickers.

Erks knew about all that. But he didn't know why he had been hired. It had something to do with a second trip for which this was the dry run. The work—he understood—was customarily performed by Chinese-Americans who brought the youths across the border as members of their families. It was some enterprise of Lucas Tenebrel which demanded Wesley Erks, so Lucas had said. Erks didn't mind. He understood that it was unusual for a white man to be making the delivery. He understood that the Chinese, the elder Chinatown residents especially, were an insular people, how to them all places could be China, how their reputedly model ghetto was a result of this insularity—enforced and chosen, both—how like sticks caught in a drain they were coated with the residue of history, and how much they would distrust and resent his kind: *bok guey,* white devils. Understanding all this, he understood that he knew virtually nothing about them.

Erks had dark hair and a pleasant, even-featured face, quick to laughter, the skin a little coarse and faintly swarthy. He was half Greek. He had a gentle manner, but a certain rural gauntness of jaw and narrowness of eye, a squint, an eye for land and weather and crops, for knowing when a cow would calve or a sheep be prime for shearing, for spotting the scutter of a grouse in brush, or at a distance for seeing doves on a wire, or the hump of a coyote's back behind a rock, an eye used to sighting down a fence line and the barrel of a shotgun. He was from eastern Washington, a country of high desert, sagebrush, pine, rivers, and basalt extrusion. A husband and a father and by trade a machinist, he was in fact what might be called a high-class jack-of-all-trades and took on what came his way, and by his reputation for hard work and for doing a job right, he managed to do well for himself. He'd spent two years at the University of Washington, but left because it was "too slow"—not that he didn't like studies: he liked to read, he liked history, he was fixed on West Coast history, he was practically a scholar—and he had worked as a carpenter and driven combines and dusted crops with his father's old biplane and seeded clouds, and farmed, and bought and sold timber land, and lately had delivered goods for Lucas—bundles and cases, mostly cocaine, and now persons, illegal aliens, for reasons unknown.

He had a pragmatic outlook, a knack for turning a personal profit. He had a tendency to stand his ground if he was unsure rather than back off, which amounted at times to what his wife, Ruby, called his rigidity. Speculation for him, whether with money or with ideas, was governed by what was known, by one absolute, and his conclusions, once arrived at, usually became givens, the corner posts driven deep into the ground from which he strung his corrals. His own measure was mortality and mortality was an everyday occurrence: he had seen geese, shot and plucked, rotten inside, and possums, coons, skunks, porcupines, and dogs dead at the roadside, and bats, poisoned, littering the floor of a hayloft, calves dead at the trough, crows and magpies working over a deer carcass in the woods, and crops spoiled by too much water, or not enough, or by frost, early and late, or by ground squirrels; he had seen ground squirrels "bombed" out of their burrows, and sheep slaughtered by coyotes and coyotes by men and hawks circling the body of a drowned woman, washed up on the banks of the Columbia, and his father dead, electrocuted in his shop and still standing, one hand up at a socket as if saluting farewell to his son, who stood astonished in the doorway. Erks saw people, their words and habits and obsessions

14

and their exchanges, their lives in the light of their mortality. It gave him distance and sometimes an advantage.

The woman, her finger marking a place in the book and her body coming up straight then settling like a stone, broke the silence: "Low."

One of the youths bowed.

"Choy."

A second youth bowed.

"Pang."

The third youth, whom Erks had been calling Wong, did the same, but turned his head, too, and grinned sheepishly at Erks.

Erks laughed aloud, shifting his feet.

The woman wheeled and stared at him, or through him, as if he weren't there, as if she fixed on some indecipherable point in the space that his body occupied, or on some pea-sized core, a molecule, a bull's-eye of which Erks had been previously unaware. He looked back into her bright almond-shaped eyes. She did not like his laughter, clearly, and she did not understand it, though she had seen that it was over a matter between himself and Wong, or Pang. That was, no doubt, enough—that there was something, anything, between them. He had violated a taboo. Her disapproval at once missed the mark and overwhelmed it. It was Erks himself that she didn't like—*bok guey*—but whatever it was in him that she viewed, or how she viewed him, was as utterly untranslatable to Erks as she was herself, or so it was until she shifted her weight ever so slightly back onto her heels and raised and turned her face so that she looked at him archly, from a slant, out of the sides of her eyes.

Physically, it was an almost imperceptible gesture, but with it a point emerged from her anger; like a knife, the woman in her poked through the expensive tweed suit and the compactness, the economy of her bearing, and the composed skin on her face, through the Chinese surface. The silence and intensity and deadlock of their bodies, six feet apart, mounted to a sexual level, keen, brutal, miscegenetic, and racist, like a gaze between a wolf and a dog stumbling upon each other. She bristled with animal energy. His breath caught in his throat.

She jerked around and abruptly began a tirade in Chinese directed at the three youths, or perhaps at the man. Perhaps—more likely—it was about Erks. Perhaps it was not a tirade. Perhaps it was her way. Erks could not tell. Her words rang, but the man continued to beam and the three youths faced her with equanimity. Her words were a torrent, and shrill enough, it seemed, to shake the cobwebs and layers of dust, and they were without cadence, and the emotion they carried, if any, was as foreign to Erks as were the words themselves. He was invisible again, removed from the room. To his right a window was bisected by the diffuse ceiling of fog almost like a porthole crossed by water. Above, the sky was blue and the tops of the high-rise buildings and the bay and the distant hills were clearly visible. Erks stepped over to the window and looked down, finding Chinatown still cloaked by fog.

He heard his name spoken once by the woman, and again; then in the midst of the torrent she spoke clearly in English: "When the American brings Ginarn Taam." She stopped and the silence swelled.

Startled, Erks turned to her. "Me?" he asked, baffled by what had brought them to this point. He did not know the name—Ginarn Taam—but wary of showing a weak side, he said, "He comes here?"

The woman opened the drawer of the desk and removed a small stack of bills, and laid them in a fan on the table with the corners exposed so he could see, counting them out in a mechanical voice: "One hundred, two hundred, three hundred . . ." When she reached fifteen hundred she squared the bills back into a stack and handed them to him. "For money such as this Ginarn Taam comes to me. Safely."

He slipped the bills into an inside pocket of his coat.

The woman picked up the telephone receiver and dialed part of a number, then stopped and looked back at him. He smiled, testing her, but her face was composed again, guarded. She waited—for what, she gave no indication: for him to leave, maybe. He did. He glanced at the three youths as he left, but they

16

stared at the opposite wall, or at the closed door in that wall. There were three such doors in the room, or four, counting the one which led out to the stairway, the three interior doors shut and bolted. Erks left by the fourth door and descended the stairway to the alley.

"Above all the same grim condition to keep friends with himself—Here is a task for all that a man has of fortitude and delicacy," read the plaque below the bronze frigate on the memorial to Robert Louis Stevenson. It was a passage from the writer's work and to Erks, who sat on a bench in Portsmouth Square, killing time, the words seemed to have the ring of truth, but he could not locate the root of the truth. The words "fortitude and delicacy" he liked. He liked such words when they described character.

In a half hour he would catch a cab to the airport. The fog had cleared with surprising rapidity and Chinese men, most of them elderly—the bachelors, the remnant of the Bachelor Society—had come out into the sun. Some had gathered around the concrete checker tables and others sat in groups of two or three on the benches, speaking at great length to one another in Chinese. It was clear to Erks that they passed their days in this fashion. The suits they wore, the varying qualities, were doubtless a gauge of their financial condition—most were worn thin— but the men were alike in that they all wore suits, a gauge of their sense of decorum. Across the street in the lot the Datsun was gone, removed, taken, as he had been told it would be. At his feet was a package and next to that his valise, the crowbar snug against the leather.

He had walked the streets of Chinatown for over an hour, window shopping. There were stores which catered to the residents, located mostly in the alleys, and on the main streets stores for the tourist trade—curio shops, import shops, art and furniture shops, jewelers, restaurants, and more restaurants. In one jeweler's window, two large rocks were displayed next to each other, labeled "Chinese Jade" and "Canadian Jade."

The narrow streets and sidewalks, the density of the tene-

17

ments, and at the intersections the crush of pedestrians—though it was not yet the tourist season—and, of course, the presence of the Chinese themselves, gave Chinatown the character for which it was renowned, a character founded on the architecture of a ghetto, on a history of poverty. San Francisco's Chinatown and New Orleans' French Quarter, Erks had heard, were the two most lucrative tourist attractions in the country. The Japanese had moved into Chinatown and were on the brink of dominating it at the time they were removed to detention camps during World War II. The detention of the Japanese had saved Chinatown for the Chinese.

There was a parable in this.

Following the war, the Chinese New Year became a public event. A Miss Chinatown Contest was instituted. Restaurants were enlarged, refurbished, and new ones opened up. White people learned how Japanese and Chinese looked different. In the package at his feet were items Erks had purchased in a Chinese mercantile: a kite from Taiwan for his boy and for Ruby an electric rice cooker made in Japan.

Portsmouth Square was a place for watchers.

The man who had seemed to stand on top of the bushes when Erks first arrived remained in the park, pacing back and forth with great deliberation over a low hillock, his hands behind his back, clasping a pipe. His age was difficult to ascertain. He could have been fifty or a hard thirty-five. He, too, wore a suit, or a worn mismatched set—coat and trousers—under his frayed topcoat, and his shoes were worn and too large and when he moved his heels lifted, revealing large holes in the socks. Unlike the others in the park, he met no one, spoke to no one, and no one spoke to him.

He stopped, his body in repose against the gray front of the Buddha Universal Church across Washington Street, and gazed upward—at what, Erks still couldn't tell; not, now, at the fog; at the top of a high-rise in the financial district, perhaps, at the sky, at nothing. It was a compelling posture. The man took no notice of Erks, who studied him closely: his head was extremely well

18

shaped, the bone finely articulated, elegant, rounded from the crown to the brow, his chin and nose definite, his cheeks rather sunken, and lined. The lines extended down around his mouth and formed arcs that traced back onto his gaunt neck. He had a wisp of a beard. He was thin. Erks wondered if he ate at all. He had an air of great calm and intelligence, an attitude that made his indigence recede, an attitude of impeccability, or so it seemed to Erks, for whom the man began to take on a haunting meaning, as was the way with chance encounters whenever he traveled.

The man put his pipe to his lips and sucked on it. He removed the pipe and smiled as if in amusement at forgetting that it was empty, but the gesture, Erks knew, was one often repeated. It was as if the man were just short of mad, his expression ironic and showing, thus, his distance. He could have been here for days. He seemed larger than he was. He seemed to be in a quandary, his life caught in some deep conundrum. He seemed to be the essence of Chinatown. On the one hand, Erks wished to help him, to reduce his own distance from the man, and he actually considered slipping the man a bill; on the other hand, he appreciated the distance, himself from the man, the man from himself, and himself—Erks, the traveler—from himself, the two men like two points in space triangulated by magic. Erks imagined that the man was on the brink of resolving his difficulty, that the subject of his interior dialogue drew near its conclusion.

19

2

The room smelled of fried chicken and baking cake. The light of sunset flooded the kitchen and made the six-horse Mercury outboard motor sparkle. Erks, back home from San Francisco, had tuned the motor and cleaned it. Now he had it up on the butcher table and was waxing the paint. Ruby stood at the counter near the sink, near the window through which the light streamed. She had carrot sticks and green onions packed, and potato salad in a plastic bin, a thermos full of apple juice and one full of water and another ready for coffee in the morning, the chocolate cake in the oven, and now she wrapped the pieces of fried chicken in foil. Her new rice cooker stood just to one side. The kitchen was silent except for the squeak of Erks' rubbing and the crinkling of foil, the low soughing of the wind outside, and occasionally a grunt from the dog that slept on the linoleum floor at the mouth of the hallway, its muzzle between its front paws. The quiet was big. It extended through the windows out across the wheat fields to the hills.

A cat, a calico, slept on top of the refrigerator. If the cat were to move, the dog, a kidney-colored Weimaraner, would awaken. If the cat were to jump, the dog would leap to its feet. If the cat were to run across the floor, the dog would chase it. If the cat were to stop, the dog would freeze just out of reach of the cat's claws. Friendly enough, the dog and the cat seemed to be under an unfriendly spell.

Erks and Ruby had planned a fishing trip to Rock Lake for tomorrow. The boat was on the trailer and the trailer hitched to their GMC wagon. In the morning the motor would be mounted on the boat, the food packed into a basket, the basket and tackle box and a cooler of beer and the worms, which Erks had yet to dig, loaded into the back of the GMC, the poles snapped into a rack. They would leave at five in the dark.

Rock Lake was a favorite spot for Erks and Ruby—thirty-five miles south of where they lived outside Davenport, Washington. A natural lake, one of the deepest in the region, on the map an elongation of blue between Pine City and Ewan, Rock Lake was dangerous because of its depth and its winds and the rock out-croppings, but the fishing was excellent, as was the goose hunting in the fall.

"I wish Lucas had told you when you make the next run," Ruby said.

Erks looked up at Ruby. The dog opened its eyes and perked its ears. Ruby's brown hair glistened because of the window at her side. She looked at her work: a square of aluminum foil and a chicken thigh, golden and warm to the touch, encrusted with corn flour and oats. Her lower lip stuck out as if she were pouting. It was her way in concentration.

"Those Chinese are the damnedest people," Erks said.

"We have to get that alfalfa seeded," Ruby said.

"It's too wet."

"True." She folded and creased the foil around the thigh. "It could even snow."

"Strangest damn kids, they followed me around like sheep. They wouldn't talk to me, though, or couldn't speak English. Not a word. They hardly talked to each other even in Chinese if I was around. I called one of them by the wrong name all the way down." Erks smiled.

"I don't know, Wes," she said.

"It does make you wonder what the hell they do when they get there."

"Cocaine is one thing, but a load of people, Wes, I don't

21

know." Ruby was a strong, well-built woman, about five feet six. She could look big at times. "Bad as it is, cocaine doesn't talk at all."

"It leaves a trail."

"They won't?"

"Christ, I don't know." Erks dug his rag into the can of paste wax.

"I don't trust Lucas." Ruby had never met Lucas, but by conversation he had become a presence in the house, a haunting made forceful by his absence.

"We couldn't make in ten years off that alfalfa field what I'm going to make off this."

She looked up. "We could make a good living off the shop."

His face clouded and she was sorry she'd said it. The machine shop, the metal building just across the drive, was filled with expensive equipment and haunted by the apparition of his dead father.

She changed tack. "You're getting more than you thought?"

He nodded.

"You've talked to Lucas?"

"Nope. But I'm bringing somebody down, a heavyweight."

Ruby faced him, a drumstick in her hand.

He answered the question she hadn't asked: "I don't know who, but they want him in Chinatown. They want him bad."

"Maybe it's Lin Piao."

Erks grunted, contemplating the possibility.

"Aren't they right-wing, those California Chinese?"

He grinned. "Christ, I guess so. Last time I talked to Lucas he said something about the Triad."

"The what!"

Erks stared.

"Do you know what the Triad is?"

"Do you?"

"Enough to know that you don't want to get mixed up in it. We don't need the money, Wes."

"We can use it."

"That's crazy. Lucas would use you."

22

The eight-year-old boy, Matt, in bed in his room down the hall, called out plaintively. His father's return and the promise of the trip had excited him and he craved attention. Outside, the wind gusted, riffling the pages of a book which was propped up in the window sill. The tension between Erks and Ruby had come from next to nowhere, slipped out of the geniality like a rat out of a cupboard.

"Nobody uses me. For seventy-five hundred I'd haul corpses across the border for the devil."

Ruby glared. Matt called again, then appeared in his doorway, dressed in white long johns and grinning sheepishly. He was fair-skinned, but had hair and eyes as dark as his father's. The dog turned its head and sniffed as Erks stepped over it. Ruby stared at Erks' back, then, once he had picked up Matt and carried him into the bedroom, at the dark vacant doorway.

It was spring. April. Day to day, the light arrived earlier and stayed longer, at noon the sun swinging toward the center it would never attain. Too far north. Even at solstice the sun would hang southerly like a ball in a sling. At noon it would flood the kitchen floors through the windows. In the evening the light would touch the ceiling in the northeast corner.

A great deal of rain, little heat, and this year snow still not out of the question, as Ruby had said. The *Almanac* advised to expect it, advised that it would be a year for root vegetables. Sparrows, swallows, and starlings flocked, it seemed, with great hesitation. In the evening ducks could be seen moving north and south as if unable to decide. The irises were late, as were the daffodils, tulips, and plum blossoms. The trees were just budding now, the flower stalks just appearing—bright, pale spears puncturing the soil from underneath.

Ruby, washing up the dishes, looked through the kitchen window at the lilac bushes in the yard. The limbs were still bare. The bushes looked like tumbleweeds, like tangles of wire, but at the tips of the limbs there was a slight enlargement and a lightening of color. The blossoming of lilac bushes is taken as a sign, the time of a spring festival here—in Spokane, the city of the region,

23

thirty miles east—but this year the occasion, the beauty contest, and the parade would predate the blossoms. The local newspapers ran insinuating stories on the impending glacial age and told of the ineluctable movement of ice down along the old corridors.

A vigorous woman, quick and deft, she washed dishes at the kitchen sink. The work was calming. The sound of Erks' voice in Matt's bedroom, low, the words indistinguishable, was pleasant to hear. Occasionally the boy's voice, bright and interrogative, interrupted; once or twice the boy laughed and Ruby imagined Erks' thick fingers going for Matt's ribs under flannel pajamas or squeezing a small knee. Outside, the breeze rose. The air blew through the open kitchen window and chilled her hands when she lifted them from the soapy water, and when the wind was right it carried strains of Alice Smith's violin from the house up the road. Buoyant in the spring, the air could carry the cries of hawks, of coyotes from the hills at night, and Alice Smith, who played horribly, could sound as though she were practicing on Ruby's front porch.

Ruby heard his footsteps, then the refrigerator door opening. The pop tops of two beer cans sprang, one for him, one for her. In the window she saw the reflection of his head and upper body grow larger as he approached her from the back. He set the cans down on the counter and put his arms around her waist, his fingers touching her hips, his cheek her ear.

"Except you," he said softly. "You can use me."

"Why do they want him?"

"Who?"

Ruby's fingertips toyed with the surface of the dishwater. "What's-his-name, the man, why do they want him?"

"Ginarn Taam, I think," he said, pronouncing the last name correctly but not knowing how it might be spelled.

She relented and leaned, pressing the back of her body into the front of his. "And he's with the Triad, or what? Who wants who?"

"I've got no idea. He's somebody." He slid his hands down the fronts of her legs.

She was a reader. The book, an account of mass murders, was propped up in the corner of the window sill so that she could read as she worked if she wished. The breeze turned the pages slowly, then they came to rest, the book open to a photograph of Sharon Tate.

She sat on the floor with her legs folded beneath her. Her nose was fine and straight, her eyes and arched eyebrows dark, her forehead high, a dome. She stared straight into the eye of the camera. Because of her position—she was leaning forward, her arms were drawn back—her breasts hung downward, earthy, mammalian, and scarcely contained by the light fabric. Her dress had crept up her thighs. And her abdomen was full and also stretched the fabric to its limit. It was a pose, all right, sultry and statuesque.

Erks—and millions of others—had seen this photograph before and had been arrested by the sense of having been with her in secret after her death, by the sense of a flying thing in the night, a spinning box, a small bursting bomb, a loose soul fluttering wildly like a bat. The hazard of her death marked the accidence of all lives.

Ruby twisted and looked up at him—looking. "Nice, huh?"

"Dead."

The breeze gusted again, riffling the pages. The photograph was replaced by type.

"Why do you read that trash?"

Ruby stiffened. "Why not?"

He put his hand on her belly, a peace offering.

Ruby revolved and tugged on Erks' belt buckle. "You should know."

Erks chuckled.

He saw the movement through the window first, a shape flitting across the lawn past the lilac bushes and up one side of the cottonwood which stood in the center of the yard. Illuminated by the storm light, the shape was ball-like, hustling, darker than the cottonwood bark and glimpsed as the movement of something turning away.

"What's wrong?" Ruby asked.

25

From outside came the shrill scream of a fighting cat. The cat on the refrigerator, the calico, leapt instantly to the floor and hurtled across the kitchen and through a slit in the screen door and vanished, and then the dog, on his feet and scrabbling on the waxed linoleum, chased the cat.

Ruby cried out, "Rex! Rex!"

But the dog rounded the butcher table and slid, his feet outpacing his progress, and practically tore the screen door off its hinges and vanished after the cat. For an instant Erks and Ruby were paralyzed. There was a second scream, or a pair of them, blood-curdling and guttural, and then the dog, snarling.

"My God!" she said.

Ruby rushed past Erks and followed the dog. He followed her, catching the screen door and throwing it open again. The cat, the calico, was up in the cottonwood, the white trunk and leafless, rising limbs like swords in the night, and the dog was half up, jumping, clawing the bark, snarling and yipping crazily at the crotch of limbs where the cat was, or two cats, snarling themselves, hissing and screaming and knocking against the wood, fighting something, another cat, an animal. Though there was light from the storm light and the moon, the action in the cottonwood was sound without shape, pure sound, and invisible, incredible mobility.

Ruby went straight for the tree, calling the cat's name. "Iris. Iris?"

"Don't put your hand in there."

Ruby reached up and put her hand right in.

"Damn it, Ruby!"

Ruby, feeling bark and harsh whipping fur, and something hard and thrashing, something of bone, jumped back. A shape, a dark thick blot, a rounded oblong thing, hurtled out of the tree and down, hit, rolled, and darted across the lawn. The dog lunged after it, following it out of the light into the dark toward the canyon. Ruby cried out again, "Rex!" The dog's running paws could be heard against dirt, then briefly there was a bout of snarling, more running paws, dwindling, then nothing.

"Rex!" Erks called. But for the wind, it was silent.

26

Ruby held one hand in the other like a fish and scrutinized it. Remarkably, it was unscathed.

"That was dumb, Ruby."

"That was no cat," she said.

The storm light rocked, the perimeter of light rocked; standing in it was like standing in a boat. Ruby moved for the tree and grabbed a limb and hauled herself partway up and clutched the trunk with her legs. Two pairs of eyes gleamed from the hollow of the crotch, two cats, Iris and a young black-and-white male saved from last fall's litter. They were still. Ruby reached into the crotch and took them down one at a time, setting the first one, the male, gently on the ground, then she went after the second, and holding the second, Iris, picked up the first again. She cuddled them both and pressed her face into their wet fur. The two cats' hearts pounded wildly against her hands.

Ruby had spread out a towel on the kitchen counter and placed the cats on it. The calico, Iris, sat upright, panting. One ear was shredded and she had a gash on her side.

"She'll be all right," Ruby said to Erks. "This other one, I don't know." She wet a washcloth and wrung it out, then brought a bottle of rubbing alcohol down from the shelf. "Iris was protecting him. And Rex was protecting Iris." Ruby looked at him, her eyes bright. She had a streak of blood on her cheek. "Isn't that something?"

Ruby had a way with animals, a way of handling them, of identifying with them, a way even, at times, of being like them —intent, fervent, remote, and prime.

The second cat, the young male, lay on its side. Large square chunks of flesh had been torn out of it, along the back, the sides, and one out of the belly. The last was like a window, the flesh rose-colored. Behind it the dark shape of an organ was visible. Just above the hip was a protuberance, a gross swelling of the kidney, perhaps, or the spleen. The cat was motionless, its mouth open, the eyes already glassy.

Ruby stroked him lightly with her fingertips. The cat convulsed slowly, drew its legs inward, then pushed them back out

27

again. It gagged. Ruby stepped back quickly. "He's a goner."

At her side, Erks grunted. He went out into the back porch, then returned, holding his hunting coat and gun case. He slipped into the coat and slid the gun out of the case. It was a shotgun, a twelve-gauge automatic.

The calico stared fixedly at Ruby as she swabbed the gash on its side. "You'll be all right," she told the cat.

Down the hall in his bedroom, Matt called from his sleep. The wind rattled a branch against a window. Erks removed shells from his pockets and slid them into the chamber. The action snapped with each injection.

"You think it's the possum?"

They had lost eggs and even hens to a possum.

"Could be. It was big, though." Erks moved for the door. "Rex'll tree it, I bet."

"Take this one," Ruby said, gesturing at the male cat with the swab.

Erks grimaced.

Ruby smiled and leaned back against the counter. Even when braless, her breasts parted the cloth between buttons.

Erks picked up the male gently, sliding his hand under it, and carried it in his palm like an offering, the cat alive but inert. Outside, he leaned the gun up against the house, knelt, and as was his way, said a prayer. "Take this cat," he whispered. He stroked the cat, then gripped it and banged its head against a concrete step. The cat wrenched, knotted and unknotted in Erks' hand. It fell still. Erks moved to the incinerator and laid the body down softly in the ashes.

He picked up the gun and crossed the lawn, passing out from under the storm light and around the chicken shed, skirting the vegetable garden. He bent and eased through the barbed-wire fence and moved across the flat toward the scrub pine in the path of the dog. To his right was the backside of the big metal building, the machine shop, darker than the sky and looming. Just ahead of him was the old biplane, tied down, the fuselage covered with tarps, but because of the long slits, the silver-colored wings, it looked like a thing afloat. Erks had flown the plane rarely, lately not at all.

It had belonged to his father, old Xerxes, the name not even the surname but the one used in this country and shortened to Erks before Erks was born. For years his father, an inventor, an experimenter, sporadic farmer and occasional crop duster, and, true to his Greek heritage, fixed on water, obsessive about water or about its lack, had seen the future in water for the arid horse latitude of eastern Washington and Oregon. Before the construction of Grand Coulee Dam, Erks' father had tried to "call" the rain with fires and balloons, then with aerial explosives chucked out of the biplane by hand, and, later, with seeding—silver iodide crystals scattered like grain across the clouds. The dam he had greeted with violent, conflicting emotions: the idea of water for irrigation he liked, and the electricity, the uses of electricity on such a scale fascinated him, but the encroachment of agencies and the power of the government, that scale, and particularly the eagerness with which the public received that bureaucratic scale, he despised. Better, he would say, to carry the water here in buckets and make power by treadmill than to have it so delivered. Exiled from his home, a revolutionary, a klepht out of the Pindus Mountains, which were also called the *Agrapha*—meaning the not written, the uncoded, for the people there refused to pay taxes, refused to be coded—the old man was obsessive about his independence, too.

It had been a contradiction—Erks knew—his father's attitude toward Grand Coulee. He himself—Erks—had not found a way to resolve the same or like contradictions except to stand off from them, nor had he escaped the old man's fierce sense of independence, nor the old man's death, which had turned Erks away from the project he had shared in chiefly for the old man's sake to begin with, though he had not quite believed in it—the machine shop, that is, gathering the collection of machinery from various sheds and buying new and putting it all into one building, converting thirty-five years' worth of a fly-by-night operation into a legitimate one—nor had he thought the old man really

29

believed in it, either, going legitimate, putting a sign up and a listing in the Yellow Pages. It was a thing to do, and to be done without heat, done even coldly so far as the objective was concerned. That was what Ruby had not understood about it, his coldness toward it. The old man had died touching the path of electricity in the new shop. And now Erks ran goods for Lucas Tenebrel.

He went around the plane, poised on its struts like a breeding mantis, a big mechanical spook that shook the dust off memory. He went into the pine stand and stopped at the edge of the flat and listened: the wind coiled out of the ravine, smelling of water and carrying the faint sounds of the Weimaraner's snarls. He began the descent, holding the gun aloft in one hand, keeping the other hand free for support on the steep trail. He slid as much as he walked and had to grab at rocks and weeds and tree trunks to brake himself. He stopped once, hugging a pine tree, to listen. The volume of the snarling had increased. He scrambled downward and came out of the trees and stopped at the edge of a rock abutment that looked down on a basalt shelf.

The dog was there, as was the animal, a possum, big, a grandfather, big as a big coon. It was in the center of the shelf, hunched and still, a lighter patch on the dark rock, and the dog, distracted by Erks' appearance, turned, a supple, glossy presence, its nose shiny. The basalt shelf, he knew from having been here in daylight, was rimmed on three sides by the abutment. On the fourth side was a sheer cliff which fell into the ravine. At one corner, between the abutment and the cliff, was a trail, or a continuation of the trail, or more correctly, a water runoff employed as a path by deer. The possum moved suddenly for the trail, but the dog jumped and cut it off, and attacked, snarling viciously. It rolled the possum. Erks saw the belly, lighter yet, flit by. The possum hissed and counterattacked. The violent flurry of movements was lost to Erks in the darkness, then the dog rose. The light hunk, the possum, clung to its chest like a big tick, plucky. The dog arched, snarling, and tore at the possum. The possum dropped and scurried backward, back into the center of the shelf. The dog circled the possum slowly. The possum hissed. The dog circled alongside the rock wall. Erks couldn't see the dog.

He fumbled in his pocket for the flashlight, found it, switched it on, and swept the wall with the beam and found the dog, circling, lifting one foot at a time, moving by inches. The dog had small shiny flecks on its chest—wounds, Erks figured, torn out by the possum's teeth. He squatted, watched, and held the gun, butt on the ground, forepiece against his knee, the cold barrel touching the side of his forehead. The wind had stiffened. It soughed and blew up out of the ravine and bent the pines and made them creak. A few drops of rain spattered against his face. The cloud blew across the moon like a ragged drape.

The dog circled the possum warily, the possum the pivot point, circling itself, or circling with its front legs and hunching its hindquarters around, for it was wounded, too, wounded in the hips. The dog passed under the ledge beneath Erks and he leaned forward to look. He couldn't see the dog. The possum, however, faced him, hissing gutturally. Its long, bared teeth flashed in the beam. Its snout was long and bewhiskered, the eyes beady, the lower half of the face grotesquely puckered, primal and ugly. The dog, circling, came into view again. Circling, it held the perimeter. Its head down, plunging and feinting, it cut deeper into the inviolable region, the center of the circle, but, respecting the possum, retreated after each plunge. But it retreated less than it advanced, shortening the string. The possum countered with short, twisting, alarming lunges toward the dog's throat, pivoting, raring, and snapping, and once the possum lashed out and hung on to the dog's foreleg and the dog, enraged, attacked. Erks couldn't make out the flurry. He heard the dog yelp and he came forward on his knees, straining to see, and was about to call the dog's name when the dog retreated, safe, and took up its circling again.

Erks sweated in the cold, his body rigid. What he saw was like a dream, pure form and quickening pace, and in a world of shadows, but in the flashlight's nimbus two figures—the dog in orbit, armature to pin, to gudgeon, the possum—were lucid and

31

alive. Wounded, the possum would have escaped if it could, but the dog, working out of some attachment, some fixation or passion mounting its own logic, was bent to the kill and suddenly it moved into the center, over the possum, and spun the possum. For an instant the possum hung by its teeth from the dog's flank, then it dropped and the dog was after it, had it on its back, tearing for the belly, and as he watched, ensnared by the killing, the thought flashed through Erks' mind that no possum, no matter how big or wary or vicious, could take this Weimaraner, that the game was fixed in advance, the scenario already rehearsed in some hinterland of natural order, and now just played out here. And yet he was on his feet, breathing in gasps, caught up. It was all flurry and frantic, blurred motion, and wild noise.

Then it stopped. In the silence Erks heard himself groan. He stepped back and sucked air, then found the possum with the beam, and the dog. Head down, the dog watched the possum. The possum rolled slowly to its side and kicked. It seemed small now, the possum, and over it the dog was big and shiny, a buck dog.

"Take that possum," Erks whispered through his teeth.

The dog pawed the possum. The possum hissed and struggled halfway to its feet, swaying. The dog went after it, biting into the spine. Erks heard the bone crack. The dog, snarling, lifted the possum and shook it violently, then went down with it, lay flat and shook it, knocking it against the rock floor. It released the possum and stared at it. The possum lay still.

Erks said, "Fetch it."

Ruby waited in front of the sofa, her hands at her sides, gripping the telephone receiver in one fist. "It's Lucas," she said when Erks swung out of the hallway. She handed over the receiver. "Wes, not tomorrow."

He fingered the receiver and blinked. "Can you look at Rex?"

Ruby was annoyed. She knew it would be tomorrow. Lucas never called except on the night before. She stalked out of the living room into the kitchen, but pulled up short at the sight of the carnage, the possum on the butcher table and blood pooling beneath the stainless-steel blades of the outboard's propeller, and on the floor the dog, still excited, sniffing at the possum and prancing, proud, its coat mutilated with gashes.

"Rex!" The dog dropped its ears as if it were being scolded.

"Lucas?" she heard her husband say.

On the counter the cat growled at the possum, but kept her distance. "You damn-fool dog," Ruby said, kneeling. The dog pricked its ears, wagged its stub, and licked Ruby's face, heedless of its wounds. "Iris, shush." The cat, craving attention, began to purr.

"Out where?" Ruby heard him say.

The dog had fifteen or more wounds across its chest, shoulders, and sides, one of which was dangerously close to the throat. Against the Weimaraner's dark coat the patches of pink seemed almost decorative, like salmon-colored brooches. Ruby stood and reached for the alcohol and swabs.

"Who's the hell's Lily?" she heard him say. She listened to the pause in which Lucas presumably explained who Lily was.

The cat rubbed itself against Ruby's arm and the dog nuzzled her crotch. Ruby pushed the dog away. The dog went up on its hind legs and sniffed the possum, then came back down and looked at Ruby, its head cocked. "I see it, Rex." She knelt again and held the dog and scrutinized the neck wound. It was absolutely square, as were all the wounds. She found it remarkable, how the flesh was neatly incised by the possum's teeth as if with a razor and removed like a patch, like the lives of the other two, possum and male cat, removed like patches.

"That's not enough, Lucas," Erks said. Ruby stopped again to listen, but the words became incoherent. Outside, the wind gusted and a tree limb rubbed against the eave above the kitchen, squeaking.

Ruby swabbed gently at the exposed flesh on the neck, then cleaned the hair around the wound. The alcohol must have stung, but the dog took it without flinching. Instead, it quivered, its blood up, and Ruby had to grip the collar as she worked. It was a good dog.

"Fifteen thousand," he said, his voice clear in a lull of the wind.

The fifteen thousand was simply a bargaining point, she knew, but it was his way to make his moves startling. That was why he did well, but doing well was not his intent. Doing well was a sidelight. That, too, was why he did well. In all things he liked the surprising, speculative gesture and then to see where it led. That she didn't mind. It made living with him interesting. It could be exasperating, though, his passion, or what she had decided was his passion: he had an animal way of watching, like a coyote watching a ground squirrel, not hungry, the coyote, not hungry enough to attack, but watching in the manner of one who might attack. More than once Ruby had felt as though she were the ground squirrel and it gave her a profound sense of being alone. He had a fatal, bright focus to his watching and at times his taciturnity could be fierce.

Ruby moved down the dog's chest, swabbing the wounds one at a time. The cat had jumped from the counter to her shoulder, where it perched, leaning against her neck. Its purring was noisy in her ear and she couldn't hear her husband.

She knew who Lucas was. She didn't know what he looked like, though she'd be willing to make a guess—there'd be something sharp in his manner, a strain devoid of passion, a brittle strain in his face, something that could snap—but she believed she knew exactly who Lucas was because of his requests, or demands, delivered as if they were givens, which meant to Ruby a condition of great flux behind the demands, of uncertainty and opportunism held up by inflexible schedules and the countless little imperatives of his trade. That she did mind. That she considered immoral—a snake lying in the mouth of its lair, showing its fangs but hiding its size and breed. The illegality of his dealings with cocaine or opium or aliens she didn't really care about one way or another—it depended. Being alive seemed illegal enough to start with.

Her husband worked for Lucas, maybe, because Lucas was the embodiment of speculation, because maybe Lucas was himself inside out. To Wes the illegality meant even less—it hardly existed—and he had his father's life behind him, the old radical, klepht, old anarchist who fled his homeland as an outlaw, although over matters of family, and loyalty to friends, and religion, her husband was a moralist, much more old-fashioned than she, even rigid. Over such matters his refusal to bend could amount to foolishness. The contradiction of his mercurial qualities and his fixity didn't always make sense, but their order, the fixity first, at the core, made him finally trustworthy. It was the way he showed his size.

Ruby felt the smooth fur between the dog's front legs for wounds, then along the belly, and found one back in the hollow of abdomen and leg. The dog shifted, pulling Ruby sideways, and the cat, off balance, dug into her shoulder with its claws.

Erks' footsteps approached the kitchen. When he entered she said, "Jesus Christ, get this damn cat off me and hold your dog."

Erks looked at Ruby, cockeyed and half splayed under the bleeding dog and the wounded cat clinging to her shoulder. He chuckled and stuck a finger in his ear and revolved it. "Saint Francis?"

"Damn it."

Erks looked at the wax on his fingertip.

"Erks!"

He removed the cat and squatted beside Ruby, holding the dog while Ruby swabbed the belly wound. "I need a bath."

"So who the hell's Lily?"

"Lucas' wife. She's riding as far as Reno."

"Isn't Reno out of the way?"

"That possum put up a fight, huh?"

"Wes?"

"The whole trip is out of the way. I have to take the truck part of it. I'll be gone three days."

They were side by side, their knees and arms touching. They had turned the dog and Ruby swabbed the wounds on the other flank in silence.

"I have to meet Lucas in Rathdrum." He paused. "Tomorrow morning."

35

Ruby grunted.

"Then I go on to Vancouver."

"Your son's going to be upset." She reached for a bottle of ointment, stuck her finger into the yellow goo, and began dabbing it on, starting back with the neck wound.

"You're upset."

"That's true."

"Listen, it's going to storm. Next weekend'll be better anyhow."

"That's one thing. Your not being here is another."

He was silent. He gazed at her buttocks, taut as she leaned around the dog. He placed his hand on the small of her back.

"Save it, Wes."

When he removed his hand she nearly lost her balance and made the dog shy, so that Erks nearly lost his balance, too. They caught themselves and rocked against each other, silent. Ruby had no desire to argue about Lucas tonight. She just wanted it done, over. The two squatted next to each other for a moment and gazed at the side of the dog, but not—neither of them—focusing on it. They gazed contemplatively outward like a pair of monkeys in a zoo.

"Listen, I'm sorry," he said.

"Oh, what the hell." Ruby grasped the dog's collar. "I've got him."

Erks released the dog and went out to the porch. He returned with newspaper and the bone saw and moved the outboard motor to one side and lifted and turned the possum and slid the newspaper under it. The possum's eyes were glazed, the expression frozen, the long incisors extending over the curled, rubbery lower lip. The body had stiffened.

"Did you get the money you wanted?"

"Not yet."

"Did you mention what's-his-name?"

"Not yet."

She stood, her hands on her hips. "I'm taking Rex and Iris to the vet in the morning." Her face was flushed from the awkward work. She picked up the beer cans, abandoned on the counter, passed one to Erks and drank from the second. He watched her, her throat and belly and firm abdomen arched as she tipped the can and swallowed.

"I fly home Sunday."

She set the can down squarely on the counter.

He cut the possum's head off with the bone saw. She watched. The dog watched. The cat watched, growling at the sudden profusion of scent. Erks carried the body out to the incinerator to lay it beside the young cat. The cat was gone. Erks flashed his light on and looked inside the incinerator at the impression, the shape of the cat's body in the ashes. There were indentations leading to the impression, prints, but indecipherable because of the depth of the ash—mysterious. He laid the possum body down. Heavy, it sank an inch or two. The sound of pines in the rising wind was a whisper, but loud, a voiceless wail, all air, a white sound in the dark.

He stood in the bedroom doorway and scratched the back of his neck. Ruby lay naked on the bed, the coverlet down around her knees, her flesh prickled by the cool air which blew in through the open window, her upper body, her face turned toward the wall. One hand rested on her hip.

Erks stripped and climbed in beside her. "I put the possum head in the freezer," he said, rolling to his side against her.

Ruby sat up and bent over him, her breast squashing against his ribs. She took his penis in her mouth, squeezed his testicles with her hand, ran her tongue up and down the cord. Like a pinned thing, Erks flayed against the covers and struggled to reach her nipples. The wind puffed the curtain in the window and blew across their bodies. It smelled of rain. He knew that it could turn to snow.

He lay back, panting. Ruby slid up him, pressed her lips against his hard enough for him to feel her teeth. She lifted her hips and came down on him, the union natural. He sucked her nipples, first one, then the other. They disengaged, rolled, reengaged on their sides. She rolled away and turned her back to him, toward the wall again, groaning. It gave him a moment's pause,

37

her sound. He touched her shoulder lightly, interrogatively, stroked it, then reached around and hugged her. She rolled back and he mounted her, their rhythm quickly growing athletic, too fast. He withdrew, teased her. Insistent, she brought him back with her hands and shoved with her hips to make him strike true.

They stayed hugged together for a time, their bodies twitching, then gradually coming to rest. Erks lifted himself off her by his knees and elbows, withdrew carefully, and kicked free, and turned and lay on his back, his left leg flush against her right leg.

"When you go to the vet, have him check out the possum head."

Ruby murmured and grasped his hand and squeezed.

Erks made a count of things to do in the morning:

Move the outboard out of the kitchen.

Unhitch the boat from the truck.

Pack a suitcase.

Pack a lunch. Pack water. Pack a flashlight. Pack the binoculars.

Take the crowbar.

Check the toolbox. Check maps.

Check the oil, the battery, the radiator, the air pressure in the tires.

Stop for gas on the way. Fill the gas can.

He fell asleep first, dreaming of the road. The broken center line passed rapidly between his eyes and back through the middle of his head.

Ruby stared at the window, at the curtain, billowing, at the square of pale light, at the night, and thought of how a change in season brought a sense of juncture, of a ribwork upon time, of a cleaving. The pattern, reexperienced, was a ritual, a wafer tasted again and again.

She thought of the bend in the creek below where they lived. Water circled land there on three sides. Last year, she, Matt, and Wes had found a neighbor's calf there. The bones were covered with hide and decaying meat, the extremities only—the ends of legs, the crown of the head—turning to skeleton. Yesterday she had walked down with Matt and found the bones bare and overgrown by bunch grass and wild flowers—lupines, buttercups, grass widows. A mullein shaft had shot up through the pelvis. The bones were white, powdering ever so slightly. The bones were picked clean. Next year the bones would be gone.

They caught her attention, the bones, revisited, as would a certain sound, or kinnikinnick growing in the shade of a certain rock again, or a certain leaning tree used as a fence post, the way each year the barbed wire cut deeper into the trunk, or the spring air blowing through the window and her husband exhausted at her side, revisited. It gave her a sense of youth and then the reverse, a profound sense of displacement, of doubt, loss, age, and of sorrow.

❧3❧

The next morning.

The town of Dynamite, Washington, a town unknown to all but those who lived in it, or nearby, or to those who happened to find it in an Interior Department blowup of that section of the county, the town named therein, actually written, or to those excursionists who took the wrong turn in the road and followed it to its dead end. But these chance travelers wouldn't think the place had a name, tiny as it was, built as it was between two hills at the back side of a lake and consisting only of three houses, one, curiously, a Victorian edifice, the other two frame homes, baby sisters to the big one, and of a mechanic's shop, and a block-long brick warehouse which had no signs to name it, explain it, or to warn against what it contained—explosives, dynamite.

Inside the big house, heavy purple curtains were drawn to either side of the leaded bedroom window that overlooked the backyard. The light in the room was of a hard, washed, bleaching character. Through the window the dark branches of nut and fruit trees—almond, cherry, peach, apple—were visible, caked on the topsides with snow, and it was still snowing, heavily, re- markably. The branches of the trees were glossy on the under- sides, a tangled etching of black lines which against the sheet of white hurt the head to see. Beyond the trees the earth was barely distinguishable from the sky.

The man in bed, Albert Sandman, rolled back and eased his

head down onto the thick pillow and stared at the opposite wall, dense with roses and stalks that twined maddeningly without beginning or end. A heavy quilt was drawn up to his shoulders and his toes were strained beneath the weight. When he closed his eyes the image of tree branches against white, segmented by the window leadings, reappeared. He ran his hands down his naked ribs to his pelvis as if testing to be certain he was there. His body was warm. With one hand he cupped his testicles and gently freed the moist bag from the skin of his legs. Beside him the bed had been slept in by another; his right hand rested in the hollow. He had vague sexual recollections, but when he tried to sort them out his mind proved to be deep in a fog. He hardly knew where he was—somewhere west of the Rockies. A stranger, Sandman, motorcycling from the East Coast in the general direction of California, he had been forced off the road by the unseasonal snowstorm.

He opened his eyes and forced himself out of bed. The cold air of the room shocked his flesh. When he leaned down to pick up his leather trousers from a chair, he nearly fell over, his legs rubbery, his head leaden. He remembered now carousing until early morning in a roadside bar and drinking too much sweet wine with the young woman, a big woman, a mulatto, or Lebanese, or Polynesian, or gypsy, or something—Sandman hadn't been sure. When he had first entered the bar from the road she sat alone at a table in the corner with a glass of wine, and they found each other in the way of solitary strangers, attracted by the undefined yet tangible air of need which they put out, and which drew them together no matter how unlike their powers. He wanted a drink, a warm place to sit, and then a place to spend the night. He didn't mind testing his strength against her. A traveler had nothing to lose.

She plugged the jukebox and jerked him about the tiny dance floor for hours—wild, crazy. She bumped him against the pool table on one side, the piano on the other, stranded him, returned with more for him to drink, and offered him a place to stay. The last thing he remembered was himself sprawled in a booth, dizzy, drunk, and the woman leaning over him with concern, close, the skin of her neck and chest bright with sweat, almost blue, clay-colored.

Two mornings before while Lily was out, her dying mother had driven herself to the nearest mortuary parlor, ordered the coffin she desired for herself—a big one, hermetically sealed, satin-lined, and with chrome-plated handles and railings on the outside—and gave instructions for embalmment: "When I go, I want to be embalmed within an inch of my life," she had whispered. She collapsed on her way out, on the mortuary steps. The mortician called the sheriff, and the trouble the woman had tried to steer past her daughter was taken up, the body transported to the county morgue, where it had to be identified, tagged, claimed, even paid for, and carried back to be paid for again before the dead woman's wishes would be satisfied.

Lily's brother, Bud, had insisted that the body be transported to Rathdrum, Idaho, to be buried beside her husband. Last night Lily had gone out to drink her keening down, out in the unnatural snow to the bar. Early this morning, the mortician had called to say he couldn't transport the body to Rathdrum in this weather, and Lily called Bud, and Bud, refusing to change plans, said he'd come after the damn woman himself. By now he had arrived and was on his way back to Rathdrum with her, the body encased in the fancy coffin, its meaning now poised somewhere between dead, lamented mother and trucked meat, the second of these complicating and fueling the first, Lily's sorrow.

Of all this, Sandman knew nothing. He wasn't even sure where he was. He figured it was her place. He buttoned up his shirt and stepped into the hallway, where he met a heavy cloud, the odor of breakfast cooking somewhere. He stopped at the bathroom. It smelled of lotion and condensation covered the mirror. He took a dab of toothpaste on his finger and rubbed his teeth and gums with it, then washed his face with cold water and slicked down his hair, and wiped off the mirror with a towel, and stared at himself. A small man, five feet six, he had thick, sensual lips, heavy jowls, large ears, and his skin looked clammy. His eyes were bloodshot. His head throbbed.

He wandered into the living room, a place out of another age. Big, it had hardwood floors, high ceilings, linen wallpaper, more leaded windows, a flowered carpet, and Currier and Ives prints on the walls. He found his way to the kitchen and found Lily there, freshly bathed but still wearing a dressing gown, her face shiny and her hair frizzled. He recognized her as something from his dreams. She towered over the stove.

"We need some wood," she said. "It's in the garage."

He went out into the soft wet snow that muffled sounds. He got the wood, a stack of it which he steadied with his chin as he struggled through the garage door, then the back door of the house. He stood, clenching the wood. Snow dripped from his boots and cuffs.

"Did you see my bike?"

Lily stood at the stove with her back to him and she chuckled, but did not turn. "In the garage. Next to the woodpile."

It was true; Sandman had just seen his cycle at the head of the stack. Groggy, in pain, he felt drugged. "How did it get there?"

"We brought it back last night."

"We did?"

"I drove it." She turned and wagged a spatula at him. "You tied one on."

Sandman smiled over the wood, curling one side of his thick upper lip. Recognizing the odor, he edged over to the stove and looked. "God!" His stomach wrenched. "Liver?"

Lily held the spatula up like a placard. "Best thing in the world. Iron."

He paused. "Should I put this in the fire?"

"Not all of it, for God's sake."

Too bright, she was too bright; his head hurt. His arms had begun to tremble from the awkward weight. Slowly, he knelt and set the wood on the floor and fed and stoked the fire, then eased into a chair at the table which stood near the potbelly stove. She served him black coffee and liver and bacon, hash browns, fried onions, and eggs turned over easy so that the hash browns might have been sopped in the yolks. He had to take the food carefully, the liver especially. He had to chew slowly and swallow with deliberation so as not to gag. The liver tasted like urine. He couldn't finish it. The joints of the stove creaked from the heat and Sandman's left side cooked. He grew drowsy. He attempted to talk of his journey, to revive some image of himself—cross-country motorcyclist: a daring image, a knotted body hurtling across the expanse of the West—but overcome by incoherence, he had to stop.

Lily added cream and sugar to her second cup of coffee and put her elbows on the table and hunched forward as she stirred. "A woman needs a man. But not the way most men think," she said.

Sandman sat back, startled. She smiled at him, revealing several gold caps—too bright, too bright again. Her position opened the dressing gown so that the inner sides of her large, brown breasts were visible, and one aureole, her left, deep blue, almost black. Obscurely aroused, Sandman looked away through a window. Snow fell upon the hill and weighted down the pine trees.

"Having a man in the rooms is good, but not for what he thinks he means. Just for having his body in the rooms," Lily said. "Personally, I do enjoy the use of a man, but you didn't amount to much last night."

He stared at her in consternation.

"I thought you little guys were peppery."

His mouth dropped.

Lily leaned back and laughed. She had a rich laugh which came from the chest. "You're a character, you know."

A sensualist, Sandman was mortified.

Lily gulped her coffee and shoved the cup into the center of the table, stood, and left the kitchen. Sandman stood when she left, then sat down, then stood again and refilled his cup at the stove and sat back down. The coffee was excellent, strong and dark. He searched his mind for what he might have said or done, or not done, the night before to prompt Lily's remarks, but it was all a blur. Lily returned, dressed in a navy-blue skirt and jacket and a white blouse, and immediately opened a door and walked

44

into another adjacent room, what appeared to be a sickroom. Through the doorway Sandman saw that the bed had steel rails. Beside the bed stood a tray loaded with prescription bottles and a four-legged walking apparatus with handlebars and plastic grips. Sandman watched Lily take several packets off the shelving which lined one wall and drop them into a carpetbag she had set on the bed.

"You don't live alone?" he asked politely.

"I'm married, if that's what you mean," she replied without turning toward him.

Sandman craned his neck to look, expecting to find a paraplegic or a withered vestige of a man in a wheelchair in a corner of the room.

"My mother's room," Lily said, coming back into the kitchen. Sandman revolved in his chair. Lifting his cup to his lips, he started and spilled his coffee over his chin when Lily reached into a closet behind the wood-burning stove, removed a double-barreled shotgun, broken down to stock and barrel, and stuffed it into the valise. Lily zipped the valise shut and faced him. "Was my mother's room. I got to go. You're welcome to come or you can stay." Her head nearly touched the stovepipe which ran beneath the ceiling to the chimney flue. The big carpetbag hung like a becalmed boat from her hand.

Sandman set his cup down and wiped his chin with his sleeve. "Where to?"

"To bury my mother."

"Ah . . . I beg your pardon."

She put on a long gray coat and crouched in front of the wood-burning stove and screwed the vents shut, then turned and smiled and squinted at Sandman with one eye. "You might as well see some country."

They left the house and walked along a gravel road past the brick warehouse. Lily walked rapidly and since she was several inches the taller, Sandman was compelled to work to counter her stride. Not a word passed between them. The sky was as white as the snow it loosed upon the hills and dark pines. The air was cold in the lungs, and wet, pneumoniac. They turned up a drive which led into a hollow to the mechanic's shop and got inside one of the cars parked outside, an old De Soto. The big boxy car kicked right over and Lily swung it around, spinning out in the snow, and bounced it down the driveway and out along the road to a paved arterial and past the roadside tavern he had stopped at last night, then onto the highway and down toward Interstate 90.

"Your car?"

"My mother's. Had to get it greased."

The snow turned to slush on the highway and Lily took it easy, kept the speed under forty-five. The fan-operated heater in the old car was excellent and Sandman leaned back and unzipped his leather riding jacket and watched the country going by. Buildings accumulated along the sides of the road, pushing out the pines as they approached the city of Spokane.

"Are we going far?" he asked. He had been through Spokane and on this road going the opposite direction—south, seeking the sun—the evening before in the rain, the rain turning to snow. The snow dislodged him, stranded him. Now this—arrested.

"Nope."

Sandman looked at her, at her cheek and the side of her jaw, the bones big, the lower lip drooping, quivering slightly with the vibration of the car, but firm. Intent on the road, she didn't look at him. The car swelled with Lily's mood, not bright at all now, but brooding and dark and vivid as a carp in late-summer water spotted in the shade of a bridge, too big for shallow waters, the sharp hump of its back protruding. The slush hissed under the tires.

"Idaho," she said. "Just north of Rathdrum. What's left of it."

"That's where we're headed?"

Lily murmured.

"They've had trouble in Rathdrum?"

"Trouble?"

They turned onto the interstate, east, and Lily leaned forward and peered over the front of the car as they descended sharply into the valley through which flowed the Spokane River.

46

Erks had passed by here already this morning and had marked the valley and the river, the Spokane, a tributary of the Columbia, and the city built on the falls of the river, a place now where property was the liveliest article of exchange, where a real estate or mortgage company could be found on every other block, and in the late nineteenth century the site of military installations, and in the early nineteenth century of inland forts mounted by contesting British and American fur traders, but long before that a fishing ground, a camas-gathering ground, a common place of tribes for meeting and trade. A natural hollowing of land, a big abundant dish, the place magnetized life and settlement, and the blood of Indian nations and white settlers had flowed here as recently as a hundred years ago. So Erks had thought. So, when passing or coming to Spokane, he always thought, or something akin to it, some catechism of history, and so then he always wondered when the original magnetism had played out and how it came to be replaced by the hot and centripetal magnetism of the city built on the ancient place.

Sandman's ears popped on the way down. The city itself, climbing the bluffs to the south and burgeoning for miles up the watersheds to the north and east, was masked by the sleet. High-rise buildings, to the left, the north, built on the banks of the river, of the falls, were gray cutouts against the white sky.

Then Lily answered him: "I mean what's left of my family."

"Oh." Sandman paused. "I'm sorry." He paused again and glanced at Lily. "It's a great difficulty," he said lamely.

She didn't acknowledge his words.

Sandman felt foolish. He regarded death as a matter of the utmost delicacy and its occasion a time to align one's words as closely as possible to the mood of the bereaved, but he was utterly bewildered as to how to approach Lily. She had wound into herself and grown massive. His elbow rested on the stock of the shotgun which bulged in the carpetbag on the seat between them. He knew it. It shocked him. He did not move his elbow. The gun, carried broken down and concealed, hung like a hook in his imagination, a savage thing dragged out of a life he did not fathom.

Yesterday he had traveled the country on a motorcycle, in control, insofar as the cycle controlled even the landscape through which he moved, and so limited it, so designed it, or his perception of it. Today he found all control taken away. Lily held the wheel now. She dealt the hand. All the weight had slid to her side. Earlier, she had insulted his sexuality. No matter how considerate he might try to be of her difficulty, what really lay at the root of his uncertainty was his desire to master her, or someone, or something equal, and so restore himself. He fingered a zipper of his jacket and stared straight ahead through the windshield, the light of his eyes, set wide apart in his forehead, choked, inquisitorial, monomaniac, and carnal. He hated feeling like a fool.

The sleet shifted back to snow as they left Spokane and thickened as they began to climb the Bitterroot Range. Sandman's ears popped again. Lily didn't talk. He didn't talk. Just beyond the Idaho border they entered Post Falls, then turned left, north, and passed across a broad plateau—the Coeur d'Alene prairie. As they progressed, the mountain forest encroached steadily upon the grain and grass crop fields. They had traveled forty miles. The snow on the road deepened and Lily slowed to twenty-five. The big car tracked well, but at dips and rough spots it showed a tendency to slide and demanded her attention. They passed through Rathdrum, a railroad town built in a pocket against a mountain, then Lily pulled off onto the shoulder, stopped the car, and got out—still without speaking. Sandman waited, then followed. The snow caked the bottoms of his leather trousers and melted onto his cheeks from behind his large ears. Deep woods lined the road on both sides. Lily appeared from behind the open trunk, holding a bumper jack and a set of tire chains as if they were toys. Snowflakes clung to her frizzy hair. One chain rang softly when she dropped it into the snow beside a rear tire.

Sandman tried to operate the jack, but it jammed and Lily had to come to his aid. He slid under the car to fasten the chains

48

on the insides of the tires, but he couldn't get the locking swivels to work. Lily didn't speak. He wished she would speak. She lay down on the outside of each rear tire, first one, then the other, and fastened each on the outside, then reached in and pulled the chains taut and slipped the swivels through the links on the insides. Sandman lay under the car on his back with his hands clasped on his stomach and watched her long fingers master the chain. When the second chain was mounted she rested her cheek on her hand and peered around the tire at Sandman.

Now she spoke: "They can be tricky." She raised her eyebrows and smiled slyly at him, as if there were nothing of moment here, nothing extraordinary, as if she were relaxed in bed and just glancing up at him from a magazine. "Are you coming out of there?"

Sandman could not find the words to respond. He lay on his back and stared furiously at the transmission, which hung over his face like a bomb.

"Myself," Lily said, "I've got goose bumps you could grate a nutmeg on."

Sandman slid out and slipped off the road to relieve himself while Lily jacked the car down. The silence of the country—set off by the echoless sound of the bumper jack, ticking and cocking, ticking and cocking—the immensity of the country, the fathomless muffling of snow and himself in it, standing behind a cedar four times as broad as he was, holding his organ with fingers numbed by handling the chain, sent a shock of unalloyed terror through his body. Christ! he thought, straddling the yellow cut he had made in the snow: Christ! A man could die here, right here, and it'd be months before anybody would come by to even kick him out of the way.

"We've got five miles of this road," Lily said.

It was a climb, all right, and Lily took it slowly, trusting the chains. They had turned off the highway and were headed up a steep gravel road, around the side of a mountain. The chains rang softly like bells in rhythm, the slack of each chain swinging in time. They followed fresh tire tracks, two sets of tracks.

49

Sandman looked over the edge of the road into the deep ravine. The terrain, crowded with forest, covered with snow, the raw verticality of the terrain, communicated great density, great fervor, great compaction of energy. He arched his back and stretched out his legs. The snow had worked its way between his trousers and jacket and he felt chilled.

"Where'd you say you were from?"

"I don't believe I did."

Lily looked over at him and smiled.

"Did I?"

"What do you do in New York City?"

Sandman frowned. Lily chuckled.

"I'm a C.P.A."

"Money, huh?"

The car skidded on a turn. Lily cut the wheel and downshifted. The chains bit in, lurching the car, then she gunned it, shifting back up into third. Sandman gripped the armrest. Lily leaned toward him and leered.

"Numbers," he said. "It's company money."

Lily chuckled again. "If you work with it you know how to use it."

Pleased to be asked about himself, Sandman relaxed a little. "I'm waiting."

"I didn't think accountants rode motorcycles."

"That was part of the idea."

"Upgrade the image, huh?"

"I guess. Or get out from under the image."

"It's that bad?"

She had a way of putting him on the defensive.

"What brought you out here?"

"Why and how I got to the tavern last night I can answer. Just what I'm doing here I don't know." Feeling her eyes on him, he hesitated. What he was doing, he had thought, was living looser than his life ordinarily allowed, loose as Jack Kerouac, as Allen Ginsberg, as Ken Kesey, as loose as one of those—he thought—who had never even tried to find the bottom line of a ledger. "I wanted to travel. To see the West," he said. "I've never been out West." As he spoke, he fell prey again to the sense that he had lost all control, to a slowly tightening anxiety.

"Did you find it?"

"What?"

"The West."

He paused, then said, "Listen, why are you carrying a gun?"

They rounded a switchback and plowed into a fender-high snowdrift which had blown across the road. Lily bulled the car through the drift. Sandman looked back. A cloud of powdering snow blew up from the rear tires. They rounded another switchback, and another. The road suddenly became extremely steep, then just as suddenly it leveled out and twisted around a rock abutment to the mouth of a sloping meadow that was scattered with wrecked cars. Covered with snow, they were mounds, the wheel hubs, axles, and leaf springs exposed at ground level—artifacts, clues to the identities of the heaps. Lily stopped the car, the chains squeaking in the snow.

"What gun?" she said softly.

He looked at her. She did not look back. Her silhouette, the side of her face, cheek, chin, and brow, deep brown, smooth, was filled with adamance and powerful gloom. Again her mood filled the car—dark, too dark: she was either too bright or too dark, she was too certain, she lacked the shadow he needed to see her form. He looked away, down at what she looked at, a two-story gabled ruin of a house standing at the edge of a small apple orchard that fanned back over a hill. In the distance was snow. A fire roared in the clearing before the house and behind the fire three men and one woman were gathered. They looked up at the car, their faces like wafers in the harsh light. The woman sat against a tree. Two men were crouched over a pig that lay on the ground next to the fire and a third man stood to one side. Sandman looked back at Lily.

"Listen. Maybe I should leave."

Lily looked at him with her head down, the whites of her eyes round and glossy, and she smiled, showing her amusement as she showed her gold teeth, a glimmer, a point in her big solemn face, a slit of brightness in the night. "How?"

51

There was no answer.

Lily sighed and grabbed the handle of her carpetbag, opened her door and got out. Sandman followed. They passed a shed, then a pen. In the pen were three big yellow dogs. Hackles up and teeth bared, the dogs lunged against the hog wire, snarling. Startled, Sandman shied.

Lily charged the dogs, flailing her arms. She grabbed the hog wire and rattled it and snarled at them.

The dogs fell silent and cowered, but their upper lips swept rhythmically back and forth over their fangs. Decked with snow, patches of white on yellow, their flicking whiskers crystallized with ice, they moved away from the fence in short figure eights, the three of them interweaving on paws as light as cotton, as if about to break into dance. Their eyes, turned on Lily, had an expression of docility. The eyes looked human to Sandman, dolorous. Fangs, rippling lips, and powerful shoulders looked treacherous.

Lily swung away, her look, too, dolorous. As they went down the hill the two men at work on the pig rose and moved toward them. They were big, massive. Sandman felt himself shrinking as they came closer. One, the biggest, was younger. The other had a large birthmark on one side of his face and a shredded ear lobe, the flesh long healed and hanging in two pendants.

Lily addressed the older man in midstride: "Lucas isn't here yet?"

The man stopped and spat to one side. The second man had stopped behind the first. They were close together now, the four of them, and Sandman felt he had stepped into another forest.

"You got Mama?"

The man nodded up the hill. Sandman looked. A shiny black casket protruded from the end of a flesh-colored panel truck.

"This is Al Sandman," Lily said. "My brother Bud. My brother Zack."

Sandman stepped forward and began to raise his hand, then dropped it again when the older man looked down at him with an expression which said he'd just as soon break Sandman's back as shake his hand. Sandman moved off. The younger man, grinning foolishly, ducked behind the older man's shoulder. They were not full-blood siblings, Sandman saw, could not be. Though they shared their size, the three of them, the men were white, Caucasian. Lily was something else—Polynesian, Indian, or mulatto, or something, some mix Sandman still hadn't deciphered.

The older man spoke to Lily, his voice filled with venom. "That one over there's waiting for Lucas. What the hell makes that sonofabitch Lucas think he can do business here?"

Sandman froze.

"Him?" Lily said, nodding at the third man, behind the fire.

"Who does that sonofabitch Lucas think he is? This ain't his place."

Lily moved. Sandman followed her toward the third man, not her husband either, his prime fear quelled; none of these was her husband. They went around the fire and had to step over the outstretched legs of the woman, who sat on a board thrown down in the snow. She leaned against the tree. Sandman looked at her in amazement as they passed. She sat as if she were tied to the tree. She wore a big straw hat decorated with artificial fruit, a moth-eaten fur coat, and under the coat, which was unbuttoned, a long, old-fashioned lace gown. Her eyes were glassy.

"And that ain't his mama," the older man said at Lily's back.

She ignored him. "Wes Erks?" she said to the third man.

The third man, Erks, tipped his hat, then a troubled expression moved over his face. Sandman looked, looked at Lily. She was weeping. Tears streamed down her face. She turned away quickly and moved up onto the porch of the house, and inside, the door slapping softly behind her.

4

"She's coming!" Zack cried, beating on the pig's hock.

Stuck, bled, scaled, and scraped yesterday after the two brothers, Zack and Bud, had received word of their mother's death, scored and disemboweled last night, greased this morning, stuffed and stitched, the half-cooked sow lay on her side in the snow. The first spit had broken. A second, thicker locust spit, whittled to a point at one end, was being installed. Bud had muscled the sharp end down the throat. The spit had slid easily at first, then it snagged on a bone or a knot of tissue. Bud fought it. Zack, a retarded man of twenty-two, had rolled up his sleeve, knelt, and stuck his arm elbow-deep up the pig's ass and beamed.

"She's coming," he repeated. "She's coming, Bud!"

Zack withdrew his arm and stood. Bud rammed and twisted until the tip of the spit appeared between the buttocks, then he rose and turned his back and kicked the butt end of the spit with his heel, knocking the point out by quarter-inch distances. The tawnycolored hog's flesh quivered with each blow. Zack stood watching, one sleeve down, one sleeve up and that arm slick with grease. His face was filled with pleasure and he bounced on his toes.

Erks watched Zack, amused by his antics.

Hot fat had carved trails in the snow, canals fed from meat and seeping out from under the spine. There was a puddle of fat

54

at the small man's boot toe, Sandman, watching too. Sandman's boots had heavily embroidered dragon heads on the panels. Erks didn't know where Sandman was from, or who he was, only his name and that he had arrived with Lily, that he wore—curiously—riding leathers, that his boots, soaked already an inch above the soles, were a poor choice for this weather. He was a funny-looking little guy.

Erks had simply driven to the meeting place to which Lucas had directed him. He was on time. Lucas was late. He knew none of these people, but Lily, Lucas' wife, he saw, was sister to the two men, Bud and Zack. He hadn't even known Lucas was married before last night. That was the way with Lucas, not to tell, a precaution of business worked into his life. The young woman sitting against the tree—he figured—was Bud's wife. Earlier, he had stood near enough to hear her whispering, and thinking she spoke to him, he had leaned toward her and begged her pardon.

She looked up. "I said, O Sacred Head."

He looked at her blankly.

"I said, O Sacred Head now wounded."

A strange one. Dressed like that in yellow high heels and garish hat and a child's wooden necklace and rhinestone rings and a garish green gown and a fur coat and sitting on a board in the snow like an old dog unable to go any farther, she was just collapsed there on the spot. But she was young, not thirty. She was skin and bones. Her head hung, her shoulders were hunched, her hands drooped over her legs, and her fingers touched the snow. Her lips moved incessantly as she whispered to herself. There was little telling what crazed life her body held.

The whole show, in fact, seemed far-fetched: the run-down house and overgrown orchard, and tools scattered everywhere, and a hillside full of broken-down cars and machinery, and two men—one of them retarded, or demented, and the other beside himself with anger or frustration or pain, or something—roasting a pig outdoors, and a casket in the back of a panel truck, and snow in April. Erks hadn't anticipated this in Lucas, not this trailing

55

net, or yes, the net, dragged behind, but not dragged over this kind of ground. He felt that Lucas, though absent, had just put a joker down on the table.

To Sandman, standing beside the fire, the place was stupefying.

So. Everybody waited for Lucas. Lily—inside the house doing kitchen work, avoiding Bud, staying out of his way because between them was rift, the imbroglio wolf, and the howl of the wolf had taken its substance in the body of the woman in the casket—waited for Lucas to get here and help her get this done with. The woman at the tree, Winona, Bud's wife, if she could be said to be capable of fixing on any one thing, waited for the time Lucas would arrive and she would have to lift her body up off that board on the ground. Sandman, stranded by Lily, didn't have the faintest idea who Lucas was except that maybe he was Lily's husband, but he, too, waited, waited for something because of the strong air of waiting that cloaked the gathering, the inescapable sense that everything would turn as soon as the one they had named—Lucas—got here and something was done with the casket in the panel truck. Bud and Zack waited for Lucas, though they hated Lucas, Zack because Bud did, and Bud because Lucas was Lily's husband, because Lily, his own sister, was of a better class than himself and made so by his mother, and out of a different father than himself, because Lucas didn't even live with Lily, because Lucas was a criminal, because whenever Bud was around Lucas he always ended up feeling like a fool, and because Lucas always made him wait. And the woman in the casket waited for her son-in-law, the only man in her family who had ever been able to get anything done. Her body waited in the dark, light and dry, embalmed with a vengeance at her request, and her hands, her unnaturally big hands folded on her chest after seventy-five years of seeking occupation, and her gypsy feet, flat from seventy-five years of walking in cheap shoes, and her legs, gnarled and heaped below the knees with varicose veins, they waited, and her eyes in the hollows gorged with seventy-five years of watching, and her tired, hawkish, heavy, pilloried face, waited for Lucas to move this casket and get it down under ground where it belonged.

Erks had gone down on his hunkers and picked up a goose neck from the mud in front of him, the snow melted by heat from the fire. There was an array of bones in the mud, left from previous cookouts—shanks and joints, ribs, the light bones of fowl. Erks toyed with the goose neck as he watched Bud and Zack, poised at either end of the pig. They intended to lift it. The pig was huge. Erks judged it to weigh four hundred pounds, maybe more, but they intended to lift it. Bud was at the snout, Zack at the heavy end. The butt of the spit filled the mouth and the tip protruded six inches beyond the haunches. Unasked, Erks made no move to help. Bud's manner, he saw, prohibited aid, but Sandman moved to Bud's side.

"Here. Let me get a hand on that," Sandman said, bending over.

Erks knew what was coming. For a moment Bud didn't budge, his body giving nothing to Sandman's proximity, then he stood up straight and stared down malevolently at Sandman.

"Keep your damn hands off."

Sandman moved away quickly, startled and silent, looking up and stumbling back, off balance. Bud spat into the fire, then went down again, brought his face close to the snout of the hog and grasped the spit, and Zack followed suit, grasped his end of the spit, crouching. Together, they rose with the weight.

Bud set his feet and pivoted as Zack swung around the fire, stepping gingerly. Bud nearly lost his grip once, but caught it, groaning, his face sharpening. As he stepped sideways, as he lifted his end above one of the two forked limbs driven into the ground at either end of the fire, he did lose it. The spit slid in his hands. Bud struggled, clung to the spit with his fingertips, strove for the fork, his body quivering, crouching and lifting at once, then, as he came upright, the spit tore through his fingers and fell, striking one arm of the fork and driving into the crotch. There was a sharp crack, but the fork and spit held. The flames hissed and lengthened, licking toward the flesh of the pig.

Zack, for whom the weight seemed nothing, had been holding his end stomach-high. He lifted it and set it into the fork, stepped back, and rubbed his palms together. The addled expression on his face, a pleasant, half-stupefied mimicry of amusement, changed now to concern as he gazed at his brother, or to a second mimicry: his square jaw dropped and his broad forehead wrinkled. His small eyes receded like two pebbles in warm wax.

"Bud?" Zack said. "Hey, Bud?"

Bud stood still for a moment, bent and clutching his temples with the thumb and middle finger of his left hand. At his side, the fingers of his right hand were bleeding, scraped by the spit.

"Bud?" Zack said, stepping around the fire toward Bud. "Hey, Bud?"

Bud waved his brother off. He straightened and turned away from the fire and stared up the hill at the road.

Zack stopped, but spoke again. "Bud? Bud?"

It had hurt, the weight. It was the way with Bud. He was always lifting too much weight, shoving too much into too small a space, trying to do too much in too short a time. Already, the mortician had refused to deliver the casket and Lucas was late and the pig wouldn't be cooked in time, not even close, and he had ten plates in the house to feed maybe fifty people. Bud rolled his shoulders, stretching them, then wheeled around and shouted at the house, "Goddamn it, Lily, where's that goddamned Lucas!"

From the house there was no response.

"It's small payment, Lily!" Bud shouted, then, turning back toward the yard and addressing no one in particular, or everyone, or Lucas himself, absent, he growled, "It'd be small goddamn payment to get the preacher here on time."

Sandman stared up at the sky, his eyes widening as if about to blow out into the white.

For the sake of having something to do with his hands, Erks dug at the goose neck with his knife, cleaned out the joints and interstices of bone. Zack turned the spit with a pipe wrench until the pig was belly up. He dropped the wrench, leaned over, and stared fixedly at the pig. The fire crackled from the grease which dripped from the flesh. The animal was stuffed with apples, corn, and onions, the odor already mouth-watering and incongruous with the cold, the wet, the air of deep gloom, of stymied, arrested energy.

"We split her," Zack said, still staring, then looking up, his face wrenched with worry, he said it again: "We split her."

Erks had seen it come by as Zack had turned the pig, the fissures at the throat and abdomen, the careful stitching of the score ripped open by the fall to the fork.

Zack bent his knees and wrung his hands. "We split her, Bud."

"Yeah," Bud said. He stood beside Zack and bent over from the waist, examining the tear. "You fucker!" he said—to the pig, presumably.

"Oh, God," Zack said. "We split her." His voice broke as if he were about to cry. "God, Bud, we split her clean up."

"All right," Bud said, his voice softening. He grasped the back of Zack's head with one hand and reached up with the other hand and rapped Zack sharply on the forehead with his knuckles, three times. "It's all right."

Zack settled down.

Bud looked over at Winona. "Hey!"

Erks looked at the woman. She didn't move. Her eyes were heavy, her face pinched, her features sharp, her dirty blond hair emerging in straps from beneath the hat, her legs prickled with goose bumps.

"Get me that kit," Bud said.

Winona did not respond.

"We have to sew it up ourselves. Get me the kit."

Winona stared vacantly into the fire. "Lucas'll be here," she whined.

"Move your ass. Bring that kit!"

Winona moved, sighing like a heap of leaves, kicked. She braced herself with her hands and stood with great effort. The back of the fur coat was bare to the hide and damp. Under it her dress stuck to her legs. She reached in and picked the dress free as she moved by Erks toward the porch. Erks heard the door fall softly.

Bud looked at Erks and grinned. "She can't do nothing right."

The snowfall had slackened. It fell sparsely in big white flakes that the eye could pick out and follow. The clouds beyond the hills had begun to break, showing streaks of blue. To the west thunderclouds boiled, but they might pass by southerly.

Erks had the goose neck clean. He had pulled out his handkerchief and was polishing, actually polishing it until the vertebrae gleamed with a pale sheen. It was something to do, a little chore to finish while he waited, and in the working, as was the way, the neck became special. He became possessive of it. The neck, long and thick, was from a goose shot last fall—he guessed —for these people kept no fowl. It was a Canadian, probably, moving down the Pend Oreille River toward the Snake, the Columbia, in 4,000-mile transport to Mexico. The geese would be returning soon. The neck could be hung on his rear-view mirror, a totem to migration.

Up in the pen one of the yellow dogs worked on a knuckle bone, flashing its teeth and snarling sporadically at the other two dogs, who lay close by with their heads on their front paws and coveted the bone. Above the pen was the road and Lily's blue De Soto was parked just to one side of its mouth. The road angled up and around the rock abutment, vanished. Opposite the abutment was the sloping meadow, snow-covered and snarled with fingers of volcanic rock and junk machinery and cars. Between the dog pen and the road three vehicles were parked on a flat: Erks' new GMC and to one side of it the flesh-colored four-wheel-drive Chevy van, from the roped rear doors of which the shiny black casket with chrome-plated railings projected like a big black tongue in a strangulated face. His GMC "Jimmy"—actually a big station wagon on a truck chassis, so he called it a truck—was pulled in frontways. It was as black as the casket. Snow collected on its hood and cab top as the casket collected snow on its foot.

On the other side of the GMC was Bud's car. It fit. The late-model Plymouth had stabilizer shocks and a "When Guns Are Outlawed Only Outlaws Will Have Guns" sticker on the bumper, and a gun rack mounted between the ceiling and the back of the front seat. A sliding-action shotgun and a rifle with a scope were outlined through the windows, visible now from where Erks squatted. He had looked inside when he first arrived. That was when he had seen that it was Bud's car—by the way the man down at the fire had watched him looking at it. Under the dash it had a police band radio and a CB receiver, and hanging from the mirror were two posse comitatus badges, one for Bud —Erks figured—and one for Zack. It all fit: the posse comitatus —the Committee of Ten Thousand—and the car, neat as a tack, and the run-down house and littered yard.

Bud and Zack waited on the other side of the fire. Sandman waited, standing alone and nervously shifting his weight from one leg to the other. Erks polished vertebrae and sifted through what he could make of the catechism of this place: Bud fit it, the Idaho Panhandle. Lewis and Clark had turned circles in the vicinity, searching for the route to the Columbia, turned around three times by the Bitterroots. The tribes here—the Coeur d'A-lêne, the Kalispel and Kootenai to the north, and southward the Nez Percé—were proud, "socially developed," and, it was said, self-sufficient, savage, slow to relent. Of the transcontinental rail-roads, the Northern Pacific was the last to push through to the coast. What was to the outside a barrier was on the inside great pressure, the topography physically closing the people off, the country a wild, craggy, hard, volcanic country, the towns—mining towns originally, mostly lumber towns now—built in pockets, ravines, hollows, and up against cliffs, the people insular, and the routes of travel serpentine, following the watersheds. The tribes had traveled according to the seasons north and west to fish, northwest to dig roots, and east to hunt buffalo, and in all directions to trade, but the white people, most of them, displayed an inclination to roost and to let others occupy the paths of trade, and, thus, the Panhandle made sects as it attracted them, the Amish, the Hutterites, the Waldenses, lately hippies, castaways

61

from the sixties, those who refused, and Satanist cults, those of the darker visions. A few years back, Rathdrum itself had been declared a Satanist Zone by the sheriff's office because of a pattern of bizarre violence, murders, human chains formed across roads at night, and the debris of orgies found in the woods by day.

It was a place where migration—a sense of trade, goods, or ideas—if it was not entirely arrested was inward, impacted, heavy, where visions were wayward and dense, discovered like insects under a stone, lifted, or grubs under bark, torn off a tree. The Plymouth aside, Bud and Zack and Winona were poor woods people and unable—Erks imagined—to purchase even the idea of a life outside their own. Erks imagined that Bud drove the county roads in his car and watched for prey—hippies, the Satanists. A quasi-vigilante organization, sheriff's helpers, they claimed, the posse comitatus was a sect itself, it and the Plymouth on the level of elaborate play, but for Bud probably play locked into belief and like a gesture become a trait of character, a habit, a tic, an obsession, a way of life. Erks knew this. He knew Bud's kind, though he'd seen few with a face as grim as that one behind the pig. Actually, Erks himself was not unsympathetic to the posse comitatus, or at least to the idea of it. He did not dislike the idea of vigilante law.

The goose neck, overworked, went to pieces in his hands. The vertebrae scattered like stars in the mud between his boot toes. One by one, he picked them up and put them into the coin pocket of his coat. At his back he heard a conversation, or barely half a conversation, Lily talking to Winona inside the house. Lily's words were indecipherable and the responses Winona made, or might have made in the spaces, were inaudible.

"Winona!" Bud snapped.

Zack raked coals under the pig. Winona emerged with the kit. Erks heard the door slap, then her footsteps, and she appeared. The hem of her dress hung off kilter below the hem of the coat. She walked around the fire and set the tin kit on the ground beside Zack, trying to stay away from Bud, but Bud loomed over her and pinched the sleeve of her coat.

"What's that dress for?"

"You know. The funeral," Winona said, stepping away.

Bud leered and tugged on her sleeve, making her body list back toward him. "The funeral? Or Lucas?" He looked around, soliciting support, looked at Erks, grinning, nudged Zack with his knee and winked at Sandman. Zack looked up and began to laugh rhythmically like someone working a hand pump. Sandman smiled uncertainly. Winona shrank. Bud fingered her necklace and flipped it in her face. "Where'd you dig this trash up?"

Winona's mouth opened and closed.

"It don't match," Bud said.

Confused, Winona touched her necklace.

"Them shoes don't match."

Winona looked down at her feet.

"That dress don't fit." Bud laughed and Zack laughed with him.

Erks' mouth went dry with anger. The door slapped at his back. The plank floor of the porch creaked under weight and he watched Bud's face turn ugly as it rose to look.

"You keep your nose out!" Bud said.

"Leave Winona be," Lily said.

"It's none of your concern."

"You are my concern."

"I'll run your ass off of here."

"Run Mama, too."

Erks looked up at the casket roped into the van.

"I'll run you and your whole damn bunch down with her. I didn't ask for this."

"The hell you didn't, but Mama and me are footing the bill," Lily said, her voice remarkably calm. "As usual."

"You and Mama!" Bud said. "Not you!"

"It's me now."

Bud paused, his face compacted. The silence soaked the air. Winona edged around the fire, past Erks toward the porch, seeking refuge. Sandman shied toward Erks, but froze when Bud spoke again, pointing at the casket. "She goes where she belongs."

"She's got nowhere to go," Lily said and then she laughed,

63

a low, open laugh, and Bud jerked back as if he had been struck. "You're a damn lackey, Bud. Long as me and Mama and Lucas are here, you treat Winona right."

"Lucas!" Bud spat, then again he paused, puffing heavily, his body rigid and his face extravagant with rage at some assertion of force beyond his power to master, some threat which to Erks was visible only as an innuendo, something between him and Lily, or Lucas, unspecified but powerful.

"And now that you've got Mama where you want her for once, you treat her right," Lily said. "As to who's running who, I could jerk this farm right out from under you."

"You try and I'll kill you."

Erks blinked. The man meant what he said.

Lily laughed again, a low laugh in the throat that was filled with menace. Erks turned to look. Lily had her arm around Winona's shoulders, the younger woman, Lily, like a mother to the child. Lily's face glowed and she was smiling at Bud, then she said, "You'd never pull it off." Spoken softly, the words, too, were filled with self-certainty and menace, as if they were a dare.

"You whore," Bud snarled.

Lily was turning to take Winona inside. She swung around. "I said you don't have the guts for it, Bud."

Erks turned back to the fire, impressed by the woman.

Then she led Winona inside. The door swung shut.

Bud stared ferociously after her, at the door, over Erks' head. His face was white with rage. He didn't move a muscle. Then he snapped at Zack, "Get that shit out of the kit."

Zack took the awl, half-moon needle, pliers, and a spool of waxed thread from the tin box, then stood and leaned over the pig, holding the instruments gingerly as if they were hot.

"Bud?" he said. He reached over and touched Bud's arm.

Bud jumped as if shaken from a spell.

Zack held out the tools.

Sandman took Winona's place near Erks. "Are you a relative?" he asked.

"No," Erks replied.

"Oh. A friend of the family? You're from town? Rathdrum?"

Bud and Zack went to work on the pig, Zack repuncturing the flesh at the throat with the awl, then stitching as Bud crimped the seam ahead of Zack with one hand and with the other drew out the needle with the pliers and held it for Zack to take again.

"No. Washington," Erks said. "Davenport." He stood up to watch the work, turning his back on Sandman.

"Listen," Sandman said. "Listen, I'm sorry if I've . . ." The voice trailed off.

Erks turned back. "No matter."

"Isn't Davenport on Highway 2?"

"That's right."

"What do you do there?"

Erks lifted his hat and scratched his head, then replaced the hat. "This and that."

Sandman grinned and pressed on. "Like what?"

To be polite, he said, "A little ranching. A little welding. Crop dusting."

"No kidding? Do they still do that with biplanes?"

Erks gazed at Sandman.

"Do you own a biplane?"

He nodded.

"I'd like to see that."

"You see one and you've seen them all."

"I've never seen one up close," Sandman said. "I'm traveling on 2. Maybe I could stop by."

"Oh?"

Sandman pulled a piece of paper and pen from a pocket. "Could you give me your number?"

"It's in the book."

Sandman paused, then asked, "How do you spell your name?"

Erks spelled it. He turned his back on Sandman again. Bud and Zack breathed slowly, audibly, and in time as they worked. Erks heard the door slap softly. He looked. Sandman had moved away silently and gone inside; his silhouette was visible in the hallway, poised, leaning forward, one hand outstretched to an invisible objective—Lily. Erks hoped now that he'd been impolite enough.

The work on the hog was exacting. The space, first the throat, then the longer tear at the hollow of the abdomen, was constricted and made to appear impossibly so by Bud's and Zack's massive hands. The light tools were wedged rather than held between blunt fingers. The thread was bullied rather than guided. The two men stood awkwardly, bent from the waist, their faces averted, their feet back because of the intense heat from the coals, and yet they worked with deftness and efficiency. Everything was magnified: Bud and Zack were like gigantic surgeons, their impaled patient huge. Fighting the heat, they were engrossed and failed to hear at first the sound of an approaching car. Erks heard it, the engine rising and falling as the car negotiated the switchbacks and grade. Bud stepped back from the pig first, quickly, and then, once he had tied a whip knot at the nub of the abdomen, Zack followed suit, slapping his trouser legs.

"God!" Zack said. His face was flushed. He threw his head back and did a lumbering dance, laughing. "Thought my pants was gonna catch afire!"

Bud looked at Erks, saw him listening, then heard it himself and turned to face the mouth of the road.

Zack stopped his dance. "Is it him?"

The sound was closer now, a low, continuous whine.

"Is it him, Bud?" Zack said.

A red Buick lurched around the abutment and stopped, dipping on its shocks. The driver remained motionless for a moment, his head like an ax behind the tinted window, then he stepped out, drawing a thin briefcase off the seat, and descended toward the fire.

A tall man, as tall as Bud, taller than Lily, but thin, Lucas had a handsome face, but sharp, the skin cream-colored and from a distance appearing faintly blue in the hollows and under the lips. Up close he would be seen heavily pockmarked on the cheeks and chin. He wore a beige suit of a thick, soft material and a long sheepskin coat that fluttered behind him as he approached like a thing transported from across the desert, a large, angular, and dust-colored winged creature out of place in the snow and among dark pines. Bud and Zack were silent at the fire, their backs to Erks like two big hams. Lucas greeted Bud and nodded at the pig and smiled, his entire face creased with lines which jumped into place as if controlled by a switch—the smile of a businessman, of one who administers credits and debits and directives with his smile. Bud's face bulged. Zack bent and bobbed and shuffled around the fire after Lucas when Lucas moved toward Lily, who had come out onto the porch. Sandman and Winona stood on either side of Lily, a short pair, nuisance and gloom.

"Zack!" Bud barked.

Zack stopped in his tracks.

Bud jerked his head, motioning Zack to come back.

Lucas embraced Lily, then held her out at arms' length, gazing at her. He spoke, but Erks could not hear the words. Lily turned her head and looked at Lucas sideways, smiling faintly, amused, doubting. In her face Erks saw what he knew: that one was not to trust Lucas' charm, but that the fascination in it could be too tempting to resist. She introduced Sandman, and Lucas shook his hand, then greeted Winona, taking one of her hands in both of his, and bowing. Winona blushed, a faint fire lighting her haggard cheeks. Erks heard Bud snarl suddenly and whisper, "Shit!"

Lucas turned and addressed Bud. He had a soft, breathy voice, one which he could use to make people lean toward him and ask him to repeat himself. Not now, however: "The preacher's at the cemetery and folks are waiting. You go ahead. Lily and I'll follow."

"And Winona," Lily said.

Bud, beside himself but holding off, twisted a rag between his hands.

"I need a moment with Mr. Erks." Lucas looked at Erks and raised his eyebrows.

He drew Erks away, back up the hill. "I just flew in from Denver last night. I got to fly back tonight, then Salt Lake City. Back to Denver. I meet Lily in Reno," he said, his voice almost pure air and the words coming quickly. "You wouldn't believe the bull that's coming down," he added. Every time Erks had talked with him, Lucas had used that phrase. The incantation of his itinerary, too, was a ritual. "I'm sorry I'm late. How was the trip?"

Not to be made light of, Erks stared at him.

Lucas raised one hand, understanding. "All right."

When they reached the cars, Lucas pushed the snow off the foot of the casket with his arm and set the briefcase down, snapped it open, took out a sheaf of papers, snapped the valise shut, and spread out the sheaf on top of it. "It's a different route," he said. He traced a line on a map with the tip of his pen: "Out of Vancouver and across on Highway 1, then just east of Creston, down into Idaho on a logging road. This one." Lucas pointed to a thin, wavery road on the map. "That's why you need your truck. You meet Lily back here tomorrow morning. Before dawn. I'll have a car for you from here down to Reno. Stop in Reno, then straight over to San Francisco."

"Why?" Erks said. He meant why this route, why a logging road, for God's sake, why stop in Reno, why is Lily driving down, why doesn't she fly, why doesn't she fly with you?

"Why?" Lucas replied.

Erks took a pencil from his pocket and wrote "dawn" in the upper corner of the map. It gave him pause, the thought of what this place might be like at dawn tomorrow morning. "I want fifteen thousand if I'm carrying that extra passenger," he said.

Lucas stepped back and gazed at Erks. "The only reason Lily's going is to spell you. It's a long haul. Time is of the essence."

"That's fine. But I mean Ginarn Taam."

Lucas' expression sharpened and he rocked back on his heels, grasping the chrome-plated railing of the casket, covering his surprise by making at once a mockery of it. "I see."

"That's right. I want fifteen thousand. And I'm not driving with five other people from here in any damn Datsun. Not when your wife and I are among them."

"You didn't mention this last night."

"Nope."

There had been a flurry of activity down at the fire—the pig turned, coals raked, fuel added, and instructions, it appeared, given to Sandman by Bud—and now Bud and Zack climbed the slope toward the cars. They had pulled off their sweat shirts and put on ties and coats to match their trousers. They wore navy-blue suits, the both of them, and both suits were too small. Their wrists stuck out of the sleeves and their socks showed below the cuffs.

"The car I can handle. The money, I don't know. You want twelve-fifty more?"

"Fifteen."

"No, Wes." Lucas leaned with his elbows on the valise and the casket bobbled. "I could up it a thousand. Six thousand total. That's a lot of money."

Bud and Zack hovered ten feet away.

Erks leaned toward Lucas. "I'm carrying a lot of live weight."

"We're going," Bud said.

Lucas stood up straight.

"We're taking her," Bud said.

Lucas hesitated, then, understanding, he leaned back, grasping the railing, and laughed, a hoarse, voiceless, wheezing laugh, a quickly concocted mockery of a laugh. In the instant that Lucas' head was thrown back, Erks saw Bud's body bolt and stiffen and an expression of great venom, malicious and evil, move into his face, filling his face for an instant as his body filled the suit he wore—swelled it to the bursting point—but before Lucas brought his head down the expression had been mastered. Lucas put his fingertips on the casket and gazed at Bud. "Yes. Take Mama."

Erks and Lucas moved into the front seat of the GMC, the briefcase between them.

"I'd take twelve-five," Erks said.

"Sixty-five."

"Ten thousand."

"Seventy-five. Damn it."

"All right." He covered his surprise. It was the amount he

had wanted, but he hadn't really expected to get it. The dispatch of it was unlike Lucas, and Erks had a premonition of hazard. He covered that, too. He said, "But I want half of it now."

They did not look at each other. They looked straight down at the house. Sandman stood alone at the fire.

"Jesus, Wes."

Next to the GMC, the van started up, roaring as Bud gunned it. He backed it around behind the GMC, then headed out, still gunning it. The van fishtailed and sprayed snow over the side of the GMC and clapped it against the window next to Lucas. Startled, Erks looked. The casket rocked crazily against the ropes as the van bumped up and around the rock abutment.

Lucas smiled. "He got me."

Lily and Winona came out of the house onto the porch, stepped down and moved around the fire and headed up the hill, Lily carrying her big carpetbag and moving slowly so that Winona could keep up. They moved past Sandman toward the Buick. Sandman watched, but didn't follow.

"It's hard on Lily," Lucas said. "God knows it's hard on Lily. She's going to need to get out of here tomorrow." He paused, then added, "We got to watch that damn Bud all the time."

Erks studied Lucas' face, in silhouette against the dripping window.

This was the first time he had seen Lucas display wear.

There was an innuendo in what Lucas had said about Bud, a path into the woods. It appeared as innuendo to Erks because of what he did not know, as with Bud, but not like Bud: Bud suggested a path that stopped immediately, its dead end snarled with the teeming, gravid matter of his own anger, while Lucas suggested a path that led to path and path to road, road to route, a matter of distance, this: no distance with Bud and with Lucas great distance. The woods had made way for Lucas' diversionary routes; his kind of routes stitched the woods together. A merchant, one who stood to the side, but who, because of his distance, could see all the routes at once, who could touch them with his fingertips—like a cartographer, but it was with money that Lucas

70

embroidered, not ink—he carried the complexity of routes in his character, and only history could move the merchant's routes, or when moved, history was made. In their fixity and in their abstraction rested their cruelty for one like Bud, who was sewn in.

To understand Lucas, to get to Lucas, to close the distance, one had to crack the secret of his map, or maybe seize him when he happened by, as Bud might, or maybe catch him like this, showing wear. The mobility in his face had stopped, the jaw and cheeks were still, and the eyes trained on his wife's rising figure. There was sadness in the way his eyelids and lower lip drooped. It was as if Erks had caught Lucas asleep and discovered a tumorous growth on his side, the side that Lucas ordinarily kept covered, but the side that he could not do away with, that finally could not be gone around, his attachments, family, meaning ruin, mortality, as family—Erks knew—for whatever else it meant, must mean, too.

Lucas lit a cigarette. Still gazing at Lily, he spoke softly. "As to the half in advance, I don't carry that kind of cash."

Erks responded softly, "Yes, you do."

Inhaling, Lucas laughed. He came back to life, his face quick again.

"I'll take half now and the other half when I get to Reno."

"An installment plan? You don't trust me?"

"It. I don't trust it, and him, the one I'm carrying, and his connections, Lucas."

"Twenty-five now. Twenty-five tomorrow morning. Twenty-five in Reno."

"All right," Erks said, troubled again by the ease of the bargain.

Lucas leaned over and snapped open the briefcase and took out an envelope and paid Erks, then the folder again, opened it, and went over the instructions he had written down, telling Erks where to make the pickup in Vancouver, and when, and he gave Erks a key, for the border crossing, he said, was secured only by a lock and chain. He said that he would meet them in Reno, that Taam and Lily would get off there, and he told him where, and when, and said that the

71

three boys would go on to San Francisco. He closed the folder and handed it to Erks.

Lily and Winona passed and got into the front seat of the Buick.

Erks set the folder up on the dash. "I heard that Taam gets off in San Francisco."

Lucas' face hardened. "You forget that. Meet me in Reno. He gets off in Reno with Lily. She knows that." He paused and looked at Erks. Erks looked back. It was a quick confrontation, Erks attempting to gauge the weight of the contradiction, and Lucas—Erks sensed—gauging what he—Erks—knew.

Lucas said it: "Do you know who this man is?"

"What man?"

Lucas smiled. "I think you got me." He leaned back and blew smoke against the ceiling. "Stay on schedule. Drop him in Reno. And be careful, Wes."

Erks let them pull out first, Lucas and Lily and Winona, in the Buick. He watched the Buick turn, then glide out of sight around the abutment. He looked down at the fire. Sandman was there, stiff, holding the pipe wrench. He looked up at Erks as if in supplication. He had been left behind to turn the spit. Behind Sandman's small figure was the pig, the listing house, the orchard, the slope, the woods, and the peak of a mountain as bright as a tooth.

Erks made his count:

Valise.

Water.

Lunch.

Flashlight.

Gas can full.

Directions for the route, the pickup, the drops: in the folder.

He checked through the folder.

He checked his coat pocket to see if he still had the old directions for the drop in San Francisco.

He did.

Toolbox.

Cash: $2,800—$300 in his wallet, $2,500 from Lucas.

Maps.

Crowbar.

He poked a big finger inside his coin pocket—goose vertebrae.

He started the engine and set out for Vancouver. It was 9:30 A.M. He would get back on Interstate 90 for Seattle, over the Cascades, then drive north through customs to Vancouver.

5

Hello, you spring salmon!
Hello, you dog salmon!
Hello, you coho salmon!

Hahatsaik, greeting Captain Cook, 1778

Erks, in Vancouver that afternoon and an hour early, had parked on the edge of Chinatown and walked the three blocks down to the harbor to kill time. He moved across the tracks and up the wide ramp of a high large pier, once a Canadian National Railway pier, but now a tavern, open at nights only. The pier was empty except for Erks and a man in a straw hat sitting like a boy with his legs over the edge and his chin resting on a lower rung of the iron railing, a bottle between his legs.

It was a fine, bright day, unusual weather for the coast. Everyone Erks had spoken to—gas station attendants, the customs agent—had remarked upon the weather. Erks' feet hurt. His socks were too heavy for this weather and his feet had swelled inside his boots. Erks leaned against the railing three or four yards past the man in the straw hat and stared at the police dock below, lined with swift-looking blue-and-white launches. The ocean breeze blew in his face and under his coat, against the sweat on his ribs, chilling him. The chill felt good.

His legs ached: too long sitting. The back of his head was in a knot: too much seen, too fast, too long traveling cross-country without stop. And it had scarcely begun.

The eastern slope and the crest of the Cascades had been hit with heavy snowfall, the highway just cleared as Erks drove over and dozers still laboring on the side roads. The western slope had

had rain, the mountains, the range—extending longitudinally from northern California into British Columbia, across Oregon and Washington, its peaks upwards of 14,000 feet—a boundary between peoples, between the coast and the interior. The only natural avenue through was the Columbia River, to the south, which swung westerly and became the border between Oregon and Washington, but that avenue had to be engineered into passability. Erks left behind the high bright plateau country—home—when he climbed the mountains. The glacier, Rainier, was before him when he came through the pass. A second glacier, Baker—"Great White Watcher"—rose to the northeast as he drove toward Vancouver. With the descent into the coastal region he had developed a physical sense of blockage, of a rising impaction at the back of his head, and arriving at the coast of British Columbia, he felt scrunched, a short awkward animal journeying, a landlocked beaver. He looked out upon too much water to dam.

"My mama's here."

"Oh?" Erks said.

The man in the straw hat looked up. He had a growth of gray whiskers and large blue eyes and a ravaged expression. His head shook: the delirium tremens.

"On the water?"

"Christ, I don't know." The man looked away, then, almost moaning, he said, "She's here somewhere."

They faced west, the both of them, down along the bay.

"She's dead," the man in the straw hat said. "I'm a visitor, that's all."

"Oh," Erks said. "Where are you from?"

"She raised me here," the man said.

"Oh?" Erks said.

"I'm visiting her," the man said testily. "That's all."

Erks grinned and lifted his hat and scratched his head and squinted down quizzically at the man, who had placed his chin on the rung again. "You say your mother's here?"

The man was silent.

Erks replaced his hat and looked west again. Out of sight beyond the bay were Vancouver Island and the passageway, the Strait of Juan de Fuca. Beyond them was the Pacific. Across that was the Orient. The man in the straw hat watched for his mother. Erks saw shore, water, and a lot of history.

The Strait of Juan de Fuca was named after one of his own kind, a Greek, a pilot properly named Apostolos Valerianos, who sailed under pseudonym for the Spanish and claimed to have sailed inland for twenty days in 1592—to what would be now Saskatchewan or eastern Montana. He said he had found natives there dressed in furs and a wealth of gold, silver, and pearls. He'd found the females of the race dark and bewitching, too—Erks would guess—in his fertile imagination. Another pilot, a Portuguese, Lorenzo Ferrer de Maldonado, claimed to have come the opposite direction, to have sailed west from Hudson Bay to the Pacific in 1588, and to have passed a vessel manned by Hanseatics and loaded with brocades, silks, porcelain, feathers, precious stones, and gold. Such accounts of impossible riches aroused a fever of interest in Europe, and the Strait of Juan de Fuca, long sought after by Pacific explorers and long missed, was just missed by Cook, then, once found, misconstrued again as the opening to a water route across the continent, and confused with the Columbia, which was similarly misconstrued. The idea of an isthmus was held to rigidly for years. It charged exploration, and thus testified both to the economic drive of Europe and of the colonies, first, then of the Union, for a trade route with China, and to the inclination of the animal to resist any trespass upon its design of satisfying fantasies.

When Cook passed in March 1778, the strait was blanked with fog and he sailed north and landed at Nootka Sound on the west side of Vancouver Island. The very size of his ships—the *Resolution,* the *Victory*—it was said, led the Nootkans to mistake them for islands risen from the sea. They attributed the speed of the ships to supernatural powers—Haietlik, perhaps, the Lightning Snake, or Quawteath, or to salmon charged with magic.

Hahatsaik, a shaman, a young woman with the power of salmon, set forth in a canoe and hailed the ships:

> Hello, you spring salmon!
> Hello, you dog salmon!
> Hello, you coho salmon!

Erks thought it like the Coast tribes to grant the power to beasts. Their design of fantasies, or their myth, was located in beasts which—a people of leisure—they represented in carved poles and boxes and entire dwellings and domestic and battle implements and in the masks of ravens and eagles and man-eating bears and beavers—all incisor—which they wore for ceremonial occasions, including the greeting of Captain Cook. The beasts, they believed, were the proprietors of power. Their myth was hardly fantasy, or hardly metaphor, and maybe not even a rousing of subliminal beings, but a design of items literalized by their presence in the rich, wet, thick, abundant place where the Coast tribes lived, and so Cook's ships, seen somehow—Erks guessed—as emanations of the migratory fish, were absorbed into the design. Erks liked that, that absorption.

But Erks was an inland being. The tangled, fecund, grasping greeting of land to water and such a treatment of beasts he himself could not help seeing as something subliminal, as organs of sexual fancy, as bodies—like those of other races—that he had to insert himself into and explode inside of in order to understand. His sense of the imagery of the Coast Indians was miscegenetic. His fantasies of the Coast Indians—like the early Europeans' fantasies of the New World—were abstracted by distance, hence the warp in his perception, which had the energy of metaphor and its sexual charge. So it was that he considered the tale of how a Nootka chief—Wakiash—stole the first totem pole from the people—that is, the animals—as a tale of a backwards Eden in which animal and human exchanged places:

So the animal people began to dance. Then Wakiash sprang into the room. The dancers were ashamed. They had taken off their animal clothes and looked like men. So the animal people were silent.

But it was like the Coast tribes, too, to joke about powers, about ships looking like salmon, for they were in fact experienced and canny traders, if spendthrifts. Among themselves they had been traders; they had also traded with the Russians and Spanish prior to Cook's landing. Their potlatches were celebrations of trade, one chief outdoing another in material extravagance. The Nootkans set immediately to trading with Cook. The furs in Cook's possession were discovered to be valuable at Canton, China, and following Cook's death, his crew returned under Lieutenant Gore, and again, by diverse ships, and more crews, and more ships, again and again, and the trade with China was established and the strait discovered—but not the isthmus: the search for that went on. Other Coast tribes were located and for a time they profited—they had an "advanced" culture—by incorporating the goods, the cloth, the iron, the copper that they took for furs, which went for tea and silk. But at last they were surfeited with trade and short of pelts and overcome by the imposition of European design and distance. Trade moved inland. There was that power in distance and in a fantasy made real.

The Strait of Juan de Fuca toward which Erks and the man in the straw hat gazed passed between the Olympic Peninsula and Vancouver Island, the route to and from the ports of Vancouver and Seattle. The conduit between them and the Orient was the Japan Current—Kuroshio, the Gulf Stream of the Pacific, carrier of fish and seed and craft: "dark blue salt," it was called, "black current," "black stream." A river of the ocean, fifteen miles wide, it was separated from the waters on either side of it as if by a wall, thermally mounted, distinguished from the waters by its warmth, by its darkness, by its speed.

And because of what he was here to carry, his yellowfish, Erks found this rising from his memory to augment his catechism, that is, the skin and bones of the air in which he placed himself as he moved:

Ancient Japanese maps delineated the North Pacific, Bering's Strait, the Aleutians, the coast of America.

The Year Books of the Sung dynasty recorded that in 458 a

Buddhist monk, Hwui Shan, set out by boat in the company of four other monks and sailed to Japan, then to the Kurile Islands, to Kamchatka, to the Aleutians, to Alaska, and southward to a land that Hwui construed to be the equivalent of some 4,500 miles east of Japan. He called it Fu-sang.

Ethnographers surmised that Kuroshio was a route for "indigenous" settlement of the coast regions, an avenue through which the Mongolian aspect of Coast Indians might be traced. In artifacts, rites, and constructions of language, certain unmistakable affinities had been observed between the people of the Orient and the Coast tribes from Alaska to Mexico.

From the time of the earliest Spanish voyages into the Pacific, there had been accounts of Chinese junks lost at sea and wrecked on the West Coast, some with survivors. By way of the Kurile and Aleutian islands, the longest stretch of open sea was 200 miles.

In 1926, an 85-foot schooner, the *Ryo Yei Maru*, left Misaki, Japan. A year later it was sighted off Cape Flattery and towed to Port Townsend, Washington. The logs showed that the ship had had engine trouble a few days out of port, then was caught by a typhoon. It drifted across the Pacific on the current. Of the twelve-man crew, two bodies were found on the deck, the remaining ten, presumably, eaten by those last two.

Sailing vessels rode this current, Kuroshio, which emerged from the North Equatorial Current and passed Taiwan and the coast of Japan and flowed eastward to Yokohama, and north, turning—like the Gulf Stream off Cape Hatteras, like the petal of a great flower—and branching, it was driven south and east to the North American coast by the cold waters that funneled through Bering's Strait. Transformed into a cold current, it passed the coast of California and returned to its root, the mouth that spoke it first, the North Equatorial Current. A turbine action, a dynamo, centrifugal, the current looped Asia and Western America together as the Eastern Seaboard was stitched to Europe by the Gulf Stream, the Atlantic Drift, but even the comparison, in that order, was a matter of acculturation, of recent history, of the sense of matters trans-Atlantic—dense and hermetic—being definitive.

Kuroshio's essence lay in the atmosphere it made, in the sense it helped to shape of a certain trans-Pacific geographic skin. The Chinese Erks was to transport inland and back out again to San Francisco had traveled already under a familiar skin; they would travel a space long worn to fit by like bodies.

Erks had not expected to be searched at the border. He had not been. He was not asked to show identification.

When the officer asked him how much money he was carrying, Erks told the truth, his elbow through the window and looking out and up at the man with the freckled face and blue eyes and red hair and crisp shirt and neat, peaked hat, an Irishman—$2,800.

The officer gave him a sheet stipulating the duties to be paid on goods taken out of the country. The man's hands were freckled, too. The illegality of Erks' business was brought back into focus by the border, the 49th parallel, the legal brow, and he thought of asking: What duty on ancient physiologies?

When asked the purpose of his journey, Erks said a holiday. He remembered Lily then, her face; her dark, melancholy, amused face had impressed itself upon him, and her body—arms, legs, and belly, large and erotic—as she leaned and shook her fist, chastising Bud from the sagging porch of the big house.

"A day to be out and about," the customs officer had responded dryly, but smiling and pronouncing the words "oot" and "a boot."

"Mama tore all up and down the coast raising me," the man in the straw hat said. "I've been away a long time, all my life."

Erks, awakened as if from a trance, jerked and grunted.

"But it's not hers. It's not hers anymore—it's ours, ain't it! It's ours, not hers," the man said, clutching his bottle and looking upward, his head shaking violently, "this land of death."

"Sure," Erks said softly, seeing that he had stumbled upon a man overcome by the swelling point in his life.

"What do you know?" the man said.

Beyond the police dock were the present CNR piers. A ship from a Japanese fleet had docked and lowered its gangplank to the longest pier. Erks could see small figures descending. The ship sat deep in the water. A crane on runners rolled down the pier and raised its derrick, then lowered its cables, four of them, each with a hook. Lowered like the slender feet of an insect, the cables etched an elongating cube in the air, reaching for the cache in the hold—Datsuns, maybe. A seaplane circled slowly and landed in the bay.

Across the bay at the North Vancouver docks, cargo was stacked along the shore, outside the warehouses and beside railroad sidings, bales of it, bundles, crates, containers, tons of it on huge floating, pentagonal-like platforms. Crisscrossed and encircled by rails, heaped with coal, ore, timber, the size of the platforms dwarfed the trains, silos, holding tanks, derricks, cranes, loaders, conveyors, dozers, and docked ships. Little detail was visible to Erks because of the distance, but there were hills of material out there, quarries and small mountains carved by the dozers. An expanse of sulfur stood out, a brilliant, acid yellow patch on a dun-and-pale-blue quiltwork which appeared toy-sized, backed by skyscrapers, then by the snow-capped, Alp-like peaks of Holyburn, Grouse, and Seymour mountains. Part wilderness and part ski slope, the mountains seemed to hold the city in and the waters to let it out. The North Vancouver docks had all but supplanted the old harbor, and from where Erks stood and running several blocks down was the original site of the city, now called Gastown after a pioneer, Gassy Jack Deighton. Warehouses had been transformed into penthouses, apartments, and shops. It was a high-rent district where small articles were bought and sold, clothing, jewelry, and curios, a skin country where the avenues of trade narrowed and the patterns grew intricate, the gestures of exchange etched in a web like veins on a wrist.

Erks decided to move. He spoke to the man in the straw hat and touched him on the shoulder as he passed. The man did not budge. Erks walked a roundabout route, still killing time. He bought spices in Gastown—curry and ginger—to take home to Ruby and a forty-five-dollar model totem pole for Matt. He walked back to the GMC to store the spices. He considered taking his valise for the sake of the crowbar, but decided against it. The totem pole he carried in his inside coat pocket. It was a good foot long and bumped against his collarbone as he walked.

He moved slowly, loitered, found his street—Hastings—and his block. At the corner a small plaza had been constructed above subterranean public rest rooms—a feature of Canadian consideration. Six Indians sat in a line on a concrete bench behind a potted alder. One of them, spotting a mark, rose and approached him. Erks stopped. The man asked for a quarter. Erks didn't understand at first. The man repeated his request, naming the amount gravely, but raising it to fifty cents, as if it were not even a point to be bargained, let alone refused. Erks dipped into his pocket and gave him a quarter. The squat, toothless Indian, a Salish, perhaps, or a Kwakiutl—originators, it was said, of the Northwest secret societies, of the Cannibal Society—nodded and thanked Erks with dignity and turned his bulk and moved back around the alder.

Another group of Indians stood outside a government liquor store sharing a bottle. The streets and sidewalks were wide, the streets good for four lanes of traffic and the sidewalks for walking six abreast, and the people took possession of them. Erks moved by an open-air magazine stall that featured European and South African newspapers, and overheard the proprietor speaking animatedly in Afrikaans with a customer. The two leaned toward each other across the counter, their tipped Dutch heads like blocks of wood. Men, quite drunk, leaned against walls, white men and Indians—but no Chinese, for they would not let themselves be seen that way.

The Chinese presence was seen chiefly in the establishments, restaurants and shops, in a mercantile with an impressive plate-glass window behind which were stacked 100-pound sacks of rice, and in a ten-story building with gold-colored lettering in each window—doctors, dental mechanics, attorneys, agents, the Chinese Communist Party headquarters, all the names Chinese. He passed two Chinese teen-agers dressed snappily in denims, bright belts, and woven nylon shirts, who had stopped to admire

82

a fast car, a Trans Am. A small Chinese woman dressed in dark clothing and carrying a paper shopping bag moved quickly past him. The whole place had a lean aspect, the clean streets, buildings, façades, and window dressings sparse and solid and frugal, showing neither the flash of the Chinese trade streets in San Francisco nor the squalor of their alleys. Erks liked this spaciousness. He had no horror vacui: he had the reverse.

He stepped into a diner, where he had coffee, a roll, and bau. He looked around the diner and back into the kitchen—an expansive Chinese kitchen, big as the dining area—and out the window into the street, and he thought about his coffee—he had taken it as Canadians do, with cream and sugar—and about the cream—Canadian cream is richer, drawn here out of a resplendent, gadgety, stainless-steel machine by a waiter with a lantern-shaped jaw and the moves of a railway porter, and a toothy occupational smile which would not vanish from his face. Erks thought about his bowels—he hoped they would move—and about his feet—they hurt—and about his schedule. He wished he hadn't arrived early. He took the totem pole out of his pocket and laid it down on its back beside his saucer and leaned forward and attempted to read the pole as he sipped his coffee.

At the top of the totem pole were two human figures, back to back. They had round faces and wore tall conical hats and gazed outward at right angles to the remaining figures, below, as if protecting the flanks. In the space between the two figures was a bladelike shape, a fin, a dorsal fin. The body of the fish was invisible, overcome by the remaining figures, first one bird, then a second, one on top of another, the second larger than the first and granted thus by its scale greater importance. The first bird, judging from its short, curved, powerful beak, was an eagle. The beak of the second bird was straight and long, though, like the first, compressed inward as the medium demanded. At the second bird's sides, wings were folded forward; they changed into arms and emerged as human hands clutched on either side of the beak. This bird could have been one of any number of species, but Erks guessed it to be the raven, foremost carrier of power, capable of assuming the human form.

Below the raven the carving grew intricate. Whorls and embellishments spun and wound, grotesque faces, serpentine shapes, and fish, and three additional bladelike forms, culminating in a third large figure, the streamlined head of a sea animal, but a mammal, not a fish, a seal, or a whale, a killer whale. The blades were more fins, a pectoral fin on either side and emerging from between the raven's feet a fluke. The figure, he saw with amazement, belonged to the topmost fin. The whale plunged through the bodies of the eagle and raven and surfaced here, carrying on its hump the intricate debris. Below the whale was the bottom figure, a grizzly with a human head held upside down in its mouth, the human's mouth open and rounded as if calling into the distance.

Captivated by the ubiquitous eyes that stared back at him, by the complexity of the carving, its nucleation, Erks thought again of Wakiash, come to steal the totem pole, and of the animal people, and he himself sensed an alien presence:

> So the animal people were silent.
> They could not sing or dance.
> Something is the matter.
> Something is near us.

Erks looked up, then literally jumped with surprise. The waiter with the lantern-shaped face had approached the counter soundlessly and had been staring at the pole with Erks. The Chinese waiter looked at Erks now, smiling, his eyes soft and sad, and he shook his head slowly, telling of his inability to fathom the object on the counter.

Erks rose and put the pole back in his pocket and left the diner, and headed down the street, passing across the plaza, where the Indian, again, the same one, asked him if he could spare a quarter. Spooked, Erks gave him a dollar. Not Nootka—the whalers—not Kwakiutl, nor Carrier, nor Bella Coola, nor Salish—taken as slaves by the Nootka—but certainly Haida—the most powerful tribe, who took Salish slaves, also, and by far the shrewdest of traders—the Indian looked at Erks, then at the bill, which he folded neatly with one hand, then back at Erks, and recognizing Erks, or pretending that he hadn't recognized him in the first place, he giggled, displayed his gums. He looked back down at the bill and closed his hand on it and stepped back, nodding. Behind him his friends, a row of squat men and one woman, rose from the concrete bench behind the potted alder. They passed Erks in a file, ponderous as elephants, and headed up the sidewalk toward the liquor store.

Erks found his address next to the Chinese Theater, a red door with a sign on it advertising tourist fares to Hong Kong. The tickets, however, were to be procured at a different address up on Pender Street. So said the sign. The windows on either side of the door were blanked out with silver paint. Erks moved out and stepped under the theater marquee. He had fifteen minutes. He would give them five.

The poster advertised a movie, *The Hong Kong Butterflies*, and displayed a sequence of stills that presumably outlined a tale of garish encounters between Chinese businessmen and a colony of prostitutes. The last still showed the protagonist calmly surveying a nude woman who lay on her back with her knees spread. Erks heard a burst of laughter from within the lobby of the theater, at once muted and raucous like the cry of a crow flying over a forest. The door opened and three Indians emerged, pushing each other outward. They spoke in low bursts and broke into laughter and spread out on the sidewalk and moved past Erks. They had round heads and heavy torsos and short legs that bowed as they walked up the sidewalk, laughing. Erks watched them.

Two teen-age Japanese girls with rouge on their cheeks came toward the Indians. The girls were dressed in the latest mode, which was forties style—oversized sweaters and thick-heeled pumps and nylons and flowered ankle-length skirts of a silken material that swung with the movement of their lithe hips. They passed each other, the three men and the two girls. It was a moment. One of the men turned and pushed his nose up with a finger and closed his eyes, mocking the arrogance of the girls, then turned back and said something. The three men laughed, and spread out on the sidewalk, then came together again, rolling on their legs. Erks watched the men, and then, just beyond them, his eye was drawn to a black Lincoln Continental parked at the curb, to the man in the driver's seat straightening up to look.

Erks froze, then turned back to the poster, alert. He was being watched, and—he could tell—not watched casually, either. It was time to go. He would go now. He turned and went, moving toward the red door with a sense of his own awkwardness because he was being watched. He stared steadily at the man in the Continental, testing him. Tested, the man stared back through the tinted glass without flinching. The head revolved until it rested like a mask on the sill, a small head, the features sharp, Chinese, the skin drawn tight over sharp bones, watching something specified—himself, Erks. Erks felt the eyes on his back when he turned the knob and pushed the red door open.

They were waiting, a woman and three youths and the man. Erks had stepped into the dim room, a vestibule of sorts lit only by a single low-wattage bulb screwed into a fixture in the ceiling. He found them as if they had been waiting for hours.

"Mr. Erks?" the woman said.

Erks closed the door and looked at her without speaking. They kept women at the portals—he had no idea why. This one introduced herself.

"I am Edna Ling. These gentlemen are your passengers. There is no need to delay."

A fragilely built creature, and dressed in a pink ankle-length skirt and a white blouse, Edna Ling had a round face and bright eyes and gleaming black hair. Erks looked at his cargo. They sat on a bench directly in front of him, the three youths dressed in tight-fitting blue denim and sitting close together, their knees and shoulders touching. Like puppies, two of them eyed him with soft eyes. The third had his hands on his knees and was bent forward, staring at the floor. The man, a man of thirty-five or so, Erks' own age, or maybe a little older, sat apart from the three youths at one end of the bench. He sat erect. His pudgy hands were folded on his lap and he looked like a fish or a small-sized sea lion, like a distance swimmer—rounded body, layer of fat, clean face, and his black hair in a crew cut. He wore khaki trousers and a khaki shirt buttoned up to the neck, and a well-fitted blue coat of a soft material. At his feet was a suitcase woven out of cane or reed. It matched his woven shoes.

"Do they have names?"

"You don't know their names?"

"I don't know which is which."

"Ho, Chang, and Lee," the woman said, pointing. "Mr. Taam."

Erks leaned toward him. "Mr. Taam?"

"Taam," the man responded. He beamed and nodded deeply without moving his hands.

"Erks," Erks said, bowing himself.

"Erks," the man repeated, beaming again, and bowing. His smile was one which took over the entire face.

Erks turned to the woman. "What if I am being followed?"

The woman smiled. "You have your instructions?"

"I have my instructions, but what if I am being followed?"

She moved. Her skirt swished. She gestured respectfully at Taam. "Mr. Taam is not to be left alone."

"Those were my instructions," Erks said. "Do any of these speak English?"

The man beamed again when Erks nodded toward the bench. The three youths remained as before, two gazing at him, one at the floor.

"Of course, it is to be expected," the woman said.

"What is to be expected?"

"You see, my duty is restricted to this." She gestured with both hands, holding her palms charmingly outward. "I have no authority."

Erks stared at her.

"I am told it would do no good to lose them."

"No good to lose who?"

"It is to be expected," the woman repeated.

"I should expect to be followed. This is what you say?"

"There is no need to delay."

Erks had the sense of having begun the conversation wrong,

87

of his words and hers not matching at all. He felt lost. He stepped toward the woman and grinned. "Do you speak English?"

The woman stood her ground and laughed lightly. "Do I speak English!"

"Do you mean to say that I am being followed by your own people?"

"My own people?" the woman said incredulously. "What do you mean, my own people? Do I speak English?" Again she laughed. Her good humor gave Erks a queasy feeling.

She spoke to the youths and the man in Chinese. Taam rose first, then the youths, or two of them rose and one leaned over and nudged the third, who stared at the floor. The third started, then rose slowly. They picked up their suitcases, Taam his cane basket and the youths three identical green cases of a plastic material.

Erks put his hand over the doorknob.

"Do not change your route. Follow your instructions," the woman said. She folded her hands at her waist and stared at Erks with her eyebrows arched.

Erks reached for her and touched her hands with his fingertips. "Thank you."

She stood her ground and pursed her lips, her eyes bright as jewels.

Erks stepped out onto the sidewalk. The Lincoln was parked as before and the head above the steering wheel, peering. Erks headed down the street. Taam walked at his side and the three youths followed, but one of them lagged. Taam's body was erect and his step light, suggesting considerable agility. Each time Erks looked at him he beamed in a way that compelled Erks to smile back. When they crossed the street to head down toward the GMC, past a newspaper office, Erks glanced back, then stopped. Taam stopped at his side. One of the youths, the laggard, was still in the street, stopped at the curb, and another youth had him by the elbow, drawing him upward. The third youth looked on.

"What's wrong?" Erks said.

At his words, the second youth immediately released the laggard's arm and looked at Erks without expression. The car, the

Lincoln, had pulled out and waited at the intersection, its signal light blinking for the turn. The laggard stepped up onto the sidewalk and reeled, catching himself by the second youth's shoulder, his expression pained and his skin, Erks saw now in the daylight, possessed of an ashen quality.

"What's wrong with him?"

Taam had left his side and headed back up the sidewalk toward the youths. Erks waited. The light at the intersection changed and the Lincoln turned the corner and drove down the street at a crawl. The man in the car openly scrutinized Erks, and Taam, who had taken the laggard's suitcase and carried it under one arm, and grasped the laggard's elbow and led him forward, the other two ahead of them, the group moving toward Erks in a staggered line, a half wedge, the front youth setting a pace and the back youth, the laggard, Ho—whose name Erks did remember; the other two, Chang and Lee, he had confused already— trying his best to look respectable despite the aid, struggling weakly, it seemed, to free himself from Taam's hold. Taam looked at Erks and motioned down the street with his head. Disconnected, an armature without axis, his head light, Erks turned and moved on down the last block toward the GMC, but at an excruciatingly slow pace, a crawl, because Ho, whom Taam had released, stopped dead in his tracks several times, swaying, and Taam waited for him, and Erks, and Lee and Chang, waiting, or not waiting, not quite stopping for him. Those two were nearly abreast of Erks now.

Without touching Ho or for that matter hardly acknowledging him—in consideration for him, it seemed—Taam somehow dragged Ho along as if by the magnetism of his own motion. Each time they stopped, Erks looked back searchingly, wonderingly, unable to decipher what was wrong with Ho. In the street the Lincoln followed, stopped when they stopped, inched forward when they inched forward, forcing cars to maneuver around it, then, when the group finally got to the GMC, all of them, Ho last, the car stopped just short of the intersection with its flashers on, the man inside watching as Erks loaded the three suitcases— Taam having given over Ho's but refusing to part with his own,

89

this with a smile and a bow and by holding the basket in his two hands close to his stomach. He had climbed into the front seat and waited there now, aloof, leaving Ho to Erks. Erks glanced at the Lincoln, at the face like a gear behind the window, the expression impossible to make out, but by position, the cant of the head, like the car—fixed, forcing traffic to move around it— relentless and audacious and insolent.

He got Chang and Lee into the back seat by opening both doors, but Ho was stopped on the sidewalk, staring at the interior of the GMC as if getting inside were something insurmountable, incomprehensible. Erks spoke to him, asked him if he would get in, then if he needed a rest room, a bathroom, toilet.

"Toilet," Erks repeated, thinking the boy might understand that word.

Ho didn't move. Erks touched Ho's arm and bent to look into Ho's face, then exerted pressure on the arm, toward the GMC, but with the pressure only the arm moved in the right direction, other various parts of Ho's body, the head, the torso, one leg, inclining diverse directions, the body weak as if it were decaying matter, the arm as if it would tear away from the shoulder with any greater pressure, as if the flesh would fall away from bone and Erks would be left standing there with flimsy substance in his hand. Ho's face, moreover, was numb, unregistering. Erks looked in at Taam beseechingly. Taam, watching, motioned him away. Erks stepped back, aghast.

And then Ho moved inside, or fell inside, putting his hands on the seat first, then, half crouching, half sitting, he dragged his feet in last. Erks shut the door gently and paused for a moment. He leaned against the roof of the GMC and inhaled deeply, thinking, then exhaled. Coming up the sidewalk was the man in the straw hat. He walked unsteadily through the land of the dead, veering to and fro, and as he passed he looked directly at Erks, but, proud, pretending not to recognize him. Erks checked the street. The Lincoln was gone. He took off his hat, ran his fingers through his hair, then slipped in behind the wheel, pulled the door shut, and started the engine.

90

The three youths sat shoulder to shoulder, huddled together, as they had on the bench in the room behind the red door, leaving—strangely—a space between each outer youth and the back doors of the GMC. These three were not alike in appearance. One was much taller and, of the two shorter, one was plump and the other, Ho, had something wrong with him, but their presence still evoked a trinity. They were like dogs, shepherd or coyote pups penned up in the snow, hungry and slowed by the cold, their outlines vague and diffuse, cloudy, though within this was a definite sharpness of eyes and nose and of bone under fur and skin like stone, as secret as stone, as secret as the dry seed in the soft fibrous ball of the cotton plant. The tall one sat in the center even though he had to accommodate the drive shaft. Erks saw his face square in the rear-view mirror and the inner sides of each of the other two faces—a cheekbone of each and part of the brow—and when the GMC turned or swayed with the road the three would sway as one like a collapsing tower, and another face—that of Ho or the plump one—would come into view. Their faces were unexpressive or expressive of nothing in particular, nothing discernible except for Ho's anguish, or lonesomeness, or pain, or whatever it was: in this respect they were collective, although their features were different—the tall one's face long and angular, the plump one's eyes hooded, and Ho's face, when it rocked into Erks' view, ashen, drawn tighter than the other two, the grievance, or burden, or affliction willed into abeyance and composed along with bone just under the skin. None of the youths took notice of the landscape, which rapidly grew spectacular enough, nor of the city, nor of the roads, nor the freeway, the ramps and bridges, nor of the traffic—these, matters which Erks considered foreigners ought to take notice of—but instead stared fixedly straight ahead, glazed.

The man beside him, on the other hand, leaned forward in his seat and turned his body at times in order to follow some object which they passed—a rug retailer, the Ferris wheel at the exhibition grounds, a commuter's bench with an advertisement printed in Chinese figures. Vancouver's Chinese people, it appeared, had flourished, multiplied, and prolonged out into the suburban area of Hastings, several miles east of Chinatown. Some distance beyond Burnaby Lake, the white face of Mount Baker —"Great White Watcher"—rose into view from behind mountains to the southeast, and the man, appreciative of the sight, turned to Erks. His face quickened when their eyes met. He nodded rapidly without speaking, but looked attentively at Erks, then he turned back to gaze at the glacier. No one spoke. Erks looked at the glacier, the dome dominating the landscape, humped like the shoulder of a bull, but brilliant as pearl behind the blue of lesser mountains and against the sky, an artifact, pure geology, magnetic, holding the eye, a spellbinder.

The cane basket rested upright between the two in the front seat and squeaked lightly with the motion. The keys ticked against the dash. The totem pole, which he had set up on the dash, rocked, knocking lightly against the window. The truck ran well, the engine smooth, the suspension registering the seams in the highway. The highway, the Trans-Canada Highway, Highway 1, descended into the Fraser River valley and the country opened up noticeably. The three heads rocked gently to and fro, Ho's head slightly more inclined, his eyes closed, or the one eye, at least, visible in the rear-view mirror, which Erks, worrying over the Lincoln Continental, checked often enough. It was there some distance back, definitely there, a shiny black spot, a bead. It had been there since Vancouver, moving in and out of sight, or he thought it had, thought it had appeared again after having vanished. He thought it was the Lincoln Continental. So thinking, he became sure it was the Lincoln.

It was a contrast, the man beside him and the gagged rectitude in the back seat, a lacuna between the two areas and in Erks' understanding of their connection. He knew nothing about any of them, but sensed more about the man, what he sensed—that the man spoke English, for example—making all that he didn't know about him take on an aura of treachery. This was despite the fact that Erks had instantly liked the man and disliked the youths; liking Ginarn Taam somehow made his treachery plausible, whereas with the youths all cards were face down, the digits inside the machine and the machine—stainless steel, computerized, against the wall—registering zero, all multiplications spinning back to zero. It was a matter of language: the routes of language which Erks believed he shared with Taam were reflected in the fact that Taam knew how to sit in the front seat of a moving vehicle and how to look at a mountain, in a certain transparency of his manner, transparent to Erks, not that he saw through Taam, but that what he was familiar with showed through Taam, that he saw himself showing through Ginarn Taam. The strangeness of the three youths in the back seat was foreign to Erks, opaque.

The Port Mann Bridge, spanning the Fraser River, came into view. At the same time Mount Baker slipped behind more nearby mountains. The bridge stood out at a distance because of its paint—the arch orange, the railings and undergirdings yellow, the colors bizarre against the pale-green bottom land of the river valley and the darker green of the hillsides. It was a margin, the bridge. When one crossed it one was out of Vancouver for certain. After that came the ascent and the high country, the towns spotted every thirty or forty or fifty or even more than a hundred miles apart like rolled-up porcupines in a wilderness of wolves, their names Scotch and British and Native and descriptive of what was found, what was made and by whom and of what had always been there: Langley, Chilliwack, Cheam View, Laidlaw, Hope, Mile 55, Princeton, Hedley, Keremeos, Cawston, Chopaka, Osoyoos, Bridesville, Rock Creek, Midway, Greenwood, Eholt, Grand Forks, Christina Lake, Paulson, Kinnaird, Trail, Fruitvale, Erie, Salmo, Creston. Erks checked the rearview mirror once, and the Lincoln was there, then again, and it was gone, then, anxiously, again and again, and the Lincoln stayed gone.

But not knowing why the Lincoln had been there, if it had, or why, now that it wasn't, he felt its absence become as strong as its presence had been, stronger. Erks didn't like it. His anxiety increased with the car's absence. He found himself wishing he'd listened to Ruby for once, wishing he were home. The anxiety gnawed at him. It was like driving with engine trouble, not knowing what the trouble was, but knowing it was there, not knowing when it would make the engine stop cold, but knowing that sooner or later it would, and not having the time or the money, either one, or both, to pull over and do something about it, or pay someone to do something about it, or being out here and having to walk twenty miles to find someone to do something about it and then they might not, might not know how, might lack the parts, might simply refuse. With Erks it was time, not money, and the trouble was worse than engine trouble, more ephemeral, deeper, more mysterious, like a black horse jumping over a fence at night, caught by the eye just before vanishing, frozen, a deep, glossy flash on the buttocks, or coming the other way, light playing on the nostrils and on the froth on the neck, the image locked just short of the vanishing point on the one hand, and just inside visibility on the other, just hanging there.

Erks lifted himself up with his legs, his heels against the floorboard, stretching, then he settled, his back flat against the vinyl seat. You've got to calm down, he told himself. This is what you wanted—intrigue, fast money, motion. It has hardly begun. If all went well—he thought—they would be across the border at Creston by midnight and back as far as Rathdrum before dawn, straight through, and there he could give the wheel over to Lily.

He was hungry. His bowels promised no movement. He thought of hamburgers and french fries—traveling food. The Lincoln was not in the mirror. The three heads were, though, swaying like flowers too heavy for their stalks. His feet hurt. He guided the wheel with the heel of his hand and pushed his shoulders back into the seat.

He saw himself as if in a dream, scrambling back and forth over the fence, trying to get to the side the horse was jumping out of, but each time he landed the horse changed directions and jumped toward him, and he wondered: Why am I doing this? What am I doing here?

"It's gone," he said.

Taam looked over at him.

"Do you speak English?"

"Yes, of course." Taam smiled, showing his pink tongue in

the center of his mouth. "You do not need to worry."

Actually, Erks was astounded, not because the man had spoken—in English—but because he had expected him to speak and now he had and because the speaking had brought the inside of the truck into a new kind of focus. Objects became individuated—the cigarette lighter, for example, which Taam pushed in, and the ashtray, which he pulled out. He lit a cigarette.

"Why not?"

Taam leaned back into the corner of the seat and door and crossed his legs. Relaxed, he acted as if the GMC were his own. He did not answer, but having spoken, his demeanor had changed. He became much less the high-smiling caricatured Chinese. In the back seat, in the mirror, the three youths seemed to recede as if seen through a telescope backward. Ho's face was down and his rocking, now, was off rhythm from the other two. When they rocked one way he rocked the opposite, knocking against the tall one in the center.

"What's wrong with that boy? Is he hurt or sick?"

"It is an injury."

The man's accent, Erks observed, was very slight. "He's hurt?"

Taam surveyed Erks calmly, the cigarette poised a few inches from his lips.

"What kind of injury?"

Again he did not speak.

"Does he need a doctor?"

"We did not know."

They neared the Port Mann Bridge. To the left the Fraser was visible, a broad strip of silver across the bright-green new growth on the bottom land.

"Does he need one now?"

Taam did not speak.

Exasperated, he asked, "How bad is it, the wound?"

"Not good, probably. We did not know."

They crossed the bridge. The GMC rumbled on the corrugated surface. Below them the Fraser was choked with logs. In the mirror all Erks could see of Ho was the side of his head and the top of one ear, his chin—Erks presumed—on his chest. The tall one's eyes were shut. His head nodded. The road swung around alongside the river. Immediately, they began to climb. They would climb for miles, slowly at first, then precipitously: up the Cascades again.

"What about that car?"

Taam smiled and leaned toward Erks and touched his shoulder lightly, then straightened up and gestured with the hand that held the cigarette. "We have many miles before us." The point, the refusal, was intractable, even more intractable because of his considerable decorum.

I cannot find words to describe our situation at times. We had to pass where no human being should venture. Yet in those places there is a regular footpath impressed, or rather indented, by frequent travelling upon the very rocks.

Simon Fraser, 1808

The road rose now, rose slowly with the Fraser River. The river valley had broadened and was apportioned into small farms, their bounds dishlike, spanning the banks of the river. The spring growth in the fields was pale and soft in the late-afternoon light, the bottom land doubtless as fertile as it could be, the fertility marked by the smallness of the farms. Mount Baker had come back into view to the southeast. His eyes returned to the mirror involuntarily and repeatedly, and much of the time he was startled by the fact that the heads, truncated by the base of the mirror, were there, that they were attached to bodies, that there were in fact three bodies in the back seat and one up here beside him. When the three heads swung in the mirror according to the motion of the truck, they looked as if they were dangling from the ceiling by strings, two facing ahead, one facing down.

"Where did you learn to speak English?" he asked Taam.

"In San Francisco."

"You have visited San Francisco, then?"

It was an obviously leading question, to which Taam responded by tipping his head back, smiling, and not speaking.

"I'd like to know what's wrong with that boy," Erks said.

He glanced over and saw Taam's expression move, or not move, but change, or not change; unmoving, it moved, unchanging, it changed. Taam's round face had an expression of benign good humor, and yet in this benignity was an armed quality—the

97

intractability, the decorum again—and it remained so, but something had slid across his face, the flick of a fish's tail sending a nearly imperceptible ripple through the musculature. It was as if he wore a mask, as if the face inside the mask were howling or laughing at something heinous, but the mask, too, however fixed it was, however calm, was alive and contradictory. Erks could not remember having seen a man's face do that, refuse so fiercely and with such facility to show its power, and so displace its passion, and tell so little, and yet give so strong a sense of having something to tell. A woman's face maybe, maybe he had seen it in Ruby's face once or twice in bed after they had made love and were talking and she stopped and looked away, gripped by some alien thought or memory of which she would not speak, or in another woman's now and then, met by chance in a crowd, somebody just bumped into coming around a corner and the distracted expression, the jungle behind the eyes, having nothing to do with him but coming from her world and he had just chanced on it.

"Yes, of course. I understand your concern."

"I don't think you do. I don't understand my concern. I don't know what I'm dealing with. I'm driving this truck."

"Ho has a knife wound."

Startled, he threw back his head and glared at Taam.

"We did not know the gravity of the wound. Under these circumstances . . ."

"What are you saying?"

"I do not know."

"And we're just going to drive on?"

"What are the alternatives?"

"There's one. Get him to a doctor."

"He would refuse."

"How could he? He can hardly sit up."

"He would find the strength. He refused before when we thought the wound was just a cut." Taam paused, then added, "I understand your anger . . ."

"This is not anger."

"It is to be respected."

"My anger? Respect my anger, then."

Taam leaned forward and crushed his cigarette in the ashtray, then sat up straight and looked out his window, and so broke contact. Erks looked forward. Though the grade remained slight, they were climbing. A charter bus approached from behind and passed them. On the back was a sign: IMPALA LINES—SUN FUN TOUR TO RENO.

The river and road had swung due east. The openness of the country, the breadth of the valley, allowed a full view of Mount Baker to the south. It was that toward which Taam gazed. Soon they would climb the Cascades in earnest. The road would narrow. The country would grow precipitous and isolated, or, as Simon Fraser wrote in 1808, it would become "romantic and grotesque." Erks had to look past the back of Taam's head in order to see the glacier, Baker, which rose from the state of Washington, but made the border irrelevant. Its size and light were utterly dominating. Without it the elements of the landscape—the lesser mountains, the river, the bottom land, and, increasingly now, the rock outcroppings—would be changed. Without its dealbate and hoary white hump like the hump of a bull above the head and horn and back and flank and hide of the horizon, colors would be altered, the green less green, purple taking on more of the shade in its mixture, the black of the bark on trees high on the slope above the road less luminous, and the blue of the sky less blue, less in contrast, even less intense, as if everything in sight of it were driven to a terrible ripening. The glacier cast its net, its white, colorless shadow, over everything in sight, or maybe it had its shadow inside it, compacted, magnetic, gravitational, a dark essence inside the white not cast over things, but a whirlpool that pulled things into it.

Even when he looked at the road, Erks could feel the image draw at his temple, compelling him to address it. By being there the glacier made his attitude. That was its power, its inexplicability. It was a matter, too, of scale, of size and cold brilliance seen from a distance, and of distance itself, his distance from it, and for those who would live here, a certainty longer than their lives, big, physical, silent, literal, bright, and not even dead—a volcano.

It vanished. It hadn't become smaller. One moment it was there, then it was not, blocked out by mountains, but its light hung on in his head, a halo, memory. The road had narrowed, the road, the order that drove him away from splendor, cut now out of rock. The grade and the extremity of turns intensified and caused the three heads in the back seat to swing in and out of his sight. The river was at their left. On the right was mountainside and forest—cedars, firs, spruces, pines, and tamaracks, and a wild, incandescent undergrowth of bushes and ferns. In the open spaces water gushed from the crevasses and cascaded down rock precipices. They passed a boulder on which a word had been printed in large green figures—JADE.

Erks glanced at Taam.

Taam shrugged and raised his eyebrows, humor flickering beneath the taciturnity.

"But why would he refuse?"

"He believes that if he reaches San Francisco all difficulties will be remedied," Taam said. "It is the immigrant's dream. He is young. He says, 'In San Francisco. Take me to a San Francisco doctor.' "

"It is not a good dream," Erks said.

"It is a demonstration of the power of an idea."

"It's a damn bad idea, if you ask me," Erks said. "Look what it's doing."

"What has it done, the idea?"

"You and I are going to have to strike a compromise on this matter of Ho," Erks said, rankled.

"Everyone is a stranger to him. He does not wish to be examined by a stranger."

"That makes more sense, but it's still a bad idea."

"Perhaps."

"Well?"

Taam was silent.

Every time the truck lurched Erks found himself checking the mirror, picking the scab. Ho's head was usually down, but if the GMC lurched strongly enough he would awaken momentarily, startled, and look up, his face wrenched with pain. Erks tried to drive lightly. It was impossible. They passed more signs: JADE 2 MILES, SILVER 1 MILE, GOLD ½ MILE. They hit a scored section in the road and the truck thumped violently, and Erks checked the mirror. Ho swung toward the tall one and threw his head wildly about as if struggling under water, as if struggling for breath. His mouth was agape and then, his head still heaving, he rocked to the left, out of view. They took a hard turn and passed a sign—GOLD 500 FEET. Erks slowed, then pulled off the road into the driveway of the lapidary shop and jerked the safety brake to and turned around in his seat.

Ho's body was twisted crazily, knees, waist, shoulders, and neck. His eyes were closed. Erks looked at the other two. The tall one smiled uncertainly.

"Help him up."

The tall one did not move. The plump one's expression was fixed and he stared straight at Erks, his compact face ferocious, then, abruptly, he leaned across the tall one and slapped Ho on the cheek, hard. Ho jumped and groaned, and looked about, his eyes rolling.

Erks swung around, got out of the truck, and jerked open the back door on Ho's side, angry. He intended to take a look at the boy, to find the source of the pain, to assess its seriousness, or at least to help him up, or to draw him out of the truck, to move the luggage and let him stretch out in the back compartment, to do something, but when he put his head inside the first thing he saw was a knife blade, extended toward him by an arm, the plump one's arm, stretched across the body of the tall one. Erks froze, then recoiled in surprise, bumping his head on the top of the doorjamb. The plump one's face was rigid with fury, his lips pulled back from his teeth. The tall one stared straight ahead, did not move a muscle. Ho's head was back against the seat. He was asleep, or dazed, or in shock. The plump one raised the knife and shook it and snarled. Erks did not move, thinking: No, not here,

101

not in the back seat, not when he has a knife. He backed out. He heard the tall one speak, then the plump one, the voice tight. He shut the door, stepped to one side, and leaned against the truck. His heart was pounding.

Across the clearing a green bungalow was set between a cliff and the river. He saw the figure of a woman behind the screen door, watching. He opened the front door of the truck, removed the keys, and headed for the bungalow. The figure vanished as he approached. When he entered he saw that she had moved behind the counter at the far wall, as if for safety.

"May I help you?"

The walls of the place were lined with heavy shelves filled with rocks. The place smelled of rock, of the dust of stones, and of brewing tea. The counter and a glass case, which he passed, were filled with mementos of the Chillicoth-Caribou gold-mining days. At one end of the case were two overstuffed chairs with doilies on the arms and backs. They faced a window that looked out upon the Fraser River, a torrent, swollen by the thaw. Beside the register stood a teapot, steaming, and an empty cup.

"Yes," he said, stopping at the counter across from her. "Where would the nearest doctor be?"

"Doctor?"

"One of my passengers is unwell."

"Oh, that's a shame." She had white hair and rouged cheeks, and soft skin, and pale, watery eyes. She appeared to be about seventy, and her face displayed the genuine compassion of the elderly for infirmity, of one who knows infirmity, and seeing this glimmer in what seemed an emotional wilderness, Erks had a sudden welling of feeling.

"I don't think it's serious." He rocked back on his heels.

"You can't be too careful." She cast her gaze upon him in a way which, were he to allow himself to remain under it, could cause him to bare secrets. "You would have to go to Chillicoth or to Hope. Either way, it is a distance."

"Thank you," he said, then, "Do you sell gold?"

Without speaking, she smiled, but there was no venality in it, not a trace of the keenness of the vendor.

102

What he had uttered was turnabout, fair play. For her advice he exchanged his patronage.

She turned away softly and moved along the inside of the counter to a certain shelf, touching certain points lightly as she went. She stopped and reached over her head, ran her hands over the stones, chose one, and lifted it down.

"And jade," he said. "Do you have jade?" It was an irony, a sort of joke, the jade, which, he knew, the Chinese gold miners had unearthed here. If one carried Chinese passengers, one should buy jade.

She moved to another spot, chose another stone, then started back. At the side of the shop a door was ajar and from behind it Erks heard a man wheezing. The woman stopped and looked upward, listening—the old man not well, an old logger or miner, likely, for around here one was likely one or the other, and the woman, who knew about doctors, shoring up retirement by turning a lifelong hobby into a shop. Erks glanced through the window, his eye drawn by a log rearing, bouncing, and turning end for end in the raging river.

"Do you do much business?"

She set the stones down, each of them the size of a large book, heavy. "In the summer, yes. And you're from the States?"

"Heading home."

"This is for the boy?"

He nodded, noting that she had marked the size and carriage of the figures in his back seat. Actually, he intended to take it home to Matt.

She touched the quartz. With her, he bent to look. She ran a fingertip slowly along a thin vein in the quartz. "Gold," she said. She looked up. "This one is eight dollars. It is a winter price."

"That's fine."

She touched the second stone, the jade. "I will give you the jade for the boy. In the North the Indians carve it."

"Thank you."

From behind the door the old man wheezed again. She looked up, listening, her eyes widening.

The two stones trembled on the dash before him. He had positioned the totem pole between them and it rolled when the truck rolled and knocked lightly against the stones, and as it rolled the figures—eagle, raven, fish, and grizzly, and inside the grizzly's mouth, the upside-down head of a howling person—turned and overturned, rolled in and out of view. The totem pole rolled and the heads hanging in the rear-view mirror swung as if suspended from the ceiling. Ho sat erect, still chafed into wakefulness, maybe, but his head was cockeyed, placed on his shoulders wrong. Erks had asked and Taam told him which of the other two was which—the tall one Lee, and the plump one Chang, the one with the knife. He wouldn't confound them now. They headed for Hope. It was on the route. The Lincoln Continental had not reappeared, and while it had not slipped from Erks' mind, it had been overwhelmed, as is the way, by more immediate matters.

"Why did he do that? Chang?"

Taam blinked. "He does not wish you to interfere."

Erks snorted. "One does not interfere with such a thing. You try to make it easier."

"Of course."

"That boy pulled a knife on me."

"He is afraid."

"Of me looking at Ho?"

"He is afraid of Ho's injury. He is afraid Ho will die. He is afraid of where he is going and of the going itself, and so he is afraid of you. He is afraid of his powerlessness."

Erks grunted. He had to grant the sense of that, though it answered nothing. What was wrong here had to do with the five of them following their momentum on the road when one needed desperately to be granted his inertia to stop. What was wrong was the assumed character of their motion—that they simply went on, that they had ever begun, that the boy had ever been allowed to come with them. There was nothing to say. When they got to Hope he would stop.

He had to slow for a construction zone. A government sign

104

informed travelers that the next twenty miles of improvement would cost 7 million dollars. Dozers were at work high on the slope above the road, cutting a preparatory swath through the forest and loose rock, uprooting trees, incising the mountain. They looked like toys, the dozers, riding the shelves, dwarfed by distance, and the men at the controls dwarfed in turn by their machines. They had to start cutting high in order to leave room to work down. Soon they would drill and blow, turn the granite out to the sun, cleave it and shove it clear. They sought to match the established plane, the old road, in order to widen it. There was a history to that, too, imbedded like stone. The history was the stone over which roads had to be built, and before that rail-roads, and before that trails. But there had always been trails to the coast, hundreds of miles of them, trade routes cutting against the longitudinal grain of the mountains.

One of Erks' own kind, an itinerant, a vagrant, an adven-turer—or so Erks considered him—Simon Fraser had passed in 1808, traveling south and west to the Pacific, traversing the stone country in search of a trade route for the North West Company, which, in competition with the Hudson's Bay Company, sought to expand its fur operations west of the Rockies. Along with the others, Fraser had searched for the isthmus, the Columbia, and thought the river that took his name might be the Columbia. Almost daily, his progress was stopped to repair canoes torn by rocks, or to replace canoes broken to pieces in the rapids, and he had trouble with his men, men sick, men hanging back, men lost on the divergence of trails, men wishing to take Indian women with them, men mutinous—his men, like the river, like the land, forever swelling out of control. He lost supplies to the water, and ported his canoes as much as he rode them, and the porting was over this rugged country, so rugged that he had regularly to abandon the canoes and barter for more. The tribes advised him repeatedly not to continue. They warned him of rapids, cascades, of hostile tribes downstream, for even the most remote among them knew, however remotely, of the coast and that the tribes there were dangerous.

They had a road to the coast and over this road Fraser made

his portages, on paths "indented" in the rocks and up cliffs that overhung the river. Pieced together by way of poles hanging to each other like the shrouds of a ship, ladders tied together with twigs and withes, the ladders set precariously on top of each other and so slack that a breeze put them in motion, swinging them against the rocks, these paths were agilely negotiated by the Indians, who ran nimbly from scaffold to scaffold, but Fraser and his men, horror-struck by the peril and encumbered by their goods, their stock, their guns, their baggage, feared for their lives.

Erks had a special attachment for Fraser's journals, which were filled with the violence of dream, of visions exceeding his ideas. His language was excessive, his nouns sheer and his verbs aggressive, Brontëesque, his words on the verge of unintelligibility and yet exact in their evocation of the massive, rebellious land. Fraser himself Scotch, his grandparents immigrants to New York, then to Vermont, Jacobite in their sympathies, then his parents, loyalist in their sympathies, fled to Quebec, or his mother did. His father died in prison, and Simon Fraser, exploring the West, took on the language of the West and in so doing seemed akin to the excessive, often brutal, and yet exact language of other Westerners to come: Joaquin Miller, Norris, London, Jeffers, Ginsberg, Kerouac, Spicer, and Bukowski.

Erks felt himself on the verge of like obscurity, affected by the country, and deeply confused as to what should be done.

They had passed out of the construction area.

They approached Hope.

They neared Hope.

The bright-yellow sign of a Sunoco station, on lifters, was visible beyond the winding road and above the trees. A set of three snow-capped mountains rose to the northeast. The streets of Hope were wet from the thaw and snow hung on in patches in the shade.

He pulled into the station, bought gas, and got directions to the residence of a physician. He followed the directions and found the home, a large yellow home surrounded by a hedge. A sign on the gate said HENRY MACNEILL, M.D. The side of the yard sloped right into the Fraser River.

"I'm taking Ho in here," he said to Taam.

He gave him no time to respond, but got out, taking the keys again, and walked around the front of the truck and up the side to Chang's door, slipped the key into the lock, unlocked the door. Chang looked at him with surprise, then, beginning to understand as Erks opened the door, bent over and fumbled for the knife under his pant leg. Erks didn't give him time. He grabbed him by the shirt and jerked him out. Chang was doubled, still groping for the knife, and Erks saw it, the keen flash, the blade coming up. He shoved Chang against the side of the truck, straightening him, then hit him once, hard. He hit him with everything he had. He pivoted and sent the blow from his back and shoulder. It was more than enough to stun the boy, which was all he had intended, but came from the back and shoulder and from the hips, from his body, from his anger, from an insulted, welling, racist fury, a full blow to the side of the head.

Chang's head jerked back and banged against the GMC. Shocked, he shook his head slowly and raised his hands, holding the knife. Erks stepped back, breathing heavily. Chang brandished the knife weakly. His hands and arms moved toward his belly, the elbows bending crazily. Then the knees crumpled. Erks jumped and caught him by the arms before he hit the ground, took the knife, loaded Chang back into the seat and shut the door, then moved around the back of the GMC and opened Ho's door.

He touched Ho softly on the knee and shoulder. Ho's head, still, was inclined, insensate. At the other end of the seat Chang was sprawled half over Lee, who sat bolt upright as if Chang weren't there, nor Ho, nor Erks, nor Taam. Erks tossed the knife over the seat to the floor at Taam's feet. Taam, too, did not move, but stared forward through the windshield. Chang groaned and began to stir, his body lengthening across Lee's knees. Erks took Ho gently and slid him to the edge of the seat, pulled his legs out, put one arm under his legs and reached behind his neck with the other arm and lifted him clear. Ho's head lolled over Erks' fore-

107

arm, the mouth open, the eyes, though open, glazed, and, it seemed, sightless. He was light. The weight had been taken from him. Erks shoved the door shut with his knee and headed for the house.

The nurse resisted him. The doctor was busy, she said. He was with a patient. He was near the end of his hours. It was 4:30. Erks saw that besides being the nurse she was the doctor's wife: she had a certain female familiarity with the place, the living room made over, with the high ceiling and deep pile carpet and heavy furniture. She had children, too, maybe in the house some- where, maybe upstairs, maybe in the kitchen sitting on chairs and swinging their short legs, waiting.

"This boy needs a doctor right now," he said.

"There is a clinic." She hadn't looked at Ho yet, not closely. She began to give directions, understanding apparently that Erks was from out of town. He had to cut a picture, standing there holding a Chinese boy.

He interrupted her: "I've been to the clinic. I sat and waited for a half hour."

"Oh?" She pursed her lips.

Ho's head was lolled over Erks' right arm and his knees were folded over the left arm. His mouth was open and drool trickled down his chin. Light as he was, he felt as though he were gaining weight. It was just Erks' arms weakening, the rush of excitement subsiding.

The woman had light-red hair and a florid face and a mole on her lower cheek, and inside her white, starched outfit, a plump compact body, a little thick at the belly. She had the full lips and strong chin of a sensualist. She was about forty and she was the doctor's wife. Of this he became certain by the way she paused, forming the decision on her own for the sake of her husband.

Besides the front entryway, there were two doors in the room. One was shut. The other was ajar and it led down a hall. He moved for that door.

"I'll check with the doctor," she said quickly.

108

He didn't wait. He knocked the door open with Ho's feet and moved down the hall and immediately found an empty examining room. He had to turn sideways to enter, taking Ho in headfirst. The woman stopped right behind him, then when he entered she passed by quickly and through the doorway Erks felt the breath of air she left in her wake, heavy with antiseptic and rose water. He heard her talking already in another room, her words interrupted sporadically by the rumble of a man's voice. He dipped to lay Ho down on the examination table, but Ho tumbled and ended up sprawled face down. The boy groaned.

He turned Ho over gently and guided his body to the center of the table, then slipped his hand under Ho's head and straightened it up. The boy's eyes were open and unblinking. For an instant Erks thought he was dead. He put his palm on Ho's chest, then, feeling nothing, he bent down and brought his face close. He felt breath, slow and weak on his lips. Erks backed off. One of Ho's arms slipped off the table, making a swishing sound. Erks jumped. He lifted the arm and laid it down at the boy's side. It was a device, the arm, a hinged wand, a light length of wood. Erks touched the boy's denim jacket, and finding it damp, unbuttoned the jacket and drew it away. The boy's white shirt was bright, crimson, and wet, soaked clear around his rib cage and up to the chest.

The doctor entered and moved to the side of the table opposite Erks, and looked down at Ho, then up at Erks, and nodded without speaking. A lanky Scotchman, he had a long face and deep parallel furrows in his cheeks and around his mouth. The woman entered behind him. The doctor put his hand over Ho's forehead, then took Ho's wrist and held it, his thumb over the veins. He bent over and began unbuttoning Ho's shirt, and spoke to the woman: "Blood pressure." She turned, took the implement off a shelf, wrapped the strap around Ho's upper arm, fastened it, and began pumping the bulb.

Erks backed away from the table, put his hands in his coat pockets, and breathed deeply, relieved to have relinquished the boy. His sense of desperation gave way to hope for their expertise. His previous feelings for the boy had found ground somewhere between a resentment he had to admit—because Ho was injured and, thus, an impediment—and sympathy—because the injury at least made Ho expressive, unlike Lee, Chang, and Taam, and because, after all, it was an injury, though he hadn't seen it, didn't know its seriousness, and still hadn't, still didn't. But it was not enough—he thought—not the sympathy, not even now: cold, it was not sufficient for himself, Erks, and what was hot, his rage at Chang, mounted out of whatever was lacking in his sentiment, an insufficient polarity not unlike Chang's fear and rage, a lack in himself, a lack of vision. He didn't know what to do. He couldn't even think it through right.

He found the goose vertebrae in his right pocket, and stirred them with his finger, then picked up the smooth, angular, star-shaped pieces one at a time between his thumb and forefinger and passed them from one end of his pocket to the other, counting for luck. The woman counted, too; she held Ho's arm and frowned at her watch. The silence in the room rested heavily upon the bodies and the cumbersome outmoded medical furniture: wooden chairs, wooden cabinetry and examination table, and even the stirrups—which protruded from the end of the table and which Ho's feet did not reach—wooden.

The doctor had undone the shirt and trousers. He parted the cloth, first the jeans, which he then pulled down along with the underwear, and Erks caught a whiff of rose water and saw the dark penis limp against a leg, a foreign organ exactly like his own. The doctor parted the shirt and exposed Ho's belly, which was smeared with blood. A deep six-inch gash, still oozing, ran diagonally from a corner of the ribs and down below the navel. Erks sucked in his breath and rocked back on his heels. The doctor looked up at him, his face alert and inquiring, as if to question Erks, and Erks, feeling tested, formed denials in his mind. The doctor didn't speak, but turned to the counter and opened a cupboard. The woman removed the apparatus from Ho's arm, moved to the doctor's side and murmured. The doctor grunted in response. They had their backs to Erks. They had left Ho uncovered. The woman murmured. The doctor nodded. Erks waited with an increasing sense of foreboding,

110

and fought his desire to ask for information.

The doctor turned back, holding a syringe, swabbed Ho's arm, inserted the needle, squeezed the syringe, and withdrew the needle, then leaned over and examined Ho's eyes closely. He shone a light in his eyes, switched it off and on. The woman washed Ho's abdomen, then, gingerly, the wound. She applied ointment and taped gauze over the wound. The doctor took his stethoscope from his pocket and listened to Ho's chest, moving the scope from one point to another while the woman began wrapping more gauze around Ho's waist. The doctor straightened up and stood for a moment, ruminating, then helped the woman, the two of them passing the gauze deftly to each other on either side of Ho, and over and under, working together as Bud and Zack had worked suturing the pig, with that familiarity. Through all this Ho lay still as a lizard.

When they had used up the gauze the doctor stepped back and looked at Erks while the woman fastened the bandage. "This is a knife wound."

"I see."

"When did it happen?"

"I don't know."

The doctor paused. Erks felt himself measured by the doctor's gaze. "I'm afraid his chances would be very slight in the best hospital in Vancouver."

Now Erks paused, registering the words. "He's dying?"

"He's lost enough blood to be dead right now."

Erks looked into Ho's face. The skin was soft like a cloth drawn over furniture, his bones poking up. His nose looked brittle. His eye sockets were dark as if bruised and the eyes were like glass. Erks looked at the doctor, then at the woman, who had finished with the bandage and had pulled Ho's shirt down and his trousers and underwear back up. The bandage, then, was just housecleaning. Her early resistance had softened and she looked at Erks wonderingly with a sympathetic, vaguely stunned expression, her eyes round as spoons, perhaps reflecting his expression, but the posture of the two of them, or their position, seemed judgmental, rendered so by his position, which in this extremity

111

had to be questionable. He had, after all, carried the boy in here.

"I see."

Erks started to say something else, but stopped, then gestured with one hand, but curtailed that, too, his hand hanging awkwardly in midair. What he had started to communicate was that it wasn't personal to him, that he was only an attendant upon the affair, but he was not only that, and it was personal—any death or even any promise of death in such proximity is gravely personal. And yet still it wasn't, and not wishing to appear as though he didn't take it personally, or as though Ho's condition were not shocking, which somehow it wasn't, although he was shocked, he had choked off his response in confusion, unable to make sense, and this despite the fact that mortality was his measure, his one absolute. He felt as though he'd come in through the back door of a stage by mistake, and found himself in a familiar action, a part of the story, and willingly so, but with a sort of disconnection because he knew how to find the door back out. But then he couldn't get to the door. He wanted the doctor and his wife to know he wasn't responsible, or—the old snag of mortality—he wanted to expiate some guilt. But what guilt? Before he left, he wanted to deny something. But what was there to deny? Ho himself? That he, Erks, wasn't really here?

"He needs blood," the doctor said. "That would be his only chance."

"The clinic?"

"The clinic could administer a transfusion, but they would have to get plasma. I doubt that they could get it in time. Even if they could . . ." The doctor paused. "To put it bluntly, it is a question of where he is to die. I've given him a sedative."

Thank God—he thought—thank God for the Scotch, thank God for Scotch candor. It was fixed, then, the boy's death. The line had been crossed, and though Ho was still alive, Erks found himself on the other side of the boy's life now, viewing his death. His thoughts swarmed around one point: he had to get the body out of here.

"Maybe I should take him to the clinic."

"We can call an ambulance."

"I'll take him," he said abruptly.

He asked how much he owed and it was the woman who told him. He put a twenty-dollar bill down on the table beside Ho's head as if he had bought nails or a slab of bacon, not a diagnosis of death. He slid his arms under the boy and lifted him carefully, trying not to bend him in the middle, and brought the boy's side to rest against his chest. The weight was the same, identical to what it had been before, but different, an old friend seen after ten years, the same, but seen on the other side of a hiatus through which so much had passed.

"We'll call ahead for you," the doctor said.

"Thank you."

He found each of their faces, their eyes, and nodded his gratitude, and thought: Not only that, but he'll check to see if I've arrived, and I will not have, and then he'll call the police, for he is, after all, Scotch, and with the Scotch, with this man, matters have their order. It was taking him a long time to move.

When he began to move, the woman stopped him by coming toward him and saying, "Here." She reached up with a blanket and spread it over Ho, tucking it in gently between Ho's side and Erks' chest. "You can leave it for us at the clinic," she said.

"Thank you."

He moved, turning sideways through the doorway to clear Ho's feet, walked awkwardly down the hall and through the waiting room. He moved through the doorway and down the walk. The door shut behind him. It was amazing what people could know, what they might not, after all, ask about, what they would allow. No matter that the doctor would call the police; he and his wife had still a generosity of spirit, a remarkable willingness to permit even matters of enormity to be as they were. The fresh air sobered Erks. Overhead, the branches of a pair of walnut trees hissed in the wind, and twenty feet from him the river roared with a sound loud as a freight train coming down a grade, but it was a silver sound, clear and transparent, a glass sound in the air. Fed by the thaw, the river raged and spumed. He stopped to look at it, a black, glistening, swift thing in the twilight, and he thought of the log in the water back at the lapidary shop, then

113

pictured Ho in it, bouncing and tumbling like a weed and then suddenly doused. He considered the weight in his arms released, weightless in the torrent and brought to a quick, merciful death, the body carried back at least in the direction of the Pacific. He looked up at the house. The door was closed, the curtains drawn. He looked back at the river. It would be simple. The river would carry Ho away in an instant. Seen in a certain light, it was the best way, to do it here, now.

He couldn't move. He couldn't make his legs walk twenty feet to the river. Aghast, he wheeled and passed through the gate toward the GMC. Three heads were visible, one in front, two in back, Chang's head upright again, the three of them like three posts set upright on the seats, waiting. He moved to the back of the truck, twisted one arm in order to grasp the latch, and jerked. The tailgate fell open. He crawled in and laid Ho down gently, shoved the suitcase to one side, found his own coat, folded it, and slipped it under Ho's head, then covered him with the blanket.

They had been driving nearly an hour before he said, "In case you're wondering, Ho's condition is grave."

They entered a valley, the forest backed off briefly from the road, and they crossed a serpentine stream, crossed it again and again in rapid succession. The stream was definitely green, lime green in the green light of nearing twilight. Up to this time Erks had said nothing. He'd been closed like a fist.

Taam hadn't asked, either.

The communication of the matter had been in the form of things not said, in the fact that nothing had been said.

"Yes?"

Erks went on to say more of what was already understood between them: "The doctor gave him no chance."

"Yes, it is most unfortunate," Taam said, nodding as if he were accepting an apology from Erks.

Erks thought: Unfortunate!

They passed a series of five-acre lots alongside the stream, marked with surveying flags and advertised by a large realty sign. There were no buildings, but only the idea of them. "Maybe if you'd explained it a little more, I wouldn't have stopped," he said.

It was a lie. He knew that he would have.

"We did not know," Taam said. "I did not expect a driver of such will."

Erks took that as condescending, an insult. It jerked his head around. Taam beamed at him, squinting and showing his teeth like a squirrel, his face tight as a skin shrunken over a post, the man suddenly become ageless. He saw an ancient beast under the face, he saw it almost surfacing, the tail of the merciless dragon, whipping.

Still grinning, Taam said, "Most would ignore him."

He said, "Not easy."

The grin dropped. "Not so hard for many."

Erks looked away. A sign warned travelers to watch for deer, the forest pressed back upon the road, and the inside of the GMC darkened in the deep shade. He said, "And for you?"

"I am powerless."

Erks' neck stiffened with anger. He spoke calmly: "I nearly dumped him in the river back there. Maybe we should dump him now. We can do that."

"There is no need."

He said, "Need!"

In the corner of his eye he saw the head tip back and he imagined the macabre grin on the face again. He wondered: Is it his own mercilessness, or just a sense of mercilessness that he carries? He was unsure. Taam did not reply, and there were no further words on the matter, and nothing at all said about the obvious hazard of his stop.

What was said in the next few hours was polite talk over what they passed—the deer, for instance, which they did see, a herd of mule deer. He saw one first, peering out from the trees near the road, then several, and he told Taam to look, and they saw more, a startling, unaccountable quantity of them, their large ears erect, heads and hides pearl-colored against the green turning black in the twilight, the deer staring out from among the trees at the passing wagon as if gathered collectively to mark it as a particular thing. What was said was calculated conversation over nothing of importance in which Erks tried to find his adversary's position in what seemed increasingly an elaborate game of will. The moon came out. The wind was up. It buffeted the truck. They traversed the Cascades, the mountains and deep woods that the Coast Indians believed to be the seat of spirits: the animal people danced in the woods, in the mountains, at night, in winter, in all the hostile and hoary places.

By the time they reached the town of Osoyoos, they had traveled over 250 miles from Vancouver and 150 from Hope. Erks pulled into Osoyoos, checked his watch, and began to appreciate Lucas' schedule. They would never make Rathdrum by dawn, not on these roads, not on this mountain highway, not on the route they were to take from Creston down. It was Lucas' way, the impossible itinerary, his way of exercising control and of making people come up short. Erks parked across from a café. His passengers had to be hungry. He wasn't going to drive all night on an empty stomach.

He got out first without speaking to Taam and went around to check on Ho. He dropped the tailgate, climbed in, and kneeling, brought his face down to the boy's face. He felt for breath with his lips close enough to kiss. There was breath. Erks pulled back. A flashing neon sign played across the boy's stricken face. If anything, he had improved. Slightly less comatose, his breath stronger, he opened his mouth and closed it, and turned his head to look at Erks. Erks adjusted the blanket and paused, considering himself beseeched. He touched the boy's shoulder as if it were a lodestone. His other three passengers hadn't moved, their heads still as posts, facing away. Erks didn't know what to think. The boy watched him. Erks cupped the side of the boy's head in his hand and stroked it gently, then slid out and eased the tailgate shut, pressing so that the latch sprang softly. He moved to the front, opened his door, and found himself whispering to Taam. "Let's eat."

He shut the door again and leaned against the fender, waiting for Taam to communicate with the other two, for the three of them to organize and get out. It would take them a couple of minutes. He figured it would take Chang a couple of minutes to agree to get out. Erks waited, ruminating.

It was 9:30, dark, clear, and not at all cold, but just cool enough to make him consider his coat, which was under Ho's head.

He tried not to think about Ho.

Just down the street was an illuminated billboard that said OSOYOOS GOES SPANISH, and listed in two columns were the local merchants who had agreed—it appeared—to help Osoyoos do so. It was a chamber of commerce hype, a cause for the sake of tourism, stolen—he figured—from those who labored here, the fruit pickers. Osoyoos was a fruit-processing town. A Canadian border town, it was built on the banks of Osoyoos Lake, which was fed by the Okanagan River, which, in turn, flowed southward into Washington, past the Colville Indian Reservation, and into the Columbia above Grand Coulee. The entire Okanagan valley was a fruit-growing region that spread from Canada down into the center of Washington along the eastern foot of the Cascades —apples, peaches, cherries, pears—the land "reclaimed" by Columbia River Projects. The word "reclaimed" was a word he had never been able to understand. By whom had it been claimed before? Or disclaimed? How many times? It was—he knew—a vestige of his father's prejudice he carried, and maybe a reactionary inclination he had to demand personification of collective possession, to ask for names, to request responsibility for acts, to be literal.

Taam stepped around the front of the truck and stopped beside him while Chang and Lee went around the back. He heard their light footsteps and a sort of piling heel-and-toe sound as they stopped. They would not come beside him, would not step into view. Given the choice between furtive and direct, the two took furtive, always. Confronted with the direct, hours ago, Chang had pulled a knife.

He moved across the street toward the café without looking back at Chang or Lee, nor at Ho, no, not at the truck, not searching for the prone form, not for the space through the windows

117

above Ho, a tincture, that space of air, of Ho, which Erks, while driving, had registered through the rear-view mirror just beyond the heads of the other two, that space the slow, close, exhausted air above Ho. Even as he walked his urge was to go back and look at Ho again, to scrutinize him again as one wishes to touch a bruise again and again, testing its pain, seeking reassurance, although, with Ho, Erks did not know what would be reassuring, more or less pain. He kept walking and looked over Taam's head to the south, toward Washington, down along the valley, and thought about what reclamation did: all along the rivers—the Columbia, the Yakima, the Okanagan—orchards had been built, a patchwork on the sloping river bottoms of the arid plateau land, sagebrush country, coulee country, glacial backwash, high desert, his country. It brought growers and truckers and pickers and migrant workers—Latinos. It reclaimed them.

"It is warm," Taam said.

Erks grunted. It was in the fifties and there was no snow, not a trace, but everything was wet, the pavement, the ground, the gutters swollen with thaw. He wouldn't exactly call it warm, though.

"It is a chinook, yes?" Taam said, glancing up at Erks.

It was. A rising hard blow out of the south, broken off Kuroshio out of the Bering Strait and following the long watersheds, it was almost warm; like Kuroshio, its substance warmer than the settled substance through which it passed. It did feel good to walk in it. It lightened one's weight.

Erks opened the glass door of the café and held it for the others to pass through, Taam first, then Lee. Chang came last and, regarding himself as confronted perhaps by Erks' good manners, came toward Erks like a colt turned loose, prancing, quick, the eyes flicking. He moved with his elbows high and his body stiff, and all but collided with Erks, daring Erks to interfere with his path, but veered, just then, as Erks stood his ground. Chang swung to the side, and doing so, still not going through the doorway, his eyes fell upon the knife which Erks had picked up from where he had tossed it back in Hope—on the floorboard at Taam's feet. Erks had it under his belt above his hip, the handle

118

poking out from under his coat. Chang hung, his eyes brightening, then his body palpably gathered force to move for the knife.

It happened in an instant and all in one motion, and Erks saw what was coming and leaned forward, bracing himself, and Chang saw that and instead of lunging settled flat on his feet, gave the knife up, then moved past Erks with one shoulder cocked as if he were about to walk through a wall, not an open doorway. Erks paused, holding the door handle, gripped by a sense of futility.

A lilting, Canadian voice called from within: "The cold air, sir."

He stepped inside and joined the others in a booth next to a window. He slid in next to Taam. Chang and Lee sat opposite. He and Taam had a clear view of the chamber of commerce billboard out on the street. The waitress who had called out delivered menus and water. She was dressed up like a toreadora: a little triangular cap, tight pants, a blouse with puffed sleeves and an elastic top, and a short vest with a button on it that also said OSOYOOS GOES SPANISH. A plain girl, a strawberry blonde a year or two out of high school, she looked at Erks. She gave him a look, twisting her mouth and closing one already experienced eye.

"What do we eat?" Erks asked Taam.

The girl smiled.

"I know," he said to her. "You get all kinds."

"Not this many," she said.

Erks chuckled.

"Hamburgers," Taam said. "Two each."

"Two?"

Taam nodded. "I'll have an enchilada," he said, smiling and raising his eyebrows to make a joke of it.

Erks chuckled again. The man was acute, very quick. He'd grant him that.

He ordered the enchilada for Taam, and for himself, chicken-fried steak and coffee. He would drink lots of coffee to gird himself for the night. They ate. Chang and Lee ate as if they hadn't eaten for days. Voracious, they clutched the

119

buns and tore out big bites. They bent close to their plates, grabbing the food and shoving it into their mouths with their fingers, swallowing heavily, washing it down with gulps of water, the muscles of their necks taut, straining, grease on their chins.

Erks ate with deliberation, the meat and the mashed potatoes and beans that came with it making a weight in his stomach. He stared through the window at the billboard that reclamation had brought to the town, musing as he chewed. Reclamation had brought a little more moisture, too, a slow change in the climatic conditions of the entire region, and, actually, a slight lowering of temperature, year by year as imperceptible as a shift in the big dam itself, FDR's dam, Senator Dill's dam, Woody Guthrie's dam, Grand Coulee. Unlike his father, Erks would not curse the dam; he wouldn't praise it, either. It was there. It propelled so vast a set of designs: fisheries and salmon ladders and, in drought, tank trucks to move the fingerlings around the ladders, and electric power, and enough cable to wrap up the earth, and irrigation, and thousands of lives lived, now, in service to the dam, in a condition of having been encircled by an act of history.

He had been in the valley and up to Osoyoos in late summer and then it was a dry 105 degrees, and fruit stands had lined the road on the border side of the town, south, beyond the billboard. The stands had been operated by Latinos and the bright red-and-white signs bore the names Lopez, Gomez, Martinez, Cabrillo, Delgado. . . . They had made a pocket here: they picked the fruit, ran the stands, they established residence, and some among them had bought fruit land. They were out there on the fringes of town in the shadow of the billboard, on its dark side, living in shanties or prefabs—according to their labor, their endurance, their longevity, their luck in riding their migration to the conditions of the dam. He knew they were out there. The Canadian town fathers had said so through the spirit taken and run through a sieve to get the streamers and ensigns and the motto—OSOYOOS GOES SPANISH.

There was a parable in it which Erks couldn't place.

Taam, watching him, acute again, said, "You need not take Ho as your personal responsibility."

Startled, Erks spoke frankly. "I show that?"

Taam shrugged. "What else?"

It was true. He'd been thinking of Ho all along. Out of the big game, one glass bead flashed in the night. Ho was missing his chance to be reclaimed. Erks tongued a chunk of gristle into his cheek, and said, "I should have dumped him in that damn river."

Across the booth, Chang and Lee sat back against the cushion as still as two gorged possums hanging upside down from a limb. Their plates were spotless. Erks and Taam were barely halfway through their meals.

Taam took a bite of enchilada and said, "What is so special about the river?"

Erks paused. It was a good question. He said, "Throwing him in it would have been irrevocable for sure."

"You desire the irrevocable?"

"Now," Erks said, "yes. Now I'd settle for just about anything definite even if I had to take personal responsibility for it."

❧ 7 ❧

It was the next morning, Saturday, the morning after the burial, and Sandman had spent another night in Dynamite with Lily, or some scrap of the night. He had in sleep just ridden the edge of gloom and he awoke feeling as if he hadn't slept at all. When he got up, Lily was gone, and he found a note by which she made herself clear, scrawled in crayon and taped to the refrigerator door:

> HELP YOURSELF.
> ENJOY YOUR TRIP.

He took nothing to eat, and so—he thought—made himself clear. He had set out, but he was stopped already. He'd planned to follow the route through the Cascades to the coast, the scenic route. He'd hoped to locate Erks' place on the way and—invited or not—to drop by and see the biplane and hit him up for breakfast. Sandman was not one to stand on ceremony. He figured he was almost there, for he'd driven some 30 miles west of Spokane, but he was stopped on the shoulder of Highway 2, his cycle dead.

The bike had juice. The lights worked. The electric starter worked, turned the engine over until it flooded. He knelt on one side of the bike, then the other, and searched it as he might have searched the fringe of a tapestry for the outcome of the story it wove. He found no loose wires, no missing bolts. So far as he could tell, everything worked except the bike. He pushed it to the crest of a hill, from which he could see the town he presumed to be Davenport several miles away, a scattering of squares like dice on a floor. He jumped on the bike, let it pick up speed, then popped it into gear. It coughed, started, ran for a hundred feet, died, and rolled to a stop. He put the kickstand down, swung a leg over, and sat sidesaddle with his chin in his hands, angry, disconsolate, not quite helpless, but certainly mastered. He had a fresh chain, spark plugs, and points, and the factory tool kit packed with his gear. The spark plugs he might have mounted, given time, but he figured he'd blown a gasket, broken a rod or valve, or cracked the block—if one could crack a cycle block, if cycles had blocks. He didn't know. He felt he was the victim of a large and continuing joke.

It had been a hard two days: the snowstorm, the first night with Lily, the funeral in Idaho and the people there, the family, the guests, Bud's invited friends, a rough people out of the woods, miners or loggers, he figured, the women mean-looking and the men either huge or viciously skinny, and a third of them maimed, one on crutches and others limping, another missing an arm, a dangerous group pouring out of the cars after the funeral and coming down the hill. Sandman's teeth ground and his breath caught when he thought of them. He had done as he'd been told, tended the pig, turned it, even worried over the pig, and stoked and raked the fire until he thought he had it just right. Bud, drunk, back with the others, came straight for him, snarling about wood, too much wood, the fire too hot, about how he'd told Sandman to turn the pig and that was all. Bud came around the pig and knocked the pipe wrench from Sandman's hand and backed him clear up against the house. The others looked on, impassive, immobile as iron things in the snow, and for Sandman the whole scene froze for an instant into a picture of pure menace, the menace of the others as palpable as the hands of the one, Bud, or even more so, their menace, their refusal to help him, to stop Bud, to do something, anything, collective. Bud hit him once, the blow not quite enough to knock him out, but enough to make his legs buckle, and, dazed, he heard someone laugh, then, as Bud lifted him, he heard Lily's voice, rising, saying something that made Bud let him loose and turn on her. He fell again. Hunched over, clutching his face and staring through his fingers at the ground, he heard the harangue, something about the mother and money, something of which he had no part, but out of which he received and carried nevertheless, now, still, the next morning, a bruise on his cheek and a shoulder that ached from Bud's twisting.

Even she, Lily, though she had interceded, did not come over to help him to his feet. Through the night, even she ignored him, and he lived in a hell of isolation in the snow over by the wrecked cars, where he waited, beside himself with fury, but cold, and afraid of the house, afraid of the people who stood at the fire and drank and tore at the flesh of the roasted pig, and furious with himself for being afraid. Even after she took him back to Dynamite, Lily treated him as she might an alien thing, a monkey, a parrot, a wooden post. She made love to him, or she employed him—she had said that, that she enjoyed the use of a man, that she liked having a man in the rooms, but not for what he thought it might mean. And she did it, made use of him, but her pleasure was so out of kilter with his that he stopped midway through and lay passively or even politely on his back, amazed by her passion, which addressed some other body, not his, and, almost painful, almost asexual, admitted only herself but nothing about herself. Done, she heaved herself over to the side, pulled up the sheet and turned her back on him. His side of the bed rose like a skiff on a swell, carrying his light body, and even his dreams were madcap and unstrung and did not cut the surface of the sea.

And now this. He had the highway and the wheat fields of the high prairie at his back and before him more wheat fields and in the distance beneath the long sky the purple outlines of mountains heaping into British Columbia. Occasionally a car or truck passed and rocked the bike. It was eight in the morning. The sun climbed. The earth steamed. Patches of dark showed through the white in the fields—the high spots. He supposed his alternatives were clear enough: sit or seek help.

He slid off the bike and started walking. A young couple in

124

a flatbed truck picked him up. The woman had a lumpy face and chipped front teeth, and she scooted over on the seat for him, straddled the gearshift. Sandman watched the man's fist plunge between her legs, and out, and in again, brushing her jeans at the crotch as he worked through the gears. Sandman raised his eyes and looked coldly through the windshield. There was that, at least, he thought. There was always that, the flesh, more flesh, plenty of flesh.

They let him off where the highway widened and divided for the town.

"This is Davenport?" he asked from the road.

The woman's face hung in the window. She nodded and blinked slowly, showing a lot of mascara.

"Thanks," he said.

There were service stations on the highway. At the first, Sandman found Erks' name in the telephone book and tried the number. There was no answer. He walked from one station to another and went through the ritual questions, asking them with an insistency born of his rising frustration. He got the runaround:

We don't have a truck to haul it in.
We don't work on bikes.
There's no cycle dealer in town.
Maybe this afternoon.
Maybe Monday.
Maybe back in Spokane.
Wanna sell it?

He tried to call Erks again. There was no answer. He held the receiver away from his ear and let it ring twenty or thirty times. Erks hadn't given him the impression that he would be out of town. But he hadn't said he would be in town, either. He hadn't stayed in Rathdrum for the funeral. He'd been there to see Lily's husband—that was about all Sandman knew, or that and the fact that their business offended Bud to the quick and had a mysterious air, which, added to the biplane and the fact that Erks' place was on his route, had convinced Sandman to stop in

Davenport. Sandman liked the cryptic, the exotic, he liked to be in the know, but for now, his options were narrowing and there wasn't anything particularly exotic about his motorcycle sitting out on the highway. The address in the telephone book was a rural box number and none of the attendants could say exactly where it would be.

He was directed to Glider and Cannott's. They might work on a bike, he was told. After a six-block walk which took him back fifteen or twenty years into a section of town by the railway tracks, he found the garage, a low, dilapidated building with a sign mounted below the eaves and running the length of the wall: GLIDER & CANNOTT/BEAR ALIGNMENT/WELDING/FARM EQUIP-MENT/SMALL ENGINES/TOWING. Nailed above the words "Bear Alignment" was a metal sign with the familiar picture of the bear. The building, set back on the lot, was surrounded with cars and tractors, most in an advanced state of disrepair. A door was ajar and Sandman stepped inside into obscurity.

The place was lit only by two bare 100-watt bulbs and a row of small windows at the back, and by the slash of light that ran across the floor from the doorway to the opposite wall. It was a four-stall garage, the entire first two stalls and most of the third being taken up with tools and parts—engines, transmissions, generators, welding tanks, five- and ten-gallon drums, boxes, and shipping crates. On the walls were tool racks and pegs draped with cables, gaskets, and antiquated accessories—clean air wicks, mesh air cleaners, Red Devil filters, woven seat pads, suicide knobs with naked girls inside. . . . Small cartons and packets overflowed from the shelves, and tools—wrenches, screwdrivers, drills, measuring devices, and valve grinders—were heaped and stacked precariously on the benches. In a corner and stretching half the distance along one wall, in the darkness, Sandman saw five motorcycles, taken down, old Harley-Davidsons. The tanks and fenders lay like large cocoons on the floor before the frames, dusty and draped with cobwebs.

There was no sign of a mechanic. A pickup stood in the farthermost stall. It reared on front axle lifts, the hood removed and the engine, winched out, on the floor beside it. Beyond the truck at the corner of the building Sandman spotted light seeping from a cubbyhole. He moved toward the light, picking his way along a narrow trail which had been made, or discovered, among the parts and tools. There was no one in the cubbyhole. Manuals and parts directories lined the shelves and were stacked on the floor, thirty or forty years' worth of them, the topmost volumes coated with dust and grase. An aluminum coffeemaker, plugged in and hot, and a mug with a brown pool in the bottom, and a half-eaten package of sugar doughnuts, stood on a tin counter where ledger and receipt books were kept. The ledger was open, scrawled on, the words and numbers unreadable. It brought out the accountant in Sandman: the books needed a system, the garage needed an inventory. But a place of softness, the cubbyhole was a retreat and it had a toilet behind a ragged drape, and the chest-high counter had two smooth cups near the edge from elbows leaned on while the book work was done. On the wall was a telephone. He took the receiver off the hook and tried Erks again. There was no answer. He let it ring. Next to the telephone hung a calendar, this year's, but the photograph was an old cheesecake picture of Jane Russell, a World War II picture, a collector's item. He stared at Jane Russell.

She was on her knees, her breasts at once large and pert under a woven white shawl, probably aided by the famous brassiere Howard Hughes had engineered for her. Her expression, however playful, had a used quality. It was a pose to help the troops get through; if she had been so used once, she could be used in the imagination again and again. She looked back with a sparkle in her eyes as ruthless and all-purpose as the diamond bit that gave Hughes his start. In her eyes was the print of the man who mastered space, who turned space into coin, who spent his last years riding the silver trails of coin across space. A trail to Vegas. A trail to São Paulo. A trail back to Salt Lake City. Arcs, curvatures, parabolas. A trail to Tokyo. Hughes had died a year ago and still the news was everywhere. But the quick-freezing scheme had failed him.

Sandman had never really believed that Hughes existed. An

Easterner, Sandman saw that as mostly legendary.

It took Jane Russell to believe. In her face was the mark as true as blood of the very size of the man's big Puritanical mechanical hustle.

Sandman didn't really believe that mechanics existed, either, except as a thing that emerged from some subliminary zone to deter the blood. He believed in flesh and numbers, not in tools.

He hung up and stepped out of the cubbyhole when he heard a scraping noise. No one was apparent, but he heard a second scraping noise, the sound of rollers on concrete, and then a boot appeared from under the bumper of the pickup right in front of him. A generator was thrust out from behind the tire. It rolled and knocked against the engine.

"Hello," Sandman said.

He was answered with a grunt.

"I could use some help."

The response, again, was indecipherable, but a rise in tone suggested a question.

"I'm broken down on the highway just east of here," Sandman explained. He paused, then added, "A motorcycle . . ." but stopped short when a fistful of wrenches was thrust out from behind the tire and dropped on the concrete, clattering. Sandman stepped forward and looked down through the engine compartment. A man wearing a gray work suit and dark glasses, a pudgy man with a soft face, lay on his back on a roller board in a faint pool of light from a drop lamp. His head rested on a pad. His arms lay on the concrete at his sides. He stared back at Sandman, or so it seemed. The dark glasses made it difficult to tell for certain.

"Mr. Cannott?"

"Cannott's out," the man said. Nothing moved but his lips.

"Mr. Glider?"

Glider waited.

"I don't mean to interrupt your work."

"Oh, no. Pass me that sack." Glider pointed out from under the pickup toward the engine.

Sandman handed him the sack which was on top of the engine, passed it down through the compartment. Glider unwrapped a half-sandwich and began to eat, lying on his back, chewing slowly. Sandman waited, watching, then spoke: "I'm broken down on the highway."

"I heard that. What's the problem?"

Sandman smiled. "Mainly that I'm on foot."

Glider stopped chewing. He removed his glasses and wiped his eyes with his sleeve, then looked at Sandman. The skin around his eyes was white. "What kind of cycle?"

When Sandman told him, Glider sighed, his belly and chest rising slowly, then falling. He took another bite of sandwich and chewed with great determination, a ruminant, and stared at Sandman expressionlessly. "Cannott's out of town."

"You don't work on motorcycles?"

"I got this pickup, then Clarence Simms' Massey-Ferguson. It'd be two, three days before I could get to it."

Sandman put his arms on the pickup's radiator and leaned. He told Glider of all the places he'd tried already, then said, "Do you think you could take a minute to look at it? Or just help me get it into town?"

"Right now I've got the guts out of this pickup."

Sandman had a sinking feeling. "Would you know a man named Wes Erks? Or where he lives? Or would you know where Route One, Box Sixty-eight, would be?"

Glider pushed the last of the sandwich into his mouth, then spoke, the words choked.

"I beg your pardon?"

For no apparent reason, Glider chuckled, kicking his feet slowly, a mischievous pupa in its cocoon down in the cool under the truck. Then he put his dark glasses back on, and so, it seemed, doomed the conversation. "I said he might be able to help you."

"Who?"

"Erks." Glider knew Erks hadn't done any serious work in his shop for over a year. It was an old joke between them, sending the basket cases to each other.

"You mean Wes Erks?"

129

"I believe you mentioned him by name first."

"Is he home?"

Glider shrugged, then chuckled again. "You a friend of his?"

"I believe so."

"Do you always use folks' telephones without asking?" Glider said, grinning.

The name—W. Erks—was printed in careful letters on the rural delivery box at the foot of the drive, which passed under a large cottonwood tree and among the pines and turned inside an encirclement of lilac bushes to the front of the white house. Sandman walked up onto the recently painted deck-gray porch. The door was open, or the wooden door was open. The screen door was shut, though unlatched. The breeze blew through the house at him and whistled at his back in the pines. The screen door rattled when he knocked.

He waited. His legs sweated inside his leathers. His boots, wet from the walk in mud and melting snow, pinched his feet. Glider had told him that somebody would probably be home, or back before long. He'd told him how to get here, to head down the block and take a left and keep going past the point where the pavement gave out to gravel, but he hadn't said anything about the house being better than three miles out of town. It was a long walk. The houses had appeared less and less frequently on the flat, at the heads of pale-green wheat fields from which the snow had all but vanished, and he felt increasingly exposed, as though he were walking on a tabletop. When he had seen the green grown deeper down the road to the almost blue color of pines, and at the head of the pine stand the white house, and another house just beyond it, and past the houses and southerly the land turning, dropping out of sight into a canyon or ravine, he had thought: I'll walk that far and if neither of those places is it, I'll go up and ask, for God's sake.

He knocked again and waited. He looked around the yard. An old swing set over in a corner of the yard beneath a maple tree had been repainted and wrapped with plastic tape. The lawn had just been mowed, the rectangular flower pots spaded and raked. Tulips and daffodils were in bloom. The place was hardly landscaped, hardly manicured: the lawn, though healthy enough, had areas of dense growth and areas of thin, and the mowing had been aggressive, the blades set low, so that in places the cut was to the root, and the spaded plots, though weedless, were not quite rectangular, but black, rich, and the edges had been cut out of the lawn with a spade so that they had a rough scalloped effect. Clumps of sod banked the plots. The hedgerow which ran along two sides of the yard, and on the third side, along the drive, the lilacs, had been allowed to grow free so that the outlines were wild, and the trees, too, spaded around the trunks, but otherwise left reckless. The interest here, the care, was of a particular kind: not cosmetic, it was directed solely toward the growth of plants. It looked hectic to Sandman. It gave him the sensation of viewing a scene of struggle.

He knocked a third time.

The breeze blew through the house.

He opened the door and called, "Wes Erks?"

He was greeted by a guttural rumble and the sleek head of a dog—the Weimaraner—coming out of the silence and shadow. In an instant the head squared off against Sandman, and he saw bared teeth and yellow eyes and heard the rumble define itself into a crackling snarl. He pulled back suddenly, pushed the door shut, held it, then gingerly backed off the porch.

He walked around back and saw a woman—Ruby—at work in a vegetable garden, a big garden, huge, impressive, freshly tilled, and extending out of sight to the drop-off. Onions, lettuce, and some root vegetables were already up, long rows of new green, and one thick patch of knee-high plants, Jerusalem artichokes. The woman was planting. She had cut several rows with a hoe along string lines, and stooped, straddling a row, dropping seed, she backed toward him like someone coming down a ladder. Near her, the young boy played with a truck. He saw Sandman and retreated to his mother, touched her leg, and murmured. She looked at Sandman upside down through her legs, then stood up and turned, her eyes narrowing as she watched the intruder, the small man, wearing leather, his face bright from

131

exertion—the insect come out of Glider's pupa back under the pickup truck in town.

"Mrs. Erks?" He stopped. "My name is Albert Sandman." He moved forward.

"Watch the rows, please."

Sandman stopped again, looked at his feet, side-stepped cautiously, and moved between rows. Ruby waited at the terminus. The boy had his cheek against her waist and she cupped his head with her hand. The boy's eyes were wide, inquisitive. Ruby's expression was flat. She wore jeans and a man's shirt, and had a red bandanna bound around her head. Sandman came near, halting less than an arm's length away, near enough to touch.

"Is Wes at home?"

"You mean my husband."

"Yes," Sandman said, looking straight into her eyes. "Mr. Glider was good enough to direct me here."

"Carl Glider?" Her eyes flickered. She thought: Damn him!

Sandman backtracked. "I have a problem." Before she could respond, he crouched and poked the boy rudely in the stomach. "The little farmer, hey?" The boy turned his face into his mother's waist. "I hoped Wes might help me with it," Sandman said.

She loosed herself from Matt and stepped into the patch of Jerusalem artichokes and began pulling plants, thinning the patch. "What's the problem?"

Sandman liked that, her obstinacy. He liked obstinacy in a woman. He rose and smiled. Behind his heavy lips, the teeth were large and uneven. He saw that Erks wasn't here. He could wait. He felt better. He had begun to feel more certain. He had begun to feel the lift of his own insurgency. Beneath the obstinacy—he surmised—was great softness; inside the shell was clay, the center of the loop, the curd. He liked her obstinacy because he thought it would yield. He watched her grip a good-sized plant near the ground, then twist and pull, her small hands and wrists alive with strength, wonderfully certain. The plant came out, soil clinging to the root hairs, and she dropped it on its side. He wanted to touch her. He wanted to touch her bare shoulder, her side, her ribs under the loose-fitting shirt.

His voice was low and insinuating: "You have remarkable hands."

Touched, taken aback, and even suddenly flattered, she didn't give him the advantage of glancing down at her hands. She glared at him and wondered: Who is this or what is this strange, large-eared intruder, or wild weed, gopher, or smooth-talking stray dog, that has come into the backyard?

"I'm on a motorcycle and I've broken down, you see. I hoped Wes might give me a hand."

"My husband's a machinist, not a mechanic, and he doesn't work for the public."

"Well . . ." He showed his palms, meaning to suggest that he was hardly the public.

"And he's out of town."

Matt hummed as he rolled his toy truck on a toy road around a basket of seed packets in the dirt.

"Do you know my husband?"

Sandman lied, "Through Lucas," then added, "It's a long story. I was going to look at the biplane."

She scrutinized him. "He's with Lucas now."

Sandman took Ruby's words more exactly than she meant them, and sensed a trap. He didn't think it was so. He had seen Erks leave Rathdrum yesterday morning. He'd seen Lucas leave late last night, and he'd overheard him tell Lily that he'd see her in Reno. He didn't know where Erks had gone. He gambled and built on his lie. "You don't mean I've missed Lucas, too. I've missed him once already."

Ruby looked up at the bright sky above the house, her face set and the bones pronounced because the scarf bound up her hair. There was a shovel in the Jerusalem artichoke patch and she pulled it out of the ground and drove it in again with her foot, turned it, and plunged it back, severing the clod. The wet, turned earth teemed with worms. She watched them twist back for cover under the surface and measured Sandman in her mind, weighed him, doubted his word, suspected the worst of him, but doubted her doubt, too, and even feared for her husband, but

133

finally just wondered what in the world had dropped this loose piece on her place.

"You didn't expect to meet Lucas here."

"No. In Idaho." He gazed at her steadily. "Do you think Wes would mind if I used his tools?"

She thought: Damn! She sighed. "Where is your bike?"

Erks listened to the truck hum and to the snow tires singing on the road. All around the truck, history hummed and did its dance with its clothes off in the night. History was everywhere, in the woods and naked all up and down the highway. It filled all the paths people had made in it, all the trails of blood, a web without geometry, a tangle of routes. He was among them, moving over the skin of history. Ruby had called him a purposeful vagrant because of the journey he had undertaken, it seemed to her, under false pretenses.

His fingers were light on the steering wheel. The mysterious small man sat as calm as a cat next to him. Erks was preoccupied with Simon Fraser and an unnamed woman and with a man of Fraser's company called La Malice. The most experienced of Fraser's men, the chief of his *engagés,* but belligerent and ambitious, La Malice had been left to explore the upper reaches of the Peace River while Fraser journeyed to the Pacific. When Fraser returned to the post at what is now Prince George, he found that under La Malice's authority an Indian woman had been traded from one man to another at the post, and had come full circle back to La Malice.

Fraser was fatigued to the bone and deeply disappointed by what would be to the North West Company a useless journey charting not the headwaters of the Columbia but an unnavigable river to be called the Fraser, and a journey that for all its travail would advance him not a whit in the company. He had more travel before him, eastward across the Rockies, and La Malice was to go with him. He asked La Malice what he intended to do with the woman.

La Malice replied that as the woman had been sold to him, he knew what he had to do—meaning that one kept what one owned.

Fraser said that they could not take a woman, particularly under those circumstances, and told La Malice that he should decide to go with him without the woman or return alone to Montreal. He said this although his canoes were so poor that they had to be gummed several times a day, when he had difficult waters ahead still, and difficult portages, when he was short of provisions and desperately short of men.

The next day La Malice returned to say that he would go with Fraser, but at his own pleasure, not under obligation.

Fraser said that since he thus showed his good intentions, he could take the woman, but not as his property.

La Malice agreed and went off to the woman, whom he had left to wait for him at the edge of camp, in the shadow of the woods.

Nothing more was reported of the matter, but Erks wondered how the news was delivered to the woman, and what was her emotional stake, her preference, for she had been treated from the beginning as an article of exchange—as a canoe or pelt or a box of beads—and then bartered between the two men in a fashion that had more to do with their shuffling for power, for leverage and purchase, for standing in the eyes of the Montreal office, than it had to do with her. He thought of how it came out in the world of the *Journal*—the teeming, aggressive, and truncated world in which the whole picture was never given, but only a chain of rocks and rapids and untraversable cliffs and broken canoes: it came out, somehow, on a moral pivot made by Fraser —take the woman, but not as your property—and this turning more on the expense of La Malice than for the sake of the woman. It came from a man—Fraser—who himself regarded the "savages" with the half-shocked and debasing sexual eye with which one might regard the backside of a hairy ape in a zoo, and who was interested really in only one thing, to find a trade route for furs, a route to express the purpose of his vagrancy, and who himself had journeyed under false pretenses—those of there being easy access to the Columbia and hence to the sea, of the enduring design of a satisfying fantasy, of there being, still, a continuous strait through the Rockies to the sea—and who had been duped, who had traveled a route much of which is still today merely charted, hardly traveled. It came out as a journey through the anarchic woods and water, the stone, the dark, the cold, the land of spirits, and yet there stood that moral position filled with light and oxygen: Take her, but not as your own.

Erks had a growing sense of having screwed himself up. He'd at once begun this journey with too little regard for what he carried and then quickly had become too involved with the trouble in the truck to find his way through it. He'd taken on the trouble of his passengers as his own, and now was unable to see clearly what the trouble was, unable even to ask Taam a sensible question about it.

He had to come up with something other than the nagging questions which since Vancouver he had directly or indirectly asked:

"What happened to Ho?"

"What do we do with Ho?"

"Why did Chang attack me?"

"Why was the Lincoln following us?"

"Why did it stop following us?"

He had to find a way to get to the questions he had not asked:

"Did the Lincoln stop following us?"

"Did Chang stab Ho?"

"Just what am I transporting?"

"What part does the Triad have in this?"

"What the hell is the Triad?"

"Who are you?"

He had not felt the weight of Ruby's objection until now. She herself—he thought—had not known its weight. Searching to understand what he did and what she thought of it, or why she objected, Ruby had called him a "purposeful vagrant" as he went out to the truck early in the morning. It left him at least a cut above Lucas, whom she called simply a vagrant. She knew he didn't have time to ask her what she meant. He knew she didn't object to the illegality of the journey. The laws against illegal aliens and those who delivered them she, too, would see as a matter of pressure politics, hardly of morality, a matter of barriers mounted on the face of geography, hardly of the fluidity of human movement, and yet he felt demeaned and duped by the lack of light and oxygen in his awareness of his passengers, especially for Taam, even for Ho. . . .

And what Ruby had called him was afloat in his thoughts.

He lacked a ground to stake it down.

But what was the alternative?

It was night. The night had dropped itself on them with great dexterity.

Although the moon was not full, its complete circularity had been visible back in Osoyoos because of the angle of the sun, which had not quite set yet. The moon's paler portion of less than a quarter which then was still in the earth's shadow had gathered light from the bias. As the earth turned, the moon's one quarter faded until it was invisible, or until it was as dark as the night in which the moon, flat on one side, hung like a cam. It looked like a stilled cam connected to machinery hidden behind the black casement. It was that bright, that metallic.

Now only the implication of the complete circle remained, an implication of the whole left in the mind, a suggested fringe of light, a negative silhouette, the missing piece dissolved to the other side of the margin. The moon trembled with the motion of the truck and moved around the windows according to the direction of the road. In open spaces the wind knocked the truck. The snow tires sang on the pavement. Erks had the heater on, and

138

Chang and Lee, perhaps, had fallen asleep, their heads tipped toward each other in the softness of the night mirror. The road, lit by the headlights, passed under the truck like a ribbon on a spool. Erks drove and talked to Taam, feeling like a ghost, feeling as if he weren't really there.

He had asked Taam where he was from and Taam had said Nevada, but that he'd been raised in San Francisco. When Erks asked if that meant he was really from San Francisco, he had said, "Who isn't?" Erks heard the irony in his voice and in the glow off the instrument panel saw Taam's body move, the head nodding at the joke.

"I'm not."

"Clearly," Taam said, nodding again.

He did not ask Erks where he was from. He did not mind being asked about himself, it seemed, but he kept his distance and held the conversation where he wanted it by not returning the questions.

"You're going home?"

"For a time."

"How long have you been gone?"

Taam pushed in the cigarette lighter. "Seven years."

"A long time."

"Yes."

The lighter snapped out. Erks saw the red trail of the lighter, then the quick flare on the cigarette in Taam's mouth. The odor of burning tobacco wafted through the truck.

"My father has died, you see. I am returning to honor his memory."

"That's hard."

"He was over ninety."

"That doesn't make it easier," he said, speaking as one who knew, and he thought: We'll be a threesome when we pick up Lily.

"No. Not for the living."

The death of the man's father only enshrouded certain questions deeper in mystery. But through Taam's words Erks sensed a dark, angular thing forming under the cover, a thick thing

139

turning like a mole in its tunnel, an incipient thing with wings like a bat about to flit loose.

"And you will stay?"

"In the States?" Taam paused. "It was not my intent."

"But now you have second thoughts?"

"Not second thoughts, no. But one must be prepared to change. I have my father's affairs to set in order."

"In Reno?"

Taam did not reply.

He probed again: "May I ask why you are entering the country in this fashion?"

The cigarette glowed when Taam inhaled. "When you leave illegally, you must enter illegally."

"Logical enough."

Taam's chuckle made Erks glance at him, and Taam looked back, his eyes glossy in the dark. "I am a fugitive from justice." He chuckled again and Erks saw the head nodding. "I am at large, so to speak." He repeated it—"At large"—and chuckled yet again.

Erks looked back at the road. "There are some who seem anxious for you to surface."

"Oh? There are many who await the return of one illusion or another."

Taam tapped his cigarette against the ashtray. They paused for a time. The road swung and the moon slipped around until it hung in the windshield like a chipped eye.

"There's a town not far from here," Erks said. "Cheesaw, just across the border. According to the locals, it's named after a tribe of half-Chinese Indians."

He glanced at Taam, checking. He saw Taam's head lift as if to look askance, and his teeth catching light.

Erks went on: "They say that a group of Chinese miners on their way to Vancouver to return home to China traded their women to the Indians in what is now Cheesaw. They feared the snow. They wanted to make time before winter hit. The women became part of the tribe and so the tribe, they say, and the town, were called Cheesaw."

140

"Do you wish to provoke me?"

Now, looking at the road, he smiled. "But it is not a true story."

"It is a story about sex," Taam said, pronouncing the word —sex—with a strong and curious lisp, making a joke. "You people like to make up stories about the heathens interbreeding. It is a way to enjoy what you fear to admit about yourselves. You call it what—dark meat?"

Erks looked and saw the teeth again. "The truth is that the town's named after a miner who settled there, Cheesaw. But the other story's the one that's told."

"Of course. The miners had no women. If they had had women maybe they wouldn't have wanted to go home. The story of my people in this country in the old days is a story of no women. That is what is not told, their aching for a woman." Then he chuckled and said, "Why do you think they worked so hard?"

Erks was stopped. It was true he had tried to provoke the man, to force him off balance. After a while he said, "Maybe the question is why did you leave illegally."

The answer came quickly. "To escape the illusion of myself."

"Which was?"

Taam laughed, the sound a series of voiceless breaths in the throat, and too many of them for comfort, monotonous and macabre. "Do you want me to die?"

They paused again. Mystified by Taam's remark, or half mystified—he understood what was said, he didn't understand why it was said—Erks found that obscure conversation and interminable road and endless night made long pauses a gain instead of a loss. A large bird flew into the light in front of the truck, rising from the bank on the left, and seeing the truck, it pumped its wings and veered upward, but hit the windshield high on Taam's side with a thump. The glass cracked. Erks let the truck roll to a stop on the shoulder and got out to check. He ran his fingers along the radiation of cracks and looked in at Taam's rounded form in the dark, soft and without detail. He stepped away and took a deep breath.

He walked back to see if he could find the bird—for a

141

breather, really. He found it in the center of his lane, the incipient thing, maybe, the dark angular thing broken loose out of nowhere, and now dead, the life whacked out of it as quickly as it had been seen. He picked it up. It was a common screech owl. The large body was warm and limp in his hands, the wing and back feathers slick and brittle, the breast feathers downy at his fingertips. One long wing hung down, shattered at the joint.

The truck was up the road, the lights on, purring like a live thing. Otherwise, the road was empty, as it had been for miles. Holding the bird, looking at the truck, he felt that he looked at himself. Certainly he looked at his predicament, his truck, the vehicle of their conveyance, and watching himself, he had the sense of being watched, the sense, again, of points in space, of triangulation. The third point—he thought—was Taam, or something seeing from the position of the yellow man's filmy words, but when he turned to toss the bird into the ditch he saw it, a large thing darker than the dark in the trees and brush just the other side of the ditch. He froze. The hair on his neck prickled.

It stood erect and it was big, one shoulder and a massive head vaguely silhouetted against snow behind the trees. It didn't move. He couldn't see its eyes, but by its utter stillness and seemingly inclined posture, he felt that it stared at him. He could not get himself to move. He couldn't get his feet to lift off the ground. He thought: A bear, a grizzly, it has to be a bear. He did get his eyes to move. He glanced at the truck, gauging the distance—fifty yards. He looked back and managed to whistle softly at the thing. He whistled again, louder. It did not move, and he thought: It's not there, it's just a trick of night, moon, shadow, and my bad bearings. He leaned forward and chucked the owl at it. He heard the bird land and then it did move. The brush crackled and the body heaved sideways as gently as a tree falling through space, a hillside sliding, as the earth itself, heaving, all of mountain and forest and night condensed and drawn into the quiet, terrible, sideways movement of the beast. It was big, bigger even than he had thought, too big for any bear he had heard about, and he saw it outlined more clearly against the snow, one leg rising ponderously and setting down, and the second leg, and the head not broad enough for bear, too ovoid, too humanoid, and the head tipped slightly like that of a man looking at him askance, and one arm dangling free, and then the body pausing, then turning toward him, moving forward to the very edge of the ditch, and as it came Erks smelled a stench, a terrific carrion reek. He was filled with the strange, powerful terror of night he hadn't known since his boyhood.

He moved. He did not will it, could not, but his body moved and walked back to the truck, not too fast, not too slow, his legs stiff, and he thought: It has to be bear, don't startle it, don't run, don't look back. He knew the way of predators—to gaze, to make their own triangulation, to test strength or fleetness, or fear, or sickness, or weakness by looking—and the way of prey—to either look back or not, and if looking back, then granting the fear and the weakness. He did not look back. He listened. He heard everything, a distant bird and the wind in the trees, and snow sporadically falling off limbs in the thaw, and the truck in front of him, running, and he heard nothing at all, the awesome silence filling a definite space right at his back. The haunting touched his shoulders. His scalp tingled. When he reached the door, he slid in fast, put the truck in gear, and drove.

So the animal people were silent.

"And what of Ho?" he said after a time, desiring to speak, to say something, just about anything, but not about what he had just seen or not seen. "He has no illusions." It came out angry. He hadn't meant it to. He went on, "Or do you just take all of your illusions with you to the grave along with your shoe size when you're from Hong Kong?"

Taam said, "In China a chief occupation was to shatter illusions."

Erks was stopped again. Taam meant Red China, and he meant himself. Erks had considered earlier that Taam was coming from Red China. In fact, at one point—reflecting on the attitude of the woman in San Francisco and Ruby's joke about Lin Piao—he had even seen sense in it, but attaching little importance to the possibility and considering it unlikely for Lucas to be so connected, he had put the thought to rest. Now the obvious struck him: if true, it was the most salient fact about Taam. It meant that Lucas had put him not just in the shade of the underworld, but in a shade further darkened by politics. He said, "You mean Communist China?"

"But in Hong Kong," Taam said, "and in Taiwan and Japan, the chief occupation has become to supply the illusions of your people."

Erks let that pass as cant. "You've been in Communist China?"

"For seven years."

"What does this mean?"

He saw Taam's head turn and felt the steady gaze, but the man would not speak further.

All through the night, the moon had crept around the windows of the truck according to the truck's direction and its own canted, westward trajectory. There were flags on it, spare parts, and a moon rover, a specimen collector—stalled in its tracks, presumably—and even footprints that went just so far into the landscape, but the moon still looked like an eye in the window to Erks, or like an old coin worn down on one side, or a mask with a piece of the chin broken off, or like the head of a cannibalized ghost. The moon had risen from a point east by southeast, and since the GMC drove the loop in the highway around mountain summits between Christina Lake and Burnt Flat and was heading south now, the moon, past its zenith, rode the windshield high and to the right, shone through the star-shaped fracture, and cast an aura around Taam's erect head.

They had traveled a good distance since Osoyoos. They were in the Selkirk Range and had passed through Burnt Flat. They neared the foot of the Rockies and the town of Creston, from which they would head for the U.S. border. He had stopped for gas back in Grand Forks and filled both tanks—35 gallons, easily enough to reach Rathdrum. Since Grand Forks, they had passed

144

through Christina Lake, Lafferty, Paulson, Rossland, Trail, Montrose, Fruitvale, and Salmo, and then Burnt Flat. It was almost four in the morning and Erks was tired. Chang and Lee were asleep, but not Taam. Tired as Erks was, he sensed the hard wakefulness next to him like a raw spot on his skin.

From the back of the truck, from Ho, an air of slow dissolution emanated, a palpable densening of the darkness, and of the silence that loaded up the space inside the GMC with stunned, soporific pressure. The motion of the truck was like a boat, its hum and roll with the road, the action of the suspension repetitious as a chant, a boat in the dark, a boat in a dream following a trail of froth, the broken, endless white line. The steering wheel was about to crumble in his hands, the floorboards about to slide away from his feet. The consciousness of Ho dwindled to nothing, a phantom harborage of shadow.

Erks' head jerked when Taam spoke. He didn't understand the words.

Taam chuckled. "I said we will be turning soon."

Erks shook his head, then dug the thumb and middle finger of one hand into his eyes and rubbed. The truck veered. He caught the wheel one-handed, dropped his other hand from his eyes, and steadied the truck. The road was graded steeply from the center for drainage and the wheel maintained a rightward pressure. Released, the truck would have plummeted into the ditch. Erks had to blink repeatedly to keep images from doubling. He saw the sign for the junction of Highways 3 and 3-A, then the sign for Creston, and he stopped at the intersection, and waited a moment, though there was not a car in sight, not in any direction.

"We're turning now," he said.

He took the turn, right. Immediately, the lights of Creston became visible, or not the lights themselves, but their glow caught in the atmosphere above the depression, the double delta, the watershed between the Kootenay and Goat rivers.

"Just after Creston, we turn off the highway," Taam said.

Erks' attention snapped. "Oh?"

145

"That was my understanding."

"You know the route?"

"Do you mean have I been on it?"

"Have you?"

"No. The drive is new to me."

"I mean do you know the route we are traveling. I mean the itinerary."

"Yes."

"Thank you."

"I beg your pardon."

"You can help me watch for the turn."

And then, though he had learned by now that the closer he probed the more elusive his objective became, but drawn to what he considered paradox, and paradox, like nonsense rhyme, increasing its attraction through repeitition, he started over again: "What do you mean, your illusion of yourself?" And again it came out sounding angry.

Taam paused. "It was a joke. I did not mean to offend you."

"What does it mean?"

Taam paused again. "It was a joke, you see, referring to those who fear casting aside their illusions as they fear their death."

Now Erks paused. The words grew wild as he turned them over to try to make them sensible. From a rise the lights of Creston became properly visible, lying low, glittering hard and bright in the wind-scoured night.

"You fear your death?"

"Me?" Taam said as if surprised that Erks did mean him. "Who does not?"

But Erks had meant actually. He had meant some specific danger, threat of revenge, or something political, or criminal, he didn't know what—the possibilities that occurred to him seemed either too personal or too outrageous to name. He was himself— he saw—from some deep uncertainty and still unidentified embarrassment, chary of the realities certain words might call out.

"You were right to say what you did about Ho," Taam said.

"That he has no illusions?"

"Yes. To say it."

146

The cause of his probing—Erks realized—was not just the attraction of paradox, and not just curiosity over the routing of his baggage, and not even just the treatment of Ho, but the sense he had of something awful on the man's conscience, some obsession that the evasion and silences covered—a dismembered torso under the sheet. The probing, he saw, went toward lifting the sheet and viewing the remains. So seeing, he felt himself chastened, but still drawn toward the spook. He had the necromancer in him. If he saw history—whether collective or personal—as alive, then, too, he saw the living as dead. In this man at his right there was something as dead as the boy in the back promised to be.

"And right to stop at the doctor's?"

"Well . . ." He saw the hands gesturing, catching light off the dash. "As I said, I did not expect a driver of such will."

He meant it—Erks felt—this time as some kind of compliment, or even as an apology. "The doctor has probably called the police."

"Yes. That was the danger."

"And the danger outweighed the cause?"

"No," Taam said. "You were right."

They neared Creston. One could locate the lights now and decipher the names in neon. But the thing Erks had almost touched withdrew and hid. What Taam meant by his being right was the façade of an edifice otherwise enshrouded in fog.

They found the road. Four miles south of town, they saw the landmark, a sign announcing the distance to the border crossing by highway—six miles—and then a half mile farther the gravel road rose abruptly off the left of the highway, as the instructions had said it would. Erks took it. The truck bounced on ruts and loose rock. He slowed to twenty-five. They had, the instructions said, 15 miles of this, a winding logging road that would lead them to the border, to a chain and lock for which Lucas had given him the key, and then onto U.S. 95.

147

The road dipped into a hollow and they passed a farmhouse, the barnyard illuminated by a storm light, the place Canadian and neat. Two tractors and assorted implements stood in a row and the front walls of the outbuildings formed a straightedge along the driveway, the very look of the place momentarily reassuring, a symmetry clipped out of the deranging woods. But beyond the house the road deteriorated. The gravel thinned, the snow deepened, and the road wound through a sudden, rising series of switchbacks. He slowed to fifteen and still had to bully the wheel. He stopped, reached over Taam's suitcase, and put the truck into four-wheel drive, clutching twice, and started up again, feeling all four wheels grab. The headlights slid over the forest that crowded the road, a confounding wall on either side, or, at cutouts in the grade, they probed the sky, and at a cutout he saw it: behind and below the truck he saw two moving beams poking like two long white ribs out of the belly of the woods. He looked in disbelief. He looked at the road in front of him, doubting what he had seen, what he knew it was. He tried to make it into something else, then, registering the truth, he looked back and down again. Come out of nowhere, a pair of headlights followed them.

He went into a turn, came out, and jacked the truck up to twenty.

Taam's face turned to him.

"Someone's behind us."

Taam looked back over the seat.

"You can't see now."

Behind them was the dark, only the darkness beyond the corner, but—certain—he said, "They're there."

They reached another curve and he had the truck up to twenty-five. He took the turn hard, and then on the straightaway pushed it up to thirty, and braked for the next turn, and accelerated halfway around, and thought of Ho, of the oozing wound, the slit skin that would part with the motion, of the margin between Ho's life and death, of the beating Ho took back there. When he glanced down the slope he saw the lights again.

"There," he said. "Look."

148

Taam looked.

The lights vanished.

"Did you see?"

"I saw."

Taam opened his basket and rummaged inside it. He came out with a black blot, a bag or pouch. Erks heard it unzipped. Out of the pouch came something that caught light.

He took another turn.

"Do you know how to use a gun?" Taam asked.

"A gun?"

Erks braked for another turn, kept the speed down, and looked at the large item in Taam's hands. He heard a snap—the clip, pushed to—then Taam set the gun between them on the basket. Erks switched on the dome light. Even all alone, without even being used, the weapon was excessive, a .45. He glanced at Taam. Taam looked at him. Taam's face, jiggling with the lurching truck, was calm, even contemplative. Erks switched the light off and accelerated.

"I guess I know how to use a gun," he said. "But it's your damn gun. I don't carry a gun."

"I had thought you might be more adept."

Given time to consider, he might have counted that another insult. "My idea was to outrun these people."

Taam said nothing.

"Do we want to stop and meet them, gun and all?"

"No," Taam said quickly, as if judging Erks capable of it. "Do not stop."

He might have thought it amazing, the gun, that Taam had produced it and thus acknowledged that he could produce a gun, that he would carry such a gun, but there was no time for thought. The gun was simply there now, making the basket squeak. Erks wished he had more weight in the back of the truck. He wished he knew the road. Good as the truck was, he wished he were driving something made out of a little less iron. He caught glimpses of the headlights below, then, when they reached what appeared to be the crest of the slope, he got a good look at the headlights. The vehicle had not lost ground.

They descended. The road was deeply rutted from the runoff, and soft. They must have come over to the south side of the mountain now. He wasn't sure. He could see no moon, no stars, and though the sun rose somewhere out there, its light was yet too diffuse to be sure of its course. The road turned like a screw, further obscuring his sense of direction, except that when the mud changed to ice he figured they were in the shade of the south, either the east side or the north. The ice made better driving than the mud. More than once the truck slid in the mud toward the drop-off and Erks had to draw it back, but carefully so as not to break the back end loose. It was the ruts he had particularly to watch. He had to pick them up in the headlights and try to ride them crossways so the wheels wouldn't trap.

"It is not the police," he said.

The swerving and bouncing jolted Erks' body and when he checked the mirror for the headlights behind them he saw Chang and Lee's lurching heads, but not the headlights. In the periphery of his vision he saw Taam's jumping form.

"The police have had all night to stop us. Whoever in the hell this is was waiting for us," he said. He told himself that, not Taam. Taam knew already. "And they're damn sure chasing us."

The engine roared and dropped according to his pressure on the accelerator, and the chassis creaked, and the baggage bounced and rattled. He pictured Ho, the light body turning and bunching up against the back of the seat. He looked forward to a mark, the dwindling point of his headlights that poked out through a hole in the wall. Periodically he glanced through the mirror or through the side windows, looked back for the lights poking in from behind, which were sometimes there and sometimes not. He held the wheel steady, held the wheel to hold the truck steady on the uncertain road, and steadied himself with the wheel, which was like a hinge between two heavy ends, himself and the truck, and the truck sought to follow the ruts and he sought to ride them over their seams, the union between himself and the truck loose, crazy.

The road dropped sharply into the bottom. The mud changed to ice, then to snow, nearly a foot of it. He saw the headlights above them, not losing ground. He pushed the truck harder, trying to widen the gap, and didn't see the chain suspended across the road until he was nearly on top of it. He jammed the brakes, slid, and hit the chain, not hard, but hard enough to jolt truck and passengers and to unload the dashboard of jade, gold, and totem pole, and to throw Taam's basket and the pistol off the seat. The chain had held. He shoved the gearshift into reverse and backed the truck off.

He got out, fishing for the key in his pants pocket, found it, ran for the chain. He went to the wrong end first. He went to the other end and tried the key in the heavy padlock, but the lock was frozen. He fished for matches, found none, and ran back to the truck, to Taam's side, and jerked the door open, saying, "Matches!" Taam was bent over picking things up from the floor. He sat up and reached into his pocket, but Erks found matches first in the glove box, ran back to the lock, lit a match, and held it under the keyhole. Moisture dripped out, dousing the match. From up the road he heard the engine surge and ice crackling under tires.

He tried the key. It wouldn't turn. He held another match under the lock, and hearing the vehicle, looked up and saw its lights sweeping the trees on a turn. Moisture doused the match. He tried the key. It turned the tumblers and the lock popped open. He freed the chain, dropped it, ran back to the truck, drove the truck through, and got out again to put the chain back. He picked up the chain. Headlights came down the hill, bouncing.

It took leverage to pull the chain taut. He had to swing around and brace himself with one knee against the post to pull the heavy chain, then he had to lean over, clutching the weight, and fasten it to the ring with the lock. The ring was attached to the post with a clasp and a bolt driven completely through the post. Erks could make it out, the glint of the bolt in the gray light. The post was a twelve-by-twelve, and sunk, he figured, several feet in the ground and imbedded in concrete. He was strangely impressed by that and by the government-gauge hardware—heavy, the best—even as he heard the vehicle whining closer and saw the lights enlarging and when the lock, iced up again,

151

wouldn't shut. Each time he pressed it shut, it popped open. He had to get it shut. He straddled the chain, the 49th parallel, the border, or some point in the twenty-foot buffer zone, one leg in Canada maybe, one in the U.S., the chain marking out thirty feet of the longest ungarrisoned border in the world, but this thirty feet garrisoned, had better be garrisoned. He needed it garrisoned right now, and—he thought—to garrison it I might have used the gun to at least startle those people into wariness, but he had left the gun in the truck, had not granted its use. He held the bit against the post and banged the bottom of the lock furiously with the heel of his hand. It wouldn't grab. He stood, held the bit against the post, and kicked the lock with his heel. He felt the snap through the casing. He tugged on the lock. It held.

He let his right hand drop, throbbing, and looked up the road. The vehicle had come down into the bottom. It was a jeep. It had to be. Its headlights were set high and close together. They lurched and carved figures in the air. Wet snow hissed under the tires. Erks sprinted for the truck, jumped in, and gunned it, the tires throwing chunks of ice against the fenders. He saw the jeep in the mirror. It gained, came close as if to ram him from behind.

But there's the chain, he thought. Accelerating, drawing back on the raw edge of nerve to drive this road, he thought: The chain, the chain, for God's sake—and thinking that, he saw that the jeep—intentionally or unintentionally—was going to run the chain. But he must have been seen at the chain. Now he was afraid.

Still accelerating, his foot deep into the arc of the pedal, he watched the jeep in the mirror bearing down on his back in the dark, the alight weight hurtling toward them, and then it hit. He saw the headlights heave upward, then go to one side, lighting the woods, and he heard, faintly, a crack, and the grate of metal against metal. The headlights swung and dropped. A taillight came into view. But the motion of the thing did not stop. The taillight vanished and he saw headlights again, but whether the chain had broken or not, whether the car moved on its own power or not, whether moving forward or not, and with what intent, what power, what knowledge, he didn't know. There was only the certain and unexplainable movement like a bear shot in the throat, but still, impossibly, turning around slowly on a path.

Spooked, Erks roared around a turn and the truck lurched crazily, and he told himself: Slow down, don't lose this truck now —but driven by his fear, or fury, or just by the speed, he did not slow down. Behind him was the gray of dawn. The chain had to have held. The jeep had to be damaged, the axle sheared, an oil line torn, a fender pushed against a tire, anything. . . . Knowing that the jeep could not be behind him made him afraid. Now that they must have been safe, his fright gained ground. The incline here was more gradual, the road straighter, and the surface in better condition. Though soft, it had been recently graded. He worked the truck up to fifty on a straightaway.

They passed a logging camp, a gathering of pickup trucks, dozers, loaders, and one building. Several men stood outside around a fire that blazed in an ashcan. One man stood next to a dozer near the road, holding a thermos. He raised the thermos in greeting as the GMC approached, or half raised it, then truncated the gesture, or the gesture was foreshortened by the speed with which the GMC came abreast. As the GMC passed, Erks caught it in a glimpse, the expression on the man's face, and the faces of the other men by the fire, rising in surprise, and the man by the dozer pumping the thermos up and down and gesturing downward with his other hand, meaning slow down. Erks did not, or he slowed just enough to make the turn just ahead, then sped up again, and then the look the man had given him registered with a snap, like the lock catching. It was the snap of sanity, this contact, coming out of what seemed a dream, this contact with the outside like a protrusion, a thing to be touched so as to be certain one was, after all, *there,* that the gesturing man had not meant slow down on general principle, but something specific—slow down because if you don't . . .

Erks jerked his foot off the accelerator and braked, and immediately he saw in front of him a ninety-degree turn he was never going to make, and above that a streak of gray, something solid, something indecipherable, a fence, a ledge, a barrier—he didn't know what. He gripped the wheel, shoved the brake down, and the truck bounced and bottomed, and bounced again so violently that Erks jammed his head on the ceiling. The truck slid and bottomed, and bounced and bottomed, and bounced upward and sideways and came out on a surface—the surface of what, he didn't know—and skidded, and stopped.

They were on the highway, stopped at a slant with the right front wheel nearly off the shoulder. The engine was dead. He turned his head slowly, testing, and said, "Jesus!"

Next to him, Taam was half off the seat, hanging onto the ledge of the dashboard. He pulled himself up awkwardly and looked around, then grinned at Erks. "Did we shake them?"

The back seat was empty. Erks looked over and saw Lee sprawled flat on his back and Chang just rising from his knees. Lee kicked a leg slowly and Chang rose, slid onto the seat. Lee followed, struggling at first to free his body from the cramped space. When they both were on the seat they shifted toward each other in the center. Heaped like that on the floor, and disentangling themselves, and sitting like that on the seat, and now gazing back at him in their comic, melancholy way, they seemed enchanted. Erks turned back. Ho, he expected, was dead.

He started the truck, straightened it out, parked on the shoulder, and let it run for a moment, listening for damage. He heard none. Taam picked up his basket from the floor, then the other articles, jade, gold, totem pole, pistol, pouch. The floorboard on his side was littered with cartridges. Erks turned the engine off, got out, and looked for headlights. He saw none, no headlights, no vehicles, neither up the highway nor down. Off the shoulder on which the GMC was parked, the steep slope fell to a ravine into which the GMC would have plummeted had it traveled barely a yard farther. This moment—that he was here, not down there—he owed to the logger with the thermos, to that instrument of reality and distance, but—cold, deep in fatigue and yet alert—Erks was unamazed. The ravine was deep enough in shadow to make its bottom indiscernible. Its walls dripped. The air was filled with the sound of thaw, the compounded trickling of snow and ice off the walls and from the bottom a crashing.

He did not look into the rear window of the truck, did not look at Ho. He walked across the highway to look up the road— or path, or deer trail, or simply country, or whatever it was— from which they had emerged. It was country, just that, a fifty-yard stretch of rock and bramble and bush and small tree running between the highway and the corner he had missed. The logging road ran parallel to the highway for as far as he could see. It intersected with the highway, presumably, at some point out of sight. The GMC had jumped the gap between them. He saw the tracks, the thrown rocks, torn bushes and split saplings, scrapes between hollows where the truck had bottomed. If his speed had been greater, they would be in the ravine; if less, they would be out there, hung up. There were no headlights on the logging road, either, no elongating glimmer out of the darkness. Above the logging road the tips of pines and tamaracks and cedars raked the sky, and in the distance, all around, were the humps of hills and mountains, gray cutouts against the graying sky. They surrounded him, the mountains, like the uneven rim of a bowl. It was a magnificent country, northern Idaho, airy and translucent, filled with oxygen, and, everywhere, the sound of water, of the cold slowly bending.

Now he returned to the truck. He pulled the latch and let the tailgate drop. Ho lay rolled up against the back of the seat, his head turned into the seam of seat and platform, his legs bent awkwardly along the side of the compartment. Erks touched him. He was warm. Erks took him gently by the shoulder and waist and rolled him to his back, then by the legs, and straightened them so he lay diagonally across the compartment again. He was alive. Nothing had changed.

Ho's eyelids flickered weakly. The eyes were like pearls. The face was brittle. The body, when moved, had been supple, or fiberless, giving no resistance but that of weight. Erks touched his abdomen. The jeans were wet again, sticky with blood. Erks put the jacket under Ho's head and covered him with the blanket, then sat back on his haunches and stared at him, aghast, but, still, unamazed.

Outside, the landscape trickled and ran. Night fled. Spirits

155

fled. There was just Ho here. Winter fled and wept for itself as it ran.

The jeep came around the turn in the logging road while he sat with Ho. And still unamazed, almost as though he expected it, he roused himself and slid out. One headlight on and one off, and moving slowly, the jeep had a front wheel loose. Not just out of alignment, but loose, something broken, the wheel wobbled crazily and a fender was bent into it. It was a military-style jeep. Open, it was painted olive green and had five-gallon cans mounted on the bumper. It stopped. Erks saw a large man in a bowler hat and cream-colored knee-length topcoat emerge from the passenger side, stand behind the door, and look up at him. Erks shut his tailgate softly, pressed it with his knee until the latch snapped, and looked again.

He saw the dome of the man's hat above the jeep, cocking to see like the head of a heron, looking up, then at the stretch between the logging road and highway, then down the logging road, then up again. Erks moved for his door. Taam was stretched across the seat, peering out the window. Chang and Lee had turned to see. Behind the steering wheel of the jeep he saw the outline of another head, looking. Everybody looked. Then the man in the bowler hat looked down the logging road again and his head lifted a little as if he spoke to the man behind the wheel. The man behind the wheel nodded. Erks sensed an action forming. The man in the bowler hat turned and bent into the back of the jeep. Quickly, Erks opened his door, slid half onto the seat and started the engine.

With one foot still on the pavement, he looked back. The man had straightened up. The barrel of a rifle was silhouetted above the jeep, barrel and scope beside the round hat, then the rifle lowered to rest on top of the door.

"Go," Taam said.

He did. He pulled his foot in and clutched, and shifted into first, and sank his other foot into the accelerator, and went, lurched the truck forward, and, going, he looked back and caught a glimpse of the rifle barrel again, not leveled, but poised above the jeep. He saw the man looking at a car that had pulled up right in front of the jeep. Erks slowed.

"Go!" Taam said.

"Look," he said.

The car was a black Continental. The man with the gun climbed into the jeep. Erks looked forward and back, from the road in front of him to the car and jeep behind. He saw two figures emerge from the car. The jeep backed up, and then appeared to turn, to move forward as if to swing around the car. It was hard to tell for certain, the pace of the truck outreaching the registration of movement at the rear. Erks watched the mirror. The highway dipped and in the mirror the land swelled and swallowed the jeep and car.

The road looped down the Kootenai River valley, the land deep brown in patches, or dun, or white with snow, or green. The tires of the truck hissed on the wet pavement. The day had a high sky. Clouds floated in the blue and to the south and west collected against mountain peaks. To their left—east—was a clear-cut mountain slope, the discarded trees, the snags, like black sticks stuck in the snow.

At fifty-five, the truck had gone into a jaw-rattling shimmy, the wheels knocked out of alignment. He let it drop back to just over fifty. They wouldn't make time. There weren't many they could outrun, either, but maybe the jeep with that unstrung wheel. He found himself still unamazed, numbed, and regarding the chase and the episode with jeep, rifle, and car almost as something remote from him, the shock of it a blunt blow to the body the effect of which had yet to be reckoned.

"I suppose we're safe now," he said.

"Safe?"

"The men in the Lincoln work for you?"

"No one works for me."

"But they were there. All night, most likely. They circled around ahead of us."

"Most likely."

"They know the itinerary, too."

157

It was obvious, and Taam didn't respond.

"They're for protection?"

"I suppose so."

"Like the gun you carry. You won't use it. You just acquire its advantage?"

The gun still jiggled on the basket between them, loaded.

Taam smiled. "It might seem to be so." Then he added, "The men in the car wish me to reach Reno. That is all. It is a matter of business for them."

"And the jeep? Business?"

Taam did not reply.

"Why the hell didn't your businessmen intercept that jeep on the other side of the border?"

"I don't know," Taam said softly.

The tone of his voice made Erks look over and he was greeted by the grin again, the same mask-like grin that stretched cheeks, flattened eyelids and bulged the eyeballs, and showed tooth and blue gum, but the face the grin made seemed a good deal less macabre than it had last night, and more melancholy, more shell-like, and seemed to cover not some ancient beast, but simply something unspeakable. It was more obviously a cover and acknowledged itself as such as if Taam said through it: This Oriental mask I take on is a sham, but I have to hold on to it. The man had told the truth. His reasons for not knowing had to be a good deal more elaborate than Erks' own, but Erks sensed that Taam truly did not know why they'd been left to drive headlong on a logging road across the border with a jeep and a man with a rifle on their tail.

Erks looked away. He still wanted to bring something out into the light. Just about anything would do. "I'd nearly decided that Chang must've stabbed Ho," he said, "but maybe not. . . ."

"He did not," Taam said, and from the tone of voice Erks could tell that he'd dropped the grin. "And yet he and Lee both are deeply ashamed."

"Ashamed!"

"You must understand that their shame is his death, and their helplessness."

158

"But at whose hands?"

"At my hands."

He does not mean that—Erks thought—he means only that he takes responsibility. The responsibility he will not share, not its explanation in words. That he covets, that secret and all that adheres to it, all that goes unspoken he covets. But the shame, the payment in flesh, he will share, even with me, for God's sake.

Erks had meant to find out if Ho's injury was the result of a previous skirmish with the men in the jeep, or their like, but, annoyed, he said, "All right, I can understand the shame. I'm damned if I understand why Ho has been treated so lightly."

"It is not so," Taam said. "It is a terrible predicament. We are running. We have absolutely no leverage but the distance between us and them, you see. Otherwise we are helpless."

Stymied, Erks stared at the road. It was impossible to follow a straight line in conversation with the man. The moon, nearly exhausted of its light, so pale as to be nearly invisible, set behind mountains in equiposition to the rise of the sun, but not truly an equiposition, not solstice. It was apparently so because of the fierce topography's interruption to perspective. The sun, too, so far, was so pale as to be nearly invisible, its light given as if out of habit.

Around the turn and up sharply over the rock abutment, then down, the big ramshackle house rose into view. Erks pulled up beside a station wagon and stopped, turned the engine off and looked down the hill. On the other side of the station wagon was the Plymouth, on the other side of that the flesh-colored van, the back empty, he had seen as he drove by, but the doors ajar and ropes hanging loose from the hinges to the ground. He looked down at the dog pen, the grounds, the house.

Lily appeared in the doorway. She looked large, then she looked smaller as she stepped down from the porch and began to climb the hill. Because of the sudden thaw, the ground had been gouged out with the walking of people and the place was littered with paper cups and plates and empty beer cans and bottles, two beer kegs in large basins: fresh debris added to the

159

old—rusted cans and hunks of metal, tools, boxes and crates, stacks of wood, rolls of wire, junk. The skeleton of the hog was where the fire had been, or the skeleton and what remained of flesh, the butt end still fixed to a forked stick and the other end, the head, on the ground, the spine and ribs picked clean, drying, white in the morning light, but the head intact, and the hooves, and the back lower legs still dark with meat as if half-alive legs struggled to kick a live head back into action.

Lily grew larger. The three dogs danced behind the wire as she passed. She raised a hand in greeting to the GMC.

"Let's get out and stretch," Erks said to Taam. "Tell them." He got out himself, stepped into the sharp April air. There was a ringing sound of hammered metal, continuing without pause.

He stretched his back and shoulders, then bent forward, loosening up the backs of his legs. When he stopped and stood square, his head reeled. He took off his hat and rubbed his head vigorously, then his eyes. His scalp tingled. He put his hat on the seat of the GMC. The air felt good on his head. Chang and Lee got out the other side and stood with Taam. The hammering continued. It sounded like cold chisel work over among the junk cars.

It was.

Bud was out among the wrecks at work on the axle of a wheel tractor, because he wanted the wheel and tire for another tractor, but he had been unable to turn the bolts and instead of devising a way to soak them—that would take time—instead of taking a torch to the heavy bolts—he'd have to borrow one, for his was broken—instead of getting his bolt breaker—he couldn't find it; it probably wouldn't have been heavy enough, anyway— he was cutting the axle off with a hacksaw and cold chisel, using them alternately, cutting with the saw, then spreading the cut with the chisel, which he struck with a short-handled five-pound sledge. He figured that if he could get the wheel off, he could lay it flat and then soak the bolts. It was roundabout, his way of making a hard enough job harder, and he had no reason to do this job over any number of other jobs—cleaning up the yard, for

160

example, which he had left to Winona—but had chosen it probably because he wanted to force something, to break something, to pound something. The pounding, the sharp ringing, had prevented him from hearing Erks drive up.

He and Zack were on their knees on either side of the axle, under the tractor, scrunched down. Zack held the ten-inch chisel in his fists and Bud pounded it. Zack's face was calm and blank. His eyes blinked with each blow. Bud's face was knotted as tight as his hands around the short handle of the sledge and dark from a night of drinking and barely any sleep, dark with rage.

Erks got his valise and leaned into the truck to organize his things—jade, gold, and totem pole, maps, miscellaneous items, two of his boy's toy cars. He found the pistol, packed into the pouch and left on the seat. It gave him pause. Taam had taken his basket. Erks didn't know what to do with the gun. He didn't want to leave it in the truck, but he wasn't sure he wanted to force it back on Taam. He dropped it into the valise. He drew back out and found Lily there—eye level. She wore her navy-blue outfit and the big flowered carpetbag hung from her arm.

She smiled. "Good trip?"

He grimaced. "Do you have a toilet in the house?"

She swung the carpetbag gently. "That bad? Second door on the left."

He spoke to Taam over the hood. "Do you hear? Second door on the left."

He saw Taam watching Lily. Lily, somber, watched Erks. Erks nodded at Taam. Taam gestured to Chang and Lee and started down to the house. They followed him.

"You're a little short with them," Lily said.

"We've got a problem."

He moved to the back of the GMC and opened the gate. Lily followed. Seeing Ho, she whistled softly.

"He looks bad."

"He's damn close to dead is what he is."

He felt he knew exactly the keys her thoughts touched and the questions struck like cogs.

161

"How?"

"Are we driving that wagon?"

She nodded.

"Let's move him."

Her eyes widened.

He stepped back, softening his position. "Listen, we're going to have to take him somewhere. Let's move him. The truth is I don't know how."

"All right." She lowered her head and looked at him with her eyes rolled upward. She moved to the station wagon, opened the door, threw in her bag, lowered the rear window, then went around and opened the tailgate. He pulled Ho partway out of the truck by the feet, holding the legs straight. Lily came over and bent, looking.

"Take him. But easy," Erks said. "He's belly hurt."

He pulled Ho farther out. Lily slipped a hand under Ho's waist, then one under his neck, cradling his head in her hand, and she lifted, handling him easily. They moved to the back of the station wagon. Lily slid inside, still holding Ho. They set Ho down, and bending over the tailgate, over Ho, Erks caught a waft of stench. He backed out and straightened up.

Inside the compartment, Lily slid her hand inside Ho's jacket and touched his stomach. She took her hand out and looked at it, then rubbed it on the carpet.

"He's bleeding."

Erks nodded.

"What happened?"

"He's been cut. Stabbed." He heard the cold chisel ringing and thought of steel, steel and flesh and bone.

"Now?"

He sighed.

She held Ho's wrist. "This boy's blood is shallow. There's nothing there. He's right down to the bottom of the bowl."

He told her about the stop in Hope and what the doctor had said and how Taam resisted it. As he spoke, she set the wrist down and settled back, her legs folded half under her and one hand

162

resting on Ho's shoulder. She listened, her face calm. Her skin had a glow to it.

"He must have a lot on his mind," she said, meaning Taam.

He didn't agree. It was more as if Taam had one thing on his mind, or more like half the circuits in Taam's head had no connection to the reality Erks knew.

"You took a chance stopping."

"Do you know what you're saying?"

She looked down at Ho, then back up at Erks, and smiled, but with the smile lay the icy composure before risk Erks had seen the day before when she'd faced her brother down. She said, "Yes."

He matched her: "If you don't know a place to take him here, then I'll find a place. The schedule can go to hell." He paused, then added, "We do not continue under these circumstances."

She gazed at him, considering. In her Erks saw a resiliency and pragmatism somehow akin to what he was accustomed to sighting—fence lines, machinery, or Ruby running a five-horse tiller over the garden. But out of the gravid intertwining of what she knew about Taam and he didn't, and out of what he hadn't told her yet about the trip, and out of whatever lay between Lucas and her, out from behind the candor in what she'd just said, something else protruded as the man with the thermos, telling him to stop, had protruded from the forest. With Lily it was something complex and yet unnamable, something he saw could be dangerous but that he might trust, maybe even had better trust. One thing was certain: they were here enmeshed already and not even on their way yet.

"All right," she said. The look in her face told him he'd damn better know she agreed at her pleasure, though, not from obligation.

He did not dislike that.

"If you'll fetch that blanket, I'll cover him."

He got the blanket and his valise out of the truck and returned, and handed the blanket in. She glanced at his valise, at the crowbar strapped to its side, and smiled wryly.

He shrugged. "I'd like to wash up before we go."

She covered Ho, drawing the blanket lightly over him. He looked like a board under it. She pulled her skirt up over her knees and crawled out to the gate and grunted when she sat and swung her legs around to get out.

"After we get him taken care of, I could use some sleep."

He walked down the hill to the house. He passed Taam, Chang, and Lee going the other way. Taam had his basket. They were tired, too, even Taam, who spurned sleep. He looked at Erks and nodded, his eyelids heavy. As he descended, Erks saw Bud standing at the back of a tractor, over among the wrecks about twenty yards away. He held a short-handled sledge in one hand, and because of the grip of his hand, his size, and the ugly look on his face, the sledge looked a great deal more like a weapon than a tool. The head of the other one—Zack—appeared from around the wheel of the tractor, knee level to Bud. Bud glowered, but did not move, as if leashed, somehow held in abeyance by Lily—Erks figured—held back, maybe, just by the promise of her departure. He said something. The other one craned his neck to look at Taam, Chang, and Lee, and Bud said something else, something degrading, Erks figured.

"Chinks," Bud had said to Zack.

And he spoke again. "Take a good look," he said. "Lousy low-down, goddamn yellow-bellied slant-eyed Chinks, Zack. Don't never turn your back on one."

Erks passed the pig carcass, then mounted the porch and came up to the woman—Winona—almost without seeing her, then, seeing her, he shied in surprise. She sat—or half lay—on a chair next to the door, her head lolled back, at her sides her arms turned insides up, her legs askew. As if dead. Then her eyes rolled, looked at him. They followed him as he passed and entered.

The tub had a rust stain down one end from the drip of the tap, as did the sink, and the toilet bowl was encrusted with brown, and on the floor the linoleum was torn and damp and the planks showed through in patches, and chunks of plaster had fallen from the ceiling. The tiny window was cracked and dark with dirt, and the sill had an inch of packed grime on it. The house was that way, clearly, once, a place of substance, certainly spacious, but for how many years he couldn't guess just a place for bodies to come into and use. He rubbed the condensation off the center of the mirror with the heel of his hand and peered at himself.

He did not look good. His eyes were bloodshot, his cheeks slack. He stripped to the waist, washed his chest, his neck and face, and then he shaved. It felt better, anyway, to be half clean. He bent and rinsed the lather off his face with cold water. The tightening of his skin felt good. He pulled the plug. However untidy the place was, the plumbing was excellent. The water in the bowl turned as the drain sucked it down.

That was Bud's work, he figured. The plumbing—he thought —excellent, of course, and probably the kitchen outlets, and the flues for the wood stove, and the roof, and a quantity of shelves in the pantry, these, measures of Bud's competence: his work, or that of the other one—Zack—under Bud's tutelage. Erks dropped his pants and sat on the toilet. He relaxed, closed his eyes, and waited. The entire house—he thought—a mass of confusion and disarray, but the essentials, the animal needs, subjected to Bud's competence. He made his count:

Valise.

Crowbar.

Jade, gold, and totem pole: in the valise.

He recalled his lunch, untouched: in the valise.

Flashlight, binoculars, directions, maps: all in the valise.

The old directions for the drop in San Francisco. He couldn't place them. Not in the valise. Then he remembered—his coat pocket.

Water, gas can, toolbox, he would leave in the truck. He might regret the tools.

Cash: $2,500 from Lucas in his wallet, intact, but the $300 of his own he had cut into. And he remembered then. He had another $2,500 coming from Lily here, right now.

Chang's knife: in the valise.

Taam's pistol: in the valise. He opened his eyes and looked through the dirty window.

And his own authority, what little he had, probably abdicated, requisitioned by Lily.

And the goose vertebrae, about which he had forgotten until just now, here, in the pocket of his coat that hung on a hook. He had a sudden urge to locate them for certain.

His bowels moved, the hurt wonderful and large.

Whilst we were eating, an Indian standing by, and looking with great derision at our eating dogs, threw a poor half-starved puppy almost into Captain Lewis's plate, laughing heartily at the humour of it. Captain Lewis took up the animal and flung it with great force into the fellow's face, and seizing his toma-hawk, threatened to cut him down if he dared to repeat such insolence. He immediately withdrew, apparently much mor-tified, and we continued our repast of dog very quietly.

Expedition of Lewis and Clark

Lee and Chang sat in the back seat of the station wagon. Taam sat with Lily up front, and Erks sat upright in the compartment, looking backward and ready to stretch out beside Ho. Lily started the car. Bud and Zack had stalked across the slope below the car. Gog and Magog, the two huge beings moved stiffly as if they did drag chain, Zack behind Bud, their knees rising and falling in unison. They went down to the house, then went back into the field among the junks, and, momentarily, Erks heard the dull pinging of the hammer through the windows of the car. Just behind the pig carcass stood Winona, roused by Bud. Immobile, she clutched a bundle of trash. Behind her small figure was the great sagging house, the orchard, the slope, the woods, and the peak of a mountain mottled with snow and forest and dun-col-ored field. Erks' body rocked when Lily pulled the car out, and as they swung around to the abutment, he had a glimpse of Zack's wide back inside the wheel of the tractor, at the axle, and over his shoulder Bud's face like a fist, and between them the head of the sledge rising and falling.

The car's suspension was soft. It rose over the abutment as if over a swell, and the house, and Zack's back, and the pig, and Winona, and then the orchard, the peak of the mountain, van-ished.

167

Erks rocked to and fro on his buttocks. He had his knees up and his arms were wrapped around them. He felt like a child, sitting in the back with someone else driving. He was dog-tired, nearly insensible with fatigue, but wished to stay awake until Lily took Ho to the doctor in Coeur d'Alene as she had promised.

He removed his coat and lay back, and drew his coat over his upper body. He looked at Ho. Ho's eyes were just open, or one eye was—the eye Erks could see—the iris a slit beneath the lid, and glossy, unnaturally bright against the skin, a ruby in a limestone mask. Ho's face shook with the motion of the car, and his body rocked stiffly as Lily bulled the car across the ruts. Erks looked at the ceiling. It was a Vista Cruiser, the station wagon, and the sky and puffs of clouds raced down either side of the roof, visible through the long tinted runners of glass, the clouds, the very sky, blown in off Kuroshio, the sky over a high country of timber broken by meadow, Coeur d'Alêne country, Spokane River drainage. The city to the south was named after the tribe.

They were camas gatherers, the Coeur d'Alênes—the camas, or quamash, a lily, the root edible and sweet, a staple, ground, stored, and used to make a bread. They were lodge builders, horsemen, and hunters. Not as wealthy as their neighbors, they lived at a hub from which the country allowed the radii—the Spokanes, Kalispels, Flatheads, Nez Percés—greater strength, but the Coeur d'Alênes were wealthy enough, strong enough not to be mastered. They traveled west to fish with the Spokanes and south and east to hunt bison in the manner of the Nez Percé. They knew the trade routes. It was a country that allowed a comfortable margin of existence, but not luxury, not like the coast—no time for totem poles, no time for potlatch, no time for excess, no time for man-eating ritual. Spirits here were as daily as digging sticks and baskets and rabbit-skin robes and oxygen and sharp mountain light.

His place.

He tried to stay awake by rehearsing this data of where he was, in fact just fifty miles from home.

Considering the desert distances ahead in Oregon and Nevada, he regretted the gas can, too, not just the tools. They might need the gas can to string together Nevada towns. He thought of saying something to Lily, but could not rouse himself.

He stuck his finger in his coat pocket and gently stirred the goose vertebrae, the fractions of the lost integer, crumbs of the whole neck once outstretched to ride and buck the wind.

He felt like a child. He remembered the money. He had to ask about the money due him. He couldn't get his jaw to move. He closed his eyes and the light condensed to a luminous oval that moved in to fill his head. He struggled to stay awake. He fell asleep, abdicating everything.

Bud and Zack crouched over the axle in the deep shade of wheel, housing, and engine, their big bodies jammed into the awkward space. A hydraulic jack, mounted beneath the axle between where they worked and the tractor body, lifted the wheel off the ground so that in time, when they cut past a certain point, the weight of the wheel would pull the cut open. Zack did the sawing. Bud did the pounding not because Zack couldn't do that —he was younger and stronger, a bull, he could work forever— but because he was easily distracted. If Zack were to see a magpie land in the field or a trickle of moisture running down the engine housing, or observe that he had a shirt button undone, he might lose concentration, but keep swinging the sledge and miss the chisel entirely and smash Bud's hands.

Zack had just taken his stint sawing. They were more than halfway through the axle. Soon it would bend. Bud pounded on the chisel which Zack held to the crack made in the axle, the strokes sure and rhythmic and slow enough to allow time for Zack to set the chisel, and, to Zack, Bud broached his resentment, the infliction over which he kept vigil, his words growing more aggravated with each blow of the sledge. Both of them were wet to the thighs from kneeling in the mud. Though the sun was bright, it was cold in the shade under the tractor.

"It's us that gets the brunt of it."

The chisel rang when he struck it with the sledge.

"It's us that holds the funeral and the wake and Winona has to clean up afterwards."

169

He said that even though he knew that since he had jerked Winona to her feet and told her to clean up the yard she had probably done nothing, or at best moved two pieces of trash from one place to another and that with no idea of making a place for trash, no system, just moving it, and even though he knew Lily had cleaned up the kitchen before and after the wake. But he knew, too, or believed, that Lily had done that just to stay out of his way, so as to be occupied in case he wanted to talk with her, and he had, and she had refused except to reproach him when she said it was she who had paid the bill for Mama's funeral.

He had it wrong already less than a day later. Lily had said she had paid half the bill, she and her dead mother. That and her sorrow Bud passed over and he actually thought he had paid— or would pay—all costs, and this when he might or might not pay his half. To get the money out of Bud, the mortician would have to bill and bill him again, then send warning notices, then turn the bill over to a collection agency and with each notice Bud's anger would mount. The matter of halves between himself and Lily was part of his resentment, his infliction.

He struck the chisel. The chisel rang.

"Who the hell does she think she is, acting like we owe her something just because Mama's dead!"

The chisel rang when he struck it.

"Her and Lucas and their goddamn money, who the hell do they think they are coming around here . . ."

The chisel rang.

". . . with their damn stooges, high and mighty."

The chisel rang.

"When you and me do the work."

The chisel rang.

"And Winona."

And still Winona, whom Bud included because it was convenient to his lie, a lie that twisted fact, but that twisting was in the bleached part of the lie, turned up to the sun and uttered. There was more twisting in the dark part of the lie, at its root: Bud gave Winona no credit, no acknowledgment, because he himself was overworked, scratching for survival and for the survival of those

170

he considered his charges, Winona and Zack, and the more he worked and worried the more single-minded he became and the less he allowed them their own work and worry and so Winona could hardly work and her worry was incessant and utterly diffuse, without location, because the goal—to please Bud, to quiet Bud, to make Bud gentle for once—was completely unattainable, and so Bud lied her right out of existence. He could lie her back, though, as he had when he said, "And Winona," and then the two halves of the lie conjoined to make the truth about Bud and to make Winona's presence doubly hollow.

But she was present. She was his wife. She had religion.

The chisel rang.

"Who raised that hog?"

The chisel rang.

"Who cooked that hog?"

The chisel rang.

"Who dug that damn hole, Zack, who dug it for Mama in the snow?"

Bud grunted when he swung the sledge. The chisel rang, stinging Zack's fingers. The sharp sound echoing back and forth against the tractor wheel and the engine stung his ears. Though Zack did not doubt his brother, not a word of it, not even what he could not understand—being an idiot, or, technically, a moron —and though he did not doubt his brother's competence, nor his love, worry filled Zack's face because he did not doubt Bud's anger either, because he knew what it could make Bud do— something crazy, something that could hurt. Zack loosened up his hands at the wrists so that if he was hit with the sledge his hands would give, and not resist, but, loyal, still held the chisel, although its position in the slot became uncertain, which Bud saw.

Bud reached over and rapped Zack sharply on the forehead. "Hold that damn chisel straight."

Zack held the chisel straight.

Bud grunted and struck the chisel.

"Our sister brings goddamn illegal Gooks into this country."

The chisel rang.

"And Lily gets half this farm."

That was it, his aggravation and present infliction, the matter of inheritance, the farm, which was Bud's because he had lived on it all his life, because he worked it, and before him his father had, and before that his grandfather, who had bought it for $2.00 an acre. Rapt with thought, Bud let the sledge fall to his knee. He stared over Zack's head at the hill, his face dazzled. After his mother had left, after his father had died, he had raised his brother on the farm, but all those years—a fact Bud had never fully considered until now, or had willfully ignored, avoided, but now coming back on him—his mother had held the title and paid the taxes. Now he had said it, that he owned half and his sister owned half, the fact that had been seething in him for four days, seeking expression.

To no one, to the air, he said it again: "She gets half this farm."

The wheel sank without sound and touched the ground softly. Its weight buckled the axle and opened up the slit.

Bud's great-grandfather, a French-Canadian, had been what was called a "freeman," that is, one engaged as a *voyageur* for the North West Fur Company and who preferred after the termination of his engagement to remain in "Indian country" rather than return to Montreal. But even a freeman had to deal with the company, and—militaristic, imperialistic—the company took on the aura of the Queen and regarded land it had explored as its own. Bud's great-grandfather sold his furs at a company post and received payment in goods only at the rate of a regulated tariff. He took a Blackfeet wife and roved these parts and received the contempt of white men of "position." Worthless, depraved, wayward, backsliding, they called his kind, those who chose to minimize their relations with the company and to live in the wilderness scores of years ahead of the settlers. At every opportunity they cheated the company, circumvented the company, and, later, with the weight of settlers, helped to break the company, as, later yet, the Wobblies strove—though they failed—to break the grip of the mining companies. Bud's half-breed grandfather

172

and his father had worked off and on in the mines to shore up the finances of the farm, and so had Bud himself—down in Kellogg. His father had been a Wobbly. From this background, maybe, Bud took his single-minded anger, his outlaw monomania for independence, for unaccountability, for being his own law.

But Bud did not see himself in the light of the ironies of his own history—his Blackfeet great-grandmother, his Wobbly father. . . .

His roots in this country went back as far as a white man's could go, and his monomania was in a way the raw residue of manifest destiny, untransformed, but subliminal and tied up in a knot, pent up in the dark, dangerous.

"What're we gonna do?" Zack said. He meant with the tractor wheel.

"Somethin'," Bud said.

"Okay, Bud," Zack said. "You say when." Then, recognizing the expression on Bud's face, he said, "Okay, Bud. Okay, okay."

They sat for a moment like two bears between the engine and wheel, Zack, worried, eyeing Bud, and Bud staring at the cut in the axle, then Bud lurched and shoved out from under the tractor. He grunted and went up on one knee, and stood, and looked down the slope at Winona.

She was in the clearing near the pig carcass, holding a paper sack she had filled with cans and bottles. She held it against her chest with one hand. She held the bottom of the sack with her other hand because it was wet. She saw Bud and bent over to pick up another can, but halfway down she lost a bottle from the top of the sack. She straightened up, looked at Bud, and shrugged, but did not smile.

Bud didn't move. The sledge hung from his hand.

Winona understood. As she stared at Bud, her mouth opened, making a hollow below the two hollows of her eyes.

Zack crawled over the sheared axle and alongside the wheel out of the shade. On his knees, he reached up and touched Bud's hand, then tugged gently on the sledge. "Easy," he said. "Easy."

Bud released the sledge.

Zack took it. "Easy," he said.

Bud started down the slope.

Winona squirmed. She didn't flee. As if fastened to the spot, and hugging the sack of trash now, her body began to writhe and her face twisted. One can fell through the bottom of the sack, then another. . . .

Zack held the head of the sledge in his lap and flipped the handle up so that it knocked him lightly on the brow. He closed his eyes and in his mind heard the sounds he had heard before, heard what was coming—Bud grunting and sometimes the thuds of his blows and Winona groaning and sometimes crying out, her wail from the bedroom which Zack might even hear from here, her voice coming right out of the house—and what he had seen —Bud's body hunched over hers, shoving, shoving, shoving at her insides. . . . Zack kept knocking himself lightly on the brow. "Easy, boy. Easy now."

Roused not by noise or jostling, but by the lack of noise, the quiet, and by the lack of motion, and by a presence—Lily's—Erks awoke from thick, anarchic dreams to see the blade of a shovel sail toward his face. More asleep than awake, he remembered no detail of his dreams, only the sense of having heard voices speaking a foreign tongue and the quality of tumult, at once abstract and physical, as abstract, physical, indifferent, and fathomless as the place where they had stopped, which Erks did not see: a mixed country of timber and rock and agricultural clearing. Its round, glaciated hills, if seen from a vantage point, were low under the sky, rolled endlessly before the eye, and receded only as the earth's curve took them from view. But if seen from the watersheds that the roads followed, the hills were big, they obscured the view, they replaced each other, and, looming up, they looked the same, one after another, so that among them one felt lost in a sea of high, soft swells, each unidentifiable from the next, and in their brutal feminine rhythm, the same great, incipient, slumbering, coiling violence of the landscape which Erks had felt even in sleep—its light, its intense gravity.

More asleep than awake, his eyes just slitted open—as Ho's

had been for, it seemed, days—Erks did see darkness down by his feet, a figure, leaning inward—Lily. He had no will to consider her, and the lustrous metal spade did not surprise him, but merged with his dreams. The head of the shovel moved past him, hung in the air, turned, then lowered, and settled between himself and Ho. He felt the soft thud on the floorboard, and he glimpsed Ho hardly there, only his shape like a two-by-four on edge under the blanket, and that did not surprise or rouse him, either—that Ho was still there, not handed over. At his feet, the dark figure withdrew into the light.

Erks was helpless. His legs and arms felt dead, beyond his power to move. The air had a familiar smell, acrid and sulfuric, which Erks did not have to remember to register: a lumber mill. The tailgate swung shut, clicked, and he fell back into a swooning sleep, the shovel, now, turning the heavy stuff of his dreams toward a spinning radial blade, and he heard a whine, or he did not hear a whine, but the hum of the rear window rising automatically. In his dream he heard the long, high, lonesome whine of the blade singing past the rafters of the mill.

In the driver's seat, Lily watched the rear window so as to release the switch before the window shut completely. The man would need ventilation. She watched through the rear-view mirror and suffered the same obstruction Erks had suffered for miles, two heads drawn together in the center, but the station wagon had a convex, wide-angle mirror, and the heads were small. The heads now were even tipped toward each other, the shoulders touching, the two brows almost touching.

They amused Lily.

Erks, too, had been amused at first. But as he drove he had increasingly seen them as just what they were in the mirror, an obstruction, a blockage that wouldn't budge, and their very existence, the fact that they even had lives—somewhere!—and that these mute lives were in his hands, had become to Erks a weight as obscure as Taam's, as heavy as Ho's. . . . And as Ho's weight had increased, Chang and Lee had refused or been unable to lighten the weight of Ho on Erks, and Taam had refused, too. Taam could have explained Ho's injury. Any one of them could

175

have done something—anything!—to help. Instead, all Erks had received was obscurity, and Chang's violence, then Chang holding the violence back, and Taam saying they all shared the shame without naming the cause of it. Finally, Erks' will to penetrate, to understand, had been obstructed until he had actually begun to consider giving up trying to understand.

He didn't give it up. That would have been unlike himself. He slept, but now his dream had that whine in it, and an incomplete syllogism, too, on which images hung surreal as fruit:

1. Any kind of density makes weight.
2. To understand is to lighten weight.

And his dream had a seeking motion in it that wound snakelike through a desert in which Ho lay, pale as death, and it slithered over Ho, and around him, and up white mesquite trees from which hung white possums and bleached goose bones, and transparent salmon, looking for something even more talismanic, the third and conclusive proposition, something prime and remote that would draw the dream to a bead.

And yet even as Erks dreamed, Ho had crossed the last margin. Ho's last residue of youth and strength had been found, tapped, and exhausted, the last stratum had buckled, and below it Ho had plunged. Ho was dead now, which Erks did not know, although he heard the whine, the call out of bones rising from the earth and soaring lighter than air, Ho's soul, seeking the chinook. No one but Erks heard that.

When Lily had pulled up in front of the doctor's office in Coeur d'Alene as she had promised Erks she would, and got out of the car, and, on her way to the tailgate, glanced through the tinted window at the shapes, Ho and Erks, something in the stiff angulation of Ho's head from his body had thrown her again, blown her physically off course. She had rocked, then come back, tugged to the window. She cupped her hands to look. Ho's eyes were wide, glaring, his mouth agape, the upper lip caught on his teeth so that his expression was a leering grimace. One arm had worked out from under the blanket, and his neck twisted impossibly. Lily looked up, still uncertain, and found that Taam had turned in his seat to watch her intently, and she watched him, finding her own intentness in his. And then, sensing something in Taam's watching, Chang and Lee turned to look at Lily, and seeing her, Chang raised himself and looked over the seat at Ho, then back at Lily, close to her, right through the glass, and she watched him and saw his lips pulled back and his eyes widened, all this, these flickering gestures of communality, seen by Lily through the glass like the inside of an aquarium, fins, gills, eyes fluttering, noiseless, and a dead one on the bottom.

She pulled away. The certainty gathered in her face. She stared at the sky and thought: As well as I know this doctor, a half-dead boy would be hard to explain. A dead one I cannot try to explain.

So decided, she had opened Chang's door, reached over the seat, and pulled the blanket up over Ho's arm, over his face. Chang, Lee, and Taam watched her. Erks slept. Lily swung the door shut and stepped back to the front door, got in, and drove.

The doctor's office in Coeur d'Alene was an hour out of the farm.

Thirty miles later she stopped in Plummer to buy a shovel.

Bodies, she had determined, were customarily buried.

This was where Erks had smelled sulfur in his sleep—Plummer, Idaho, 433 souls.

A cluster of houses, a bar, and the store were built mostly on a flat spot on one side of the highway, and on the other side, on a slope, was Pacific Crown Lumber Products. Logs lay in tremendous stacks all around the mill, but the store, which Lily entered, had only what was needed and little more: food, clothing, hardware, over-the-counter drugs, and items in bulk—sugar, flour, sacks of dried beans, gallon cans of vegetables. A cord had been run from one end of the store to the other to hold hats, but strung to it were only four. The place was airy, smelled of soap, and had high windows through which the light streamed over half-empty shelves to the floor. Though picturesque, the store was grim in its spareness. The hats—two of them were the black, high-crowned variety favored by young Indians, or by young tourists who believed they were favored by Indians, and two were cheap cowboy hats—and two dark-haired girls with their mouths against the edge of the cooler, choosing Popsicles, told Lily about the town. The girls shied when she approached and looked up at her with the wide, measuring eyes of children who are on their own early. The proprietor smiled when she came up to the counter with the shovel and five bottles of Nesbitt's orangeade.

"Digging is hot work."

Lily murmured.

The storekeeper eyed her, inwardly weighing, probably, the question Lily had come to expect: A Negro? A breed-Negro, for God's sake? Or what?

He was bald and lean. Lily imagined that there were stories told about dealing credit with this man. When the mill shut down his accounts did not. About sixty, he had lost an index finger and his face was weathered. With work he had earned this inside job, and in pride what he had earned would come to be set against what others could not. The price on the shovel was outrageous —$24.95.

He said, "Wild flowers?"

"Rocks," Lily countered.

"Rocks?" The man leaned forward on the counter and grinned again, but slowly now, suspicious, careful not to be caught unawares. "Folks come through this time of year digging wild flowers to put in their gardens. It's against the law."

"That's why I put rocks in mine."

The man opened his mouth and grinned. His skin crinkled all the way up to the center of his bald head. Then he closed his mouth and the humor vanished.

In the man Lily saw her brother, Bud, that ferocity, but couched and neatly cushioned under a businessman's good manners. When she asked he opened the bottles with a church key attached to a string that hung from the side of the cash register. It was an old brass register, portentous and lavish, and it would ring when the change drawer popped open. The man struck the keys methodically with his middle fingers, this motion of the

178

man, and the motions of Pacific Crown's paymaster across the road, the two controlling ganglia of the town. Behind Lily stood the two Indian girls, clutching Popsicles, dwarfed by her size. The change door popped open and the register rang brilliantly. The man looked up and smiled. Lily passed over the money. The two girls scattered when she turned, then approached the counter, peering just over it with wide eyes, and set their Popsicles down. Lily moved along the aisle, carrying the shovel over her shoulder and the five bottles by sticking her fingers into the ends. She heard the man's voice at her back, the condescending lilt of one who hated children. Lily opened the door with her knee and moved out into the hard light.

She laid the shovel in the back between Erks and the body. She returned to the driver's seat and raised the rear window, careful to leave ventilation. She pulled her door shut and drove.

"I bought the shovel."

"So I see," Taam said. "But where are we to do it?"

She shifted her weight, settled, and looked around. The town, a sputter in the hills, had vanished as abruptly as it had appeared. For no apparent reason the highway had widened into four lanes and before them lay a vista of the land, the defiles and the crests of hills dark with timber. In this land a body buried was an eel in the ocean.

"Pass two of these back," Lily said, touching the bottles she had set in a row between Taam's basket and the back of the seat. On top of the basket lay her carpetbag, heavy with gun.

Taam passed two back, one for Chang, one for Lee. "We should not bury him near the highway. We should certainly not bury him in view of the highway," he said.

Lily handed a bottle to Taam and took one herself. The last —Erks'—she nestled between the seat and her buttock so it wouldn't spill. She took a swig of hers, then put the bottle between her legs, denting her skirt. She drove with the butt of one palm on the wheel, with a smoothness that bespoke her size and bearing.

"Of course not."

179

"Or even off the highway, who knows who might pass by. It will take time. Suspicions are easily aroused."

"How much guarantee do you need?"

But his anxiety fueled her own. She was still under the power of her mother's death. And she had instructions from Lucas which had to do with death. These instructions she could hardly bear to recall, let alone think clearly about, or understand how she had agreed to them. The death of the boy seemed more of the same, an extension. Death wouldn't stop. She felt pushed off balance. To right herself she felt she would need to shed something, to slough something off. Or she needed to be shed, to be sloughed off herself.

"I believe that no matter where we stop we will be visited," Taam said.

"We could wait for dark."

"Even then . . ." He spread his hands.

"You're nervous."

It was true. In Lily's presence Taam displayed an apprehensiveness that he had not with Erks. Her manner allowed him— or most anyone besides her brother—to do so without fear of being judged. Erks' moral nature—in which matters were constantly sorted, weighed, judged—prohibited showing fear. Lily would grant her own weakness, even her own duplicity. Erks strove to overcome weakness. He did not fully understand this in himself, although he'd been told of it many times by Ruby when she was annoyed—but his wife also liked it in him, his strictness. He did not understand that what he saw as Taam's secretive posing, and that of Chang and Lee, that what he saw as Oriental in the people, and as the arcane tangle of this entire business, was in part rubbed off himself through what he forced the boys and mostly Taam to be. But Taam himself was taciturn and strict. The two of them together compounded what was similar in their natures: a chemistry. They hadn't discovered the way yet to locate the common ground between themselves.

"I suppose I am," Taam said, smiling.

"Do you mean that you've been followed?"

She asked it although she knew it was so.

"We," Taam said, shifting his weight toward her. "It's me they want, but we are being followed."

"By who?"

"The Triad." He spoke it softly, placing no weight on the word, and so doing, placed a lot of weight on the word.

Lily looked sharply at him.

He looked back at her without speaking.

"They're on our ass right now?"

"Probably."

She knew this, too. Lucas had told her. But because of the bearing of her instructions on this fact, she instinctively checked the mirror. Behind them the road was empty. She took a swallow of orangeade, then set the bottle between her legs and fingered the lip.

"And Jui is following us . . . not Jui himself, of course, but . . ."

And she knew that, but she said, "I thought we were working for Jui, me and Lucas and Erks."

"I believe Jui is protecting us."

"And you leave that to him?"

Now he told her about the border crossing, road, chain, and chase, and how it was thanks to Erks that they'd escaped, how whoever had chased them had been met afterward by the men in the Lincoln. He told her that there had been an attempt on him in Vancouver, just before Erks arrived, that Ho, himself a Triad novice, along with Chang and Lee, had been stabbed because of his traveling companion—himself, Taam—and that at first no one had known Ho had even been stabbed, that Ho had minimized the wound, that when they saw it was serious Ho had refused to see a doctor.

Taam told Lily all this with apparent guilelessness.

But Lily had the growing impression that it was the reverse, that the guilelessness was to cover an expert sounding of her position.

"I'd call that a lapse," she said, referring to the fact that Ho hadn't been taken to a doctor earlier.

"Yes," Taam said.

He told her that they'd stopped at Hope, how Erks had been confused, how Erks was angry.

"I heard about that."

They rounded a bend. On their right an entire series of hills had been burned off and fallen trees littered the slopes.

"Have you told him?" she asked.

"About the Triad?"

She nodded.

"No. At first, I did not put abandoning us beyond him."

"Not Erks."

"So I saw."

She glanced at Taam. "And then?"

"Perhaps I did not wish to alarm him further."

"How bad does the Triad want you?"

He displayed his apprehension again: "That's the trouble. As you know, there is no question of degree with the Triad. It is either yes or no."

He lit a cigarette. He had openly acknowledged part of what she did know, which she couldn't deny. The man was deft. She felt that with the slightest touch now he could have got her to reveal the rest of what she knew. She eyed the heavy cloud of smoke that circled slowly over his lap, then gathered and vanished in a thin stream out his wind wing.

He changed the subject. "The boys want Ho buried properly."

In the rear-view mirror she saw the bottoms of two bottles poised, the orange disks in the middles of two tilted faces. She looked back at the road and sighed. "What the hell does properly mean?"

"It is something we cannot do."

"Then they'll have to get used to what we can do."

"It is not easy for them."

"But that doesn't matter." She swung her head toward him. Her drooping eyelids and heavy lower lip carried what was not easy for her, her own turpitude, guile, and grief. "The boy is dead."

They had before them Tensed, Viola, Moscow, Genesee,

182

then Lewiston, and to Lewiston 85 miles of this country, but opening to great flatland, to cattle and sheep, wheat, peas, alfalfa, and grass crops. Beyond Lewiston was the high desert shared by Idaho, Washington, Oregon, Nevada, and California, the shared condition indicative of the fact that in the old days no territory had wished to lay claim to its desolation.

Lying downhill, his head full of blood, Erks awoke, groggy, and tried to raise himself, but fell back because of the steepness of the cant of the car and bumped his head on the blade of the shovel. His head reeled. He struggled up, trembling, clutching with sleeper's desperation the seat behind Chang and Lee, then positioned himself between the back of the seat and the hump of the spare tire, his back against the wall of the compartment. He was profoundly confused as to where he was. The back of the car was warm—an incubator in which some foul smell was being nurtured.

He saw Chang and Lee. He saw Lily and Taam. Through the front windshield he saw cloudless sky and the rim of the canyon wall opposite, precipitous, beige-colored and blue. The car negotiated a grade, switchback after switchback, and Lily fluttered the brake. He looked down at the shovel. Remembering, he looked at Ho and knew at once, the body still as metal under the blanket. He closed his eyes and rubbed the bump on his head, then looked again and reached out and drew the blanket down from Ho's face. His body wrenched at the sight. He pulled the blanket up, leaned back, and stared through a window, wishing for sleep.

Dirt runouts were cut into the slope above the road, rising at better than forty-five degrees, these, safety valves for trucks with failed brakes. Signs dotted the road, marking the distance to the next runout, and the road had skid burns leading into the runouts, and the runouts had been gouged by wheels. The fact that they had been used told a story of panic. Descending even in a car, slowly, under Lily's care, the road had to it a catching panic. He realized where they were, the Lewiston Grade, 2,000 feet of sudden downhill that took better than two steep miles of corners to cover. Being here seemed at once a longer and a shorter distance than they should have come. Tired as he was, the little sleep he'd had was as bad as none. His body ached. With the twisting road, Ho's body rocked, but, stiff, it rocked as a single piece under the blanket, head, arm, and foot rocking in unison, the same as the shovel rocking on the arch of the blade without swivel. Erks felt leaden and filled with the slow panic of dreams.

They caught up with a truck. Lily slowed and shifted the automatic transmission down and still had to use the brake. In front of them, the rear of the semi-trailer swung with the road, but over the sides, over the banks and down precipices, Erks had at intervals perspectives of the canyon bottom: first a coil of the Snake River, then the junction of the Snake and the Clearwater, and then the town itself, a piece of it glittering in the sun. They wound down the wall, the grade slackening into foothills. Lily passed the truck and the smell of brakes, hot, cut through the rank odor in the back of the car. Lily saw him in the mirror and waved. Still half stupefied, he couldn't respond. They crossed the bridge, drove past a hydroelectric plant, the river there spanned by a dam, and dynamos and transformers mounted in close formation upon the banks. They entered the town, or the first of two sister towns on either side of the Snake, one in Idaho, one in Washington, Lewiston and Clarkston. They entered Lewiston, a blast of color, heat, power line, and motion, and Erks came to consciousness clambering crab-like over the ribs of time.

The towns were a seaport. The locks that carried the Snake and Columbia 450 miles to Portland had been recently completed. Lumber, ore, but mostly wheat were shipped out of here by water. The Nez Percé had followed water routes to this place, a gathering ground, a place to greet the salmon run. Lewis and Clark had arrived by water. A new road to replace the Grade was under construction, but the Grade exemplified the difficulty of an approach by land. Prototypical towns, an axis, pivot, radiant, several times a boom town, both of them—although Lewiston had usually been the stronger—and now they boomed again, both, but the Army Corps of Engineers had favored Clarkston with the port. The history showed, its spokes like those of a

184

wagon wheel half buried in sand. Levels of topology poked through the skin: the antiquated routing of the roads of approach —once mule-skinner trails—the loaded barges, water and dynamo, narrow streets and on them cowboys in straw hats, and Indians. The buildings of Lewiston still stood wall to wall like a Western set, and they had—the brick, and even the new aluminum and plastic façades—the bright, blown-dry quality of the sagebrush country that surrounded the place.

His kind of place.

They stopped for gas. Lily opened the back for him. He got out and stood for a moment, rocking. It was warm. Taam scooted over for him in the front. Erks eased his body onto the seat. Lily returned and they drove across the Snake into Clarkston, passing a marker that stated that Lewis and Clark had camped on that very bank. Lewis and Clark had passed by here twice—Erks remembered—once on their way to the Pacific, and again on their way back, both times desperately short of food, eating dogs and horses, seeking replenishment, which they received both times from the Nez Percé, or Chopunnish, as the tribe then was called. The facts stuck in Erks' mind and would not budge.

Lily turned into an alley and pulled up behind a restaurant, the Jade Lantern. They left Ho out in the car, locked in, covered, beside his shovel.

The place was crowded, the main dining room full, and they were relegated to a foyer-like affair between the dining room and kitchen. They sat around the table, just the three of them, cramped, himself, Lee, and Chang. Taam had gone over to the kitchen, Lily to the rest room. There were so many people in the place that the conversations dinned in Erks' ears. The ladies' room was right behind the chair he had chosen and when Lily wanted in she banged his chair with the door. She was in a hurry. He slid forward to let her by.

He could see the Chinese in the kitchen, a family of at least six. The father had come to the serving counter and spoke animatedly with Taam. They gesticulated with their arms as they spoke. Behind the father, the others hustled the food. At Erks'

185

side, Lee and Chang sat still and—it struck him—now that Chang had calmed down, or now that he had Chang's knife, the two of them had seemed increasingly like the earlier three, Low, Choy, and Wong, or Pang, in their way of being there and not being there at once, and in the way they just sat there under the skin of their race, but, for now, so unlike the fast action in the kitchen with the pots and pans. So maybe it wasn't race, after all, or not just race, but too much travel and all this strangeness. That was what he thought, looking at them, but not letting them know he looked, though they knew, of course, but also knew, as is the way, that he looked with the pretense of their not knowing, so they acted maybe as if they didn't know. He looked at them in just the way they sat there, doing it, but not doing it, and—he thought—they looked the way he felt, too, half asleep, and thick, and invisible. Something began to happen as if there were a sheet of glass between them and someone was drawing a picture on it and sooner or later they would have to look and then see each other through the picture—a flirtation with contact. When Lily came back out she banged the back of his chair with the door and the noise was like the noise of that glass breaking. He jumped. She touched his shoulder and apologized.

She sat opposite him. Erks sighed, then stretched his legs out under the table, and leaned against his chair, tipping it back on two legs. The idea was that if someone wanted in the rest room, or out, he could drop the chair quickly and be out of the way. Lily put her elbows on the table and leaned, her face coming forward as if to counterpoise his shift in weight.

"Are you with us?"

Erks closed his eyes and opened them. "Just about. So is Ho."

"I stopped in Coeur d'Alene. He was dead. I couldn't take him in dead."

"He's out in the car, for God's sake."

"He's covered up."

"He stinks."

"He can't stink yet."

"He stinks, damn it."

"We'll bury him."

Erks rubbed the stubble on his neck. The noise of the restaurant made it possible to speak as if in private. Chang and Lee stared across the table right through the conversation as if they weren't there. "It's not noon now. It's warm out. When?"

She bridled. "What do you suggest?"

He suggested nothing. At the moment everything was impossible. A woman came out of the ladies' room and banged his chair. He dropped it onto four legs. The woman walked by and out of the foyer into the throng of eaters.

"Where the hell did she come from?"

Lily grinned.

Two Chinese men entered the foyer, a short one and a tall one. Erks saw them instantly and stiffened. They stood out, as Erks and Lily and their group stood out, because the clientele in the place was entirely white, and not just white, but rural and boom-town white—shirtsleeves, bolo ties, bouffant hairdos, and thick arms. The floor help was white. Only the kitchen was Chinese, and only half the food—the menu offered hamburgers, steaks, Caesar salads, and club sandwiches, too. Cat-like, the two men moved to a table against the opposite wall and sat down. They looked around, the tall one coolly and the short one with darting glances—big cat and small—but both investigations came to dwell on Erks' table. It seemed to Erks that the small one nodded at him. He wasn't sure.

He held his face blank, saying: I don't think you meant me.

The two men looked over at Taam. The short one Erks felt he had seen somewhere before. Very small, he had a square jaw and extremely sharp cheekbones, pinched, dimpled, as if the bone were about to poke through, and the clothes he wore were too large; the coat of his pin-striped suit hung on his body like a rug on a pitchfork.

Watching Erks, Lily's face had quickened into a question.

"Somebody chased us across the border."

She nodded. "I heard."

"Don't look now, but we have visitors."

She didn't look. "Not surprising."

"Oh?"

She didn't speak.

"Did he tell you that whoever chased us tried to use a gun on us, that they were met by somebody else?"

"Taam says we have two shadows, friendly and unfriendly."

"I figured that out, but how do you tell them apart?"

Lily, who had not moved, whose elbows still rested on the table, whose head still hung forward, smiled at him, showing gold teeth. "Is that some kind of joke?"

Erks rubbed his neck again, then tipped his chair back. He saw Taam turning away from the counter to come to the table. "He's attracting a lot of attention."

"He's considered valuable."

The question How? How is he valuable? Erks let rest. He asked, "Then why is this trip so damn slipshod?"

Taam slipped behind Lily and sat softly in the chair between Lily and Erks. "The owner is preparing us a special dinner," he said, then he leaned toward Lee across the table and broke into Chinese. For a moment Lee sneaked out from under his skin. His face brightened. Then he sneaked back in. Taam straightened up. "The owner is Mike Lee. You see?" he said in English.

Lily reached out and touched Taam's arm, but spoke to Erks: "If you mean how come we're out in the open like this, the idea was for us to blend in with the background. It's the old trick. Make yourself so obvious that you're not noticed."

That covered only part of what he had meant, and he wasn't sure he even believed it for what it did cover, and further, considering the well-fed citizens of Lewiston and Clarkston who crowded the restaurant, businessmen and families out for lunch on a Saturday, and the two over by the wall—kangaroos in a world of bears—and themselves, himself, the large woman, two scared kids who didn't seem to know a word of English and showed it, and Taam, who, here, in public, looked increasingly derelict in his rumpled clothes, and tired, and older than he was, more and more like an old bird on the skids, out on the street, more and more like one of those he had seen in Portsmouth Square, the bachelors, the lost bachelors, Erks had to smile at the absurdity of it.

Lily pulled back and almost smiled. Formidable, she held it in.

She intrigued him.

Taam had grown watchful.

"That hasn't worked from the beginning," Erks said.

"If it is the two gentlemen you are concerned about," Taam said, "there is no reason to worry." He looked over at the two. The small one—alert—raised his fingers from the table and waggled them.

Erks saw that.

Lily did not.

Taam turned to her. "They are with Jui."

Erks didn't have the faintest idea who Jui was.

But Lily swung around in her chair and stared at the two men. The one raised his fingers again. Lily turned back and crossed her arms, her face suddenly somber.

Erks had to let his chair down for a woman who wanted the ladies' room. "What I mean is I don't understand why I've got the feeling that this business is so rough around the edges when the schedule's so damn tight. Something's not connecting."

"With who?" Lily said. She didn't move. She looked angry. But she was one of those with whom it was hard to tell, one who looked only possibly angry and who then suddenly either wasn't at all or was very angry. She motioned at Taam with her eyes. "He says the Triad's after him."

Erks paused. He tipped his chair back on two legs again and touched the table with one hand for balance and thought: The Triad again. What had been a question, a possibility, a danger that had seemed alien or mythic and thus more conversational than actual, one of the list of cogs he might have struck to try to find a path into the center of what he was engaged in, gravitated toward certainty and became, feasibly, the center. He still didn't know what it was—an Asian Mafia, an opium-based syndicate, one of those secret societies that snaked in and out of Chinese history. He imagined that the odd life or two in its way would not be counted. "Of course it is," he said dryly.

Her face gave a little.

189

Erks sighed. "Who the hell is Jui?"

"You're working for him."

"I thought I was working for your husband."

Again, her face gave. She almost smiled. "He's only the purveyor."

He gripped the table edge now, his fingers whitening, and he spoke sharply. "I like to know who I'm working for."

Lily didn't speak.

He glanced at Taam, who listened without moving, as quick and as still as a lizard on a rock, the object of purveyance. Taam's bright eyes looked a little wild in his fatigue-worn face. They held too much light. Stony, they looked as if they could be burned through from the inside by light. Erks looked away and stared at the seam of the opposite wall and ceiling, but held the image of Taam in his mind and left the figure in the periphery of his vision to whiteness bright as the light off diamonds. He had the sense of something else about to be known, of some logic about to close, something even more specific than would be knowing what the Triad was or who Jui was or who the two men across the room were—a third proposition, out of his dream. But it wouldn't come out. It teased, but he couldn't quite shake it loose.

He heard the toilet flush behind the wall. He let his chair down and said to Lily, "Listen, I get jumpy over such things. I'm just a country boy after a little cash."

"The hell you are."

Their meal arrived—rice, sweet and sour pork, curried shrimp, and fried vegetables piled in separate bowls, and egg rolls arranged neatly on a platter and coated with an amber-colored sauce, and for Chang and Lee hamburgers and a pile of french fries each. The waitress, a large woman with dyed red hair, unloaded it from a tray to the table, but she looked as though she would have been more comfortable unloading hay from a truck. She bulled things around to make room, and gave Erks and Lily the hamburgers and empty plates to the others.

When Erks and Lily switched with Chang and Lee, the waitress stopped and said, "Well!"

She poured their tea, moving around the table and jockeying for access. She puffed as she leaned and thrust her arm in front of their faces. Erks, who had moved his chair back to make room for her, was banged by the rest-room door. The woman emerged, apologizing out of a cloud of perfume. Then two more appeared and wanted in. Then one wanted out. For a moment the waitress disappeared behind the open door. When it swung shut she was there, standing against the wall like a pedestrian waiting for a green light. She came at Erks' cup last, poured his tea, then hung on to his shoulder as she leaned to set the teapot in the center of the table. She stood back and asked if they needed anything else. Her question had the weight of a final judgment.

"Chopsticks," Taam said.

When she left, Erks said, "The hell I am what?"

Now Lily smiled, her large face breaking open. "A country boy."

Lee and Chang set to their food immediately. They leaned into their plates and worked at eating. They were invisible.

"I had twenty-five hundred dollars coming in Rathdrum," Erks said.

The smile dropped.

"That was the arrangement," he said.

"Lucas didn't tell me. Lucas didn't leave me that kind of money."

"I noticed you didn't force any on me."

She put her hands on the edge of the table and pushed back, glowering.

He was annoyed, but he liked Lily. He liked the way she looked—strong arms and large adamant face that could twist into any expression. He liked the way she looked now, as though she could get tough any moment. He said, "What the hell kind of operation is this? I've got another twenty-five hundred coming in Reno. I want that five thousand dollars in Reno."

The waitress returned with chopsticks and said, "Deal me in."

Her joke was met with silence and leaden looks.

191

She stood with her hands on her hips and surveyed them as if to curse them for their bad manners.

The chopsticks were dusty. Lily was adept with them. Erks was not. The pork he liked, small chunks of ribs, the meat savory. He liked the bite down to the bone. The curried shrimp was hot enough to make him fear for his bowels. He used the chopsticks out of deference, though he felt as if he were eating with a pair of pliers. They were too small, too light. He wanted to clutch the sticks and jab the food.

Seeing his difficulty, Taam held up his hand and clicked the tips of his chopsticks rapidly, then slid them out of his hand and showed Erks how he held the hand, and slid the sticks back in, showing where the fingers went, all this without words. He bowed as one who has performed a balancing act, but grinned sadly, too, under his crazy eyes, as one who mocks the feat as nothing. Erks chuckled at his expression. Lily looked up from her plate, the whites of her eyes large under the irises, mournful, her nose long-looking, but at the same time she curled her lip away from her front teeth like an animal. It came out looking like a sexual advance to Erks, like her face went with a body in bed hiking itself up higher for a better hold.

He tried the chopsticks according to Taam's example. They were easier to manage for a while. Chang and Lee finished their hamburgers and raided the Chinese dinner, took up the bowls and scooped the remains onto their plates, set the bowls back, empty, and ate with the chopsticks the waitress had left them even though they had ordered hamburgers. They ate fast, the food moved on a direct course between plate and mouth, this eating and the taking not a breach. The food was there. The boys were hungry. Therefore, they took the food. It was a syllogism of the flesh without the warp of good manners. But Lily looked at Erks again and raised her eyebrows, not in disapproval, but faintly amazed, or amused; it was hard to tell which because mourning was there, too, hanging on. Erks was fascinated by the way her grief came out erotic.

Mike Lee, the proprietor, visited their table to ask if the meal had been satisfactory. Taam spoke to him in Chinese. Mike Lee looked pleased. A small man, stooped, Mike Lee had a complexion that showed too much time spent in the kitchen. His translucent white shirt was stained with food. While he remained, the red-haired waitress stationed herself one table over and talked to friends, busy as the restaurant was.

A lady came out of the bathroom and banged the back of Erks' chair. Mike Lee greeted the lady. "Hello, Mrs. Watson."

The waitress spoke over the noise, telling her friends about how she felt weak, how she awoke in the middle of the night unable to breathe, how she feared for her life. She told how the doctors thought it was gallstones, the kidney, then the thyroid, the pituitary. "Then they wanted to do an exploratory," she said.

"We can do that," a man at the table said.

"My eye," the waitress said.

The waitress had Erks' attention, and Taam's and Mike Lee's, and others in the foyer awaited the man's response to her. Even Lily, her back to the waitress, smiled as she listened.

"On the spot," the man said. He motioned at the table. "Stretch out."

The waitress doubled up, bent over the food, then straightened, laughing. She collected herself and posed, one hand on her hip and the other touching the hair at her neck. "Over my dead body."

The people in the foyer laughed, but Erks, watching Lily, saw her smile drop and her eyes widen, and her body rock back ever so slightly as if struck by something soft. There was a crash from the main dining room, the sound of a tray of dishes dropped, then silence, there and in the foyer, then a roar in the dining room, but muted by distance—a disconnected echo of laughter that rose and ebbed.

Unperturbed, Mike Lee said, "Considering her health, she has a lot of spirit." He nodded at Taam, then at Erks, marked them.

Strange—Erks thought—how he granted the waitress that —spirit—and how she held her ground even though her employer stood at the next table. They had an understanding, clearly, his abdication of power matched by her servility, his tolerance of her matched by hers of him, this, somehow, a racial compromise arrived at—a modus vivendi—but out of the sense of compromise emanated a bad air, the air of confusion and bad faith.

Erks ate the last of his shrimp with his fork. The shrimp was cold. Mike Lee left them. The waitress spoke softly with her friends. The voices in the restaurant rose again to a monotonous din. Erks felt a wave of anger, violent and irrational, undefined, a path of possible action zinging out into space.

. . . and seizing his tomahawk, threatened to cut him down if he dared to repeat such insolence . . .

Erks felt that way.

His monomania, his own fierce independence and the lawlessness rubbed off on him from where he had lived, threatened to come out.

But at whom it was directed, at what insolence, he still didn't know.

He stared at the two Chinese men against the wall. They were finishing their meal—steak, which they ate with knives and forks—and, staring, Erks remembered the small one, but the head only, and not connected to the body, the head like something mechanical cocked behind the tinted window of the Continental in Vancouver.

"He drives the Lincoln," Erks said abruptly, pointing. "He's been with us all along."

The small one saw him point and nodded, as if to say: I do mean you.

Erks kept looking, but as if he looked and had pointed at something on the wall behind the man.

"Yes," Taam said.

He turned to Taam. "They know our itinerary."

"Obviously. From Jui."

"Who got it from Lucas?"

Taam shrugged. "Or gave it to him."

194

"And the others back on the logging road? The jeep? That's the Triad?"

"It is possible."

He put his elbows on the table and leaned toward Taam. "But you believe so."

Taam leaned toward him, matched him, and hissed, "Yes."

"And they know the itinerary, too."

"They should not."

Erks pulled back. "They damn sure knew part of it."

Taam did not move. He fingered his teacup and looked directly at Erks. He said, "They are not here."

Something came out of a remote place and snapped like the tip of a whip—the third proposition out of his dream: In order to understand, the missing component must be added.

He remembered all three:

1. Any kind of density makes weight.

2. To understand is to lighten weight.

3. In order to understand, the missing component must be added.

Though a paradox, it came out clear and did, momentarily, lighten his weight when he translated it this way: It's the snake itself, it's Lucas. Lucas is setting us up.

That became utterly certain in his mind. Then what had been lightened quickly grew heavy again through the uncertainties attached to the now known peril.

He looked at Lily, but did not say it all: "We've been set up."

She stared at him, then looked away, then looked back again with formidability in her eyes. She cocked her head as if she were about to snort. "Let's go."

Taam began to move.

Erks did not. He thought: She knows already.

"But I've got to get in there again," Lily said, pointing over his shoulder at the door to the ladies' room.

She got up and he had to move for her.

As soft as ghosts, Lee and Chang followed Taam out. Erks was left to the cash register. The cashier had to go to retrieve the

195

bill from the waitress. The two Chinese gentlemen, the tall one and the small one in the too-large suit that swung as he moved briskly inside it, had risen when those at Erks' table rose, then had followed Erks to the cashier, and stood at his back, waiting to pay. The small one—he felt—waited for him to turn, would greet him with a show of manners if he did, would in some way acknowledge himself as the one seen in Vancouver, or even in the second car at the border crossing. He felt as if the small one were jiggling something to get his attention. He felt the eyes on his back. He did not turn, but he had the sense of triangulation again—a real model for his syllogism: somewhere out at an angle from himself and the small one was a third point, and invisible lines of transit led to that point, and lodged in the point was the solution, some strange and phantom and exculpatory meat—dog, himself—his joints gnawed not by Taam, after all, but by Lucas Tenebrel. There was a whole scene in it, a sinister episode that had not come out from under the skin, that ought not to be allowed out. To face it would be perilous.

He heard a light voice: "Sir?"

The cashier, a girl with a long nose and sad eyes, took his money.

When she gave him change, she let her eyes linger on his, as if to say, "Take me with you."

He thought: My God, do I carry that air?

He looked past her through the doorway into the main dining room, at the crowd organized according to the tables they hunched over.

The cashier caught his eye and said sadly, "Good-bye."

10

He waited for Lily at the door and together they walked out into the heat and alongside the building toward the car.

Alone with him, she responded to what she'd refused to respond to in the restaurant. "So you think we've been set up," she said.

He regarded her response as a probe. He said, "I know we've been set up."

She swayed away from him, then swayed back, touching his arm with hers.

"Lucas was awfully damn insistent about sticking to the schedule," he said.

She murmured.

He thought it again: She's known this all along.

"I bet he told you to stop at this restaurant."

"Nope."

It was strange. She was lying about something. Yet he still didn't distrust her. He would have to wait.

They continued to the car without speaking further. The two Chinese gentlemen were right behind them. They got into a mud-smeared Continental parked not far from the station wagon. Taam, Chang, and Lee were waiting at the station wagon. Erks drove. The Continental, which the small one drove, followed them out of the lot, out of Clarkston, across the river, and out of Lewiston, out up the hill to the flatland en route to Lapwai.

197

On the high flatland, the brush country, the car in the mirror dwindled to a black dot and became interchangeable with other dots, indecipherable, lost in space, as uncertain as an ache in the chest, as storm clouds, as a bull in spring pasture. There seemed no relief from such uncertainty.

The place, the pair of towns, they had left behind was an armature—the rivers its method of dexterousness, the rivers digital—and a pivot, and prototypical, and through time, as with all gathering places, protean: its perimeters were elastic, its form, its face, changed, mask upon mask. The town of Lewiston—Erks knew—was founded illegally on the Lemhi Reservation. The treaty stipulated that no white man could erect a building on the reservation, but the Snake River, which bounded the reservation, was an avenue of trade, its bed, its course, *put* there by Pliocene lava flow and downwarp, the canyons later excavated by the waters of Pleistocene glaciation. Its course knitted the rugged inland country together, linked the Spokane and Coeur d'Alene country, interior British Columbia, and the Salmon and Clearwater rivers to the Columbia, and then to the Pacific. The Snake translated directly into trade, and, thus, into coin. At first salmon was the coinage, then fur, then in the 1860s it was gold—the Clearwater and Salmon River strikes.

Miners flooded Nez Percé land, staking "claims." One chief, Eagle-of-Light, brought his people just short of war. Another, Lawyer, resisted any white establishment on the east bank of the Snake. It would bring sickness to his people, and whiskey. But the Indians, too, their grazing lands increasingly infringed upon, were tempted by trade. It was an impediment to have to cross the Snake there. So permission was extracted from some Nez Percé—not all—and a trading establishment was built—but never chartered. So beset, the Nez Percé pulled back and the town of Lewiston was the result.

The Chinese, released from the railroad by the pounding of the golden spike at Promontory, followed the white miners here, and, though heavily taxed, worked passed-over or "played-out" placer claims with success. The Chinese had a different—Asiatic

198

—view of acceptable profit margin. The white settlers were enraged by their success. One summer the bodies of 32 Chinese miners were discovered along a 10-mile stretch of the Clearwater. The history of the Chinese in such places was one of influx and forced withdrawal. But a few, such as Mike Lee's father, maybe, or his grandfather, or his wife's grandfather, had hung on. Somehow, Mike Lee and his family had come to be there.

A quintessential property of money was its synergy, its way of compounding itself, its way of tying different interests together, its ability to travel and to cause travel. The Chinese miners had hoped to take the coin back to China. The river routes, roads and highways, the paths, the air, the very wind, were all veins of coin. Horse was coin. Boat, car, wire, radio wave, laser beam, and gun were coin. Taam, traveling, sitting next to him, was coin. Because of coin, Taam on the one hand, and then Chang and Lee on the other, though they rode in the same car, traveled in opposite directions, to different worlds. And in the center, at their intersection, was Ho—a quintessential property of both migration and coin—dead.

Erks shuddered and straightened up behind the wheel.

He thought about the horse: How it began on this continent, then crossed the ancient land bridge to China, how the Chinese tamed the horse, and the Turks, and Greeks. How the horse traveled to Europe, how it went to Spain, how it came back by water to Mexico and Peru, a cargo of the conquistadores, how it traveled north to this country, how it transformed certain tribes, among them the Nez Percé, from gatherers and fishermen, from groups loosely knit together, to unified, nomadic tribes. How the horse increased their range, opened up exchange and trade with outlying tribes, how its possession became a sign of wealth, how an elaborate game developed around stealing it, how battles were fought over it, and how, because of the distance it granted, it granted, too, a greater sense of abstraction, how the ability to cross space meant not just that one could cross it, but also that one could reflect upon the idea of its crossability, upon the idea of mobility and the ways of extending it for profit and adventure.

Traveling in company made unity, the going and coming made unity for both those who went and those who waited behind. The movement of peoples along the routes was a melody played over the land form, and under their movement by horse gathered the accouterments—blanket, bridle, hackamore, legging, skid pole, teepee, buffalo meat, and stories of the journeys.

Distance was melody.

And the harmony that accompanied this melody was power. Contraband was rhythm.

Erks felt the effect of time spent together. Lily sat next to the window and Taam between them, and Lee and Chang in the rear-view mirror, minimized by the convex mirror, their two heads cocked toward each other emblematic of the time endured together, and himself at the wheel, not just a carrier but synergized by his cargo, and Ho in the back . . . Ho, a melody truncated in midcourse, a note held in midair rising to a whine, his dream of San Francisco, his innocence, afloat forever above the land.

They crossed Lapwai Creek, then entered Lapwai itself, the central town of the Nez Percé Reservation, for many, once, a place of exile. Now the town had a granary, a shopping center, and a new tract of homes, square, identical, and cheap. Children, their limbs and faces and black hair bright in the sun, played in the packed earth streets and bare yards. Gardens, recently turned, were gray-colored. Outside Lapwai were small farmsteads, the homes sparse and weather-beaten, and the yards littered with machinery, spare parts, oil drums. . . .

"We could pull off anywhere along here," Erks said.

He glanced over at Lily on the other side of Taam. Her largeness and softness outlined him—a lightly shaded area to his density, this not so much a matter of skin as of mystery. In Taam mystery was still dense and hidden, atomic. But beside Erks, Taam's body seemed buoyant, balanced by his feet on the drive shaft housing, and he had a curious odor, a blend of perspiration, soiled clothes, and lilac—foreign and sweet. His cane basket rested between his feet and Lily's on the floor, creaking softly with the motion. Lily's carpetbag was between her feet and the door. Each of them refused to part with these accouterments. Neither of them responded to his words, except that Erks sensed a certain quickening in Taam, a response forming. Taam glanced up. Lily stared straight ahead through the windshield.

"We could pull over somewhere along here and bury Ho," Erks said.

Now she spoke: "Folks watch over small farms."

"We can pull off on one of these roads." Every few miles they passed a road that led into the hills.

"Pull into somebody's farm?"

Now Lily looked at Erks and he glanced at her. Her large face was a lament and in her drooping eyelids and lips lay a roosting menace that Erks could not read. He did not speak.

"We don't want to be caught burying a dead one," she said. "We'd have to run."

Again Erks did not speak, but glanced over at her and leered, not saying it, but meaning: And what do you call this?

She understood. Her face brightened for a moment and she shifted position, leaned back, put one elbow out through her open window and stretched the other arm along the top of the seat behind Taam. Her fingers nearly touched Erks' shoulder. It was hot. The wind made her curly hair dance, but her face remained formidable. Taam lit a cigarette. The diffuse smoke scattered and blew out the four windows.

They passed by the town of Winchester, and through a forested country of hills and canyons, through Craigmont, and they crossed Lawyer Creek. The land opened, allowing marginal farming. There, some fifty miles beyond Lewiston, Erks spoke again. "We could bury Ho here."

Lily responded quickly. "There's a lot of rock."

It was true enough. There were quantities of surface rock— basalt—and the presence of that rock on the surface, placed as he knew it was in huge sheets, cleavages, molten once, meant rock under the surface. Stopping here to dig meant taking a chance on rock or going into a field some farmer had carved out of a pocket amongst the tree and rock. It was also true that in the

201

last hour of traveling there had been plenty of places to bury Ho, considering it would take only a few feet of open earth, or even plenty of secluded places to simply dump him.

"We don't want to bury him shallow," she said.

He didn't know why not.

It was over eighty degrees, and Lily had undone the top two or three buttons of her dress for the sake of the breeze.

"We don't want to bury him shallow," she repeated. "We've got to bury him deep."

Erks gazed at the road, then into the mirror. Lee and Chang dozed, taken by the soporific motion of the car. Between himself and Lily, Taam was wide awake, light and silent, listening, a watcher, an organ of reception. The man never slept.

"If we don't bury Ho now," Erks said, "we'll hit the Salmon and there'll be nothing but rock."

"It doesn't matter. We'll be out of that before dark," Lily said.

She was stalling.

"Dark?" he said.

Lily leaned back in the seat. The cushions under Erks shifted with her movement. She rubbed her shoulder under the dress. "It's not hot enough yet," she said. "These bones can't get too much heat." Then, in a voice that took Erks a second to place— it seemed to come from the back of the car, from nowhere—she said, "How thy garments are warm when ye quieteth the earth by the south wind."

He paused. "The Bible?"

She chuckled. "The chinook."

He paused again and thought: Religion?

He said, "It's hot to have a corpse in the back of a car."

Lily stuck her head completely out the window and held her face to the wind.

They entered the canyon of the Salmon—once called "River of No Return" because steamships venturing up from the Snake were unable to negotiate the rapids back downstream.

Another hour passed, the hours driving receipts on a prong:

202

one went through them and quickly lost count. Between words the silence in the car could have been five minutes or an hour. The time had little effect upon the words, as Erks had observed last night in British Columbia; here it was even more true because of his fatigue and the light and the space. A silence in time made the next word no more or less surprising, nor was it surprising if there were no words at all. It was, now, early afternoon, the center of the day: the perimeters of day, dawn and dusk, seemed separated from the present by an endless chasm.

Again, Lily sat with one arm along the seat behind Taam, and Erks felt the pressure of her hand on his shoulder. He felt it after it was there, discovered it. She began toying with his shirt, running a fingertip slowly back and forth along a seam. It made him tighten up at first, then, as it continued, he relaxed. She had her head against the doorpost and her eyes were half closed. She ran her hand up the back of his neck and began tugging gently at his hair.

They had been in the canyon for some time, and by force of the shade of the cliffs on either side of the road, the air had cooled. Lily had rolled her window up most of the way, and Erks his, but fearing the corpse, he had rolled the rear window down another few inches. The basalt cliffs were boggling, their closeness, the strength of their outline to the sky, their ruggedness, and mostly their size, their effect upon the car, road, and even the river, of profound diminution. In the river the fish spawned, their migration a well-directed movement between feeding ground and the ground where they bred and died. The fast, careening river seemed to Erks to be a link in the vast chain of apparent miracles with which he was encircled. Wild, bleak, enchanted, the landscape made him long not to be anywhere else. Lily toyed with his hair. She twisted and untwisted the strands, and tugged gently, and separated the mats by running her fingers slowly through them, groomed him as a monkey grooms a mate. He didn't know what to make of it. He allowed it.

Lily gave up tugging on his hair and took to massaging his neck and the back of his scalp. Aroused, Erks looked over Taam at her, and she, alerted, or expectant, looked back, and held his eyes with a look of having been wounded—the grieving in her jaw and cheeks—and of seeking comfort and wishing to give comfort, and in her eyes—he thought—this unaccountable striving for contact mounted to a sexual address. It was a look that took him completely in. It seemed a revelation, but it revealed only itself, only the look itself, only that it was there and not why, or it revealed that she could give such a look, but the reason behind it was as unaccountable to Erks as the message in her touch. So distracted, he felt a hand lightly touch his and drag rightward. He jumped. He had allowed the car to drift over the line. Taam did not release his hand until the course had been corrected, then Taam looked up at him, laughing soundlessly, his teeth showing. Lily's caresses ceased. When Erks looked over he saw her fast asleep.

Taam said, "I'd like you to wait for me in Reno."

"Oh?"

"Behind where we will stop is a parking lot. In the parking lot is a stall with my father's name on it—Chiang Taam." He spelled the name. "Wait there." He reached into his pocket and produced a key, which he held out. "There should be a car in the stall that we can take."

The key was bright blue, a duplicate. Erks took it, put it into his breast pocket, and buttoned the pocket, but said, "My instructions were to take the boys straight to San Francisco."

Taam's body swayed against Erks, the touch of his shoulder delicate as the sunlight playing against the cliffs. He said, "Yes. But wait and I will go with you."

They emerged from the canyon at Riggins and stopped for gas. Lily used the rest room again. She came out and sat on the front fender of the station wagon so that the car tipped on its shocks. Chang, Lee, and Taam waited inside the car. Lily asked Erks if he wanted her to drive for a while. Erks stood to one side, warily eyeing the attendant, a boy, who held the nozzle to the tube and had a clear view into the back of the wagon. Erks said no—thinking he'd have to sleep later for the sake of the night

204

drive to San Francisco, thinking he'd be damned if he'd turn the wheel over until they got the corpse out of the car. The smell of running gasoline was metallic in the hot air. Lily stretched, arched her back, rolled her shoulders, threw her head back, and held the pose of a coquette, bizarre in a woman of her size.

Relaxing, she swung her face in Erks' direction and grinned, two gold teeth points of light at the corners of her mouth. "Tough guy, huh?"

He looked away.

She liked Erks. She liked the way he looked standing there with his hat pulled down almost to his eyes. She liked his dark hair and gray eyes and angular body and strong features—Italian, or French, or Spanish, or Portuguese, something Mediterranean. She liked his taciturnity, his way of withholding, and what she saw in him without having had to see much of it—his competence. She'd like to have that kind of man, a kind she was not accustomed to, someone with that stolidity—tending to the prosaic—and who yet had, as she sensed Erks did, a ragged aspect, something under the surface which one would not want to offend because, if angered, his redress might be overpowering. She might even like that, being overpowered, or certainly sexually overpowered. It would help her to forget herself.

She wished she'd met him under different circumstances. She wished she didn't feel hunted by things she could not bring herself to think clearly about—her mother, her brothers, but mainly what Erks had said, that Lucas was setting them up, which she knew was true. She was privy to it. She had agreed . . . but exactly what she had agreed to she couldn't now even name in her thoughts. Whenever she came close to naming it in thought her mind pulled up short and seized. She stared at Erks' leg, or just short of it, focusing on a point just above the car's fuel spout and the nozzle where the mirage-like vapors of gasoline made the air look liquid. She recognized that she had to name it in order to deal with it. Even when in the act of agreeing to Lucas' request—one day at her mother's place—she had doubted herself, then—the next day—her mother died and she'd lost track of both doubt and agreement, and now, escorting Taam, she was snarled in her agreement—doing it, traveling, carrying a gun—and her doubt had come gnawing back.

She considered that she liked Erks so much because she wanted to make him into a force to match Lucas, that she was actually trying to tease him into becoming that force. She did like him. But she wanted more than that. She wanted something to touch while she looked at Lucas with the hot, hostile, close scrutiny of a wife with other interests.

But she'd tried that before. She'd been with Lucas for three years, actually married, the condition of the marriage fast action and manipulation, its method indirection, and the expectation of romantic betrayal so constant that it wasn't even betrayal anymore. She'd spent the last four months living with her ailing mother and hadn't missed Lucas or his fast action. Between herself and him the emotional colors were washed out.

She hated being manipulated.

She had a habit of taking up with manipulative men—like Sandman.

She wondered how Lucas had trusted her with this in the first place. Maybe he hadn't. Maybe his powers of cruelty extended to her. So considering, she saw that she might betray him, that she might revive the fire in betrayal. But if she betrayed him he wouldn't trust her again and that—losing that part of herself which was made by his expectation of who she was—was hard to slough off. She could decide nothing.

She stared at the spinning digits on the gas tank—measure and price—and wished she could transform herself on the spot. She wished it were possible for her to fall in love with one like Erks, to become whatever it would take to do so: circumstances or no circumstances, it was impossible, and her desire was as irrational as her inability to name what she was doing here, or as lunatic as her feeling about Ho, who she wished were alive. Dead, she didn't want to let him go. She hadn't even known Ho, but only his corpse, and hanging on to it, manipulated by it, using it as some kind of touchstone, retentive about it, refusing to agree to bury it the way she did, was lunatic, but even knowing that,

206

she couldn't seem to do anything about it. She wished she weren't on the rag. She wished she weren't so pulled into herself. She wished she could think straight. She wished Taam would disappear. She wished Erks would beat the hell out of her.

"Not so tough," he said, turning his head. "I'll need the sleep later."

"What if I need it later?"

The nozzle clicked off and gas spat out of the tank.

Erks scratched under his hat. "Maybe you need it now."

He looked away and she saw his face suddenly harden.

The attendant, the boy, had washed the windows and came back to the nozzle to work the price up to a round figure. "What do you got in the back?" he said.

Come out of nowhere, and likely an idle question to him, it made Lily's blood run cold.

"A dead collie," Erks said without looking at the boy.

"A what?"

He spoke again, looking out across the street. "My dog. We let him out on the highway and somebody hit him."

"Too bad," the attendant said, looking in the back again.

Now Erks turned to the boy. "Yeah. Is there a pet cemetery around here?"

"A what?"

Lily turned her back to keep from laughing, and so doing, saw what Erks must have seen, a dark-green car pulled up across the street, waiting, and two men wearing city hats in the front seat, large men, featureless and stationary in the shade, like blots, and not even looking back, but forward, just sitting there as if impregnable, waiting. It was them. She felt Erks' eyes on her back like a curse.

They drove.

The car did not visibly follow them.

Erks asked, "Did everybody see that green Ford?"

The silence was an assent.

He glanced at Taam. "Would you say they were friendly?"

207

Lily stared straight ahead through the windshield.

Taam said, "I would say probably not."

"I'd say they're the same two out of the jeep."

"Possibly."

"What are they waiting for?"

"Opportunity."

The distance between towns, Riggins and Cambridge, was ninety miles, and between those points were three additional towns, New Meadows, Tamarack, and Council, the space between each town widening with the land, which widened before the eye, the terrain letting loose of timber and, beyond Cambridge, opening into the high plain, desert, the Great Basin shared by four states, or even by five if Utah was counted—Bannock space, Shoshone space, Paiute space, Washo, Mono, Gosiute space, Ute space, the space of the gatherers, the American *agrapha,* the unwritten—a land whose settlement showed as it had for centuries the thin power of the land to uphold dwelling, the great power, instead, residing in space. Outside Cambridge, they were on the verge of Bannock space.

They passed through Midvale, a town consisting of two short parallel lines of brick buildings, facing each other, the back of one line to the northeast, to the winter wind, the back of the other to the southwest, to the chinook. The buildings gave the town the air of defense against the space outside, the waste, the wilds. . . . And inside the car, an air of fear and of defense against what would not show itself, and a density of dreams, windows open because of the heat, and the air from the outside blew through the odor of death, menses, lilac, and sweating bodies.

Lily had her arm up on the back of the seat again.

She did not touch him.

They entered Weiser, which appeared at first to be another ten-block burg, but wasn't. It had an appendage on the southern side, a tongue of tract houses built into the fields, the fields irrigated. The town, in fact, was another axis, an upper pivot for reclaimed desert running from here south and southeast into Boise. He stopped for gas at the edge of the appendage where

208

the fields came up to the road, mixed in with buildings. He watched the attendant, watched the road for the Lincoln, for the Ford, for Chinese. He pulled the car away from the tanks and parked, left Chang and Lee in the back seat and Lily to the rest room, and walked with Taam across the road to a fruit stand. They bought bananas, apples, peaches, a box of strawberries, and Australian beer.

Outside the store, he stopped and took two peaches out of the sack, handed one to Taam and bit into one himself. Its sweetness stung the insides of his cheeks. Chewing, he gazed at the field across the street, beside and beyond the gas station. It was planted with lettuce, cabbage, young tomatoes, and maybe strawberries. A group of five field workers, dwarfed by the distance, worked slowly toward them.

"You should not be concerned with Ho," Taam said. "We will bury him at dusk."

"Why wait?"

"It will be cool then."

Erks grunted. His eyes were drawn to the gas station, to a large, dark figure moving inside it.

"From here to Oregon by our route the land is cultivated," Taam said. "We would have to drive into the hills. By dusk we will be into the hills."

Inside the gas station, the dark figure—Lily—stood near the plate-glass window. She had one hand to her head, as if holding a telephone receiver.

Erks said, "Look in the station."

Noting Erks' gaze, Taam had already looked. "I see."

"She's on the telephone."

"Yes."

"Who the hell is she calling?"

"I don't know."

"Does it worry you?"

"Yes."

They paused, watching. In a moment, Lily moved and reached up to the wall, a gesture of hanging a receiver on its hooks. She turned and suddenly brought her face close to the glass and stared outward, seemingly at them, then she backed off and vanished into the shadows.

"It worries me," Erks said.

"We have to wait."

It made him nervous to hear Taam name what he had resolved earlier—to wait. He said, "I don't like this kind of waiting."

Taam looked at him. "She's troubled."

"I can see that. I don't like waiting for her to work it out. I don't know what she's working out."

Taam did not respond. He looked away, as if silenced by hearing Erks name what he had considered.

They paused again. Something grew between them, an emanation of something wild they both knew was there.

"How long will you be in Reno?" Erks asked.

"About an hour."

"I've got to stop and get the money owed me, anyway. But one hour after we arrive, I'm going on to San Francisco."

A wild polar bear hung between them, big and white and silent, but pitting its weight against the chains that held it.

"Another peach?" Erks said.

Taam took one.

Erks took one for himself.

The field workers moved closer. Both men ate their peaches and watched the graceful steady movement.

"Illegals?" Erks said.

Taam looked up, his face set and showing perhaps just a hint of anger. "Possibly."

Erks spat his peach pit in the gutter.

They crossed the street to the car. Lily hadn't returned yet. Erks opened the tailgate to get to his valise, and bending over Ho, gagged. He caught hold of the valise, fished his binoculars out, shoved the valise back, and coming out, straightened and took a deep breath, his eyes watering. He moved to the front of the car and focused the binoculars on the field workers. There were five, a family, and they all wore wide-brimmed straw hats and flowing shirts that hung down to midthigh. They formed a phalanx, a man in front, and all carried long tools which they

handled lightly in the manner of the blind with their canes. All
five wore sacks slung waist-level from straps that passed over
their shoulders, and their motion had an accord and grace. The
grace he saw straightaway. It held him rapt. The utility and
economy of the movement took him some time to discern.

The man was in front—point guard—and he uprooted weeds
with his hoe. Behind him and to his right, the older girl also
uprooted weeds with a hoe, and behind the two of them in a
wedge, staggered, the woman, a second girl, and a young boy
picked up the weeds with their tools, but none of them removed
the weeds from his or her own tool. To do so would have wasted
motion, for the tools were several feet long, long enough to reach
the ground in front of them. Instead, they held the grasping
mechanism of the tool before another, and passed the weeds,
according to a pattern, forward, backward, or sideways, and not
always to the same person, but according to the position of each,
and so each person had two duties, two of them hoeing and three
picking up weeds, and all five removing weeds from another's
tool and dropping it into his or her own sack. The motion of tools,
the long handles flickering in the sunlight, rising, falling, crossing,
and the steady progress of the group accounted for the intricate
beauty of the motion.

Erks saw the man stop and look up, seeing him watching
through binoculars. The others stopped. Erks lowered the
binoculars. The family resumed. Reduced in Erks' vision, their
labor seemed easy, a delicate and elegant dance in the field.

For fifty miles, or an hour, they drove through the agricultural land, the "reclaimed" land, a watershed, the crops watered
from the Snake and its tributaries, the Weiser, the Big and Little
Willow, the Payette, the Boise. . . . Almost everything was grown
in the region: orchard crops, potatoes, onions, lettuce, tomatoes,
wheat, alfalfa and grass crops, cotton, corn, hops . . . . Dairy Cattle
supplanted range cattle, Holsteins, black and white, bright as
magpies in the watered fields. Thanks to the water, the farming
was at once intense and on a vast scale.

The fruit he had bought was devoured, Lee and Chang,

211

again, ravenous. He, Taam, and Lily drank the beer. Little was said. Everyone waited. It was hot, a dry baking heat.

Having smelled Ho in Weiser, he now could smell nothing but Ho. Having smelled Ho, he couldn't tell whether Ho really smelled that bad, if his odor really filled the car. It was like the smell of food one has vomited, a lingering waft of it like a stain. The windows were down, but that didn't help. The fruit smelled like Ho and he quit eating it. The beer smelled like Ho, but he drank to slake his thirst.

They came south of Parma, then the Silver City Mountains rose into view to the southwest, then at Homedale they crossed the Snake again, the river there tamed, slow and wide. The Silver City Range loomed larger, blue against the sky, then they entered the range, climbed it, the land turning to desert again— table plateaus and butte formations with igneous protrusions, dun and pale blue and heavily eroded. The growth consisted of sagebrush and bunch grass—range country growth. They entered the southeast corner of Oregon, crossed Succor Creek, passed through the Sheavilles, then Jordan Valley—a settlement of Basques—and headed west along the path of Crooked Creek. The sun, a flaming red disk, looked heavy as it sank behind a blood-colored mist of dust.

Suddenly, Lily said, "It's not just him who needs protection."

It was a remark to which Erks could not imagine a response.

She leaned forward and looked at him, her head sideways.

"It's not just him," she said, motioning at Taam with her thumb. "It's us. All of us need protection." She looked away, out her window.

Between them Taam was like light.

Erks said, "Let's help everybody out by getting rid of the body. Goddamn it, let's start with that."

Then just outside the town of Rome—but it was impossible to be anywhere but outside the town of Rome unless one stood inside the gas station right next to the cash register, it, the gas station, and the two farms erected on the river comprising the only buildings which would fall in sight were one to position oneself in what one might construe as *inside* town—just before

212

they reached Rome, when what there was of the town had come into sight, then Lily said, "All right. There's a road."

Erks slowed and turned off the highway, north, onto a dirt road that ran parallel to the water, the Owyhee, continuing a mile or so until a conjunction of rivers came into view in the dusk, Jordan Creek meeting the Owyhee, the waters high on the banks. He felt Taam's body alerted next to him, and in the rear-view mirror saw the eyes of Chang and Lee—watchful. He stopped the car in clear view of the water, got out, opened the tailgate, grasped the shovel, and bending into the wagon, dry-gagged at the stench. He recoiled, dragging the shovel out, then hoisted the shovel to his shoulder and walked toward the Owyhee just upstream from the confluence, and began digging on the crest of the bank.

Lily's door swung open like a wing. She got out and stretched, took several steps toward Erks, then stopped. Erks' figure was in silhouette, long and rangy and black against the sun, and bending, the shovel plunging and lifting. The sand, tossed to the side, flickered, and the blade of the shovel flashed. Taam slid out of the car. A back door swung open and Lee and Chang stepped out of the car, and they all stood, silent and disconnected, peopling the desert.

Erks dug rapidly at first in a fury of relief, flinging the heavy sand. But his arms were weak from sitting too long. He slowed and became methodical. He gauged the ground, six feet by four, and went around the perimeter once with the shovel, then began working in earnest, moving deliberately across the surface, deepening the hole with each stage and keeping the walls vertical. The work was calming, but because of the nature of the task, or because of the events surrounding it, or because of the desert at twilight—big, swelling with quiet, looming—or because of the rhythmic effect of shoveling and the sound—the quick plunge and the hiss of the sand tossed off the blade—Erks found himself in a strange state of sensitivity so that he started when he heard the cry of an owl overhead, and then, when Lily came up from behind and spoke, he jumped violently.

"I can take a turn."

213

Erks grunted, thinking: She grants that we are digging a grave.

"You don't think he'll get washed out here?"

He kept shoveling, but between strokes said, "It's April. . . . It's high water now. . . . It's not . . . a dry year. . . ." And the words became grunts between strokes, barely articulated, but the words "a dry year" ran repeatedly through his mind as he worked.

After a time, Lily said, "Let's bury him deep," and he stopped in exasperation. He had shoveled the hole better than knee-deep, but when he looked up at her, he softened. Her expression was one of great confusion, but swallowed, as if she were trying to swallow her confusion. Behind her Chang and Lee watched like twins, their faces strained. Taam had moved upstream and he squatted on the bank at a place where the currents eddied and swirled and made a pool—a good place to fish, Erks thought. Taam gazed into the water, dark in the paling light.

"Do you want me to spell you?" Lily asked.

He removed his shirt. Though twilight, it was still warm. Soon enough the sand would lose its heat, but for now it was warm. He took the key Taam had given him out of the shirt pocket and put it in his pants pocket, then tossed the shirt up over the pile and looked at Lily, thinking: No, he'd keep on shoveling, and, then, unaware of his own expression, he saw its reflection in Lily's response, the recoiling of one who had seen something ugly.

"All right," he said.

He jumped out.

She eased in and shoveled.

He hunkered in the sand. At his back, Lee and Chang stood in silence. In the distance, he heard coyotes yip, then cease. In a few minutes they yipped again, and ceased. The intermittent sound left small holes in the cloak of silence. Then there was only the swish of sand off the shovel, the faint spume of water. The desert, up to now an expanse seen traveling through it, so known, and now known stopped in it, a place of light even at dusk, its sheen moved inward to the unknown, and he was a hump on it,

214

and over at the bank, Taam a like hump, a part of it protruding
—that was all—and between them a woman working, digging
out the hole at its center and throwing out random shots of glitter
—his geometry laid to waste by a method at once more driving
and more rococo. At his back those two watched who showed no
mark of their watching.

The hump at the water shifted. Taam came over for a turn
with the shovel.

Lily climbed out and strayed off.

Taam turned the cup she had made back into a rectangle.
Erks couldn't see that. From where he sat he couldn't see the
bottom of the hole, but he did see the motion of the man's arms
and shoulders, and thus he could envision the routing of the
blade of the shovel, the short, accurate strokes that bit into the
wall and turned earth out. And each shovelful flung landed just
over the peak of the mound so that the dirt would not roll back.
Erks liked that. He hadn't expected it in Taam. It revived something in himself. Knowing how to dig a hole was as much a
measure as a fence line strung true, a foundation laid plumb, a
socket slicked square, a clean head shot. He hadn't expected
Taam's strength, either, the man not soft as he appeared in his
loose pants and the shirt that bloused at his waist, but powerful
in the hands and upper body, and agile, too, which showed when
he leapt out.

He stuck the shovel into the mound and said, "Enough?"

Erks said, "Lily wants it deep."

Taam looked into the hole, which was belly-deep. "What we
shovel out has to be shoveled back."

"True."

"We do not want to be too long here."

"No," Erks said. "I'll dig a little more."

He threw the shovel in, and followed it himself, finding the
bottom of the hole as he had envisioned it. When he looked up,
Taam was gone. He worked and thought of him, Taam, who was
still the point around which matters gathered, and of Lily, one
of those matters coiling right now. So he thought: facts, enigmas,
and images, bred in a quiet turmoil as he dug the hole. Often

215

when he worked he formed a resolution. Now he could not. He needed more weight fused onto the mysteries.

He soon had the grave shoulder-high—deep enough. He trimmed the bottoms of the walls and shoveled out the last loose sand, which, as he approached the level of the riverbed, had grown increasingly wet, and, thus, heavy. His shoulders and arms ached, and the soles of his boots were damp, and he had sand in his hair. It felt good. He looked up. He could not see over the sand heaped around the edges of the hole. A bat flew low over his head. He tossed the shovel out, waited a moment, then called. No one responded and for an instant he felt a quickening of fright, or not actually fright, not nearly that close, but once removed, the idea of fright as if remembered from childhood, only the idea of the fear of being stranded in a carefully prepared hole, for, though awkwardly, he could have climbed out. Doing so, he would have kicked dirt back in.

Lee and Chang's heads appeared.

"Give me a hand up."

They didn't move.

He held his hand out, beckoning them.

They backed off.

"Hey!" he said, even the anger in his voice instantly swallowed by a great deal of air.

Lily appeared and looked down at him, and tried to make a joke, "You do nice work." But her voice and face wouldn't get in line with the words.

"Give me a hand out."

She did. She pulled as he sprang. He found himself drawn close to her. He backed off, making space. She handed him his shirt, which he put on. Chang and Lee waited. He checked for Taam and saw that he had returned to where he'd been before —a hump again, studying the water. Bats darted over his head in jerks of dark against the light-colored land. The bats dipped into the eddy to drink, then rose clumsily and flitted away.

Lily said, "What's he doing?"

Erks said, "Let's get that boy."

They did. They went to get Ho, the two of them, Lee and

216

Chang following on their heels, mute, and they found Ho already disturbed, the body moved sideways in the compartment of the station wagon.

"I think the boys have tried," Lily murmured.

Erks grabbed the legs and pulled, sliding Ho out to the tail-gate, then an arm, dragging the body sideways so it could be handled. It seemed insulting. With the dragging the blanket pulled off, and the shirt, unbuttoned, parted and twisted under the head. Lily caught the legs, and Erks the shoulders, the body reeking and stiff, and bending over the boy to heft, he saw a glossy patch high on the ribs, a half-foot square, running from the ribs over to the breast, and looking, trying to discern the glossy patch in the weak light, he thought: He's been bleeding—then he thought: No, not after he was dead, not there, and it's square, why is it square? He released one shoulder and touched the place gingerly with a fingertip, and pulled back, startled, and said, "What the hell?"

"What?" Lily said.

"Jesus," he said, looking again, unable to fathom it. He reached for his valise and dragged it over, and dug down past gun, totem pole, and jade for his flashlight, found it, and turned the beam on Ho, bent over, and looked and saw what he thought he had touched, the square of flesh, muscular tissue bared, the skin peeled off. He straightened up, dumfounded.

Beside him now, Lily looked. "He's been skinned," she said, her voice an appalled whisper.

He saw several white flakes on the carpet of the compart-ment, picked one up and looked at it under the light—a piece of skin, moist and curled.

"Why?" she said.

She did not say who. Tacit, that was understood. He glanced at Chang and Lee, who stood some ten yards away, a tall one and a short one side by side, flat in the faint light, and looking away, looking into the desert.

She said, "They were in here while you were digging."

He put the piece of skin in his shirt pocket and returned the flashlight to his valise, and said, "Let's put him in the hole."

The body felt at once loose and stiff, the slackening in hiding just under rigor and waiting to come out. They held the weight gingerly and firmly and walked to the grave, dragging the blanket the doctor's wife had given him—Mrs. MacNeill—that scene strangely coming back to him, the woman lifting the blanket to cover the boy in his arms. He and Lily paused, holding Ho at the verge, and looked at each other, uncertain as to what to do—ease the body down, slide it in, or go in with it to set it down, or just drop it—and they looked around at Chang and Lee and at Taam, who had come to the spot. No one spoke. It was a moment, emblazing the day that had gone by.

They swung the body a little and dropped it. The body fell with a thud. Even in the bottom the face was revealed, stiff and grimacing, and the chest, glossy in the dark, the legs sheathed in blanket and curled gracefully like a cocoon toward one corner. No one moved. The hole had become a grave. Erks was filled with a sense of his detachment. Lily bent over and gathered up a handful of sand, which she sprinkled over Ho, then she stood again. Everybody stood—profoundly awkward—each one waiting on the others, and as in the restaurant in Clarkston, Erks felt the moral weight of diverse customs stacking up behind each set of eyes.

Impatient, Erks said, "Take this boy." The words snarled in his throat. He reached for the shovel, but found that Lily held it firm. His body hung off balance.

She moved, breaking the power between them, and began to shovel dirt into the grave, the first shovelfuls landing on Ho's feet and ankles. She worked up the legs. Chang and Lee looked at her out of the sides of their eyes as at one who was committing an atrocity. In the faint light their rigid postures and their faces showed enmity toward one whose place it clearly was not to fill the grave, and then Chang moved, reached into his jacket pocket and came out with something that flashed, something metal, and Erks stiffened, thinking: A knife, again!—but Chang flung the object into the grave and it landed on Ho's neck under the chin —a shiny triangular-shaped thing like a badge, a talisman, something—he surmised—that showed attachment to Ho, or his attachments, but thrown, too, as if to dare Lily. Oblivious, she kept shoveling. Chang and Lee stared at her. Their eyes glittered.

Erks turned away. He went down to the bank where Taam had hunkered, and sat there himself, gazed into the dark, flowing water, and listened to the water, and to the faint, rhythmic swish of sand from the shovel. The desert had gone from red to dark, and now, as the moon rose—one day short of full—the sands and sagebrush took on a silver sheen. He heard a voice speaking in Chinese—Taam's voice. The sounds seemed awkward and block-like in the mouth, and soft, and intoned, chanted. Listening, lost in a reverie of mysteries, and watching the water, he started when he heard singing come from all around him in the desert. His hair prickled and he froze, then realized that it was coyotes, their yipping mixed with the Chinese. He relaxed. Then listening, knowing what it was, he froze again and again his hair prickled at the beauty of it, the hidden circuitry of the desert rising at night to show itself. Rapt, he jumped violently when a body leapt out of the brush behind him and dove into the water in front of him.

The water broke white around the body, which rolled, then vanished under the surface. When the body did not reappear, Erks stood and stepped forward, but stopped, confused. He watched. A head broke surface and a face appeared, and hands reached up to smooth back hair, the figure barely discernible, but unmistakably Lily. Erks looked up at the grave. Against the sky, three bodies were silhouetted. One of them shoveled sand. The speaking in Chinese continued, an oration, maybe, a eulogy. The coyotes continued, caught up by their song. Erks looked back at Lily. Bats, startled away by her plunge, returned and dipped at the water around her. She took a turn or two in the pool, her body bright as a wet stone, elastic as a fish, shimmering, dark and electric.

She stood up in the waist-deep water, naked. Erks watched. She waded to the bank, the water roiling around her knees, then her ankles, and stepping in the sand, she bent, then straightened up, dripping with water, her breasts and one side of her body, cheek, arm, hip, and leg, brighter than the other side in the

219

moonlight and behind her bats dipping in the water. She veered and came toward him, the moon at her back now, and the front of her indiscernible as to detail, big and glossy, rippling with dark. Aroused, his body quickened as she came near. He sensed the drift toward coupling and his mind raced around a point, gudgeon or moral nexus, and the answer came out: No, I won't do this.

Nearly up to him, her breasts, midriff, and eyes shone and became distinguishable, her form frank and melancholy and powerfully erotic, and he felt his morality caving, a slow slide, the matter still hanging up on objections he could not relinquish, but sliding, and then her body swung sideways, as if repelled, and she went past him and into the bushes at his back. He stared forward. He heard her in the bushes. He heard coyotes fighting over a kill. He heard Taam speaking in Chinese. She had been near enough to touch, near enough to hold a leg. He saw bats dipping in the water and thought: It is as if that much satisfies her, as if that was all she wanted.

It was not so. Brought herself to the verge, she desisted, held back by death and menses, and respect, her sense of his morality and of her capacity for betrayal. Dressed, she came out and sat next to him. Her shoulder touched his, familiar, but unexotic to him, and to her, perhaps, sisterly.

"I owe you an apology," she said.

"Oh?"

"We could have buried the boy anytime today."

"I guess there's less worry at dark."

"That's not what I mean. I mean I didn't want to bury him." She paused as if waiting for the words to come. "I didn't want to let him go." She paused again and sighed heavily. "It sounds crazy, but I wanted to carry a dead thing. It was in myself. I have death in myself—my mother, you see, and . . ." She trailed off, then began again. "In a way I was glad when he died, not just because of his suffering, but because then I had death with me. I did not want to let this death go away from me."

She stopped. They sat still and stared at the desert. The

water lapped. The seconds that passed seemed long.

"I wanted to keep it," she said.

He said nothing. A solitary coyote yipped. Above the desert were the moon and stars. His face felt like a window.

"Taam chased me off," she said. "The boys didn't want me filling that grave. I'm all right now."

He said, "Ho was their own kind."

"Yes."

"I want to see Lucas in Reno."

"I know."

She shifted and looked up at the sky, holding her knees and leaning back, and didn't touch him with her shoulder anymore, and said, "Now that I've got rid of Mama and the boy, I feel like I'm carrying Lucas dead. Like I've got his husk rattling around inside. I've got to get rid of it, too. And I—"

He interrupted: "That's none of my concern. I want to see him about money. I want you to take me to him."

"I know that. But it is your concern. There's more to it than you think."

"If there's something you have to do, then do it," Erks said.

"Listen. It was either you or him."

Startled, Erks didn't respond. At their backs, the shoveling and the talk or chanting had ceased. It was time to move. The lone coyote yipped once, the sound like a solitary note taken out of a long melody and played sharply on an oboe at great distance.

Chang and Lee were already in the back seat of the car and Taam stood at the front door. Lily was with Erks at the back. He shoved in his valise, and was about to close the tailgate when he heard something, a crackle of brush, then, looking, saw past the sound, way down the road, something large and darker than sand on the road. Car-sized—he thought, the thought a shock. Then, looking at the sound, he saw a glint just ten yards away, and he thought: Someone, something is there. He thought he saw some-body crouched, and in hand something that glinted. Instantly, he thought: Gun—and in the same instant he heard Lily gasp at his side, and seeing Taam standing in full view at the side of the car, seeing a certain angulation of glint and intent in the dark—the gun pointing at Taam—and Taam just standing there, not seeing, exposed, vulnerable, not even paying attention, a posture that filled Erks with rage, he reached and pulled his crowbar free of the Jiffy strap and in one motion wheeled and threw it, prying end first, hard, at the shape. He heard it hit with a thud, heard a grunt, then he shouted at Taam—something incoherent, a caw —then he ran, circling around the person and coming up from behind, and saw him hunched forward, looking sideways, a big, round face, wrenched with pain, under a bowler hat. In his hand was a gun.

Erks kicked him in the face. The man fell back, lost his hat, struggled, and Erks kicked him on the side of the head, hard, a soccer kick off the instep and heel of his boot. He heard something crunch. The man—a big man, wrestler-sized—flattened out. Erks bent to snatch up the gun and crowbar. The man moaned and rolled his head and looked up at Erks with milky-colored eyes, the face slack, pale, massive and eerie. . . .

Arrested, Erks stopped for an instant and stared, the gun in one hand, the crowbar in the other. Then he moved, left the man, ran back to the car, threw the gun and crowbar in the back, swung the tailgate shut, and went quickly up the side, and shouted at Lily, who was half on her seat, bent over, and hadn't shut her door yet. He jumped in, started the car, and took off down the road. Lily pulled her door shut. He saw a dark car parked, and, his lights playing on it, saw that it was the Ford, and inside it, a figure. He slowed as if to stop, a decoy. It didn't work. The car turned into their path. He sped up and swung off the road into the sand to get around the car. The station wagon spun out and fishtailed. Fighting it, he heard something snap together, and glimpsed Lily lifting a shotgun. She came up with it, the double barrels rising and swinging and nearly touching Taam's chin and hesitating there, and as the station wagon slid sideways and the Ford turned like an insect, awkwardly keeping its nose on the prey, he saw the barrels not moving and felt something delicate and something ponderous hanging in balance, Taam's head and the chamber and butt of the gun, and the weight of the one who held it. Then the gun moved to his own head, and past it, and became delicate, too, arched like a second hand. The gun changed ends. The barrel went out the window. They were abreast of the Ford. Lily leaned into the gun and fired, the sound inside the station wagon like an explosion inside the nose and in some remote place—glass shattering.

He sank his foot into the accelerator and bounced the station wagon back up onto the road. In the mirror he saw the Ford straddling the road, stopped. He expected gunshots. He heard nothing, or just the engine of the station wagon in the silence, and stones, kicked up against the undercarriage, and a ringing left by the shotgun. The station wagon smelled of gunpowder.

They passed another car, a Continental, going the other way.

They turned onto the highway.

Lily set the shotgun butt down on the floor between her legs.

"Your friends were late again," he said.

Taam looked up.

"You're awfully lucky," Erks said. "We're awfully damn lucky. That one was going to shoot you."

"Yes," Taam said. "I am deeply grateful."

"Why did you just stand there? Why didn't you move?"

Taam said nothing. He only shifted in the seat.

Erks said, "How the hell did they know we were there?"

Taam touched his arm lightly. "We have to stop for gas."

Erks glanced at the gauge. It marked virtually empty.

"Shit!"

They had nearly passed through the magical center that delineated one side of outside Rome from the other. He braked and turned into the station and spoke now to Lily. "Stash that gun."

He got out to hustle the attendant, the proprietor, a man who wanted to talk. He asked where they were headed. He spoke of the weather, the night, the moon. He tried to sell Erks rocks. He said he had geodes, agate, and tourmaline. Erks responded perfunctorily and stood at the tailgate so as to be near the pistol he had tossed in the back. Now he would have used a gun. No one came.

From Rome, he drove. But he would have to stop to get some sleep for the sake of the haul to San Francisco. The face of their assailant was stuck in his mind—Oriental, expansive across the cheeks, and more than just pale, actually white, and the hair, a crazy shock of it loose from under the lost hat, white, too, and the eyes milk-colored.

He told Taam.

Taam said, "It's the albino."

"You know him?"

"Of him."

The headlights made a tunnel and beyond that the desert was lit by the moon, which had the effect of making the desert look white, or silver, or as though in daylight the desert could be white as snow.

"How did they know we were there?"

The question was intended for Lily.

She didn't reply.

Taam said, "They probably knew we were carrying a body. They probably knew where we had to stop for gas."

Erks leaned forward and looked at Lily.

She shifted, but kept staring through the windshield.

Between them, Taam was the fulcrum point.

Finally she spoke. "Taam's right."

"Oh?"

"I called him, but he told me where to stop. He said to stop just past Rome. But we didn't. I told you to pull off before Rome. They found us, that's all."

"Him?"

"Lucas."

At his side, Erks felt Taam's body rise.

"I was confused," she said.

"But your confusion was used to Lucas' advantage."

"Not now. Not finally. Back there it was yours, damn it. Ours."

224

Despite everything, he liked the fact that she refused to grovel.

He said, "All right."

Except for cars coming the opposite direction—two or three of them—they had the road to themselves. An hour out of Rome, he stopped on the shoulder to change with Lily. "Get this rig into Reno," he said. They moved fast, not wishing to waste a moment. He got into the back, lay down, and pulled his hat over his face and tried his best to be drowsy. She drove. He was not the least bit drowsy. Drowsiness he needed, the lip to the mouth of sleep. He could not get comfortable. He was cramped even without Ho, without the shovel—and that, the shovel, he realized with a jolt, they had left at the grave, their extraordinary measures rendered meaningless by a shovel left stuck in the sand right where the grave had been dug. He would not mention it. He would forget it. He could not forget it.

He sat up again and looked for headlights out the back window. There were none, but only the desert, magical and silver, as flat and spacious as the ocean, and the car like a boat—soft suspension—but here in the back compartment a certain rigidity as if felt through deck from bow and in their wake a dark cut of road through the expanse. He liked the desert. If he could have slept, his dreams might not have troubled him. It was hard to fall asleep when one feared for one's life. They crossed the Nevada line. On one side was a general store. On the other side the town of McDermitt welcomed them with neon: Dancing, Cocktails, Slots, Roulette. . . . It passed suddenly, a splash of glitter out of the bright sand. The others in the car were silent. But he sensed in the car an air of community, desperate, unavoidable, the result of attack and their common frailty. He lay down on his side like a child and fell into a deep, fermenting reverie, then into sleep. His dreams were calm, as abstract as the desert itself—the desert route to Winnemucca, the road an endless line, straight, and the desert slightly canted like a dish resting on a knife because of the mountains to the east, the Santa Rosas. The mountains slowly closed in on the route, constricted the alkali basin in the shape

225

of a V, the apex Winnemucca, and they lifted the edge of the desert on one side. It took a lot of space to live here. A dream here took up a lot of space. It was Paiute space. "Diggers," they were called. They knew the distance from root to root. The roots became points in Erks' abstract dream.

He slept through to Winnemucca and awoke there, startled, when Lily stopped for gas. He didn't get out. He propped himself up on his elbow and looked out from under the brim of his hat in a daze and saw an incandescent parabola of façades and neon —24-hour restaurants, cafés, clubs, casinos—and directly across the street a place with a line of wooden Indians out front and a flashing sign that spelled out KIDDIE FUNLAND, a place to stash children while the parents gambled. A small sign advertised "Childcare Specialists," and through the plate-glass windows Erks saw brightly lit pinball machines, an arcade, a whole training ground. . . . He saw no children. The inside of the place was a chemical densening of the town itself, a hot spot, a dime-sized rash on the desert. What McDermitt had hinted at, Winnemucca fully promised Reno would fulfill.

The car rocked when Lily got back in. Erks watched as they hooked onto Interstate 80, the road to Reno, the road to San Francisco, and back the other direction to Salt Lake City. The road followed the watersheds—dry and wet—it followed the course of the Central Pacific Railroad. They passed a switching yard. There was a myriad of rails in this town, a lot of trains waiting on the tracks in this town, which was another terminus, another axis, named after a Northern Paiute who wished to fight, father of Sarah, who became herself wife of John Truckee. . . .

Erks, his mind alive with space, did not exactly sleep. He lay back, pulled his hat over his face, and neither thought nor dreamed, nothing that rational or that irrational; it was not so much sleep as a kind of half-wakeful meditation, luminous and true, which refreshed the mind: the Paiutes had lived here, and there had been little of the hierarchic in their lives, not in social structure, not in matters of the spirit, not in what they ate—

226

cottontail and jackrabbit, gopher, rat, muskrat, mouse, squirrel, chipmunk, raccoon, bobcat, badger, beaver, dove, blackbird, owl, woodpecker, robin, bluebird, quail, loon, duck, goose, mud hen, grouse, trout, sunfish, ant, caterpillar, bee egg, cricket and grasshopper, and wada, and sunflower, camas, chokecherry, blueberry, and horse. . . . For years the Paiutes, dwellers of this place, the American *agrapha*, the unwritten, had regarded the horse as something to eat.

The Paiutes took on the color of all things alive and the way and speed of all things alive, thus took the desert inside their skin. There was no time here, not enough time for anything in the old days, no time to be alive here where the margin of survival was toe-high, no time for dancing. "Diggers," they were called, and the weak were allowed to die, deformed infants and the infirm were sometimes killed, and the rites of burial were condensed to next to nothing by utility, the need to move on, to keep moving, no time, no time for anything, only space.

Maybe Taam had seen Ho in the same way from the start, maybe from that perspective of necessity. And Lily . . . she had her necessities. By degrees, Erks fell deeper into a sleep as white and timeless as the South Pole, then, by degrees, he awoke, and sat up, and leaned against the window, half slept, half watched as they passed the towns and exits to towns: Nightingale, Hotsprings, Fernley and Wadsworth, the exit to the Walker Reservation by route of the Wovoka Highway. . . . He was awakened by the lights, bursts of them inhaling the phosphorescence of the desert. He did not move, his body cramped and twisted in knots. He did not move to find the ache.

He heard snatches of conversation from the front seat, the words ghostly, as indefinite as ghosts. He heard Lily say something, then Taam. Had he even been able to make out the words, he would likely have been too groggy to grasp them.

They passed by Fernley. A mining operation emitted swirling white dust from its white towers. North of here, between here and the southern tip of Pyramid Lake, lay the Big Bend of the Truckee River and the site of battle between whites and Northern Paiutes. He remembered, he meditated: the Paiutes became hierarchic, or gathered around their chiefs, only for seasonal gatherings—for antelope or deer drives, rabbit drives, during the fishing season—or for war. White men shot the "Diggers" like coyotes in the desert, but later, when the Paiutes came together for war, then they rode horses and wore hide clothing, and took commands from Chief Numaga—who, like Joseph, the Nez Percé, seeing the ultimate powerlessness of Indian against white, had not wanted war. Numaga had argued with Winnemucca over war, protested war by fasting to the brink of death, but, like the legend of Joseph, the Nez Percé, Numaga was a master strategist, too, and he defeated in 1860 first the Susanville posse, then fought mustered troops to a standstill in the hills, employing, like the Nez Percé on their famous "retreat," all the principles of guerrilla strategy, the feint, false advance, and collapsing withdrawal suited to the desert, to rock and sand, the warriors vanishing before the soldiers' eyes into the space of their merciless and exquisite desert.

Erks fell asleep, then awoke when he heard Lily speak his name. He didn't remember what else she had said.

He could not hear Taam.

At Clark Station they passed a power plant, vast and sudden, incandescent. Then the illuminated road signs began in earnest their conversation with travelers: Nevada Lodge, Harrah's Club, the Eldorado, Ponderosa Ranch, Sambo's, McDonald's, Red Garter Steak House, Sundowner Casino . . . Jesse Beck's Hotel and Casino, Harrah's Automobile Collection . . . Club Cal Neva, Motel Mark Twain . . . They were within a few miles of Reno.

He heard Lily say, "I don't like it."

He heard Taam murmur some assent, some assurance.

He heard her say, "But I don't know how else to do it."

They talked about a door, something about a door, the sense lost to Erks. He looked at his watch—it was 1:15 A.M.—then, moving, straightening up, he groaned. His body hurt. "Do what?"

No response.

They had passed through Sparks and now approached Reno.

The lights of Reno were visible, making a halo in the sky. The station wagon penetrated Reno's sprawl.

He heard one word out of Lily's statement: ". . . money . . ."

He heard Taam this time: "That's good."

"What?" Erks said.

No response.

They entered Reno. Lily swung the car off Interstate 80 and down the ramp onto Wells, then turned onto East 2nd, and Erks, sitting up in the back, rocked with the turns. His body tingled, fully awake. He made note of the streets so he could get back out of town. The lights came up on him from behind, intensifying as they approached the center of town. The voices in the front seat had ceased. Erks looked out to the side, holding his face close to the window. The streets were crazy with neon and full of people. Lily stopped at the intersection of East 2nd and Center and Erks looked out at Harrah's Casino, a Rolls-Royce in the window, wide doors open to the street, and rows of slot machines, blackjack tables, and people inside and loitering just outside in the half light, an underwater light, the light of fog.

Lily turned. Just past the Cal Neva, she turned up an alley and from where Erks sat the lights dwindled to a slot at the end of the alley. The car stopped. The walls on either side were high and close. Erks saw Lily and then Taam moving to get out.

Suddenly claustrophobic, he said, "Hey!" It came out a croak. "Open the damn window!"

Lily looked at him through the glass. Her voice was muted. "Sorry."

❧ 11 ❧

Ruby sat at the dining room table with coffee, considering the diseases that tainted leaves, infested root and stalk, and fulminated in the fruit.

Fungus, mildew, rust, ring rot, bulb rot, neck rot, soft rot, cottony rot, white rot, black scurf, canker and curly top, virus and mosaic, club root, blight, wilt, drop, scab, and smut.

Through the window she stared at the lilac, not fully leafed out, not in bloom, late, but the tips of stalks were swelled and ready to bud. It would not be long, any day now. Lilacs drew aphids and mildew. Nasturtiums could repel the aphids. Mildew the lilacs would survive, but out in the garden it would ruin the heads of broccoli and cauliflower. Planting always carried these matters to her mind—disease and pest; they rode in on the tail of planting time and gained a morbid sway. Too cool yet to show them, the soil held them secret from last year, the spores in their niduses, the larvae in their cocoons. Only fire could touch them now. Just when the seedlings took hold, these possibilities of scourge would steal from the ground and across the fields and out of the woods to feed.

Wireworm, spider mite, grasshopper and aphid, onion thrips, cabbage looper, bean weevil, hornworm, fly moth, maggot, cutworm, beetle, earwig, and slug.

Bird.
Gopher.
Mole.
Porcupine.
Possum.
Skunk.
Deer.
Coyote.

The truth was that the coyotes were no threat except when they lured Rex away or broke into the chicken coop, and besides, Wes had a feeling for them. All the possum did was attack chickens and, it seemed, cats. The chickens were a liability. Skunks, too, bothered them, and the eggs, and sprayed the dog, but porcupines only girdled the tops of young pines or shot the dog with needles, though Ruby had known a porcupine to nibble off a cabbage head, and what deer came up from the creek bottom to feed in the meadows were still arresting, astonishing when they leaped away, though last spring one had come over the fence and eaten off the early lettuce and chard, and the birds—especially swallows, martins, and nighthawks, which ate aphids, and the hummingbirds, which ate ants, lice, and caterpillars, and the woodpeckers and flickers, which drilled for bugs, and the wrens, and others, many others, and the pair of barn owls, which ate gophers—she actually encouraged, though they—the birds—did eat their share of berries, too. She fed the birds in the winter to keep them near. Gophers and moles she could do without. The gophers ate the plants. The moles ate the earthworms. She wanted the worms. Gophers and moles she trapped—with marginal success—but did not poison because she wanted the birds. The balance was so complex, and her leverage so uncertain, but even that, the hazard of it all, she did finally love, or she did most of the time. Not now. Something was wrong. Maybe it was just the morbid power of spring, the long, rising slant of light which raised a sadness sharper than the dullest hours of autumn and on its heels the hot, dark quickening of memory. Beyond the lilac

231

she saw Walter Hugaboon's winter wheat, the distant field light green, seedling-colored, a backdrop to the snarled web of dark-green lilac leaf and dark-gray branch. A good year so far, good promise, the wheat thrived. The snow would do no damage. A hard frost could.

It grew later in the morning. Ruby sipped coffee and told herself to get a grip on herself. She didn't know what was wrong. It wasn't the stranger out in her husband's shop. What was wrong had been wrong before he got here, though he didn't help. His deviousness didn't help at all. And it wasn't just Wes being gone, or the book on mass murder she'd been reading, or even the season, the weather, but something in addition which collected all matters, or governed them, and raised this concupiscent, libidinous longing, a finger curled out of a deep, melancholy hollow. She looked at her hands, gathered around the coffee mug. They looked old.

She had driven the man out to get the motorcycle, which, she observed immediately, was pointed west, not east.

"Didn't you say you were headed for Idaho?"

Sandman had anticipated this: "I tried to get back to town."

Ruby turned a U and stopped the pickup just past the bike, then backed up to it. She had noted the New York plates. Parked there on the shoulder of the highway, the bike looked light enough. They took the front end first, gripping the frame and fork members on either side, but it was far from light, and surprised by the weight, they had to set it back down. Matt watched them solemnly through the rear window of the pickup.

"We have to get it in," she said. "Every time we try it'll get harder."

Sandman nodded and rubbed his hands together. "All right."

They tried again, struggled, held on, and got the front wheel over the lip of the pickup bed, then held the cycle to balance it. Ruby moved to the back wheel. Sandman followed. They shoved, gaining about a foot on the fulcrum point and lifting the front wheel up off the bed. The cycle rested on the frame and pointed crazily upward like a grasshopper reaching for a leaf. They grabbed the back of the cycle, lifted and shoved. The cycle slid forward on the skid plate and rocked, and Ruby clutched at it, strained against the weight, which Sandman seemed to be relinquishing. "Push," she said. "Goddamn it, push!" They pushed and lifted, though she felt—still—the weight going away from her, toward what should have been his share, and clutching desperately at it, she saw cloudless sky, and beyond his head silhouettes of mountains, steaming fields, and grinding against the weight, doubling, bowing to hang on, her forehead nearly touching the fender, she saw spoke, sprocket, dark chain and chrome hub, then felt the weight rest. They had it up, balanced, the rear wheel hanging just free over the edge of the bed.

She stood up straight. She arched her back and looked up. From the strain, she saw the sky filled with dancing slivers of light.

"You are strong," he said.

Ruby glared at him through the spokes of the wheel. "Then you didn't plan to stop in Davenport."

"I beg your pardon."

"You had driven by. You didn't plan to stop in Davenport."

"Ah, I see." His upper lip curled, showing his teeth. "I expected to meet Wes and Lucas in Idaho."

"This morning?"

"When I broke down I hoped to catch him here. Besides," he said, raising his eyebrows and nodding his large head, "I broke down."

"Wes left yesterday."

He paused and smiled again. "I wouldn't know about that. I was to meet them in Idaho."

She stared at him, then took hold of the motorcycle. "Let's get this thing in."

They lifted and pushed it in so that the front wheel thumped against the head of the bed. She climbed into the bed to tie the bike down. He waited on the ground. She saw that it was possible: Wes had told her that he would go through Rathdrum again today, but she knew the man was lying about something. She didn't know what, or what to make of it, or what danger it posed, if any, or with what gravity the man should be taken. Probably none. At the least, it was insulting, the man cutting a runway into her life. She jerked the rope around a post and tied a loop knot.

He waited on the ground. Pressed, he had taken his chances. Lucky, what he said had let him out. He had no idea how. The steady breeze, the building chinook, blew into his face, the wind of ghosts and lies.

They drove back. Ruby wondered why she granted him the foothold of his broken-down machine. In her distraction, she hadn't suggested that he try to start it again before they loaded it. She didn't even ask what was wrong with the machine until they were almost to the farm.

And he said, "I don't know yet."

"What do you think?"

He shrugged.

"What was the problem?"

"It wouldn't run."

"What did it do?"

He lowered his heavy eyelids and lifted his chin so that he looked like an embossed figure on an old coin against the window frame, affected, and he spoke languidly. "It died. I ran it down a hill. It started and died again."

Matt sat between them, silent, his bright, watchful eyes just above the level of the dash. Ruby touched his head softly, his hair, smooth and dark. The boy didn't move.

"How long have you known Lucas?"

"Only in business."

She paused. "What is your business?"

"I am an accountant."

She looked at him, finding him haughty, a pretender, a malingerer, and detesting his condescension, but thinking: That, too, could be—and she asked the same question Lily had asked: "On a motorcycle?"

"I should be in a Jaguar?"

She braked and downshifted for the turn into the driveway. The motorcycle rocked gently against the rope in the bed. "All the way from New York?"

"Why not?" he said, smiling heavily. "Income tax is federal."

She spoke without thinking and immediately regretted it: "So is interstate crime."

Her hands looked old. Her short, powerful fingers were chafed, wrinkled, and knobby at the knuckles. From washing dishes, watering stock, from digging her fingers into the ground to plant, from contact with the wet, her skin was dry. She could feel the calluses on her palms against the coffee mug. As if left out to the weather, her hands showed wear beyond her years. She stared at them as if they were disembodied things, two old birds lying on their sides.

She supposed she'd have to take something out for the stranger to eat.

Sandman had found a milk case and moved it over to the cycle so he could sit. He looked up as soon as Ruby came in the door, her body slanting through the space of light and scattering the motes. She carried a tray.

Matt sat on top of a bench against the wall, playing with one of his father's magnetic screwdrivers and a small heap of steel shavings. She set a plate with a sandwich and a glass of milk down next to him, then passed a plate and a glass of iced tea to Sandman.

"I hope you eat ham sandwiches."

"Thank you," Sandman said, holding the plate and glass against his chest like bricks.

She eyed his work. He had rolled her husband's tool case over and tools and parts were scattered on the floor around him. She eyed the parts, finding among them no sense, no continuity —several bolts, an engine inspection cover, the battery cover, a piece off the seat. On the bike he had the seat raised and several wires disconnected.

"Did you check the gas?"

An amazed expression filled Sandman's face, and he set the

235

plate and glass down and rose and unscrewed the cap and peered into the tank, then looked at her, relieved. "It has gas."

"Do you have juice?"

Sandman smiled, curled his upper lip as if to suck something through his teeth. "Juice?"

"Do your lights work?"

He flipped the switch on. They didn't work.

"You'll have to connect those wires to see."

"Oh?"

He sat down, reconnected the wires, stood, and flipped the switch on again. The lights worked.

"Try to start it."

He switched on the electric starter. The engine whined, kicked over and ran for an instant, then died.

"How's your compression?"

Sandman stared at her.

"Kick it."

He looked uncertainly at the side of the bike, at the kick starter with which the bike had come equipped in addition to the electrics. She tried it herself. It resisted her leg, sliding and catching on the tangs of the gear.

She squatted beside the bike, pulled the spark plug cables, held them against the engine casing, and told him to turn the bike over again. She held her face close to see. When he turned the starter a sharp jolt ran through her fingers and she saw the spark, strong and blue.

"You've got good spark."

"How do you know?"

"I thought you said you could fix this yourself."

"I suppose I could."

"Let's check the gas line."

She pointed at it.

He stared at it.

She picked up a crescent wrench and handed it to him.

He used it awkwardly to back the nut off the flange.

"Now turn the engine over again, quickly. Just touch it."

He did so and the line spurted gasoline.

"You see. You've got gas. You've got compression and spark and you've got gas. There's nothing much wrong with this machine."

Sandman took a bite of his sandwich.

Jesus—she thought—I've got to get rid of him. "How's your air filter?"

She pointed at it and handed him another wrench.

He pulled the cover off and the filter fell out. It was nearly black with dirt.

"Good Christ!" she said. "If you took your carburetor apart do you think you could put it back together?"

"Oh, sure."

She looked at him askance.

"Where'd you learn all this?"

"I used to race stock cars."

"No kidding?"

"Just like you do Lucas Tenebrel's income tax."

He backed off several steps, nodding like a rooster. "We all have our specialties."

"Uh huh." She looked up at the ceiling of the metal building, up at the cobwebs which spanned rafters and joists, then down at him. "This is what you do. Pull the plugs and check them, wash that filter in gas, then dry it, take your carburetor down and clean it and blow it dry."

She got him a can of gas to clean the filter and showed him where the carburetor cleaner was and how to use it. "But don't put your hands in it," she said. "It's strong." She showed him the air hose to dry the parts off with and how to pull the carburetor and told him just how far to break it down—not far. The more she said, the more his fortification was attacked, the more the animus within the walls stiffened, the more he wished to strike and conquer. He followed her closely, stood near, cloyed, and even allowed his fingers to linger on her hands when she gave him a socket wrench to fit the plugs. He gazed at her with wide, steady eyes.

"Call me when you've done that."

He stood and sipped his tea.

She looked around the metal building. She hadn't been in the shop for some time. Her husband was here, embodied by the packed shelves, and by the saws and lathes and drills and punches which stood on the concrete floor, and up against the far wall his acetylene and arc welders, and jacks, chains, portable winch, axle stands, countless parts and tools, hosing and cable. He was here in the orderly arrangement of equipment, and the floor, though even he used the shop rarely now, was swept clean. A drill punch stood poised, a big thing shaped like a C clamp, with a table and a velocitized mouth. Attached to a rafter above it was the fluorescent light fixture her husband's father had been installing a year ago, standing on the drill press table, and the line to the socket had somehow tapped the feed conduit to the power machinery —600 amps of juice—and her husband had come through the doorway to find him there, and she after him, hearing her husband's choked shout, and they both stood, stopped cold by the sight of the old man thus, singed, grounded by the drill press, and dead of a charge which, it was said, had melted the bone in his legs. She saw him now as if he were there still, one hand lifted to salute them, his face rubbery. She could still hear the low, incessant crackling, and she could still smell singed hair and flesh and the frightening, spacious odor of ozone.

In that agony her husband was here, in that and in the idle equipment, behemoth on the floor, and in the stacks of steel plate and rod and angle iron which with his father he had fabricated and machined. They had been starting a business. It had been a better time in a way. Though pressed for money and driven half frantic by work, it had been better than this, with him gone half the time and traipsing all over the country, but then—she thought—it was not that she minded his travels, or how he made his money, really, or being home by herself—on the contrary, the world spun too fast on its axis for her to mind any of that—but that somehow she minded its being done for the sake of Lucas and the likes of this one, Sandman. No matter what Sandman claimed, whether or not he was lying, it hardly mattered; he was a bad fit, he couldn't wear who he was, whatever that was, and

238

whether or not he was associated with Lucas—whom she didn't know—in fact or by his lies, that didn't matter either because he was just the sort to gravitate to what she thought Lucas was, the image of command, the fin of a shark splitting the surface of the deep, but in fact all sham, fin only, no shark, the fin fake, hooked up below the surface to some blunt machine. Sandman—like Lucas, who showed his wallet—was just the type, Lucas' shadow, showing his motorcycle or his teeth behind his thick lips or his leather pants or even the bruise on his face, who had to have someone like her husband or herself to prop him up. Was that it? What in God's name was it? Incomplete enough herself, for God's sake, she didn't like having this one around trying to fill out himself with her substance, or her husband's. Was that it? The world did not spin too fast on its axis to object to larceny of her own bone and flesh. Was that it?

She glanced at her son. He played with the screwdriver, stirred the shavings. He held the screwdriver up and gazed at the fan of magnetized shavings attached to the tip, transfixed.

"Mama," he said, "how do these hairs hang on?"

"Eat your sandwich, Matt," she said softly. "It's magnetism."

The boy didn't move. At her side Sandman shifted, made his presence conspicuous. Annoyed with Sandman, she spoke sharply to the boy. "You," she said, pointing, and instantly regretting her tone. "Eat your sandwich."

In the bathroom Ruby washed her hands and face, loosened the top of the shirt and washed her neck and shoulders, and combed her hair slowly, took off the scarf and combed her hair down until it shone and her scalp tingled, then tied the scarf back on and crammed her hair under it. She took out the bottle of lanolin—pure lanolin, dense as pine tar, the oil of wool, sheep hair. Sheepherders' hands, she'd heard, were the softest hands in the world.

She rubbed a glob of it into her palms, slowly breaking it down, and worked it up to her wrists and on the backs of her hands and around her fingers. It took several minutes. She put

239

the stool cover down and sat. She took off her sandals and rubbed lanolin into her chafed, leather-hard feet, the right foot first, around the heel and ball, between toes. It made her calf tingle. She switched feet. Bemused, she stared at the packet of contraceptive pills left open on the shelf above the bathtub, but untouched for a week, her cycle dropped halfway through. Without thinking, without willing it, she had gone off the pill. She had thought of it four days ago, shocked at first by her omission, then intrigued by it, and she hadn't resumed. Was that it? What was it? Slowly, she stroked her feet, the skin lubricated now, the pleasure almost sexual. Above the shelf, the rising chinook hissed through the ajar window. She hadn't told Wes about the pills.

She planted two rows of broccoli, a row of cauliflower, one each of lettuce, chard, and spinach. She cut furrows with the hoe along the string lines she had set up, then dropped the seed into each row, hoed a thin layer of dirt back on each, and tamped methodically with the hoe. Matt came back out to play with his trucks. He'd been good all day, model, in fact, as was his way when he was disturbed.

She stood at the head of the row and surveyed her work, the wind whipping the tails of her shirt. Tomorrow was the full moon, tonight the thirteenth day waxing gibbous, today and tomorrow the last days to plant the early leaf vegetables, which in seeding required the light of the moon. Monday she would plant potatoes, beets, parsnips, kohlrabi, turnips and carrots. Her toes, sticking through the sandals, were dirty again. Matt's trousers were wet and grimy. She had dinner to fix. She had to deal with the bugbear in her husband's shop. Beyond the end of the garden was the fence, the chicken shed, and the heavily timbered slope where the land vanished from sight down into the ravine where Wes and Rex had killed the possum. The rooster crowed from the far side of the shed, his cry smooth as brass, but distant and tossed by the wind, elaborate as lace, as sad as pipe. As twilight approached, the sky grew metallic. The wind seemed to come out of the big hole in the ground to fill the sky. The big hole seemed to suck the color of the sky down into its darkness.

It neared 6:30. She had finished in the garden, watered the stock, put a casserole in the oven, and washed the kitchen floor. The light dwindled. Sandman hadn't shown. She walked across the corridor of wind from the house to the shop and saw him at the far wall, gazing through a window, his back to her. He had put his jacket on and he looked like a dwarf, small body, large head. He didn't hear her come in. He had turned on the fluorescent light above the cycle. The carburetor was spread out in pieces on the newspaper. She squatted, then knelt to study the pieces. The wind, the high chinook, whirled around the walls of the shop.

"I see you got everything else back on," she said.

She heard his feet turn on the concrete, then his footsteps approaching. He had taken the carburetor down farther than he needed to, but it was clean. He stopped beside her. She saw leather legs and outlandish boots. She picked up the float and bowl, and without looking up, said, "These go together."

She put them together, screwed in spring and bracket, and cupping the bowl in the palm of her hand, eyed the remaining pieces—needles, tiny bolts and nuts, valves, flanges, and gaskets —and touched some of them lightly with a fingertip, turned and rearranged them. She had never assembled a carburetor. What had been offhanded in her earlier mechanical advice had now become a jeopardy. She tried to put the pieces in order, to arrange them in an exploded version of the whole. The whole asserted itself and she became more certain. As she grew more certain, the pieces became radiant, the bright, tiny innards the clockwork of the aluminum nutshell she held in her hand. All around her the metal building sighed from the pressure of wind.

Sandman sat on the milk case and watched. Because of her position, the shirt flared between buttons and he could see one naked breast, the soft, tear-shaped prolongation of her nipple. It was not just his nature, but her armored manner, too, her rapt attention as she put the carburetor together—as she actually put it together—and the juxtaposition of flesh and metal, of carnality and steel parts, that fueled his furious desire. She assembled what was to him still subliminal, impossible, and littered—the carburetor. Her nipples rubbed against the inside of her shirt as she moved her hands.

She had the carburetor together and began bolting it onto the engine. The ratchet ticked as she turned in the bolts, then the bolts made a high squeaking sound as she tightened them down.

"Try it now."

"Start it?"

"Turn it over."

He stood and turned the switch on. The engine whined without catching.

She threw up a hand, then found the screwdriver and backed the needle out. "Try again."

The engine coughed.

She backed the needle out another turn. "Again."

The engine kicked over and caught, ran, and kept running, but roughly.

Sandman nodded and smiled, then posed with his hands at his waist and looked down at her, his eyes hooded by his heavy lids.

Ruby reached across, grabbed the throttle, and gunned the bike. "Keep it running!"

He put his hand on the throttle next to hers.

She bent over the carburetor and backed out the needle, enriching the mixture, and listened. When the sputter flattened out, she kept turning until it began to choke and almost died, then turned it back quickly, and rolled the needle slowly to and fro until she found dead center, the heart of the sound, a pulse as tangible as heartbeat.

She looked up. "Now rev it."

He gave it a little gas.

"Gun the fucker!" She stood and shoved his hand off the throttle and unwound it until the engine roared, blanking out all sound of wind. The engine had a wobble, a large undulation of sound. "Hold it!" she shouted.

He did so, but at arm's length and wincing at the noise.

She went to work on the main jet. She knew about this, main and low-speed jets. The rest of it had been luck. As she backed the needle out, the wobble narrowed to nothing and the roar of the engine was transformed into pure scream which rattled the metal walls of the shop. She stayed on her knees for a moment, listening. The sound made the bones in her head buzz and ran down her back and she felt an ache in her legs. She rose, swaying slightly. They were surrounded by a fog of blue exhaust.

"Damn!" she said, taken by her success. "I'll be damned!"

He mouthed the word: "What?"

She pushed his hand off the throttle. The engine burbled down to idle. She goosed the engine, let it drop back, and goosed it again. The whine arched gracefully. When she switched the cycle off, it was as if the floor of the building had dropped fifty feet into the ground and briefly the sound of the wind was airy, decorative. She felt light.

Disappointed, he said, "That's remarkable."

With the work, half her hair had fallen free of the scarf and she had a grease smudge on her cheek. Her face glowed. She looked strong enough to break the spine of a large dog across her knee.

Sandman hadn't expected this. The black of night filled the windows at Ruby's back. With the carburetor off, he had felt assured of the night. Before she came in, he had watched the sun go down over the flatland to the west, and had felt once again the menace of this space, big and violent and empty. Even with the carburetor on, he had not expected the bike to run, believing as he did in the insolubility of mechanical trouble. But the cycle ran. That became a given, a sum arrived at, and his mind turned to ways of accommodating to this sum certain matters—food, the hour, the wind, where to sleep, comfort, affection. He searched for words to establish his position; whether lies or not, it didn't matter. Words he regarded as numbers, as things one looked down on like so many beads to be arranged according to need, as fluid integers, as flimsy as ideas, as consumable as flesh. He ran his eyes coldly up Ruby's body.

243

"You have quite a touch."

"Touch?" She gazed at him fiercely, but she could have gazed at just about anything, a fence post, a stuffed polar bear, a mask carved into a tree. The wind raged. The building boomed.

"Yes," he said. His bottom lip drooped and the upper one curled. "It's late."

"Touch," she said, unable to imagine what he meant by that, touch. "Well." Incapable of anything beyond monosyllables, she stared over his shoulder through the doorway at a spot of light in the darkness, bright, sharp, mobile as flame, and as she watched in something like terror, the light elongated into a blade, came nearer, took on a light-colored ragged shape, still moving, like a corn stalk dancing in the night, a phantom out of the warm chinook, a spirit, an idea which for an instant she thought came faster than it did, flew straight for her face. It was the light of the moon, she saw now, playing on white pajamas, Matt, running. He became himself in the doorway, and kept coming, and she watched, terrifically moved, finding him to be as strange who he was as he had been before he became so, her boy. He threw himself against her and clutched her leg.

She cradled his head in her hand. "Matt?"

"I'm scared."

Alarmed, she held his head tighter. "Of what, Matt?"

"The house is shaking."

"It's only the wind," she said, then straight to Sandman, "I can give you a bite to eat before you go."

He scratched his belly slowly through the leather, low, near the crotch. "In this wind?"

Wireworm.
Spider mite.
Mosaic.
Black scurf.
Cabbage looper.
Skunk.

"We eat in the house," she said, and he laughed immediately and insistently, too eagerly, curling his lips grotesquely, alert to any movement, any scutter in the brush, and she saw her joke, what she had even known was a joke, but had not intended for laughter. The grip of Matt's arms on her leg had tightened and it struck her quite suddenly—it was not the wind; this man had made the boy afraid of the wind.

"I would appreciate something to eat," he said. He touched his ear lobe and swayed toward her, a leather thing. "I wish I'd had the chance to talk to your husband. I doubt that there's much point now in my going on to Idaho."

Not even remotely tempted by the man's obvious proposition, but complimented as if by the devil, she was gratified even as one might be gratified by the craving expressions of a sadist. His tenacity made her feel vicious. One had to root out such mischief. To do so was a reparation. Outside, the wind soughed and wound, and blew everything that was light against what was not light, and tossed the flesh up against scruples. "The wind will die. Have something to eat and go to hell."

❧12❧

So the older Maps of America make the Land from the Mage-
lane Straits to the South Sea, runne much West, when as they
rather are contracted somewhat Easterly from the North. The
like is justly supposed of their false placing, Quivira, and I know
not (nor they neither) what Countries they make in America,
to run so farre North-westward, which Sir Francis Drakes Voyage in that Sea (his Nova Albion, being little further Westward
than Aquatulco) plainely evince to be otherwise. Yeah the late
Map of California found to be an Iland, the Savages discourses
in all the Countries Northwards and Westwards from Virginia:
fame whereof filled my friend Master Dermer with so much
confidence, that hearing of strange Ships which came thither
for a kinde of Ure, or earth, the men using forkes in their diet,
with Caldrons to dresse their meate, &c. things nothing suit-
able to any parts of America, hee supposed them to come from
the East, neere to China or Japan, and therefore he made a
Voyage purpose to discover: but crossed with divers disasters,
hee return to Virginia, frustrate of accomplishment that yeare,
but fuller of confidence, as in a Letter from Virginia he sig-
nified to me, where death ended that his designe soone after.
But how often are the usuall Charts rejected by experience in
these Navigations, in this worke recorded? Painters and Poets
are not alwayes the best Oracles.

Master Brigges, in Purchas His Pilgrimes

The alley was dark, but gathered garish off-light from the town
so that from inside the back of the Vista Cruiser everything
looked ultraviolet, or as if he were in a bathysphere underwater.
Lily's face pulled back from the window, a planet-shaped sea
creature in the weird light, blue with yellow highlights. Erks
turned and saw Taam moving around the front of the car toward
a door which led into a building. His khaki trousers and cane
basket and his face looked yellow. Anything lighter than the
darkness of the alley and the side of the brick building took up
light from the air. Then Lily, carrying her carpetbag . . . He saw

her pass alongside the car, a giant squid-sized purple fish with yellow highlights swimming on its tail, and he thought: She's screwing me. He whirled around and felt for the latch to the tailgate, found it, pulled it and kicked the gate. It didn't move.

He jerked back around and climbed over the seat next to Chang, going headfirst, then dragging his legs over and bracing himself with his hands on Chang's legs, and he felt Chang's body go hard, stiffening for a fight, and, his knees on the edge of the seat now, he grasped Chang's arms near the shoulders and felt them about to thrash loose, and, their faces nearly touching, he saw Chang's head reared back and his lips curled, his eyes and teeth shining in the strange light—a creature that could bite. He thought: Steady, steady, son—and still holding the boy with one hand, he reached out with the other, located the door handle, swung the door open, slid out, found ground, straightened up, and saw Taam vanish through the doorway into the building, and behind him Lily, going in.

He moved after her, calling, "Hey!"

She went in.

He caught the door to the building by the knob before it fell shut, and hesitated, searching the darkness within. He saw Lily, her body moving away from him, then, over her shoulder or to one side of her, he saw a shaft of light from a door opened at the other end of what appeared to be a hallway, and he saw Taam slowly becoming visible as he approached the light. A small figure flitted into the end of the hall and fell against Taam. Taam and the figure embraced, the two diminutive in the distance, silhouettes, or one tangled silhouette. He heard a cry—a woman —something he had not considered—a woman, a wife, a sister, or a mother awaiting Taam's return. At either end of the dark cord, the hallway, there was light, an embrace at one end passing light from body to body in a knot, and himself at the other end, an organ of reception, a tablet, seeking light, and then Lily's body swayed between them, blocking out the light.

He moved forward, meaning to follow, but as soon as he moved, something came slowly sideways, a massive thing sliding gently out of greater darkness into the doorway like an embankment slipping, then filling the doorway, a man, coming forward now, growing discernible, head, arms, hands, and looming torso, a doorkeeper, then the face, broad and unreadable, the eyes catching light. Erks found himself releasing the door. The man stepped back and the door shut. Erks stood for a moment, then tried the door. It was locked. He stood for another moment, ruminating, regarding himself as the greatest of fools.

But he did what Taam had said, drove down the alley, found the small lot with a stall marked as Taam had said it would be and a car in it, a Cadillac. He parked the station wagon, got out, and tried the key Taam had given him on the Cadillac. It opened the door. He tried it on the ignition. The engine started and purred just like a Cadillac—a great deal of waiting, heavily insulated power. He went back to the station wagon to roust the boys and gather up the goods. Lily had left her shotgun and a box of shells in the front, the barrel of the gun propped against the far door —the mark of her counterfeit, her refuse. Without knowing exactly why, he broke the shotgun down and packed it and the shells into his valise. They joined the two pistols, those of Taam and the man in the bowler hat, and Chang's knife, the totem pole, the two stones . . . specimens.

He locked up the station wagon and kept the key, and then packed the boys' two suitcases into the back seat of the Cadillac. He locked the Cadillac. He did these things, made the transfer systematically as if it were procedure without knowing to what the procedure was connected—to some slippage, some vestige. . . . He had his doubts as to whether or not he would find either car when he returned, or Taam, but he intended to look for Lucas himself—that, too, a procedure he must follow. He had on his coat and hat and would not leave his valise. Despite the guns, the crowbar, he would carry it. It was heavy when he lifted it.

The three of them walked back up the alley and past the door toward the light. There was a rising buzzing sound, a sound everywhere in the air as the trailing of neon was everywhere, and both sound and neon took the air over when Erks and the boys stepped out of the alley and onto the street among the night

248

population, the diehards, those who considered half-past one on Sunday morning the time to run on luck, those for whom this hour might as well have been day. The people thronged the sidewalks and the casinos.

He moved a distance down the block, then entered the casino—the Royale—behind which he surmised the hallway from the alley must have passed. The place was wired together with noise and light. Chang and Lee stayed close, stopping when he stopped, moving when he moved. He attempted to locate inside what he had seen from the outside. They moved inward, then laterally in the direction of the alley among the crowd and ranks of slot machines, over which Erks, because of his height, could see. When he found a vantage point he stopped to reconnoiter.

At his back and extending to the street were the quarter slots, then the half-dollar slots, and he stood among the dollar slots, and before him were the blackjack tables, then roulette and craps. The stakes increased inward to the center—a long cashier's cage. At one end of the cage a girl in a bikini stood on a platform and spun the keno wheel and above her head a computerized board flashed numbers. Beside her a man in a powder-blue suit spoke into a microphone, his voice haranguing constantly just over the din, announcing what round of keno this was, what the winning number was, who was singing in the lounge, what began next and what began after that. . . . From either side of the cage and along the length of the back wall ran a waist-high barrier. Behind it were several secure-looking doors, and two big men in red blazers—former athletes from the looks of them, retired linemen or punched-out heavyweights. One opened a gate in the barrier for a small man in a black suit, then a door. The man in the suit went inside to the offices, the corridors. . . .

Erks considered that he could simply go up to the cage and ask to see Lucas, or Taam. But wariness kept him from it, a sense of risk in being marked as one to so inquire, in so committing himself.

To his right the casino stretched through an archway. He wanted to investigate that, and he glanced back to draw Chang

249

and Lee with him, but stopped, attracted by their interest in an old woman in a baggy purple double-knit dress at the slot machine next to them. He'd been looking right over her head. Her pallid skin hung in folds, and she was heavily made up—lips, eyes, and cheeks colored. She looked like death trying to pass for life. Her hands shook when she reached into her worn canvas purse and took out a silver dollar. She fumbled with the coin before slipping it into the slot. She edged forward and listened to the coin fall, then grasped the lever and swung it down with all her strength—a woman's gesture. The lever could have been the handle of a wringer washer or an iron lowered to a shirt, or an oven door, opened, the motion, however arduous to her, a familiar one. When she released the lever, she hung on to the machine for balance. Her lips moved as the figures spun.

With Chang and Lee, Erks watched the dead thing come to life. He thought: This interests them. The woman was oblivious to their watching. They could have touched her and she would not have known. She spoke, her body swaying, the words not audible, a secret code, maybe, a glossolalia, or maybe a specter sang to the woman and she translated for the machine.

Chang and Lee leaned toward her. When the figures came up in the machine's favor, Chang and Lee leaned back and the woman recommenced the ritual, reached into her purse, took out another coin. Erks touched Lee and beckoned the two of them to come with him through the archway. They turned to follow. They had a light of amusement in their eyes—the first time Erks had seen that in them—a small light behind the chips of stone. He himself had found the noise, the clatter, and the air of excitement moving into his blood, and the sight of chips stacked on tables—money. One could quickly be overcome here.

He gazed at the wall as he moved. What transpired on the other side of it he wanted to measure even if he could not see it, or directly know it.

A thick-set man in his late thirties worked with a stack of papers at the head of a long table. He looked to be a breed, half Chinese, half white. He had heavy lips and a patch of orange freckles on each of his cheeks, but Oriental eyes heavily magnified by a pair of horn-rimmed glasses, which gave him the owlish look of an accountant, a bureaucrat, a permanent underling, of one who spent his life among the papers and documents left in the trails of other lives. He looked like one who had begun as a wrestler and ended up a clerk. His hands were large and soft, and they moved gently through the papers, and they had freckles on their backs, too.

A contract lawyer, his name was Freckles U. His tie was undone, his collar unbuttoned, his French cuffs soiled, and his hair stuck out in tufts over his ears. He was late. The principals were here and Hiram Chow, his boss, had just arrived. U moved quickly through the stack of papers before him, checked each sheet, then set it on one of five stacks to his left, and—obsessive —each time he added a sheet to a stack he picked up the stack and squared it off by striking it sharply on two sides against the table, set the stack back down, then looked up and nodded down the table to the small man—Chow—as if to reassure him that it would be only a moment or two longer. U had the stacks to his left in line, each equidistant from the next. To his right was a pad to which he turned periodically to make notes or compute figures, and on the floor to his right stood two small metal wastebaskets, one filled to the brim, the other virtually empty. Systematic, he had filled one before starting on the second.

The papers directly in front of him were records, wills, titles, contracts, legal descriptions, lists of encumbrances, of debts, credits, assets, itemized lists of equipment, descriptive lists, inventories. . . . The stacks were organized according to categories of the proceedings about to begin. Several times U encountered a sheet he considered unnecessary. He would hold it in front of his face, studying it, then abruptly crumple it into a wad and drop it to his right. A wad pinged in the empty basket when he dropped it. That sound, and the crumpling, and the scratching of U's pen, and the rapping of stacks against the table, and occasionally a sound of movement from one of those who waited—a chair creaking, cloth rustling, a match struck—were the only sounds in the vaulted room, and these sounds bracketed by si-

251

lence, individuated, sharp as a book dropped in church.

To U's right and around the corner of the table sat Taam, and to Taam's right a woman in her sixties, his mother, and three chairs down from her Hiram Chow, and two chairs down from him sat Lucas in a white suit and royal-blue tie and pearl stickpin. Before him on the table lay a straw Panama hat with a blue band to match the tie. He was out of season again, resplendent, a creature blown in from a tropical land. Across from Chow sat Jui, smoking a cigar, with one side of the table entirely to himself. He tapped his cigar lightly against an ashtray. A match scratched, then hissed, when Taam struck it to light a cigarette. Ice clinked in a glass. The glass clicked when Chow set it back on the table. U squared off a stack of papers, rapping it twice, set it down, looked up and nodded to Chow. A small man, Chow had a face as exact as a set of calipers, and he looked back sharply at U. U nodded again, and blinked, then turned to the papers. No one spoke. Smoke from Taam's cigarette hung almost motionlessly above the table, diffuse and incorporating the thicker ribbons of smoke from Jui's cigar, the entire cloud slowly expanding and rising toward the high, paneled ceiling.

The table had ornate legs and a finish high enough to reflect images, and glasses down either side of its length, and pitchers of water, and cut-glass ashtrays, and it was long enough to accommodate twenty or more persons. There were just these six seated at it, but in the room there was one more: A large Chinese man with arms that hung away from his sides and hands that looked like bludgeons stood against the wall, guarding one of the two doors in the room. He wore a turtleneck and sports coat and mauve trousers under which his thighs bulged. He had a glazed expression. Outside the door, through a corridor, outside another door and through the cage, the play continued, raucous in the casino. Not a sound of it could be heard here, but a few minutes ago, when Chow had entered, there had been a soft shriek from it in between the opening and closing of the door. The second door was on the opposite wall, behind U, and outside that door a foyer in which another guard was stationed, and outside the foyer the hallway that led to the alley. As soon as he had stepped

252

from the alley into the hallway, Taam had become in effect a prisoner of the Triad.

Taam had folded his hands and from between fingers the cigarette protruded, trailing smoke. Jui looked at him. Taam's face was becalmed. He looked tired. He looked as if he weren't even here, as if he had let his body stay and sent his spirit—his shen—out to wander somewhere else: out over the Pacific, back on the highway, out in the streets of Reno. Jui was mystified by him. Jui distrusted him. Jui feared for him. Jui wished he would act more as if he was looking out for himself.

Jui himself didn't move, or only his hand with the cigar and his watchful eyes moved.

Taam's mother didn't move. She had an air of dignity, the poise of one who understands suffering.

Chow didn't move.

Lucas didn't move.

The guard looked inanimate.

The atmosphere was funereal and strangely disconnected. The activity with the papers at the head of the table neared a close, U like a gravedigger behind schedule and working in the presence of the mourners, who out of a sense of taboo would not exhibit their impatience.

Earlier, out in the foyer, Lucas had spoken to Jui and told him that he wished to sit in on the exchange. Jui had said that the meeting was not open. Lucas had pressed and Jui had told him that he'd have to talk to Chow but that Chow probably wouldn't arrive until the meeting was under way. Lucas said that he'd already spoken to Chow and that Chow had said it would be all right if it was all right with Jui. That had stymied Jui, Chow's gesture, his own power granted ascendancy by one whose power was greater, one with whose power he was at war, and also the menace in the gesture, for the fact that Lucas had spoken to Chow meant—so far as Jui was concerned—the reverse, that Chow had spoken to Lucas, and that now, through Lucas, Chow was putting him—Jui—on notice, but for what Jui didn't quite know. Jui had been trapped by a sense of decorum and by a greater but undefined sense of omen.

Jui, of course, knew Lucas' business—running cheap trans-continental labor, aliens, Latin Americans, Islanders, and now Asians, to Los Angeles, New Jersey, Philadelphia, Baltimore, San Francisco, to work in warehouses, car washes, restaurants. . . . That was how Lucas had come recommended to Jui. And Jui knew very well—being engaged in the same business himself but in a capacity by which the likes of Lucas worked as his agents, his runners—that a business such as Lucas' sought to enlarge, as a decimal seeks the digit, as alleys seek streets, and streets the thoroughfare, and that Lucas was courting Chow. He understood now why Lucas had wanted to be in Reno himself for the deliv-ery. He understood how the route of Taam's journey had come to be known to Chow's men. Jui looked at Lucas. Behind the flamboyant dress and stilled face, Jui saw one not unlike himself, vigilant, probing for soft spots, but the duplication come from an unexpected quarter—here, a white man, whom he had hired for Taam because he was white, a camouflage, given permission by Chow to be here.

As he looked, there was a shallow trail of a smile on the scar side of Jui's ugly face. Lucas looked back, his face electric and his eyes bright, an acknowledgment without motion. Before him Jui saw one whose superior soul—his shen—was at one with his in-ferior soul—his p'o. Lucas was unlike Taam, who let his shen wander and so endanger itself even when he was awake. Jui saw danger.

Jui looked away. The entire room was subdued, conserva-tive, the walls paneled, the rug a deep maroon-blue-and-cream floral pattern, the furnishings weighty, wooden, rich, the cush-ions various shades of brown, the lighting refracted from chande-liers, and over the windows heavy curtains were drawn. The place was familiar to Jui. He drew on his cigar and scanned a set of photographs on the opposite wall, five of them, all but one of which displayed a historical interest: a photograph of old Reno, a photograph of a Paiute encampment on Pyramid Lake, one of a Central Pacific trestle under construction in the Sierras, an-other of a coolie tent town on the Central Pacific line. . . . At his back—Jui knew—were more photographs. One of them showed

254

a youthful Chiang Taam, whose room this had been, standing with Dr. Sun Yat-sen. Jui's eyes returned to the center photograph on the wall before him, which was identical to the photograph in his San Francisco apartment. It showed the board of directors of the Chinese Benevolent Society, the Chinese Six Companies. Chiang Taam was among the figures. So was Jui. Chow was not.

U rapped a stack of papers sharply against the table, twice, set the stack down, then leaned back in his chair and sighed heavily. He was ready. The attention of those in the room began to turn toward him, but about it, still, there was little focus, only shifts of the eyes and slight movements of bodies. Taken together, the attention of the people at the table and even of the guard at the door had a curious, diffuse, and confused character. Disconnected, the people seemed articulations of a remote structure, yet to be brought into play, or they were disembodiments of a whole that was buried in some other place.

U leaned toward the stack nearest him and spoke in Chinese, his voice a raspy whisper, but he had scarcely begun when Chow's head jerked.

"In English, Freckles," Chow said, flicking his hand at Lucas. "And begin with the property."

"But it would be irregular for the heirs to sell property which they have not inherited," U said, whispering again.

"We've waited long enough!"

U flinched. He picked up a different stack and, holding it, spoke to Taam but looked at Chow: "Does Mr. Taam wish to examine the documents pertaining to the sale?"

Taam stubbed out his cigarette and, watching his hand, said, "No."

U said, "We have an offer of six hundred fifty thousand dollars and a preliminary acceptance from Mrs. Chiang Taam. Does Mr. Taam accept this?"

Taam looked up, his face impassive, stilled.

Jui wished he would show some conviction.

Taam shifted slightly toward his mother, looked down the table at Jui, and said, "I do not."

Then Jui, softly, to Taam's mother, said, "You agreed to that?"

She gazed at Jui, her eyes widening slightly.

Jui looked across at Chow. "We agreed on eight hundred thousand."

Chow said, "You sell for what the market will bear."

Jui pointed his cigar at Chow. "When the market's so provisional, maybe you don't sell at all."

Chow smiled.

Jui turned back to Taam's mother and asked, "Why?"

She said, "My son is with me."

"You were threatened?" He paused. He knew that it was so, that she had been threatened with her son's life, and specifically, not just the blanket threat that had been in effect for better than seven years. She had told him. His surprise was feigned, or not even feigned: everybody knew that he knew, but he wanted Chow to know that he was feigning. He wanted the haze cast by pretense. He nodded at Taam. "He was threatened?"

Taam's mother gazed at Jui. Her expression showed penetration and intelligence, and disdain, and mortification, the look of one not used to being in this position, to being so manipulated, and it showed an inward weighing of some balance of which she would not speak.

Jui imagined he knew what the inward balance was—her husband's fortune, her husband's life, and her son's betrayal on the one side, and on the other side just what she had said—that her son was back with her. He was sure he knew which way she wanted the balance to tip now—toward the son. And Jui wished to help her, but—he reminded himself—it was out of friendship.

That was all.

He was not otherwise obliged.

He had brought the younger Taam this far.

He had laid the groundwork for the sale.

The threat to the widow was a violation of the agreement he had made with Chow, but had not surprised Jui, nor had the actual attempts against Taam on the road, though they were a disappointment. It was to avoid them that he had hired Lucas, because Lucas had a reputation for efficiency, because he was white, because, being white, he operated outside Jui's and Chow's circuits—or so Jui had thought—because Jui had hoped that Chow wouldn't know who Lucas Tenebrel was or even how to find out. And Jui had taken Lucas' recommendation for a driver—Erks, who, Jui would say, was either very good or very lucky—and Lucas' suggestion that his wife—Lily—ride half the journey armed, and Jui had seen that Taam himself was armed, and that his—Jui's—own men stayed with the car, all of which had seemed a little ludicrous to Jui, but maybe outlandish enough to work, and it had, though just barely, so far. . . .

He turned to Chow. "This property was not placed on the market. On the market it would go for a million and a quarter."

Chow smiled again. "But in this case the market is provisional, Jui."

"No market is that provisional."

Chow paused as if to let the foolishness of Jui's statement sink in. Then he said, "What do you suggest?"

Jui grew enraged, as was expected of him. His burly body and bulbous face gave the impression of one about to spring. He looked as if he was about to rise and throw himself across the table and grab the man. "I'll buy it myself! I'll pay the eight hundred thousand!"

Chow did not speak, but stared at Jui with an expression made of ice, this, too, the very expression expected of Chow. The entire proceeding, in fact, was like a masquerade for what was known and preordained, and played out at this strange hour— one-thirty in the morning—in the quarters of a dead man. Jui eased back in his chair and waited for whatever it was over which he had an omen to break surface. The widow did not move. Lucas sat still, a light left burning. The guard at the door was asleep on his feet.

Taam moved, leaned over and spoke softly to U.

The lawyer looked up with a startled expression, listened to Taam, then touched a stack of papers, chose several pages, and passed them over. The attention of those in the room shifted again, toward Taam, but almost imperceptibly, moving like the

257

hour hand of a clock, or the eye of an octopus slowly opening on the bottom of the deep.

Chang and Lee followed Erks through the archway which had appeared to be a passageway from one part of the casino to another. They moved down a row between slot machines and Erks had to excuse himself repeatedly because of the bulky valise. They came out at the end of a bar. He stopped there. Chang and Lee stopped with him and looked up with the vaguely quizzical expressions of those following a motion to which they were bound but did not understand, like small children taken to town. Erks looked around.

Here the slot machines and blackjack tables—of which there were only four—were much older than those on the other side of the archway, and the change girls wore slacks and looked seasoned, and the solitary blackjack dealer—for only one table was in play—was a matronly black woman. The bar was out in the open, right next to him, not in a "lounge," and the back bar had ornate wood cabinets and leaded mirrors—antique, out of another age, or would have been had time been material here. Through the archway he saw the keno wheel spinning and the scores of heads bent toward the slot machines. He saw, then, what was most obvious about this side of the archway, that the clientele was black and Oriental and Indian, that whites were in a minority, that the archway marked an invisible racial boundary, the change from one side to the other as unexpected and definite as the ground of a dream changing midstream.

Near where he stood a black man in work clothes sat at the bar sipping the beer half of a boilermaker. "What place is this?" Erks asked him.

The man glanced up. "The name? . . . The Dragon."

Erks gestured toward the archway. "It's a different place from that over there."

"You bet."

"Who owns this place?"

The man shrugged.

The back wall of the casino was not barricaded and it had a door. Erks looked back through the archway and mentally lined up the back wall in the Royale with the wall in this casino.

"Tong," the man at the bar said. "I think the guy's name is Tong."

Erks turned. The man had swung around on his stool.

"Yeah, Joe Tong . . . Bill Tong . . . Charlie Tong . . ."

Erks had a light-headed sensation—the mark of the small man with the swimmer's body who had sat next to him in the car. Charlie Tong . . . Chiang Taam. This was the place.

"What about that door?" he asked, pointing. "Where does it go?"

The man looked down at Erks' valise, then up, grinning. "Toilets. You the plumber?"

Erks touched the brim of his hat. "Thanks."

Chang and Lee followed him across the casino and through the door, where they found the two rest rooms, a door for each, but a third door, too, which had a green EXIT sign over it. Erks tried the door. It was open. They stepped into a tiny cubicle, lit only by the light that came through the door left open behind them and a green EXIT sign over another door. Erks felt demeaned, just like a vagrant, but he tried the door. They found themselves in a spacious white room brightly lit by fluorescent fixtures, and across the room, seated at a table next to another door, was a Chinese man in a dark suit and patent-leather boots. He had a face like a frog—low brow, squashed nose, flat, protruding lips—and he was big: another big one. His chair was tipped back against the wall, his legs hung over the front, and his feet were square on the floor.

The man spoke, his lips moving like plates. "You again."

They approached, Erks' boots and the boys' shoes clattering in the empty room. He put it together—this man and the one sliding sideways into the doorway out in the alley—probably one and the same. He felt expected, and demeaned. When he stopped the boys stopped right behind him. "I'm looking for Lucas Tenebrel."

The man had a fly swatter. He leaned toward the table and

killed a fly, then brushed the fly onto the floor. Dead flies were scattered at his feet. "Who?"

"I said I want to see Lucas Tenebrel."

The fly buzzed on the floor. The man looked over the edge of his chair and squashed it with his boot. "Never seen anything like this place for flies," he said. "You can't even drink a cup of coffee without keeping your hand over the top."

The place was spotless, brilliant, antiseptic, apparently in the process of being remodeled, the walls and ceiling freshly painted white, new white tiling on the floor. All along the walls—Erks saw —outlets had been installed, and in one far corner stood a fortress of cartons, large cartons and small, with the names of electrical specialists printed on them: Southwire, Elcon, Alcan, Honeywell, Corning, General Electric, Leviton, I.B.M. . . . The room, already, had the breath of ozone, but it had flies, too, flies on the ceiling, flies on the walls, flies that buzzed around Chang and Lee's heads, one that landed on Erks' cheek.

"Don't know anybody by that name," the man said.

"He's here. Maybe with one named Taam."

"Maybe?"

"Tenebrel owes me money."

"You could go back and check, but you'd have to get by me, then Baker down the hall, and then Liu. . . ." He stopped, slowly lifted the fly swatter, then slapped. He brushed another fly off the table to the floor. He looked back at Erks and blinked slowly— a large amphibian at the edge of a world. "And Perkins and Jenkins, and five security guards. If it was me, I'd forget it."

Even without the threat, or the invitation to test the man's muscle, Erks had a deadening feeling, or a sense of trucking something inert, an unrecoverable arrears, a flotsam, and of what little rapacity he had left taken away from him by purposelessness. He wasn't even sure he cared about the money. He was sure he'd lost his chance for it here as soon as the door in the alley closed on Lily.

But he said, "If I could get what's owed me, there'd be a percentage in it."

"Look, nobody's really interested in you," the man said. He

glanced down at the valise, then up, and smiled, his flat lips curling. "Crowbar or no crowbar. If I was you, I'd just get those two to San Francisco and go on home."

"Tell Lucas I want that money."

Lily had told Lucas. She'd followed Taam down the hall to the foyer outside the room where the meeting took place, the door between them then open, and a man at work with papers in the other room and Taam over in the corner with a woman— his mother, she took it—their reunion, it had seemed, strained. The woman held Taam's arm. From time to time they would speak, then look away, their faces masked, then they would speak again, then look away . . . like a sea, rising and ebbing over a rock. Lucas had met Lily and she'd told him.

"He'll get it," Lucas had said.

"If he doesn't get it now, he says he'll leave the boys and go home."

"No, he won't. How was the trip?"

"What about Erks?"

"He'll get his money."

"You didn't expect him to make it?"

Lucas stared.

"I want a divorce."

Lucas opened his mouth, his cheeks clicking, then he closed it again before speaking. "Right now?"

"Tomorrow morning."

"There's plenty of time, then," he said, the words filled with irony.

"Look . . ."

"I can't talk about that now, for Christ's sake."

"I'm not asking you to talk."

"Not now, Lily."

"I'm telling you now. That's all."

He had grasped her arm and leaned toward her and whispered fiercely, his breath heavy with mint. "I'll tell *you* what. You didn't follow directions. You turned off at the wrong place. And you were supposed to waste him. I gave my word."

She pulled back. "That's what I'm saying, Lucas. I can't play ball in your league."

"Bullshit."

"What about Erks?"

"I said he'll get it."

"Where are you staying?"

"The Sheraton."

"Then I'll meet you in the morning."

She left, went back out through the alley, and walked several blocks, found a hotel room. She bathed and thought of sleeping, but changed and went out to play the numbers, a little blackjack, a little roulette, craps. . . . She liked the dice, the feel of them and the roll against the wall and the barker and the people pressed around the table, instantly familiar, like witnesses at the scene of an accident.

She rolled deuces.

A stranger bought her a drink.

When she finished her business with Lucas she supposed she would strike out for home. She thought of her brother Bud, how, if he could have seen it for what it was, he would actually have approved of everything she'd had a hand in: burying Ho as properly as possible, betraying Lucas on what Lucas had named and that she could name now—that her job was to set Taam up and then, if someone else hadn't, by the time they neared Reno, to waste him. Erks and Taam both, she felt, had somehow known, and known also that she wouldn't do it. Lucas must have been desperate, to have not understood what he was asking her to do. That she had ever agreed seemed eerie. High life and cocaine runs and transcontinental hotel stops were one thing; murder was another. And yet the former seemed eerie, too.

She stopped, the dice in her hand. She'd just come out of a morass back into herself. It was just herself here.

The people awaited her throw.

It was amazing what one could almost become, or actually become. One could take on any idea, any notion, and become it. Maybe Lucas had been right about her. Maybe it was just Taam she couldn't murder. Maybe it was the chance element of Taam

Lucas hadn't foreseen. Maybe she could murder a man. So thinking, she felt a weight lift. She rolled deuces.

The stranger bought her another drink.

On the other side of the table a woman—drunk and losing and hating it—wept like a child, like an actress on TV. Everyone pretended that she wasn't there.

And Bud would have approved of her sloughing off Lucas. He didn't approve of divorce. If he could have said it, he would have said that he believed in everlasting union. But he would never say that. He would have approved of her divorce if he could have understood the tangle it was built on, but he couldn't because he had his own tangle, and were she to try to tell him about hers, he wouldn't approve. She wouldn't tell him. She liked it the way it was with the wolf between them, snarling from the end of its taut chain.

The stranger was clutching her arm.

She would divorce Lucas and go home to tease the wolf for a while.

From here, home seemed an extraordinary place: her mother's house, leaded windows and potbelly stove, a nearby warehouse loaded to the gills with explosives, or her brothers in Rathdrum, yellow dogs, pig carcass, mountainside, spoiled orchard, leaning porch, Winona, rutted road.

Chang and Lee sat opposite Erks in a booth in the Money Tree. The restaurant was on the second floor and from the booth they could look over the railing at the main floor. Toward the entryways and windows, the slots were alight and still noisy, but because of the advancing hour about half the blackjack and dice tables were covered. Others were in play. Erks, Chang, and Lee could look down and see the heads, the hands, and the cards, chips, and silver dollars passed over felts, and the dice, rolled across numbers.

He'd lost something besides the money and, at the moment, it felt like the will to survive. He was that tired. Everything looked so small on the main floor, cards, coins, chips, and dice, and the hands that touched them, and the heads of the faithful, of the most relentless out of the multitude, bent, as if in prayer. Whatever Erks had lost, he felt that he had found Xanadu, or one of Coronado's Seven Cities of Cibola, or the Kingdom of Anian, or Jules Verne's Villa Francia, or, legendary auxiliary of Cibola, the City of Quivira, or any one of these places invented as heavenly in order to detain inescapable loss.

Coronado had spent two years searching the Southwest for Cibola, and when he came to the place cartographers had marked for it, he found no gold, no emeralds, no high-walled houses, no doorposts studded with turquoise, but only squat dwellings made out of adobe—clay. He did hear word there—or so he claimed—of another place, far in the interior, the fabulous City of Quivira, and this second place, Quivira, filled the vacuum left in the imagination by the reality of the first, Cibola. The news spread. Quivira's melody hit the sixteenth-century European charts. Everybody looked for Quivira; Cabeza de Vaca searched for it, and Fray Marcos de Niza, and the Negro Estavan de Dorantes, and Castaneda, and Viscaino, and Brigges, and others, and many others, and Balboa, and Drake. . . . While he sought the sister fantasy, the Northwest Passage, the Strait of Anian, the trade route to China, Drake kept an eye out for the glitter of Quivira. And one of his—Erks'—own race, Apostolos Valerianos, or Juan de Fuca, claimed to have sailed under the Spanish flag and to have discovered the isthmus, the Strait of Anian, and to have sailed inland to Quivira.

It was doubted that de Fuca had ever sailed Pacific waters at all. Erks considered that the true ground, the old Greek's imagination in which a legend flowered. And to suit the legend, which came to be collectively held, and, thus, certain, the cartographers moved Quivira around, out of the Southwest to Kansas, and up to Saskatchewan, and back to the Pacific Coast, up and down between the fortieth parallel to the fiftieth, and then inland again to places not known, not yet *explored* or written, to places in which the fantastic remained conceivable. Whenever a discovery was made, it became a discovery of where Quivira was not. Quivira was discovery seen in a mirror, a floating design not ever to be trespassed upon, a hermetic place made out of greed

264

and filled with a contagion, the breath of false religion.

It wasn't just the money he'd lost. He was also losing the desire to even have it. But he would wait for Taam. He could fix on that one point. He had become certain as to where that sympathy rested.

"Hamburgers again?" he said, pulling back from the railing and turning to face them. "Do you boys want hamburgers?"

He had their attention.

"Two hamburgers each?" he said, holding up two fingers.

"Two," Lee said, holding up two fingers and nodding, the word barely recognizable, but certainly there though the vowel twisted crazily around the consonant.

Erks grinned, pleased with Lee.

Lee grinned back. Even Chang became less invisible and took on an expression which with the proper provocation looked as if it could have turned into a smile.

Chang and Lee had two hamburgers apiece and quantities of french fries. Erks ordered a hamburger for himself. The keno girl came by while they ate and Erks bought numbers for Chang and Lee—not knowing himself how to play.

"It's the same as bingo," the girl said. Dressed in a low-cut, sequined body suit and netted stockings, heavily made up, heavy with scent, sluggish, she reached across the table to take the keno cards out from behind the salt-and-pepper rack and, utterly bored, showed him how to play.

Erks pointed out the numbers on the cards to Chang and Lee, then pointed to the board mounted on the wall. The boys seemed to understand, but were confused by the numbers.

It occurred to Erks that he had traveled the isthmus, not by water, but by land to this place, Reno, a place of riches, a place where money was not even money, where there was no time, but only space, an oasis of space where time and money and one's losses were not counted.

There was a parable in it.

That Reno, and likewise Winnemucca, and Las Vegas down south, were constructed in the desert, in the timeless, un-hierarchic, barren, merciless Paiute space of the old days, was

265

somehow fitting, logical, even inevitable. The cities, implanted in the Western imagination, then made real, a place for Howard Hughes, a place for Lucas, for Lily, and for the ghost of the old woman at the slot machine . . .

And for himself, a place to be weary and filled with disgust and to relearn what he'd long prided himself in knowing—that he was only mortal, a man of dust.

The boys finished eating and Lee looked at Erks as if he wished to speak.

"Yes?" Erks said.

Lee said something that sounded remotely English.

Erks couldn't make it out.

Lee spoke again, the words twisted, vowels curling the wrong direction and consonants in unlikely places, but Erks thought he recognized it—"San Francisco."

He said it. "San Francisco?"

Lee nodded rapidly.

"By morning," Erks said.

"San Francisco?" Lee said, improving on his pronunciation.

"By morning. At dawn. When the cock crows," he said, smiling.

"No," Lee said. He struggled to find a word, his tongue wrenching. "This . . . this San Francisco?"

Erks understood. "No. This is Reno." Amazed, he paused, and smiled, amused and amazed by the look of expectation on Lee's face, by his delusion, his confusion of sister cities, by his wonderful innocence, his and Chang's, these two, one of whom had pulled a knife on him, and both who for some dark reason had skinned a patch of flesh off a corpse. "Reno," Erks said. "San Francisco tomorrow. Later. By morning. Five, maybe six hours. By dawn. By light," he said. "At light."

Lee looked bewildered.

On their way out, Erks stopped to show them blackjack. He sat them down at a table, choosing one with a Chinese dealer, gave them money, and had them play. He stood between them and reached out and touched cards for them to play. They began to understand, but laughed when they lost or won, laughed when silver dollars either came or went—it made no difference. They understood gambling. The young Chinese woman, the dealer, was amused by them. Chang and Lee advanced their pots by several dollars each.

"They are new to the country," Erks said to the young woman.

"Yes."

"I am taking them to San Francisco," he said.

"Yes."

He gazed at her, a strikingly beautiful woman. "Can you speak to them?"

"Yes."

"Will you?"

She did. They spoke back.

"They think this is San Francisco," she said.

"Yes," Erks said. "Did you tell them the truth?"

"Yes," the woman said.

"Tell them we will be in San Francisco by morning."

The woman spoke to them.

"Thank you," Erks said.

"Yes," the woman said.

Chang and Lee lost their pots, everything.

"All things are equal here," Erks said.

"Yes," the woman said.

Two months ago, Chiang Taam had told Jui, "The power of my learning is dead. The world has changed. Your learning is alive."

Chiang's compliment had made Jui feel ill at ease. He hadn't believed it. He hadn't understood it. He hadn't known what Chiang meant by his learning, the learning of the marketplace, of the streets, of transcontinental smuggling, what he knew from books all but wrenched out of the Chinatown public schools that otherwise had tried to keep him in the dark. It wasn't that Jui distrusted Chiang's word. He might be mystified, but never distrustful. He left that to the others, who took Chiang's past too

267

seriously, who distrusted that for which the man should have been revered, who forgot that every generation had its feet in a different age.

As Chiang had grown older, he'd spent most of his time in Reno, but when he chose to come to San Francisco, his presence had seemed to Jui to have the aura of a visitation. And now, in the days since his death, he seemed even more than he'd been alive—to Jui and, Jui believed, to some others: the interest in the casino was not strictly economic, but, for the Triad and for Hiram Chow in particular, a vendetta, a raid on a corpse, an opportunity to dismantle the dead man's fortune.

This was what made Jui uncertain: raids could unexpectedly take any available avenue.

Chow would not own the casino—the Dragon—any more than he owned the adjacent casino—the Royale—or the tenements in San Francisco. He was only the Triad's San Francisco dragoman, literalizer, lever, channel. . . . And yet for Chow the raid was personal, though attached to an international cloud of interests, owners, liabilities. . . .

The same day in this room, two months ago . . . It was the last time Jui would see Chiang. Chiang had asked him to come. The old man had said, "If my son returns, you and he will be enemies."

Jui had protested.

Chiang waved him off, his hand rising and falling slowly, then resting on the table for support. "His life is governed by ideas, you see. He would die for them. He is as I was when I was young. He has taken that part of his father and wishes to fulfill it."

"You expect him back?" Jui had asked.

Frail as a leaf, but standing, Chiang paused and hardly seemed to breathe, then went on: "But if he returns, a last kindness you could do for me would be to help him, help him to be safe at the first, at least."

Jui had agreed without hesitation.

"Do you understand what I mean?" the old man had said. "I mean arrange for his return if he wishes it."

It was a plea from one who never pleaded.

Taam, the son, had lost weight in the seven years since Jui had seen him. He looked the way the old man looked as a young man in the photograph with Dr. Sun. He acted as the old man had acted for as long as Jui had known the old man—nearly twenty-five years, through which time the old man had always seemed old. The son acted withdrawn, haughty, as if he were hardly here, so like the old man, but so far as the old man was concerned, Jui had attributed the behavior to age and position, and, later, to the tragedy of the son—Ginarn's arrest, imprisonment, his flight from the country, and the crime behind it, a Triad burning in Chinatown. Ginarn had had a bookstore that sold Maoist publications and served as a meeting place for an organization that called itself a research project but which everyone knew was an extremist league, the place and the man in defiance of old Chiang, and, from the start, marked. . . . The Triad had burned it. But for the old man, the younger Taam would have been killed straightaway, not just burned out, and even so, several had been killed, children, and Ginarn's wife, burned to death. Two days later a Triad man, the torchman, was found dead in a street, hunted down and shot by Taam.

To have opened a radical bookstore was one thing—perhaps forgivable now, commonplace enough, but not eight or nine years ago. To have organized rebels was another thing. The loss of Taam's bride was tragic, but to have killed a Triad member was clearly unforgivable. To have fled, then, to Communist China was forbidden. To have stayed there by choice was heinous.

What Jui had said about the value of the casino was true. The Dragon might have brought in a million and a quarter, or, were the purchaser to carry the encumbrances against it, somewhat under a million. But this or whatever amount would be less, also, the expenses connected with arranging to get Taam out of China, then out of Hong Kong, and for hiring Lucas Tenebrel to deliver two loads of boys to San Francisco and Taam here, and, second, less some abstract figure—it seemed to be in the vicinity of $100,-000—for Chow's promise that the Triad would lift the execution order against Taam. It was an uneasy agreement. Jui had set the price at $800,000, knowing that he could offer more himself should the opportunity to buy the casino arise. Chow had made a low offer in private to the widow. But the widow refused to agree to anything until her son was safe. Despite his promise, Chow had tried to have Taam killed before he arrived, which Jui had anticipated by sending his own men out as protection, though, fearing possible violence and subsequent reprisals, his instructions to his men had been contradictory: "If they try to kill Taam, stop them, but don't tangle with them."

By long-standing custom—tacit—it came out this way: up to the time of sale, duplicity was expected, but once they met in Reno promises were to be honored. So Jui had explained it to the widow.

But if Chow had succeeded in killing Taam the sale would have fallen through. This made Chow's behavior puzzling. Possibly, Chow only meant to frighten Taam and his mother, and so ensure the lower price. But there was another custom, or even an imperative: those who murdered Triad members were executed. Jui had never heard of such a one being spared, and from the start he had doubted that Chow had the power to do so.

Jui had feared this all along.

And yet things might have been easier with Taam dead.

Or if Jui managed to buy the casino, the deal would also be off, and Taam would certainly be executed. Jui had hoped to buy the casino years ago, years before Chiang had spoken to him. It was an old longing that Jui could not suppress.

But Chiang had said, "Help him to be safe at first. . . ."

Jui had brought Ginarn this far. . . .

All this passed through Jui's mind—or not exactly passed, not in so many words, but dwelled on his mind, for he had rehearsed it, trying to find a way to see to the safety of Taam and the security of the widow, to live up to his promise to Chiang and still get the casino, to get out from behind Chow's shadow . . . trying to find a path out through the encirclements. . . . The complexity of it was absorbed into the omen that rested on his mind as he, with the others, turned and stared at Taam with the startled attention of one awakened in the middle of the night. Taam had taken out a pen and begun signing the papers U had passed to him.

Chow broke the silence. "What are you doing?"

Taam looked up. He'd lit another cigarette. Smoke trailed upward. "You are interested in speed?"

"Meaning what?"

"I am signing the papers. Any amount in excess of eight hundred thousand is acceptable."

Lucas' chair creaked. He put his elbows on the table and said, "If negotiations are to be reopened, I would like to make an offer."

Jui's body jerked. "What!"

Chow said, "We have decided not to buy the casino."

"Then why are you here?"

"We have decided that we do not need the scrutiny owning another casino would bring."

Jui said, "I've not heard this."

Chow shrugged, a gesture designed to infuriate Jui.

Jui paused, digesting the information. It was possible that Chow was lying. It was possible that he told the truth. It was clear that Jui's premonition was taking shape.

Lucas said, "I would pay eight and a half."

Jui said, "Who is this man?"

Chow said, "He is on equal footing with you."

Jui smiled, or leered, or the scar side of his face twisted. "And what can he pay? We have no guarantees. He has no place here."

"He can pay."

"With whose money?"

Lucas reached down and lifted a valise onto the table, snapped open the catches, and shoved it across the table toward Jui. Jui pushed it back into the center as if it were a distasteful substance. It sat there, filled with bundles of bills, perhaps, or perhaps a solitary bank draft rested in its satin bottom, or letters of guarantee.

"My advice," Jui said, turning to the head of the table, "would be not to sell at this time. You're being railroaded."

Taam said, "We've been railroaded from the start. You're being railroaded now."

Jui stared. It was true.

Taam said, "You could offer nine hundred thousand."

Jui—grievously insulted—opened his mouth to speak, but closed it and looked down at Lucas, then at Chow, the widow, then at Taam, and said, "All right."

Taam rose from his chair and touched his mother lightly on the shoulder and said, "I'm going. I've signed. Anything in excess of nine hundred thousand we accept."

And he turned and went; carrying his basket, he walked toward the door behind U, the second door.

"But where?" Jui said.

Taam opened the door and went out, moving as if he were going nowhere in particular—to get a drink, to wash his hands, to take a turn about the building—or as if he weren't even here going somewhere, had never been here, or as if he'd been here only as an onlooker who had grown bored with the proceedings.

Jui stared through the doorway at Taam's form and thought: He's going. But they'll stop him now. Chow will call out to have him stopped. The room was silent. No one moved. All watched. Jui watched Taam cross the foyer, his shoes silent on the carpet, then turn into the hallway and vanish, his soles squeaking lightly in the hall, the sound receding, then vanishing. Jui thought again: He's going—then, suddenly realizing that if Taam left he—Jui—would lose at all corners, feeling the entire machinery slowly turn and finding himself on the opposite side, finding all that he thought had been in his favor now a liability heaped in with his other liabilities, and seeing that Taam had understood this from the start, and feeling like a fool, he half rose from the table and spoke to the guard at the first door: "Stop him."

The guard looked at Chow.

Chow looked at Jui.

Jui shouted through the doorway, "Stop him!" Then, to Chow, he said, "Where the hell is Baker!"

"We would not want an incident in the casino," Chow said.

"But he's gone," Jui said.

"Yes," Chow said. "He will go to San Francisco."

Jui saw more—that Chow had never intended to buy the casino, but only used the sale as a way to get Taam back into the country in order to kill him and that Taam had understood that, too, all of it. Jui sank into his chair and looked at the widow. She sat stock still. Her eyes had widened as if to take in the whole room, as if to absorb it all. Jui leaned toward her. "I am sorry."

She stirred, as if awakened. "You're a fool, Jui! My husband was a fool to trust you!"

Erks, Chang, and Lee walked out of the Money Tree and back up the block. They entered the alley and went down it to the Cadillac. It was there. The station wagon was still there. But Erks expected to find no one. As he leaned toward the door of the Cadillac with the key, he stopped and peered inside. In the eerie light he saw the vague outline of a rounded shape just above the window sill on the passenger side. The shape did not move. Erks did not move. He peered and saw that it was a person hunched down, and on the seat beside the person he saw what appeared to be the familiar cane basket. Then the person moved and all the locks on the doors snapped up.

Erks opened the front door and whispered, "Taam?"

A voice whispered back, "Yes?"

Erks looked around. No one was in sight. Lee and Chang had slid onto the back seat. Erks pushed his valise in, then got in himself behind the wheel.

"Are we in a hurry?"

"Feasibly."

He started the engine and pulled out of the lot, and headed back toward the freeway, tense and wary again, watching for any permanence, any insolence of headlights at his tail.

13

Fifteen minutes out of Reno they passed the Last Chance Slots, crossed the California line, and traded in the electric for night. Erks had never been here before, but the smell he knew, coming through the wind wing, the savory smell of a pine forest in spring. The draft through the window was quite warm for a mountain night, warm enough to bear the pungent, bracing odor, the odor of spring, the odor of all other springs, which seemed to heap up and bear collectively upon a point—himself—and give him a profound sense of déjà vu, of melancholy, of his youth and his age. He had never been here, not on this road. He had been here, just here, driving just this way, this car, his fingers light on the steering wheel.

The road was like no road through any forest he'd been on, not even the interstate through the Cascades, Spokane to Seattle. This was a wide road, four lanes with enough space on either side for another lane, and it had a surface like a new parking lot. Canted, engineered in the path of the Central Pacific and the Donner Trail, the road had the arterial feel despite the elevation, but Erks had it nearly to himself. It was 3:30. The forest he could not see, only its density when on a curve the headlights swept it. Chang and Lee were awake, their heads erect, still and yet active in the mirror, filled with anticipation, most likely. Erks had seen them clearly when a solitary car approached from behind, hovered, then passed. He had seen Taam to his right, the small man

274

in a ball, face averted, hands over his belly, quite undignified in his sleep. Erks felt he could have been anywhere smelling this pine, his fingers guiding the Cadillac like a boat along a channel.

Forty minutes out of Reno they went by Truckee, then approached the pass. Erks read the signs—DONNER PASS, HISTORICAL MARKER, DONNER LAKE—the words bright as teeth in the night. He wished he could stop. He wished it were day. He wished he were home.

The signs beckoned the sightseer in him, then the mortal contagion, and he wished he could stop to see this place the image of which burned on the history of the West, a brand on the space—*large and without mercy.* Trapped here in the winter of 1847 by blizzards that left snow in excess of twenty feet, the some eighty immigrants from Illinois, lacking experience and provisions, and, earlier, misdirected on their route across the Nevada salt flats, and thus delayed, thus trapped, they lost animals in the snow and built a cabin on a creek hidden by snow so that their fire burned through the ice and the cabin collapsed. They sent out a party on a desperate mission, and ate what they had, the last of the animal flesh, the last provisions, then hide rugs and sinew, and a glue made of boiled bone and hide, and finally nothing, and after that themselves, the dead, the murdered, the flesh broiled, blood drunk raw or cooked, and organs, kidneys and human hearts, roasted on sticks.

Half of them perished. The other half were taken out by a series of rescue parties, the last of them not until after the thaw had begun, mid-April. The rescuers found the cabins surrounded by corpses, hacked and mutilated, the heads split open for the brains, and strewn about were members, and human hair, and bones, and torn scraps of clothing that had been cut off so the bodies could be more easily chopped up. Inside the cabins they found strips of human flesh, more bones. In the last cabin they found the German, Keseberg, the only survivor of the final group of seven, eating one of the other six, whom he had killed, boiling her blood in two kettles, and this though outside his door the snow had melted down around the frozen body of one of the oxen lost in the snow five months before.

275

With the Washos, the tribe of the Sierra Nevada who saw the Donner party from the forest, from the trees, the word for white man, it was said, was Cannibal. Of this the Washos were certain, and so named it. Erks wished he could get out to see the dark place he had read about. It was not just the horror of it that struck him—though it did, it did strike him—but also the durability of the story, its power, its quintessential property, this tale of the utter distillation of the ways of an animal of prey to one single blood lust. The party of immigrants had found themselves there in the straits of space without mercy. The car glided past the site.

So the Animal People began to dance. . . .
They had taken off their clothes and looked like men.

And Chang. And Lee. And Ho! His illusion!
And if it were cocaine—he thought—or wild horses, or a load of manure, or monkeys, or some kind of hardware, or anything unhuman, which he carried, he would drop it here and go back home, or if it were light enough like cocaine he would take that and go home and let them come to him, let them pay the five thousand dollars he had coming at home; but it was people. It was people—Chang and Lee and Taam and even Ho—who kept Erks in the car and pointing toward San Francisco. It was his own softness, his sentiment, his growing softness of feeling toward Chang and Lee, and the softness of his passengers, the softness of Chang's and Lee's illusions, and—he supposed—of his own illusions that kept him going—as well as his sense of doing right for God's sake. It could be—he thought—this very softness together with a sense of doing right or of at least doing what was necessary that turned sentiment into rage, that turned the overwhelming, soft, knitted logic of illusion into virulent, ecstatic, immoral rage—Cannibal. And Quivira—he thought—such a vision, naturally, just one step removed from Hellfire. He considered these things coolly as he drove and looked down at the road now growing just visible on its own by the first light of California dawn that slipped over the mountain at his back like honey.

And what of Taam? What of his illusion? What was his illusion? Why was he here again?

He remembered what the man with the face like a frog's in the white room had said: ". . . nobody's really interested in you."

And yet Keseberg went by the ox to Tamsen Donner's cabin. . . .

There was the story of another of them, James Reed, a leader of the party, who was banished from the train in Nevada for killing a man in a fight. Reed went ahead, reached Sutter's Fort, and made two rescue trips through the snow, delivering among others all of his family, and, later, settled in San José, where he made a California fortune buying and selling real estate.

Erks saw this, or its effulgence. He guided the car past the summit—7,240 feet—and around a sweeping curve to a point where he had a vista of the valley. It was deceptive. It looked like a huge x-ray, dark at the bottom and lighter at the top; the dark, he made out, was the grade, the mountainside, a deep, precipitous gloom, and beyond it was the valley itself, flickering, just touched by the sun, and in it a great, brighter swirl of lights— Chico, or Davis, or Petaluma, or Santa Rosa, or Vacaville, or mostly Sacramento, God knew what all—a long, carnival glow in the shape of a femur, the electric broadening of the joint, hipbone to the west, toward the ocean where it met Kuroshio, the vastness of the arch of lights exceeded only by the vastness of the space that contained it, a space without limit, falling from sight only by the lack of light and the curve of the earth.

By the time dawn had grown complete, Taam awoke. In the mirror the boys dozed, their excitement, presumably, too high an edge to hold. Taam awoke bright and bristling. He beamed at Erks, showing his teeth. Erks, tangled in his thoughts, grinned awkwardly and scratched under his hat. His legs ached, his buttocks and back ached from sitting so long in the same position, even his arms had a dull ache from touching the wheel. He was tired, still fatigued, desperately fatigued, but the dawn, the light on the hills and trees—California oak now interspersed with the pine—had been just enough to grant the gesture of awakening and he held on, acted as though it were time to wake up, as though it were possible. It was after 5:00. They had driven over a hundred miles out of Reno. They had scarcely over another hundred to go.

"Thank you for waiting," Taam said, picking up where they had left off.

It took Erks a moment to reel back the miles and understand to what Taam referred. "We are in accordance with the plan?"

"Plan? I hope not. The idea is to get out of a plan." Taam lit a cigarette and made himself comfortable.

"I was waiting for you in Reno, not for the money." He said it, then realized it was a manner of confession, not entirely true but true enough to stand as a confession.

"Thank you. Lily tried to get your money for you."

Erks glanced over and there passed between them a look concerning what they both knew Lily had been told to do and had not done, her purpose and her renunciation of it striking a balance and in the middle the woman neither one of them disliked. On the contrary.

Erks looked back at the road. "You're not afraid that they'll be waiting for you in San Francisco?"

"They?"

"There's a woman there, anyway, who's very anxious to see you."

"Oh?"

Erks raised his eyebrows.

"Ah. Rose Chew." Taam inhaled smoke and glanced mysteriously at Erks, then looked out the window with an air of great interest and exhaled, the smoke banking against the window, heavy in the sunlight.

"I bet that's the one," Erks said.

They passed through Rockland, the elevation, according to the sign, 250 feet, which Erks could hardly believe—that they had descended 7,000 feet in one hour. He had still the sense of elevation. The pines had dwindled, but the oaks had increased. The rock dwindled. The orchards and vineyards increased. Open space dwindled and rural settlement increased, the houses now

278

appearing regularly according to an unseen symmetry—or war
—of soil and economy. The oaks, the great, airy, laterally ori-
ented trees, most definitely took the ground they occupied. The
branches twined sideways like a root system. The trees seemed
to float. Under them next to nothing gathered but the sunlight,
the quickly waxing, low, yellow California sunlight that collected
on the ground like a vapor, heavier than air. Along the roadside
the manzanita increased, the leaves dust green, the branches
wine-colored.

His head felt light, as if there were too much air in it. Maybe
it was just lag, his head still up on the mountain, or left behind
in Reno, or lifted by three days on the road and abandoned,
perched precariously at the top of a stack of unexplained events.
But he had begun with lag, with misunderstanding, with an absence from what actually transpired and through three days and
nearly 2,000 miles seemed to have come no closer to it. Instead,
the lag had grown, waxed, and synergized. Outside town they
passed a vineyard, then orchards—apple, peach, cherry—the
cherry leaves a deep glossy green and startlingly intense. Watching, Erks felt like a tourist, which manner of watching he particularly despised, this casual way of seeing without design.

"She told me in no uncertain terms to bring you straight to
her."

A furtive look passed over Taam's face. "You did not mention this earlier."

"A great deal was not mentioned earlier."

"True."

"And I am to take you to her?"

Taam grinned suddenly, showing his teeth. "No, do not take
me to Rose Chew. A battle-ax, yes?"

Erks stared at the road and smiled. "Then where?"

Taam leaned across the seat and touched Erks' arm lightly.
"You remain most inquisitive."

"I'm driving."

Taam did not move, but stayed, leaning over cane basket
and valise, touching him. Erks smelled him, the odor at once
acrid and sweet, the smell of a man like himself unwashed

through days on the road. He glanced at Taam. Taam stared at him with his eyes narrowed, but soft and luminous inside the slits, and he grinned, or grimaced, showing his teeth like an animal. Erks saw his whiskers, black and sparse against the skin, like those of a pig.

"I don't mean that you have bad manners, only that you're inquisitive."

"Oh?"

In the mirror, he saw Chang and Lee move. In sleep they had sagged back against the seat, separating. Awakening, they drew toward the center again in their fanatic way and looked wildly about as if to discern where from Hong Kong they might have been brought.

The hand gripped Erks' wrist. He stiffened and looked down at the hand as if it were an inanimate thing, a buckle or clasp. He looked at Taam, who looked back, holding his wrist, examining him in the most casual fashion, as if *he* were an inanimate thing, a billboard or a bush, surveying him conditionally for whatever might chance to prove of interest.

"There," Taam said. He drew away and dragged on his cigarette. "Your curiosity is very abstract. Very cold."

Erks felt something rising to make itself known, a fin or hump out of the deep slicing the surface—cold, maybe, but hardly abstract. He thought of the tourists—not simply inquisitive, but acquisitive after the cannibal zone—who visited Donner's Pass 10 years, 20 years, 40 years, 60 years after the winter of 1847 to view the camp and rifle the ruins, finding baubles, bits of clothing, children's toys, scraps of diaries, and human bones. Then the site was made into a monument to hardship, to the death that slept with migration, to the migration that was death, to the public impulse to acquire the unnatural and mysterious.

He said, "All curiosity is carnal."

Taam grinned. "Maybe so. In any case, it's what I like about you."

Erks looked over, strangely moved, his confession about why he'd waited in Reno now matched by Taam's declaration, the *terra incognita* between them, the ground, perhaps, that Lily

280

had occupied, now moved in upon by themselves.

Taam gazed out the window. "Well. It has changed."

On the eastern outskirts of Roseville, the big airy oaks were thick, airy and thick at once, as thick—literally—as they could be, luxurious and libertine with their space, taking up enough space to leave a lot for themselves and not much else—a little grass, a little bush.

For Erks, the oaks told how much space should be employed here, how much light, how much time. The great, lateral oaks told the way. The people ignored their advice. The oaks vanished, their ground seized by exoskeleton, by the bone of the town and, on the western outskirts, by the bone of trailer courts and housing complexes, mostly houses, the roofs flat, parallel, graveled, in lots right up to the freeway, but walled off from the freeway with concrete block and from each other with either block or chain link—this, the fencing, the squares of gravel like the checks of a game board, a luminous, floating geometry of gray and steel. It took hold of the eye of the traveler. It was a weakened sperm that would not quit, faltered but would not quit, and rose, spread, broke into a million cells and stayed, and Erks wondered: My God! What do they do with themselves? Never mind the oaks, what advice do these people hear from their souls? What advice could they heed?

They rolled by at sixty and he imagined he heard the soft high cries of souls famished by the bodies that held them. Too much psyche. Not enough animus. Of course, it had changed. Change was all it had. Not enough dirt for anything else. Not enough tooth. Too much gum. Not enough bite.

"So many people," Taam said, gazing at the sprawl. "So much work. So much wealth. So much power."

Erks turned, his face showing another question.

Taam smiled and said, "I've been on this road many times. We lived in San Francisco, but much of my father's work was in Reno."

"How has it changed?"

Taam gestured at the window, indicating the obvious: project, hatchery, garrote, or so it was to Erks. But Taam said, "I

281

should not say change. It has increased. There's little change."

"That bothers you?"

Taam paused, then said, "Yes. That it just increases."

"It's different in China?"

"China still has hope."

He asked one of his questions: "You were there for political reasons?"

"What is not political?"

Of course—Erks thought—so Taam would say. But he—Erks —said, "What is not geological?"

Taam stared at Erks for a moment, then began to laugh. His body shook and his hand groped in the air before his chest. He stopped and caught his breath. "For you even the rock is carnal, yes?"

"Why not?"

Taam laughed again. Erks did not fully understand the joke, but he found the hilarity catching and laughed, too. In the mirror he saw Chang and Lee attending the commotion in the front seat.

Taam calmed himself. "I was compelled to leave the country."

"So you said."

"I'm a hunted man."

Erks looked sharply at him.

"Do you know what the Triad is?"

Erks shrugged. "That name keeps coming up. It's a secret society."

"More than that. I shot one of them, which is considered unforgivable."

"Shot?" Erks said, thinking of the gun in his valise, the gun Taam would not use.

"Yes."

"But with cause, of course."

"It was a crime of passion."

For an instant Erks thought Taam was joking again. He glanced over and saw that he wasn't. "Can't the law protect you?"

"Do you mean from the Triad?"

Erks felt the weight of the rhetorical question, but still didn't understand it. He felt, too, the man's sense of guilt, which he had felt before—something hidden under a sheet.

"Besides," Taam said, "the government wants me, too. I have doubts that the charges would hold up, but I was arraigned for murder just before I left."

"Why the hell didn't you stay in China?"

"It was time to leave."

"You ran into trouble there, too?"

"No. I did well. I became a deputy commissar to the city of Amoy. But the times were uncertain. Both Chou En-lai and Mao died last year."

Erks smiled. "I heard. So did Howard Hughes."

Taam chuckled. "An age has passed." He went on: "Even though Chou had arranged for Hua Kuo-feng to succeed him, there was turmoil. Chiang Ching and her associates were arrested last winter. My superior was removed for failing to purge the radicals fast enough. I was unsure of my position. Some considered me a hard-liner and I was a foreigner. When I received word of my father's death and that arrangements could be made for me to return, it seemed to be the time."

They paused.

Erks barely had to touch the wheel to guide the car. He'd set the cruise control at sixty, the temperature control at sixty-five. The car had tinted windows, leather upholstery, and a tray in the front mounted on swivels to keep food and drink from spilling. The front seats tipped and slid electronically to the desired position. Chang and Lee did not sit as close together as they had before, but on the wide back seat of the Cadillac they seemed closer yet. The car was virtually noiseless. It moved through the air like a hand in an expensive glove gesturing gracefully.

Erks asked, "Isn't San Francisco the wrong place for you to go?"

Taam said, "It's home."

"That's what I mean."

"I have business here."

"It can't wait?"

"No, it won't wait."

Erks sensed intransigence, the same intractable quality he'd sensed back in B.C. when he'd first tried to find out what was wrong with Ho, and the guilt again, and the same fatality he'd witnessed after they'd buried Ho when Taam, standing at the door of the car, a gun leveled at him, hadn't moved.

"My father was a political man," Taam said. "When he was young he met Sun Yat-sen in San Francisco. He went to China and fought for Dr. Sun against the Manchus, then came back here to raise money for the cause, and found that he could raise money, and did, and went on raising money, and became wealthy. It became a contradiction he never resolved, his wealth and his politics. . . . Many fathers and uncles of men now in power in Chinatown fought for Dr. Sun, or supported him, but this is forgotten. My father never forgot it and he was distrusted for it. Those who were not Triad men distrusted him because he was one. His Triad brothers distrusted him because he was of the old school."

"But it was his life, or his memory of it, not yours."

"Of course. I am trying to answer your question by his example."

"No, you're not," Erks said, looking over and smiling, knowing that one never spoke of one's father as an example. It was always personal.

"All right," Taam said, raising a hand. "My father was a Triad man, or a Hung man, as they are called. So was Dr. Sun. You are right. The Triad is an ancient secret society, a brotherhood of outlaws, one of many in China. Sun enlisted them into his party, the Kuomintang. And years later, Mao enlisted them into the Communist Party after Chiang Kai-shek had purged both the Communists and the secret societies from the Kuomintang. Mao has written of the part the secret societies took in the revolution. But then, after the revolution, in this country and in other countries outside China, the Triad became an arm of the Kuomintang again, of Taiwan, and then an Asian syndicate. So the Hung men remain criminals, but are no longer outlaws, not the way they were. It is a question of who is to benefit. Now the Hung men prey on weakness, on the poor, instead of on the powerful. They have changed the most important part of their view. They peddle drugs. That is the contradiction my father lived with. The honor I would like to show him is to resolve this contradiction."

"But it was his contradiction."

"No. It has Chinatown in its grip. In a way, since it is international, it has you in its grip . . . or would even if you weren't driving this car."

Erks didn't understand. For one thing, the information—which Taam knew intricately, first hand—was coming too quickly. For another, he didn't understand how what Taam spoke of was anything other than a cloud too expansive and nebulous to fight.

He said, "And you have a way of resolving it single-handedly?"

"I believe I have resolved it in thought."

"In thought!"

Taam grinned.

"That's why you're going back? That's why they still want to kill you?"

"What they fear is the shattering of an illusion."

Erks paused. They had been at this bend of conversation before, back in B.C. Like the road coming down the Sierras, he felt he had been right here before on ground—in the case of the Sierras—he had never seen in his life, or—in the case of the conversation—thrown back on ground that remained unfathomable and which he searched—or inquired—for some real bit of debris, or chip, or scrap of information: "You mean they think you'll turn state's evidence?"—which struck him as a good idea —"Or that you've found a way to unravel the whole organization?"—which hardly seemed possible, either in reality or in anyone's imagination—"Or what? That you're a Communist agent?"

"It is only that they're thorough. Nothing is left unresolved. That's why they're so effective. I am relatively unimportant to them, but they fear loose threads such as myself." Taam smiled. "They have an image of their purity. They are completely ruthless. They demand complete loyalty from their members. Most of all they fear the loss of fear from anyone inside or outside the organization, because fear is what stitches their perfect image together."

Erks scratched under his hat, knocking the brim down over one eye. He set the hat back straight on his head. "That sounds paradoxical to me."

"Not at all," Taam said. "It's an operable and long-used contradiction."

Erks chuckled.

They had by-passed Davis and now the road swooped through wheat fields. It was a fact he could hardly believe, that he was actually driving through wheat fields in California.

"What's the difference?"

"A paradox is imaginary because it is thought to be irresolvable. A contradiction is real because it changes, or can be changed."

Erks grunted. "What do you do with paradox?"

"Me?"

"Whoever."

Taam grinned and Erks, seeing the grin, grinned back in anticipation of whatever it was that was coming.

"Paradox is a relic of the Greeks," Taam said. "We smash relics."

Erks laughed aloud at the impish way Taam had spoken.

But the laugh didn't last.

He wondered: Does he know that I am Greek?

And he still felt chastened by what he didn't understand: a whole school of whales inside the man's body of which he saw only one spout—the words—breaking surface, and not where all the whales went, not what they ate, not how they bumped up against each other for miles underwater. It was a matter of belief, or of race, or of a language he did not know, or even of political cant, which Taam seemed to embrace half the time and to mock the other half. Erks' thoughts returned to the original question —"Why are you going back to San Francisco?"—a question he didn't want to ask again, out of deference, or politeness, and that he thought strange, to be polite over a matter that seemed a question of life and death. Taam, to whom compulsion seemed impossible, with whom every motion and word was measured, seemed to Erks to be acting compulsively. But he didn't know. He would have liked to hear Taam deny it, or explain it. He would have liked to have had the satisfaction of understanding, but he couldn't ask—still, out of politeness—and if he were to ask he expected the answer would be as incomprehensible to him as the ones already given: because it is home, because it is where the trouble arose. It would not be incomprehensible because he still thought Taam was evasive, but because Taam seemed attached to a world with which Erks had no familiarity. It seemed that the exact truth, the plainest of answers, "I am returning because . . ." was so obvious, so bright, and worn so thin, so brittle, that with the slightest touch it would crumble into incomprehensibility. It seemed that the answer would have to be left afloat, a frail boat made out of weeds, bobbing on the sea, a speck just barely in sight.

Since Roseville, they had by-passed the junction of 99 to Los Angeles, crossed the Sacramento River, and gone by Sacramento itself, the high-rise buildings and the golden dome of the capitol visible on the left, and by Bryte, and now Davis. Coming up were Dixon and Vacaville, and then the distance to the Bay Bridge would be thirty miles, another half hour, and less than an hour to Chinatown, even parked and on foot to the drop point—less than an hour.

To his amazement Erks had seen farming on a tremendous scale, and crops of great diversity: row crops, corn, lettuce, potatoes, and orchards, and the wheat, and grass crops, alfalfa, and cotton, and flax, and barley. Without witnessing it, he would not have believed the farmland could remain here, but the economics of agriculture, apparently, held delicate sway over construction, over the population, or not even that, but economics held delicate sway over agriculture. The people had to eat. Doubtless, the food was scrupulously plotted and itemized long before the seed was drilled. Husbandry had been outclassed.

There was no place for it here and no time for gathering, no room for rabbit, and too much crop for crow to damage, and hardly enough sunlight left for coyote to run in.

But perhaps—frail, delicate, looming, a thin cloud unraveling to nothing before the sun—water, or its lack, drought, held the promise of sway over economics: the return stroke. Maybe drought would win out and run this raft aground. It was the idealist in Erks, the anarchist, the held hope for the victory of nature over people, for the struggle it would force upon the people. It might bring the crow and coyote back out into the light. It might bring the scavenger back out.

"Certain contradictions do not go away," he said.

"Contradiction stays. Certain contradictions are always changing. This is in the nature of contradiction," Taam said.

"No," Erks said, thinking: That's the cant again. "The ground is mysterious. We will never understand it. We will never master the ground. The ground is permanent," and surprised at himself, he thought: I've all but said that the ground is sacred.

"But you're a cowboy."

He looked over quickly, thinking: No. I'm Greek.

Taam smiled slyly.

"You do not want to master it," Taam said. "It's your good fortune to see things the way you do, to have such respect for things, to have such a morality. But for these people," he said, gesturing at the windshield, at the unseen houses that lined the edges of the farmland and took parcels out of the fields, at the cities toward which they drove, "your way is impossible."

"But my way survives," Erks said, thinking: He doesn't understand, he doesn't understand that I don't mean it's sacred, not that way, only that it has power. So it is that Reno is Quivira, that this place we're coming to is a place of many languages, as it always has been, even back in the days of the tribes, even before that.

"More than that," Taam said. "Your way is truly American. It must be reckoned with."

"My way survives here." He thought: No, that's not it, I don't mean *my* way. He thought: I mean *the* way. And recognizing

288

that, troubled by the fact that they were talking about himself and by so doctrinaire a sentiment, his own cant, and by words that didn't say what he meant, and by what he meant—his belief about how lives lived on a ground were shaped forever by the nature of that ground—which grew unutterable and small, nothing more than a bright thing in his mind, thin, brittle, fragile. Touched, it, too, would crumble.

"Of course. But as an illusion. For you it may not be an illusion. Back where you live it may not be an illusion, though I wonder about that. Here, it certainly is. Here, your sense of bounty is changed into waste, your independence is changed into viciousness, your morality is changed into foolishness. What there is of the outlaw in you becomes fanciful here, and treacherous. It is a question of numbers, you see, of sheer numbers."

He thought: By God, that's the truth—but he said, "No matter how many of them there are, they still stand on the ground. You stand on the ground. You can't float, and they aren't angels on a pinhead, they've got to stand there. If they live in a high-rise, they've got to come down once in a while. The way you and those boys got here," he said, gesturing at the back seat with his thumb, "by hook and by crook, carrying false visas and sneaking across the border on a logging road, and following the water routes down, that's what I call truly American."

Taam chuckled. "Keep that to yourself."

"This matter of illusion is not interesting," he said, surprising himself with his directness. He thought: The problem is we're both just talking, there's no movement in these words, we're getting farther and farther apart. He felt a tremendous sense of weariness with the words. The words had lost the force in their naming. They'd become ghosts of themselves.

As if sensing that, too, or as if to answer Erks' thoughts, Taam gave the craft that was afloat a shove: "It was a fire." He paused. The tone of his voice had told Erks to attend this pause. "I opened a bookstore. It was the first place to sell Communist Chinese publications in Chinatown, and so caused a furor." He paused again. Erks looked over and saw him staring fixedly at his hands. "They burned it. And people died. My wife and I lived in the back room. She was burned to death. And in the apartments upstairs an old woman and five children were killed."

"I am sorry," Erks said, thinking: The man's sense of guilt, even if misplaced, has been fully explained.

They were silent for a time, then Erks said, "And you shot the torchman?"

"Yes. My father was a powerful man. I was outspoken, an activist, you see, during the sixties. There were many who hated me, but the burning was directed at my father, too, partly just because he was my father. In Chinatown, fire is a terrible thing. You cannot imagine what fear of fire there is in Chinatown." His voice became hoarse. "Death by fire is a terrible thing. I heard my wife screaming, and the children. I couldn't help them."

Again they were silent.

The Cadillac rolled past the fields.

"And yet the Triad chose fire as its method," Taam said, his voice rising, defiant.

"And you mean to keep on fighting them?" Erks said.

"Perhaps."

Erks looked over.

Taam grinned, showing his teeth. He looked like an animal, a boar, all tooth and bristle against his pale yellow skin. He leaned over and punched in the cigarette lighter which was built into the illuminated, chrome-plated ashtray.

They were beyond Vallejo. Cattle grazed in yellow fields on the sides of hills, the hills trailings of the Coast Range that opened up here as if intending to allow access to San Francisco Bay. The freeway had ten lanes. He had counted them, and even though it was Sunday morning, the lanes were in use, not filled, but in use, and he had to stay alert. The old oaks, now, had become curiosities in the gulleys and swales. The bay itself came into view in the distance and behind it a high gray mass—fog. He could smell it, the water, the fog. In the rear-view mirror, Chang and Lee were, as always, awake and close together, wide-eyed, taking it all in according to their way, and once, through the back window, he saw a Vista Cruiser behind them with three heads visible in the front seat. For an instant it seemed as if he, Lily, and Taam were following themselves. A car pulled between the Cadillac and Vista Cruiser, and the Vista Cruiser receded.

Erks watched the road. The hills were blond, the color of California sunlight. They passed a Union Oil refinery, tank after tank silhouetted against the gray sea sky, more behemoth than Stonehenge. They crossed the Sacramento again. It emptied into the bay. They entered the metropolis for good, the industrial emplacements first deepening, then giving way to the suburbs. They entered the joint of the long femur of light that Erks had seen from the ridge of the Sierras, the bright, phosphorescent, electric leg that came out of the ocean and lay across the land. Houses were everywhere, stretching up and down the hills and along the water. A white cloud of cigarette smoke filtered through the car.

Taam said, "So many people. So rich. So powerful. So much sadness. So much work to do."

When Erks looked he saw that Taam's eyes glistened. The pain in the face, the sorrow and the compassion, were startling. Erks looked back at the road, moved. They rode above Berkeley and down toward Oakland, toward the water, the fog.

"So what will you do? Stand trial?"

"Possibly. There is one thing I am doing for certain. I have writings on everything since I began . . . the organization I belonged to, the bookstore, the attempts to close us down, the Triad, the burning, my seven years in China . . . the solution to the contradiction we spoke of. . . ." He stopped, then went on, changing tone as if to make a joke. "They could make an exposé. A hot item. Last year I met a reporter from the *Chronicle* who came with a delegation to China. He was interested in these writings. I am taking them to him for safekeeping."

"And that's why you're returning?" Erks said, not sure whether or not Taam was in earnest. But no matter which it was, Erks sensed doom again. The man's words were really only half about what he had revealed, and half about what he would not reveal. They bore upon a fabric too ruinous to completely broach, the words like the notes of a melody, mournful in their discon-nection. It didn't seem to matter what Taam said, or what he meant: the effect would be inescapable and the same. That he made a joke of it was chilling. "For what?" Erks said. "For vindi-cation?"

He saw the Vista Cruiser in the mirror again, two lanes over and several cars back. He caught a glimpse of it and again of the three heads in the front seat like ghosts of himself, Lily, and Taam, the car a barge out of place on the freeway carrying the three *Doppelgängers* out of one more missing fabric. The car vanished. That it was there, then not there, but still there and only unseen like a thing of the shadows, he found chilling, too.

"Exactly," Taam said. "And for the sake of correction."

"And for your wife?"

"Yes, for her. And to honor my father. It is imperative that these writings be in the printer's hands."

"All right," Erks said. It was a reason, something concrete, but unsatisfying, and inexplicable as to why they had to be deliv-ered this way, by hand, by Taam himself.

"Does the Triad know about them?"

"Probably. Any other questions?"

Erks' body jerked. It didn't matter what he asked. It was a life's worth of demystification he needed. It didn't matter. He asked, "Why the hell did the boys skin a patch off of Ho?"

"They will send it to Ho's mother to be buried in the family plot."

Erks grunted and stared at the road, amazed.

They started across the Bay Bridge. The corrugated surface wailed softly under the tires of the Cadillac. In the rear-view mirror he saw the Vista Cruiser for the third time, closer now, and the three heads rigid like pumpkins on sticks. The grille of the car and the hood were splattered with mud. The car was dusty, the blue verging toward brown, and then it began to register—that the chimera was real, that it was not just any blue Vista Cruiser, but *the* Vista Cruiser, the same muddy Vista Cruiser he'd driven into Reno. It was a rivet driven in one side and now, since Reno, the fabric of space folded, and the rivet coming out the other side and crimped shut. He looked ahead, regarding himself—again—as a fool. He looked back through the mirror, then ahead.

He said, "Look behind us."

Taam looked, then turned back quickly.

Seeing Taam look, Chang and Lee turned to see.

"Is that what I think it is?" Erks asked.

They had neared the end of the bridge. Taam pointed and said, "Take this ramp."

He did. He had to swerve to make it. Behind them the Vista Cruiser swerved and followed. They descended and swung onto the Embarcadero, which ran along the waterfront. They drove past wharves, ships, warehouses, and into the fog. Erks switched on his headlights. The Vista Cruiser switched on its headlights.

Taam turned and gazed behind them, then turned back. "I think it is."

"What are we going to do?"

He glanced at Taam. Taam's face was grim. Slowly, the fog deepened, but they were still on the edge of the bank, not in its heart. The Vista Cruiser stayed with them.

Taam said, "Ultimately, there is no escape."

Erks said, "Bullshit. I can run for it. With this car I could do it."

"Speed up," Taam said.

He did.

He would have done it anyway, but he thought: Good.

The Embarcadero swung westerly. Erks pushed himself back into the seat and took a deep breath and straightened his torso. He switched lanes to pass a car, switched again and pressed the car in front of him. The car held its position. In the iridescent fog the green road signs and black pavement and yellow lines and the colors of cars were brilliant. He switched lanes again to pass, but then the traffic ahead jammed up and they slowed to a crawl.

He cursed.

"Try to pull in there," Taam said, pointing.

"It'll be worse."

But he did as he was told, trusting Taam, found an open space and lurched the car over and pulled into a drive that passed in front of the BART terminus.

"There," Taam said. "The trains are changing. I can catch one."

He stopped in a yellow zone. He saw the Vista Cruiser out on the Embarcadero, jockeying to change lanes and get in behind them.

Taam gripped his arm and said, "Thank you."

"Hurry."

Taam grasped the handle of his basket. "Thank you." He slipped out of the car.

Taam was gone.

Erks watched. He saw two men emerge from the front seat of the Vista Cruiser. He watched Taam's form hurry away—khaki pants, blue coat, pale-yellow basket, and faintly squared head. In his path were the two men, one a man Taam's height. The other, the familiar figure of the tall one in the bowler hat, glanced back at the Cadillac, the strange pallid face grimacing, red mouth and eyes as colorless as the fog, and a gauze bandage on the side of his forehead. On the walks, a crowd moved both ways, in and out of the terminus, a crush, their clothing bright in the silver air. Erks watched Taam move away and mingle with the people, then vanish altogether in the crowd, then, behind him, the two men vanished, and then, leaning close to the window, he watched the place where the forms had vanished, where they had been swallowed up, and grew uncertain as to where the place had been, the moving people like a high tide. The air was like smoke.

He pulled back behind the wheel and looked forward, deeply confused, and then heard it—a pop, muffled and small. He bent to look again. The crowd suddenly parted. The people stumbled over each other, scattering like toys, but in a frenzy, two waves of them, parting, and in the space they had abandoned was the form of Taam, hunched, crumpling like a baby, falling. The crowd froze, but among the people were two in motion, the shorter one and the big one in the bowler hat, an angular form,

294

fleeing. Then they were gone. Erks found himself out of the car and running toward Taam. He saw Taam roll on the pavement and the gore on the side of his head, a hole, gushing. He slowed, his feet, it seemed, thumping without noise, as if the sound were only reverberation, only percussion, and, his mind whirling with something like a prayer about Chang and Lee back in the car and the two in the crowd with guns, about the Vista Cruiser parked back of his car, and about the answer to why Taam had come back to San Francisco—to die—and about himself—both a mercenary and a witness now—he stopped over Taam, knelt, touched Taam's head, then cradled it with one hand, and looked into the eyes, glazed already, and still heard nothing, only a rushing sound like water, a deluge, a cataract.

But he spoke, or growled, hoarse, not hearing himself, his own words drowned out by the sound like water in his ears: "Call a doctor." He looked up at the faces, the people like figures pasted against a wall, bright and without depth. "Somebody call a doctor."

A man began picking up the contents of Taam's basket, which had broken open in the fall. The man returned them to the basket. Erks looked at the contents, a book, a comb and toothbrush, a pad, a bar of soap, a bottle of ink, a clean shirt, a thick stack of papers held together by rubber bands, then at the man, outraged—as if these were the contents of a lady's dropped purse and the man was acting cavalier. The man stopped and blinked, showing confusion the same as Erks' own, though a much weaker strain, devoid of the ties. But touched by that, Erks reached out and touched the stack of papers, picked it up, tucked it under his arm, and thought: His writings, if they knew about them they didn't want them, or they considered them unimportant, they just wanted him—and, growing rational, he thought: There is nothing for me to do here. He set Taam's head down gently on the pavement.

The rest of it was an afterthought, a closing of paths, which Erks, numbed with shock, survived.

The Vista Cruiser was gone. It had been gone when he returned to the Cadillac. The fog, blown westerly over the water by wind off the currents, heaped up against Nob Hill. It deepened as he drove along the Embarcadero. He turned left on Washington and away from the water, into the city, into the heart, the eye of the fog. The traffic, too, deepened, and he found himself gripping the wheel, leaning forward and peering into the murk, groping to locate the bumper in front of him. He tried to find the names of cross streets, but could not. He followed the traffic. When the grade steepened abruptly, he remembered, then saw on his left what seemed a space occupied by fog only —the park, Portsmouth Square—and on his right—faintly—the sign for the Golden Phoenix. He veered right, slowed, and pitched the car over the sidewalk and into the lot, stopped. Out in the street, horns wailed and changed pitch as they passed.

A Chinese boy came to the window and called, "Yes?"

Erks crammed Taam's papers into the top of his valise, shut it, then grabbed the valise and his coat and cracked the door open.

"Yes?" The boy stepped back. "For Mr. Jui?" he said, his accent thick.

Erks got out and pulled his coat on. "The keys are in it," he said, hoping that would satisfy the boy.

"Yes?"

In the street the cars were large shapes without detail, hulks, pachyderms. Blunt, ghostly figures moved slowly up and down the sidewalk. He opened the trunk and reached for the three matching suitcases. There were three. He had forgotten about that, the third suitcase. He took them all out. Chang and Lee had not moved. The attendant had vanished. He moved alongside the car and opened the door for the two, stuck his head in. "San Francisco," he said, the words strange. "California. Let's go."

They walked up Washington, past Brenham, and stopped for the light at Wentworth. Chang and Lee stood behind him, holding their suitcases, silent and wide-eyed, a tall one and a short one like two sunflowers, slim bodies and large responsive heads. He carried Ho's suitcase and his own valise. The light switched from a diffuse red orb to a green one. They headed up and turned into

296

the alley—Ross—where the fog grew still deeper, tangible as water, but he knew the way and found the number, the door with the sign advising prospective renters to contact a certain Mr. K—— at the address of a certain association. They went in. Below them in the wide room, thirty or forty women hunched over the sewing machines in the harsh fluorescent light on Sunday morning.

They climbed three flights of stairs. It was cold. The higher they climbed, the colder it grew. They walked down the hall to the farthest door, Chang and Lee right behind him, their breath quick and light. Erks knocked and instantly the door swung open, and the woman stood before them, the same woman, dressed in the same tweed suit. She glowered at Erks. He stepped aside to allow Chang and Lee to enter before him, then followed and stopped. Chang and Lee had stopped, their faces anxious. No one spoke. The Chinese man stood in the center of the room.

"Only two?" she said.

"Chang and Lee."

The woman gazed furiously at each of them, and at Erks. He waited for her to ask about Taam, and tried to prepare some response, but she opened her black book. He saw the page, a ledger, which was filled with numbers, English phrases, and Chinese figures, as before, but filled more than before, dense, the same page perhaps worked over through the three days of his journey and now a crazy patchwork spilling every which way with passages crossed out and others inserted, and lines, and arrows, a labyrinth of directives that contained, he presumed, some account of the lives he delivered, or failed to deliver.

His arms were tired. He set the suitcase and his valise down next to each other on the floor. His body was tired. He felt as if he'd been beaten with a club. The woman removed a pen from the clip on her lapel and wrote something further on the page, then snapped the book shut. Inexplicably, the Chinese man smiled at him and nodded. Chang and Lee did not move. As if reduced to the marks on the page that held them, or holding such reduction, having been so reduced all along, they stood side by side and gripped their suitcases, but their faces, however composed, were like sunflowers, the worry showing through the cover, two faces full of seeds.

Now—he thought—now we will have it out over Taam. He thought further: Now I might simply leave.

"Where is the third?" the woman said. "Where is Ho?"

Erks opened his mouth to speak. No words formed. He gestured foolishly at the third suitcase on the floor beside his valise, to which he still had his crowbar strapped. "Where is Ho?" he said, not understanding at first how she didn't know about Ho. But of course, she shouldn't have known. He said, "Ho is dead."

"Dead!" But her fury lacked something. Something was wrong.

Erks thought: Then she had learned that Taam was to be left in Reno and not brought here. Or she had not heard that he'd left Reno with Taam in Taam's father's car.

She repeated it: "Dead!"

But her venom, her power, was somehow divided, somehow falsified, and a thought came into his mind, a thought like a big monkey wrench that he struggled to manipulate, a large tool that made him feel clumsy and foolish: She knows, she doesn't know about Ho, or she pretends she doesn't, but she does know that Taam left Reno, that he is dead! She is one of them.

The woman said something to the man. The man shooed Chang and Lee into the back room, waving his arms as if he were shaking the dust out of a rug. The boys went into the room. The man followed them. The door shut. The latch clicked. The woman took an envelope out of her book and handed it to Erks.

"Your money," she said curtly.

He took it, utterly bewildered. The envelope was thick.

The door swung open behind Erks and he jumped violently. Two men entered, a burly one and a small one. The small one Erks recognized from the restaurant in Clarkston—half of Taam's protection.

The burly one stopped. "Difficulties, Mrs. Chew?"

The woman didn't speak. She raised her body, lifted her shoulders and chin, proud. Erks felt power moving palpably over to the thick-set man in the expensive suit, and he thought: I've got nothing to do with this, it's too late, it doesn't matter. He bent over, picked up his valise, and left, went along the hall and down the steps, fleeing.

They followed him. He heard their feet clattering on the stairs, then in the alley, out in the fog, they caught up with him.

"I am Jui," the burly one said. He gestured at the small man next to him. "This is Chinn. You are Mr. Erks?"

Erks glanced at them as he walked.

"And Ginarn?" Jui said. "And Ginarn Taam? It is important that we know."

Erks looked at him, walking rapidly.

They moved out of the alley and up the sidewalk, Erks and Chinn on either side of Jui. Three abreast in the fog, they forced others to lurch out into the street to avoid them. "And Ginarn? Where is Ginarn?"

"I brought him to the city."

"But where has he gone?"

"He said he came to honor his father."

"Ah! Excellent!"

"But he is dead," Erks said suddenly.

Jui stopped.

Erks kept moving.

Jui caught up with him again. "Not Ginarn."

"He was shot at the station."

Jui's face twisted with shock—presumably—but it looked vicious, as if this one had his own ax to grind, as if the presumable shock shared its location with something else, and Erks, who had wondered if he should entrust Taam's papers to this man, decided against it.

"At Embarcadero," Erks said. "At the terminal."

"Ah!"

Erks himself, carrying two deaths and miles of confusion and seeing the pain now in the man's face— What man! Who was this man, Jui, who presumably had arranged with Lucas to deliver Taam safely to Reno? And what pain, what counterfeit of it, what or whose image of pain's horror? looked away, upward, and through a hole in the fog saw the tip of the Transamerica Pyramid, the detail, the point suggesting the whole, the walls that slanted down into Chinatown on one side and on the other into the financial district.

"This is very bad."

"Did the woman know he'd left Reno?"

Jui looked up at him. "Rose Chew?"

"Did she know he'd left Reno?"

"Yes."

"With me?"

"No one knew that for certain."

"They knew. She knew."

"Yes?"

"They knew to kill him less than half an hour ago and she knew he was dead."

Again Jui stopped, and Erks stopped with him, and Chinn.

"Do you understand?" Erks said.

Jui's face filled with anger. Erks envied him the anger.

"I understand."

Erks envied him that, too, understanding, which Jui probably had although Erks knew in his bones that the man was otherwise a liar.

"I don't," Erks said. "If you do, then do something."

"Yes," Jui said. As he spoke, his meaning retreated behind the mask that switched from shock to grief to anger on his ugly face. "She was one of ours."

For his boy he bought a toy boat, a model Chinese junk to float in the bathtub or in the creek down in the ravine. For Ruby he bought a silk dress with a slit to show her leg. He went down to Portsmouth Square to sit. He shared a bench with a heavy old Chinese man whose pockets were filled with ballpoint pens, fifty or sixty of them. The playground was filled with children and attentive parents. He surveyed the people—the Chinese and the tourists—and among them found his man, the man of fine, elegant, articulated bone, wispy beard and gaunt cheeks, dressed still in the mismatched trousers and worn shoes, socks with holes, and holding his pipe. As before, exactly as before, the man had

300

the air of calm, impeccability, intactness, great intelligence, the air of being of a piece. As before, he paced slowly and thoughtfully toyed with his pipe. Erks tried to raise the sense of triangulation again, the magical location of a third point, the transection of his distance from the man and the man from him and of himself from himself. He came up with nothing. It was flat, dead. He had lost all distance, or he had only distance and nothing else. The man, clearly, had not solved his conundrum, his deep mystery, though he continued to stop and stare upward toward the wisps of fog and at the light that played with the peaks of buildings. The man, perhaps, was stark, raving mad and nothing at all drew near its conclusion.

He had to leave Chinatown. He had to get out of the park. He found Columbus Avenue and walked the half mile or so along it until he reached Washington Square, another park. The fog dissipated rapidly. He had crossed boundaries out of Chinatown and into the Italian district, and out of that into a mixed district. The more the sun shone, the more rapidly the fog dissipated: this was a certainty. Alone, Erks drew into himself.

He sat on a bench to read a newspaper, to kill time, to watch. He watched the people file into the church across the park. The sun shone through the fog—or clouds—and caught the spires of the church. Outside the park, the streets were placed so that the traffic seemed to move in a never-ending encircling motion. Between the benches and the green lay, in fact, an encircling sidewalk upon which a solitary young man in jogging sweats ran around and around. Dogs roamed the green, big dogs, wolf-hounds, borzois, Dobermans, flashy dogs. They urinated against trees and gathered in groups to sniff each other. A man with a tray on a stick went around picking up shit. Watchful, the dogs' masters moved slowly around the periphery with leashes in their hands, their positions threaded by the jogger who ran around and around.

Several young couples strolled about the green. Several more sat on blankets. On a bench several yards away from Erks, a couple argued over a third party. Two gentlemen walked diagonally across the park holding hands. The seated young couples lolled against each other, fondled each other, and it struck Erks suddenly that there were no children. Since Chinatown he had seen no children, and watching the couples, he heard again that shrill wailing sound of souls famished by their bodies, of too many bodies and not enough souls. One young couple took photographs of each other with a Polaroid camera. They would take a snapshot, wait, then look, then take another. . . . The lead story in the *Chronicle* told of a gang slaying of two homosexuals. The jogger ran around and around. The cars went around and around.

Right next to Erks was a marker that said, "U.S. Coast and Geodetic Survey. Latitude—37 47 57 N. Longitude—22 24 37 N." That much was certain.

He went through his count. A gesture now, only a gesture of ritual or retrieval:

Crowbar.

Valise.

And in the valise:

Taam's pistol.

The man in the bowler hat's pistol.

Lily's shotgun, broken down into two pieces.

Chang's knife.

He stopped. He couldn't take weapons on an airplane. He scooted down the bench next to a trash can, unstrapped the crowbar, and took Taam's writings out of the top of the valise. He checked the arguing couple near him and the park for other watchers, then deposited the weapons one at a time in the trash can. They clanked in the bottom. He returned the writings to the valise, strapped on the crowbar, and hefted the valise. It was much lighter.

And in the valise:

Maps.

Jade.

Gold.

Totem pole, the whale diving through the top and coming out the bottom.

302

Binoculars.

Taam's writings—what in his inquisition Erks had acquired.

He couldn't bring himself to remember it all.

In his wallet—at least $2,500.

In the envelope in his coat pocket—$5,000. He had counted it.

Airline ticket.

He poked with his big finger, stirred the coin pocket—goose vertebrae.

In his shirt pocket, a patch of Ho's skin.

And on the cuff of his shirt, Taam's blood.

❦14❧

Erks sank into his seat on the plane and fell asleep, even before takeoff. The jet rose, bouncing lightly on the air streams, and headed out of the bay to the northeast over the city, over the burnt-brown hills of San Leandro, and over the mouth of the Sacramento. The fresh water, what there was of it, had to get out somewhere. The salmon had to get in. The delta looked big, but in fact the Sacramento's current buckled quickly in the face of the Pacific's eastward tide. The jet rode the upper shell of the chinook inland, rose further into the still, bright cold, and followed the spine of the Coast Range.

It had been warm out in the Pacific. It had been warm in Hawaii. It had been warm on the coast of China, and hot down in Ecuador and Colombia, and China, catching the rolling expansion of air from the equator, enjoyed it and passed it on, deflected the air across the ocean, where it picked up water and blew into the Northwest, where it dropped the water in the form of fog and rain on the coast, and snow in the Cascades, the Columbia Basin, and the Rockies, and blew on, dry, still warm, across Montana and up into Alberta and Saskatchewan. The dry wind was called the chinook. The folks in Havre and Billings called it chinook while those in Spokane and Chewelah called it unseasonal snow. The folks in Spokane and Chewelah wouldn't call it chinook until it stopped snowing, but it was the same wind out of China all along.

The snow was Chinese.

The thaw was Chinese.

The fog back in San Francisco was certainly Chinese.

The wind was called chinook after a tribe, the Chinook, relatives of the Kwakiutl, and, like the Kwakiutl, trade wise, but the word—chinook—was Chehalis. The Chehalis tribe called the Chinook that—Chinook—and the white traders called them that, too. A squat, coastal people with "cradled" heads, the Chinook were well known to those who came to trade at the mouth of the Columbia because of the tribe's proximity, because of their assiduous interest in bartered goods, and because of the Chinook jargon, a trade language, a lingua franca made up of a dozen tongues, Chinook, Salish, and Nootka, and others, and later Spanish, Russian, and English, and French, but known all up and down the coast for centuries before the time of Columbus, or Drake, or Perez, or Bering, or Peter the Great, or Father Serra, or Captain Cook, before the time of Juan de Fuca's imagination, and still known, still used today in Alaska, changed and yet the same, a flexible instrument, a permeable gland, the jargon: words were added and dropped, invented according to need, and these words were used alongside strange archaisms, old survivors which no linguist can place—Chinese, maybe, Eskimo, Aleutian —the language an organ of route and collection like English, but smaller, more streamlined, quicker on its feet, like the wind itself, the chinook out of the Chinese trade winds which carried heat, and fallout from their 10-megaton model-T bombs, motes and particulates, and distillates of ancient smells from the streets of Shanghai, debris and birds. Certain cormorants, the emperor goose, Baikal teal, and Steller's eider know these winds they migrate on as well as the gray whale and chinook salmon know the current, Kuroshio.

The Chinook people, scourged by disease and whiskey, vanished into the Chehalis people. The jargon survived.

Near the end of the journey, Erks awoke. His body jerked. His gaze addressed the back of a head directly in front of him and it seemed an exceedingly strange thing, the thinning dark hair

305

combed over a bald spot. The jet hummed. It took him a moment to understand where he was.

He looked out the porthole immediately to his left, looked west across the long, luminous, delicate land toward the commanding features, the glaciers, the Three Sisters—Helena, Adams, and Hood—their bright white humps above everything else, even above the thin, broken veil of cloud. The passengers were still. The noon meal, apparently, had passed him by. To his right an elderly woman dozed. He looked back out the porthole. He knew exactly where he was.

The Three Sisters, and, directly below, the dark, authoritative cut in the skin of the earth—the Columbia, the boundary between Oregon and Washington—and just above it the coil of the Snake, told him where he was. And when he craned his neck to peer northwesterly, the two additional crests—Rainier and Baker—told him. He looked back and forth across the several hundred miles of space between Baker and Rainier and the Three Sisters, the crests like pearls set on top of the landscape, but, even so diminished by distance, big; he could see how big they were, undeniably so, like the report of a 7-millimeter gun heard from a distance, soft, muffled, but undeniably big. Legends told of the glaciers watching each other, of jealousy, pride, of marital strife among them. Helena, it was said, had moved out on Baker because Baker was always looking at the other mountains. Baker had called her back. She turned away from him. Maybe it was their light, their magic, their gravity which had awakened him.

The Three Sisters passed out of sight beneath the wing. Rainier and Baker sank slowly behind the Cascade Range as the plane dropped, glided closer to the desert ground. Above Spokane, the crests of the two glaciers were still just visible—over on the coast, near the water, 300 miles away—and Erks watched them, amazed, moved by the radiance of ice, and then they vanished. And he looked at the ground, pale brown with a sheen as if airbrushed over glass, and he was moved again by the fact that it was there still, at once inexplicably capable of being affected and yet indifferent, moved by the incredibly fragile spirit of sand and rock. The jet swung and dropped sharply into the basin. Basalt outcroppings, pine stands, buildings, and fields became distinguishable.

His place.

Inland.

Outback.

Home.

Searching for beer, Erks had his head inside the refrigerator. Ruby came out of the bedroom, wearing her bathrobe, holding it closed with one hand. Erks had on his pajamas. Matt was long in bed. Erks had spent the evening with him, playing catch, wrestling, shooting baskets out behind the shop in a hoop that was too high for the boy to reach with the ball except once out of every ten or so throws. Erks had told him he could stay home from school tomorrow, that they would go fishing. The phone had rung once, then Erks had turned off the ring.

They had been eating dinner when it rang and Ruby looked at him across the table, already angry, her eyes strong medicine. "Goddamn it, Wes, if that's Lucas . . ."

"Listen," he had said, his voice sharp. "I'm through with Lucas."

Ruby sat back in her chair. They hadn't spoken yet of his journey. His manner, his tight-lipped distance, had kept her from asking about it. He was filled with something—she knew—some story, some trouble, some determination. It would come out.

The phone kept ringing.

"So did you fix him up?" the voice said when Erks picked up the receiver.

Erks knew the voice. "Who's this?"

"Carl. Did you take care of him?"

"Take care of who, Carl?"

Glider chortled. "That guy on the Honda. He didn't say who sent him?"

"On a Honda, huh?" He looked at Ruby.

Ruby made a face.

"You sent him, huh?"

Glider laughed. This old joke between them had begun back in high school when they set each other up with a new girl in town—Ruby.

"Thanks, Carl."

Glider laughed again, delighted with himself.

When he hung up, Erks upended the telephone and turned off the ring.

"So," he said when he sat back down.

"You're through with Lucas?"

"Who'd he send over?"

"Sandman."

"Sandman?"

"He said he knew you. He said he worked for Lucas."

"Oh, Jesus," he said, remembering the name, the man who had arrived at Rathdrum with Lily. "He was lying."

"I figured."

The very thought of Sandman was an affront to Ruby. He had left without eating dinner the night before, Saturday, out in the driveway the figure in leather, a knot mounted on the machine out in the high wind against his will, riding west now, he had said, and against the grain, she had thought, the man to her a bone in the throat, and, once removed, a thing to make her think, but not long. To her husband, to Erks, Sandman was even less than that, a piece not even at the bottom of the pile, debris off the side of the heap, a little synapse that had nothing to do with the weight Erks carried, a weight as deep and intricate as brain, as soft, as dense, as vulnerable as brain, and brought back to it, thus, it suddenly hit him as he lifted a forkful of boiled carrots to his mouth. He set the fork down and turned his head away.

"Wes?" Ruby said, alarmed by the look on his face.

Matt stared at his father in astonishment.

"They killed him," Erks said hoarsely, his throat thick.

"Wes?" she said, meaning: Who? What?

"Goddamn it, Ruby, they killed him," he said, and he slammed the table with his fist with such force that the plates rattled and Ruby and Matt jumped, then he dropped his forehead to the butts of his palms, his body shaking.

308

Ruby got up and grabbed his arm. "Wes?"

"The one I was bringing down, Taam, they killed him," he said.

He played with Matt until dark. He brought out the gifts, totem pole, rocks, boat, spices, and dress with a slit up the side, then put Matt to bed, and talked with Ruby, explaining what for the moment he could of it. She went to change for bed and he looked at Taam's bundle of papers, undid the rubber bands and leafed through the pages. They were handwritten, mostly in English, but partly in Chinese.

He couldn't read. He would read later. He stared at the wall and wondered how he would find the reporter.

He followed Ruby. They stripped under the covers and held each other, their bodies warm and smooth and somber.

He shifted position and slid his knee up between her legs.

"But you're through with Lucas," she said.

"That's right."

"What'll you do?"

He looked into her face. "The machine shop, I guess."

"I'm off the pill."

"What?"

She grabbed him around the waist and tugged. "What the hell."

Afterward, they lay side by side for a long time, silent, touching hands and feet. The room was bright with the moon and their thoughts.

"I can't go to sleep." he said. "Jesus, I'm tired enough, but I can't go to sleep."

"I know."

"How about a beer?"

He had his head inside the refrigerator. "No beer?"

"In the bag on the counter. It's warm."

She went into the bathroom.

"I'll put it in the freezer for a couple minutes." He found the six-pack, carried it out to the porch, and opened the freezer door, and stepped back quickly at the sight of the possum head, which Ruby had forgotten to take in to the vet. Lips curled, incisors exposed, ferocious, the eyes beady and glazed, the head was frozen solid inside the plastic bag in the quick-freezing compartment. He set the six-pack beside it, closed the freezer, stepped outside.

The wind had blown over. It was a dead calm, the sky bright with stars and big, overpowering full moon. He heard sounds, cries like voices, but indistinguishable as to emotion. He moved out into the open toward the chicken shed in order to hear better and recognized the sound. It was often so with him: when he heard coyotes he did not recognize them at first. They were rhapsodic tonight, the many of them, their cries interwoven and dense and ornate as a gospel choir, one voice scooping up and down like a gospel obbligato, but without text, without meaning, pure glossolalia, utterly abstract and yet powerfully concrete, without tonality and yet powerfully musical, and giving to Erks a welling of feeling which, if he had been asked, he could not have named—a strong animal rise of blood.

He could not locate the sound. It seemed to come from his left side. When he turned, it still came from the left side, and he turned full around and it still came from the left side, the outrageous, delirious swoop and coil of sound, and it grew clearer, and louder, and then he thought he had placed it. When he thought he knew just what bluff overlooking the canyon the sound came from and turned to face it, riveted his attention on it, the sound vanished. He turned, tried to recover the sound, but could not. He heard only the space the sound had occupied, magically empty, and, still, abstract, but frightening as if meant personally for him.

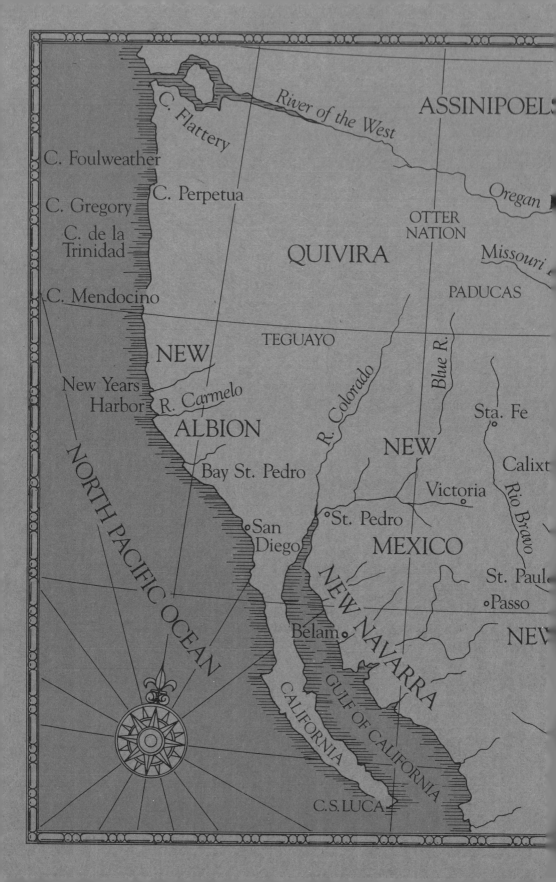